Praise for P. C. Hodgell's prior novels

God Stalk

"Out of the Haunted Lands to the city of Tai-tastigon comes Jame, one of the few remaining Kencyr left to carry on their millennium-long battle against Perimal Darkling, an entity of primal evil. Establishing herself in the city, Jame becomes an apprentice in the Thieves' Guild, make friends and enemies, and begins to develop her magical abilities. Hodgell has crafted an excellent and intricate fantasy, with humor and tragedy, and a capable and charming female hero. Highly recommended."
—*Library Journal*, September 15, 1985

"*God Stalk* by P.C. Hodgell takes some familiar elements of fantasy—a city of many gods, a Thieves' Guild, a heroine with the strange powers of an ancient race—and blends them into a delightful concoction bubbling with originality. The heroine, Jame, stumbles into the city of Tai-tastigon suffering from amnesia and the strain of headlong flight from her enemies. She finds herself in an apparently uninhabited maze, a chaos of weird supernatural effects. When the inhabitants finally appear, they're a quirky, lively, and (most of them) down-to-earth group who draw Jame into the network of their lives and concerns.
With this novel, [Hodgell] makes a promising debut, and its sequels could turn out to be major contributions to the fields."
—*Locus*, September, 1982

"It's become increasingly hard to do anything new in the high-fantasy field, but there's still a big difference between those who can only reheat the same old stew and those who can take full advantage of all that's been done before to brew up a fresh mix. Hodgell proves with this debut novel to be in the latter group.

Jame is a fully fleshed character in a rich fantasy milieu influenced by the likes of C.L. Moore and Elizabeth Lynn. Like their work, this novel and the series it begins should prove popular."

—*Publishers' Weekly*, September 21, 1982

"Those who regard fantasy as an insignificant branch of the literary tree lack understanding of the many ways in which all people approach that mystic realm we call 'reality.' Reading *God Stalk* might allow them to confront a few of their own demons. For the rest of us, whether because we are seeking ways of looking at our lives through fiction or because we simply want to explore someone else's vision, Hodgell's book is a dramatic introduction to a new world that both embodies and transcends our own."

—*The Minnesota Daily*, September 28, 1982

Dark of the Moon

"In *God Stalk*, P.C. Hodgell set in motion a convoluted plot involving such standard elements of fantasy as dark lords, thieves' guilds, and homey inns, and she transcended convention through sheer force of imagination. The sequel, *Dark of the Moon*, takes all these tendencies even further, with more convolutions, more familiar themes, and—again—a redeeming, delightful originality of vision.

Already she brings a welcome freshness and flair to a field where creativity often seems more the exception than the rule."
—*Locus*, September, 1985

"P.C. Hodgell is one of the best young fantasy writers we have and yet her work is not all that well known. This is partly due to her low productivity (two novels and a handful of short stories in the last ten years) and partly due to the difficulty and darkness of her work. Where so much of contemporary fantasy seems to consist of little more than a mindless reworking of Tolkien and Howard, Hodgell's affinities lie with the complex plotting of Mervyn Peake, the dark humor of Fritz Leiber, and the gruesomely poetic detail work of Clark Ashton Smith."
—*Fantasy Magazine*, October 1985

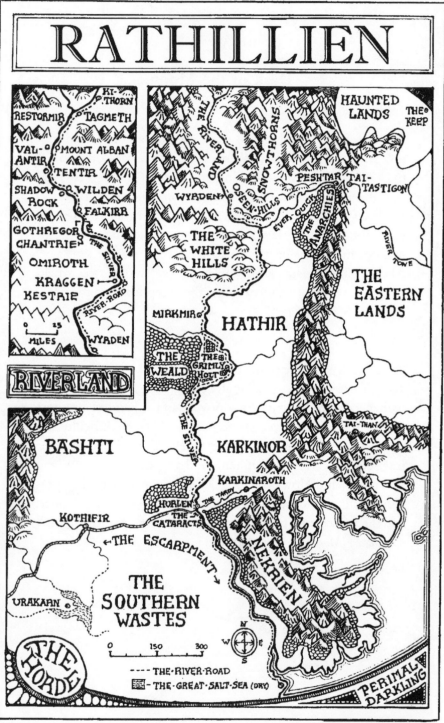

RATHILLIEN

RIVERLAND

KI-THORN
RESTORMIR · TAGMETH
VAL-ANTIR · MOUNT ALBAN
TENTIR
SHADOW ROCK · WILDEN
FALKIRR
GOTHREGOR
CHANTRIE · THE SILVER
OMIROTH
KRAGGEN
KESTRIE
RIVER·ROAD
WYADEN

0 25 MILES

THE RIVERLAND
WYADEN · OSEEN·HILLS · SNOWTHORNS
PESHTAR · TAI-TASTIGON
THE ANARCHIES
EVER·QUICK
HAUNTED LANDS
THE KEEP

THE WHITE HILLS

RIVER TONE

THE EASTERN LANDS

MIRKMIR
HATHIR

THE WEALD
THE GRIMLY HOLT

THE SILVER

BASHTI

KARKINOR
TAI-THAN

KARKINAROTH

KOTHIFIR
HURLEN
THE CATARACTS
THE TARDY

NEKRIEN

←THE ESCARPMENT→

THE SOUTHERN WASTES

URAKARN

0 150 300

N
W·E
S

THE HORDE

---- THE·RIVER·ROAD
▓ - THE·GREAT·SALT·SEA (DRY)

PERIMAL DARKLING

P.C.HODGELL

SEEKER'S MASK

BY

P. C. HODGELL

Meisha Merlin Publishing, Inc
Atlanta, GA

Seeker's Mask Copyright © 1994 by P. C. Hodgell
All maps Copyright © 2000 by P. C. Hodgell
Introduction Copyright © 2000 by Charles de Lint

SEEKER'S MASK

An MM Publishing Book
Published by Meisha Merlin Publishing, Inc.
PO Box 7
Decatur, GA   30031

Editing & interior layout by Stephen Pagel
Copyediting & proofreading by Josh Mitchell
Cover art by Kevin Murphy
Cover design by Neil Seltzer

ISBN: Hard cover   1-892065-33-9
        Soft cover   1-892065-34-7

http://www.MeishaMerlin.com

First MM Publishing edition: April 2001

Printed in the United States of America
0 9 8 7 6 5 4 3 2 1

Table of Contents

Dedication:

for Teddington Weir, who was and always will be Jorin,
and for Romney Marsh,
and for Melinda.

Introduction to
P.C. Hodgell's *Seeker's Mask*

Charles de Lint

Back in the summer of 1993, when I was asked by Alan New-comer of Hypatia Press to do an introduction for a third novel in P.C. Hodgell's Jame series, I was happily anticipating Pat's return to the field, not only with this new book, but with further volumes yet to come. I was sure that some Big Name Publisher would snap up the mass market rights and if not fame and fortune, then certainly some measure of it, would come her way.

Sadly, that didn't happen. The wonderful *Seeker's Mask* came and went, and here we are some seven years later and it's only now coming out in a more consumer-friendly (read: less expensive) edition.

But things are looking up. While Meisha Merlin isn't a Big Name Publisher, they're certainly a respected independent publishing house with better distribution than a specialty publisher such as Hypatia Press has, and they have the ability to produce both hardcover and more affordable trade paperback editions. Having already released *Dark of the Gods* (an omnibus collecting the classic *Godstalk* and *Dark of the Moon*), plus contracting a fourth volume from Pat, they're obviously committed to her work in the long term and that should make a difference.

And you, gentle reader, can make a difference as well. If you like this book as much as I think you will, tell your friends, spread the word. Let's show the publishing world that quality storytelling can still do well, even if it doesn't have a huge budget behind its publication and promotion.

Speaking of that earlier Hypatia Press edition, I was pleased to be invited to write an introduction for it at the time, and I'm happy now to have been asked by Stephen Pagel of Meisha Merlin Publications to update it for this new edition. To put what follows in context, I wrote it in September of 1993 when I was very busy juggling a number of projects—the story of my life, it seems, ever since I misplaced my spare time and have had to play catch-up every since...

* * *

And How We've Missed Her

When Alan Newcomer called up to ask if I'd write this intro-duction, the last thing I needed to do was take on a new project. It was mid-September and I was already running two weeks late on the deadline for my current novel, which in turn was threatening to make me late on a number of short fiction com-mitments, not least of which was a second Newford collec-tion due at my publisher by the beginning of October—and I still had a couple of stories to write for it as well.

So trust me on this, I wasn't looking for work. But I jumped at the chance to write this introduction all the same.

It wasn't because Alan offered me fistfuls of money. To my recollection the only time remuneration came up in the conversation was when Alan said something along the lines of, "Of course, I can't actually pay you anything for doing this." And it wasn't because of the spiffy books Alan offered to send. I'd already read his two previous publications by Hodgell in their earlier incarnations—*Child of Darkness* and *Bones*, which appeared in *Berkley Showcase II* (1980) and *Else-where III* (1984), respectively. And it certainly wasn't because I like signing my name so often in a row for a signed edition that eventually I begin to forget what my signature's supposed to look like.

(This is not as easy a thing to do as you might think when you consider I have a signature that looks more as though someone's checking to see if there's enough ink in their pen rather than one composed of letters that are actually supposed to spell out a name. Perhaps it's a legacy of my grandmother's Japanese blood and what I'm offering is less a signature and more a chop, my own quirky identifying ideograph. But I digress.)

No, the only reason I agreed was because it would give me an advance look at the manuscript of *Seeker's Mask* and after all these years (lord, has it really been eight years since the last novel?), I've been desperate to find out what happens next.

Can I assume that you've bought this because you, too, were just as enthralled with Pat Hodgell's previous two books, *God Stalk* (1982) and *Dark of the Moon* (1985)? Were you perhaps also somewhat resentful of this Ph.D. of hers that was taking her away from her fiction? Well, fret no more. Her doctorate on Sir Walter Scott's *Ivanhoe* is over and done with and finally we have a third installment in our hands, with – dare we hope? – the promise of not nearly so long a wait for the next book?

If this were a fair world, readers would be falling all over themselves in great numbers to acquire this new novel because, simply put, Pat is one of the very few true and original voices to write in the field of fantasy set in a secondary world— by which I mean high fantasy, that sub-genre inadvertently popularized by Tolkien with the publication of his *Lord of the Rings*. But fair, as they say, is only the first third of fairy tale, and like an elfin enchantment, fairness is difficult to pin down.

The truth is P.C. Hodgell isn't the household name it should be. Her wondrously dark and tangled fantasies don't command a huge audience and it has nothing to do with the high quality of her work.

Part of the blame lies with that vast monolith, the NYC publishing machine: because Pat's name didn't come up in its internal lottery where it's decided who's going to be hot and who not, her books were basically sent out to fend for themselves, wandering the byways and backroads up bookstores and libraries like itinerant rogues or adventurers. I'm sure they've had any number of grand escapades along their way and made many true, life-long friends, but without the help of those two Fairy Godmothers, Publicity and Real Publisher Support, fame and fortune has remained elusive.

It's also partly Pat's fault in the sense that her output has been so small that she and her work become easily forgotten in a world where public memory only encompasses the last big thing and all information is preferred in fifteen-second bites. (This reference to Pat's output, I should add, isn't meant in a negative sense. It's always important to follow your muse and if your muse insists on your straying from one form of creative endeavor to another, all you can do is comply. The curious thing is that you're usually better off for the break, but I digress again.)

Hopefully Pat's status in the field will change, now that her academic obligations are completed and she has the time to once again enrich our field with her singular fiction. It's all well and fine to have a rabid cult following, but I'd much rather see her do so well that she can concentrate as much of her time as feels right on the telling of tales.

And what tales she has to tell us.

If you remember, the last time we saw Jame (in *Dark of the Moon*), she had finally tracked down her twin brother Tori and now had to find a place for herself among the Kencyrs, those warrior-magicians she'd been searching for throughout the previous books. *Seeker's Mask* opens with the unruly Jame trying to fit into the constricting life found within the Women's Halls at Gothregor. Knowing Jame as we do, we also know it's a lost cause and in no time at all, she has set the quiet Women's Halls topsy-turvy, though it's not entirely her fault.

True, she finds it difficult to fit in, but she does try. Only what can you do when Shadow Guild assassins come hunting you, not to mention old ghosts from her days in Tai-tastigon, the city of a thousand gods? It doesn't help, either, that no one in the Women's Halls seems willing to help her, or that her brother will have nothing to do with her. So in no time at all she and Jorin, the blind, cat-like ounce with whom she has bonded, are off and away once more, barely one step ahead of a multitude of dangers.

Stated so simply as I have above, the bare bones of the plot undoubtedly sound like that of any one of the literally dozens of derivative fantasy novels that clog the shelves of our bookstores, but that's far from the case here. Like Guy Gavriel Kay and Patricia A. McKillip, like Jane Yolen and Jane Lindskold and a very few other talented fantasists, Pat works with the archetypes of myth and high fantasy and uses them as a means of confronting and dealing with the real world, rather than as simple escapism. Her work demands involvement from the reader, not because her prose can be so dense, or the plotlines don't always follow through in a traditionally linear sense, but because there is an underlying resonance to every action and motive and description.

You come away from one of Pat's books with your mind and heart humming. The reverberations of what you've read carry through into the world beyond the book's pages and you see things differently. Connections that originated in the novels link with our own lives, offering insights and questions, both of which are important as we make our way through the confusing morass of the world. The insights show us established paths we can take that we might not have seen before. The questions make us look a little harder so that we can forge our own routes.

Like many of us, Pat has cast her net into the pool of what went before, but unlike most, she replenishes those waters with more than what she took. You can't ask much more of an artist and for Pat's unwavering commitment to give us so much, she deserves not only our support, but our admiration and respect as well.

*   *   *

That's what I wrote about *Seeker's Mask*, seven years ago upon its first publication, and I stand by it today. Pat Hodgell is one of the original voices and great talents of our field and I couldn't be happier to see her work back in print once more, with at least a fourth novel scheduled to appear in the near future. If you're new to her work, get comfortable and allow a master storyteller to take you in hand. If you're already familiar with Jame's adventures, I hope you'll enjoy revisiting these stories as much as I have.

Charles de Lint
Ottawa
December 2000

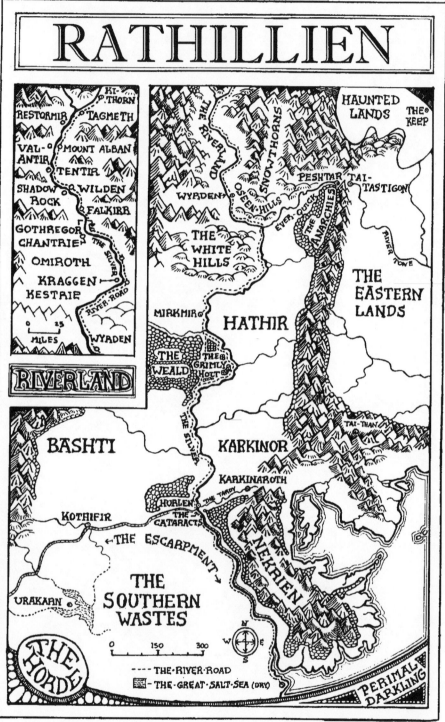

RATHILLIEN

RIVERLAND

KI-THORN
RESTORMIR · TAGMETH
VAL-ANTIR · MOUNT ALBAN
TENTIR
SHADOW ROCK · WILDEN
FALKIRR
GOTHREGOR CHANTRIE
OMIROTH
KRAGGEN
KESTRIE
THE SILVER
RIVER-ROAD
WYADEN

0 · 25
MILES

HAUNTED LANDS · THE KEEP
THE RIVERLAND
SNOWTHORNS
WYRDEN · OSEEN-HILLS
PESHTAR · TAI-TASTIGON
EVER-QUICK
THE ANARCHIES
RIVER TONE
THE WHITE HILLS
THE EASTERN LANDS
MIRKMIR
HATHIR
THE WEALD · THE GRIMLY HOLT
TAI-THAN
THE SILVER
BASHTI
KARKINOR
KARKINAROTH
THE TARDY
HURLEN
THE CATARACTS
KOTHIFIR
NEKRIEN
←THE ESCARPMENT→
THE SOUTHERN WASTES
URAKARN

0 · 150 · 300
N W E S

---- THE · RIVER · ROAD
⊞ — THE · GREAT · SALT · SEA (DRY)

THE HORDE

PERIMAL DARKLING

P.C. HODGELL

Characters
present and past

Adiraina—the Ardeth Matriarch, Adric's cousin,
    sister-kin to Kinzi

Adric—Lord Ardeth of Omiroth,
    Torisen's ally and former mentor

Aerulan—a Highborn Knorth girl killed in the
    Massacre; Jame's cousin; sister-kin to Brenwyr

Argentiel—That-Which-Preserves,
    the Second Face of the Three-Faced-God

Ashe—a scrollswoman singer who was killed by
    haunts in the White Hills and therefore
    returned as one

Bane—Ganth's son by a Kendar mistress,
    Jame's half-brother

Bashtiri Shadow Guild—a guild of assassins,
    noted for their determination and invisibility

Brant—Lord Brandan of Falkirr, Brenwyr's brother

Brenwyr—the Brandan Matriarch, Brant's sister,
    sister-kin to Aerulan

Brier Iron-thorn—a Knorth randon cadet,
    formerly a Caineron yondri

Burnt Man—Merikit avenger of the slain

Burr—Torisen's Kendar servant

Caldane—Lord Caineron of Restormir,
        Torisen's enemy

Cattila—the Caineron Matriarch,
        Caldane's great-grandmother

Chingetai—Merikit chief

Chaos Serpent—the great, primal snake said to lie
        under Rathillien, whose mouth is the
        maelstrom known as the Maw

Dianthe—the Danior Matriarch

Ganth Gray Lord—former Highlord of the Kencyrath,
        father of Jame and Torisen

Gerridon—the Master of Knorth, former Highlord
        whose treachery caused the Fall

Gorgo—a Tastigon rain god of the Old Pantheon

Graykin—(Griki) Jame's half-breed servant
        and Caldane's bastard son

Grimly—a wolver poet

Grondin—Caldane's first established son

Ham Grip-hard—Torisen's second in command
        with the Southern Host

Hawthorn—a Brandan randon captain,
        assigned to Tentir and Gorthregor

Higron—Caldane's sixth established son

Hollens—(Holly), Lord Danior of Shadow Rock,
Torisen's closest kin on the High Council,
therefore his heir presumptive

Immalai—the Arrin-ken who passed judgment on
Jame in the Ebonbane

Index—an old scrollsman, expert on the Merikit

Ishtier—a Kencyr high-priest, Jame's enemy

Jame—Jamethiel Priest's-Bane, Torisen's twin sister

Jorin—Jame's blind royal Gold ounce

Kallystine—Caldane's favorite daughter,
Torisen's limited term consort

Karidia—the Coman Matriarch

Kindrie Soul-Walker—a healer, Jame's cousin,
the Knorth Bastard

Kinzi—Jame's great-grandmother, sister-kin
to Adirania, killed in the Massacre,
the last Knorth Matriarch

Kirien—the Jaran Lordan or Heir, a scrollswoman

Logan—Gorgo's priest

Lower Town Monster—the demon created by Ishtier
around Bane's soul

Lyra—Caldane's young daughter, formerly consort
to Prince Odalian of Karkinaroth,
nicknamed "Lack-wit"

Marc—Jame's Kendar friend

Pereden—Ardeth's dead, renegade son, former
      commander of the Southern Host

Ragga—Mother Ragga, the Earth Wife of Peshtar

Rawneth—the Randir Matriarch

Regonereth—That-Which-Destroys,
      the Third Face of the Three-Faced-God

River Snake—that offspring of the Serpent's Brood
      that lies under the Silver

Rose Iron-thorn—Brier's mother

Rowan—Torisen's steward at Gothregor

Rue—a Knorth randon cadet

"Sonny"—Chingetai's son, the Merikit Favorite

Telarien—Jame's grandmother, killed in the Massacre

Tieri—Ganth's young sister, sole survivor of
      the Massacre

Tiggeri—Caldane's seventh established son

Tishooo—the Old Man, a wind from the south

Torisen—Lord Knorth of Gothregor, Black Lord
      ("Blackie"), Highlord of the Kencyrath,
      Jame's twin brother

Tungit—a Merikit shaman-elder, Index's old friend

Vant—a Knorth randon cadet

Yolindra—the Edirr Matriarch

Seeker's Mask

by

P. C. Hodgell

Part I

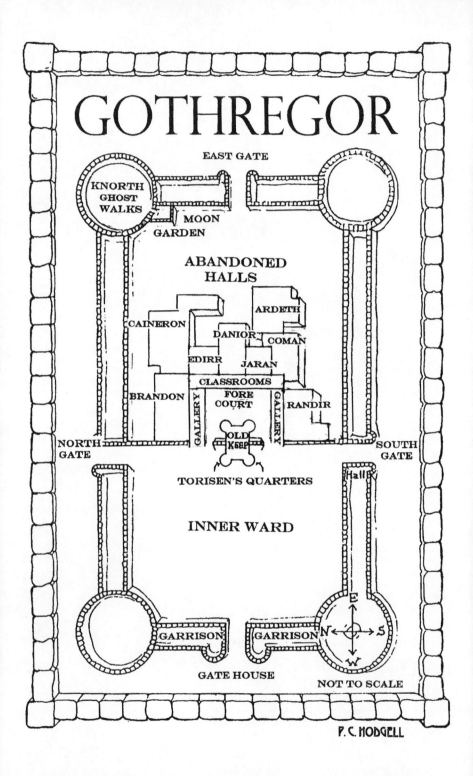

GOTHREGOR

EAST GATE

KNORTH GHOST WALKS

MOON GARDEN

ABANDONED HALLS

ARDETH

CAINERON

DANIOR

COMAN

EDIRR

JARAN

CLASSROOMS

BRANDON

GALLERY

FORE COURT

GALLERY

RANDIR

NORTH GATE

OLD KEEP

SOUTH GATE

TORISEN'S QUARTERS

Hall

INNER WARD

GARRISON

GARRISON

E

N

S

W

GATE HOUSE

NOT TO SCALE

P. C. HODGELL

I

"The first duty of a Highborn lady is obedience."

So spoke the young instructress as she swept imperiously back and forth before her even younger class. The extreme tightness of her under-skirt obliged her to walk with tiny, rapid steps, but she did this so smoothly that she might have been mounted on wheels.

"A lady's second duty is self-restraint," she said, pivoting on her toes. Her full outer skirt belled out around her, velvet pleats opening to reveal panels of rich embroidery, restraint transformed by long practice into grace.

"Her third duty is endurance."

The little girls obediently echoed the words after her, fingers busy with the knot stitch which they were currently learning, eyes downcast behind the simple veils that were appropriate to their age and rank. They had already repeated these maxims endless times, both in their home keeps and here in the Women's Halls at Gothregor—not that their teacher thought of that in terms of endurance. She herself had learned to love the simple dicta that gave shape to her life, and believed that the more often her students heard them, the better.

That had been especially true over the winter just past. Never in her short life had she seen such snows, or felt such cold, or heard such winds as had come howling down the narrow throat of the Riverland. By day, her fingers had blanched with frost even within the halls, while outside birds had plummeted frozen from the sky. At night, she had lain awake in the arms of her sister-friend, hearing the stones groan around them and the distant *boom* of ironwood trees shattering in the cold. Even on Spring's Eve, they had to dig into snow banks for the crocus with which to make their vows, guided by the flowers' violet glow beneath the ice crust.

Under these circumstances, the inmates of the halls hadn't been home since the previous autumn. True, the younger ones didn't expect to leave Gothregor before summer, but it made a difference, knowing they couldn't go home even if they wanted to. Still, thought the instructress, they had better get used to being homesick. Soon they would have to go wherever their lord sent them, to honor whatever contract he chose to make in their behalf. By then, of course, many of them would belong to the community of sister-kinship that would be their only true "home" as adults. At present, though, they were still the children of different, distant homes, in need of all the self-control that the Women's World could teach them.

Their young teacher had also felt that need, despite the warm arms of her Edirr sister. For her, the snow, the cold, and the wind of the past winter had been nothing compared to its strangeness. With most of the Kencyr Host wintering in Kothifir, the Riverland had been so *empty*. Now that the snow had finally melted, one heard first-hand accounts of things only rumored before: of weirding mist and Merikit raiders, of strange noises in the earth and air, and of arboreal drift. Why, one hunter even claimed to have heard the demented howls of the Burning Ones, avengers of the slain, far south of their usual haunts—but that was nonsense. Everyone *knew* that they and their master, the Burnt Man, were mere Merikit superstitions.

Still, things *must* improve soon, now that Kencyr were beginning to return. The Jaran Heir Kirien had passed by some weeks ago accompanied by the haunt singer Ashe, bound for the Scrollsmen's College at Mount Alban. More important, only three days ago the first of the lords had returned. That it had been Caldane, Lord Caineron of Restormir, seemed an especially good omen, since she herself was a Coman with two Caineron grandmothers. The Highlord's garrison, on the other hand, had manned the walls as if expecting an attack.

Abruptly, another memory came to her, unbidden, unwelcome. Rumor said that just after the great battle at the Cataracts, Caineron had been stricken with some mysterious illness, which his randon commander had described as "not quite feeling in touch with things"—whatever *that* meant. The health of great lords affected everyone bound to them, even distantly, as she herself was. One more thing tottering in her world, one more thing insecure...

So she glided back and forth before her class, repeating the great truths, demonstrating by her grace that the world still made sense, here in the heart of the Women's World where nothing ever changed.

Below, hooves rang on cobblestones. The windows looked down on the Forecourt, so called because it occupied the foremost open space in the Women's Halls, which themselves occupied the back half of Gothregor. At the center of the entire fortress was the old Knorth keep, whose own rear half projected into the Forecourt. A horse was clattering in through the gate which separated the court from the fortress's inner ward. But men weren't allowed here, the instructress thought, outraged. These were the *Women's* Halls, where even the Kendar guards were female.

Then she saw that the rider, although properly masked, was wearing a divided skirt and, yes, boots. Lady Brenwyr of Brandan had returned to Gothregor.

At the best of times, most people found this Highborn unnerving. The Iron Matriarch, they called her behind her back, for her rigid discipline. These past few months, however, that control had seemed to slip. Everyone had been aware of her restless comings and goings, as if even in the depths of winter she had been unable to stay either in or away from the Women's Halls for any length of time.

The instructress had heard scandalized whispers about the Iron Matriarch's traveling garb, but had never before seen it for herself. It was indecent, she thought, and yet, and yet...

She firmly believed that whatever her elders did was above criticism. The conflict between that dictum and her feelings confused and frightened her. Things should be one way or the other.

Brenwyr dismounted and disappeared into the north wing quarters of the Brandan.

"*Forget what you can't help*," the Women's World taught.

The instructress turned from the window, wiping what she had just seen from her mind.

"The fourth duty of a lady," she said firmly to the class, "is to be silent."

Traditionally, the response to this was mouthed rather than spoken. This time, however, a low but quite distinct voice in the rear of the classroom said:

"*Damn.*"

"Who was that?" demanded the instructress sharply, but she already knew. "*Now* what have you done? Come here and let me see."

The dark figure in the back row rose and glided forward into the shafts of late afternoon sunlight which fell through the windows like the memory of antique gold. Once, her gown must have glowed in such light. Now the little girls snickered as she passed, pointing out to each other the tarnished silver trim, the threadbare royal blue facings, and the rich plum velvet, dulled by age to the color of a bruise.

Once they had laughed less cautiously. The instructress remembered their taunt: "Seeker, seeker…" because of the eyeless mask with which the Matriarchs had tried to curb the newcomer's roaming. But then that blind face had turned toward the class and they had frozen, like…like the instinctive cower of small animals before a hooded hawk.

That was *not* a suitable image, the young teacher told herself sternly.

Anyway, now the oncoming figure wore a standard half-mask and ignored the children as she passed them.

But their giggles were still nervous, and so was their teacher.

For one thing, she wasn't used to pupils older than herself, if only by a few years. Worse, this elder girl was a Knorth, the Highlord's own sister. There had been no Knorth women at Gothregor for more than thirty years, since Bashtiri assassins had given the entire family a hard shove toward extinction. To have one here now, with her incredibly old, fabulously pure bloodlines, was like trying to deal with a creature of legend.

But the Matriarchs hadn't allowed her that status. Rather, they had subordinated her to her brother's limited-term consort, Kallystine, and to any teacher whose classes she was ordered to attend. This was one of them. And, really, this Knorth was so very ignorant. Why, not only had she no knowledge of needlecraft—or of any other skill which any self-respecting lady should long since have known—but she wasn't an initiate into even the lowest ring of secrecy. Therefore, the instructress spoke sharply to her, but with a strong impulse to back away as the Knorth advanced, black-gloved hands extended.

Then she saw why those hands were so oddly held: the Knorth had accidentally sewn them together.

The young teacher sighed, obscurely reassured.

"Oh, Lady Jameth. Not again. If those gloves make you so clumsy, why don't you take them off?"

"I prefer not to."

The voice was level, without emphasis, but with something so unyielding in it that the instructress felt piqued. After all, this was *her* class, and all the pupils here were under her authority.

"Don't be silly," she said sharply. "I insist."

"So do I."

The gloved hands clenched and parted, snapping the threads, diving out of sight behind the other's back.

Like two wild things escaping, the instructress thought.

For a moment, absurdly, she had been very frightened indeed, and that in turn made her angry.

"You *must* obey me!" she insisted, reaffirming the shape of her world. "The first duty of a Highborn lady…"

"…is obedience," finished that expressionless voice. "But why?"

"You mustn't ask that!"

"Why not?"

"Because...because it's forbidden!"

"That's circular reasoning. Why is it forbidden?"

This couldn't be happening. No one asked such things, especially in front of children. "All knowledge is the gift of our elders. They tell us what we need to know, when we need to know it. To demand an answer is sacrilegious."

"Not that, surely," said the Knorth. Her voice had lost its flatness, as if for the first time in weeks she was beginning to enjoy herself. "When the Three-Faced God drew the three people of the Kencyrath together to fight Perimal Darkling down the Chain of Creation, he (or she, or it) didn't give us any choice in the matter. I don't think that, ultimately, we could commit sacrilege against him if we tried. Anyway, he apparently abandoned us after our first defeat thirty millennia ago, so that we've been on our own, in retreat from threshold world to threshold world, ever since. But we still have our honor, whatever god or man does to us."

"And a lady's honor is obedience!" cried the instructress, beginning to wax hysterical. Surely *that* must clinch the argument.

"But if she faces Honor's Paradox, ordered to do something dishonorable?"

"T-that's unthinkable!"

"But it happened."

And, suddenly, she began to chant, the old dark story rolled over the room like an eclipse, the daylight dying:

"Gerridon Highlord, Master of Knorth, a proud man was he. The Three People, held he in his hands—Arrin-ken, Highborn, and Kendar. Wealth and power had he and knowledge deeper than the Sea of Stars. But he feared death. 'Dread Lord,' he said to the Shadow that Crawls, even to Perimal Darkling, ancient of enemies, 'my god regards me not. If I serve thee, wilt thou preserve me, even to the end of time?' Night bowed over him. Words they spoke. Then went my lord Gerridon to his sister and consort, Jamethiel Dream-Weaver, and said, 'Dance out the souls of the faithful, that darkness may enter in.' And she danced..."

"Stop it!" cried the instructress, hands over her ears.

But she knew all too well how that terrible story ended, as someday these children would too if their elders condescended to tell them. Two-thirds of the Kencyrath had fallen, soul-raped, and the shattered remnant had fled to the next threshold world, Rathillien. Three thousand years ago, that had been, but no lapse of time could dim the horror of that night or its repercussions in the Women's World, which paid daily for the Dream-Weaver's fall.

At least, so her elders had told her when, as a child, she had been so ill bred as to question the restrictions that were to shape her life. That was when she had first heard Jamethiel's lament with its bitter coda: "*Alas for the greed of a man and the deceit of a woman, that we should come to this!*"

It had never occurred to her before that the Dream-Weaver had fallen through obedience to her lord.

But a lady's honor *was* obedience.

Stop it, stop it. Things *must* be one way or the other.

"W-we don't discuss such questions here," she stammered, struggling to wipe them out of her mind. "We practice obedience, self-restraint, endurance, silence…"

"And knot stitches." The Knorth sighed. "Some of us do, anyway. Just the same," she added, regarding the sampler which the younger girl held, "a raised stitch like that might be useful as part of a code…"

The instructress felt herself go cold. "Shut up, *shut up*, SHUT UP!"

And her hand lashed out, as if of its own volition, to deal that masked face the hardest slap it could.

The Knorth went rigid. Her own-gloved hands were still behind her.

The nearest child, staring at them in awe, said, "Oh look, oh look!"

The teacher had fallen back a step as if shoved away by the other's sudden blaze of anger, remembering too late all she had heard about the deadly Knorth temper. She instinctively clutched the sampler to her chest as if sheltering behind it and flinched back as one of those gloved hands lashed out at her in a black and white blur.

Then the Knorth whirled about and left the room, moving with a hasty stride reduced by the tightness of her underskirt to a series of rapid jerks.

The instructress let out her breath unsteadily. She felt as if some appalling violence had just flashed past her, incredibly doing no harm.

Then the sampler fell to shreds in her grasp.

"Did you see her hands?" the little girl was babbling. "Did you see…?"

"Be quiet!" snapped her teacher. "The fourth duty of a lady is…"

But down the hall, another voice broke the rule of silence to exclaim, "Lady Jameth, be careful on that stair!"

That triggered a chorus of warnings, as the Knorth was hailed from the doorway of every classroom she passed: "Slow down!" "Walk like a lady!" "Watch your step!" "Jameth!"

The instructress reached her own door in time to see the singing mistress, nearest the steps, pop out of her room to wail, "Remember what happened the last—"

Too late.

They all saw the Knorth hop down the first two steps—which was indeed the proper way for a lady to descend—but she was still going too fast. The next moment, she pitched forward out of sight. Her sharp cry echoed up the spiral stair as she tumbled down it.

A collective sigh rose from the instructresses in the upper hall: "Oh no. Not again."

II

Adiraina, the Ardeth Matriarch, sat by a window in an upper chamber of her family's compound, stitching a letter to a five-times-great-granddaughter—one of a growing number. They did tend to accumulate, she reflected wryly, when one was over a hundred and twenty years old.

So did memories.

The spring breeze off the Snowthorns brought back an evening a lifetime ago, the child that she had been leaning on this windowsill, looking eastward over the jagged rooftops of the Women's Halls to the lights that sparkled in the Knorth family quarters, hoping for a glimpse of her new sister-friend.

Oh, Kinzi...

How short that springtime together had been, and how long the years apart afterward, as each had served her lord wherever he sent her, in whatever distant house or bed. Highborn men laughed at the token cloths which their women seemed eternally to exchange. Adiraina touched the worn shawl draped across her shoulders. It had arrived on Spring's Eve almost a century ago, after a winter's enforced silence: Kinzi's vow gift, the stitched record of her winter days. Adiraina's fingertips remembered every detail, however many knots unraveled with age.

But at last the long separation had been over when they both returned to these halls, each now the matriarch of her own house.

Memories: another evening, long after the first, standing by this window, the day's work done. Family business kept Kinzi to her quarters, but if Ganth returned soon from his hunt perhaps she could slip out.

Like children again, Adiraina had been thinking, *stealing sweet moments. What a good life we've had...*

She tried to fix on that moment, the last of happiness, but memory swept her inexorably on: cries in the darkness, and then screams as Bashtiri shadow assassins slashed their way through the unprotected tower. The blaze of Kinzi's helpless rage like a fireball in her lover's mind, suddenly extinguished. Dead, dead, Aerulan, Telarien, Kinzi—all the Knorth women but one, and her a child who must be kept hidden the rest of her unhappy life...

It would be dark there now, in those apartments built for the Highlord's family in Gothregor's massive outer wall— dark and cold and silent. The Ghost Walks, people called them, and kept their distance. At least she was spared that dismal sight: the eyes on her gray, velvet half-mask were mere embroideries in silver thread. She had been blind since adolescence.

A pity, Adiraina thought, that she couldn't also claim to be deaf.

Behind her the Danior and Coman Matriarchs, Dianthe and Karidia, were arguing again; or rather (as usual) the latter was trying to pick a fight. As always, Karidia was advancing the interests of the Caineron, on the theory that since Caldane was the most powerful Highborn in the Kencyrath, he should be given more power still with first claim on the newly-discovered Knorth, Jameth. "Dear Catti" would insist, if only she were here.

Adiraina smiled. "Dear Catti" was Cattila, the Caineron Matriarch and Caldane's great-grandmother, who had once called him the stupidest thing on two legs in the Riverland.

"Speaking of dear Caldane," she said, "has anyone heard exactly what has ailed him this past winter? 'Not quite feeling in touch with things' is not, I'm sure you'll agree, a particularly enlightening diagnosis."

She sensed rather than saw them all glance at Cattila's Ear, who sat in the shadows knitting their conversation into a scarf which she would subsequently dispatch to her mistress. Being an Ear, she of course said nothing.

"At least Lord Caineron sleeps at night," snapped Karidia. "That's more than can always be said of our fine, young Highlord or, recently, of his sister. Anyway," she continued, perhaps still thinking of lost sleep, "there's already an alliance between the Houses of Knorth and Caineron, in that Torisen has taken one of Caldane's daughters as a limited term consort."

"Yes, dear," said Yolindra, the Edirr Matriarch, from a cushioned seat by the western window where, like a cat, she took her ease in the day's last warmth. "But I wouldn't count on that if I were you. When the Highlord stopped here last fall on his way to the Cataracts, he didn't so much as send her word, much less visit her. And he's had no trouble staying away all this past winter. It sounds to me as if he's begun to slip through darling Kallystine's grip."

"Nonsense!" snapped Karidia.

"About time, I'd say," Dianthe said briskly. "I've always had the highest regard for that young man's survival instinct."

With that, she swept off to take a turn around the room, with Karidia trotting to keep up, still arguing as fiercely as increasing shortness of breath allowed.

Dear Karidia, thought Adiraina. *She has such an unfortunate tendency to yap.*

These squabbles would be amusing, if the stakes weren't so high. Ever since the Three-Faced God had created the Kencyrath over thirty millennia ago, its highlord had been Knorth. Everyone had thought that Torisen was the last of his lineage, had almost been glad of it, after the grief which his father Ganth Gray Lord had caused; but suddenly this girl, his sister, had appeared out of nowhere. It seemed inevitable that either her son or his would be the next highlord, the first in history with the blood of another house also in his veins. So far, Torisen had shown the impeccable instincts with which Dianthe credited him by refusing to give anyone a legitimate Knorth heir. It was unlikely, though, that the lords would permit him to be so evasive with his sister. If ambitious Lord

Caineron did secure the girl's first contract with the option for a child, young Torisen Black Lord was not apt to get much older. That he would be better off dead than his sister would be alive under Caineron's roof, Adiraina knew perfectly well, but she gave it little consideration: in the Women's World, after all, one obeyed and endured.

Karidia trotted by, still trying to keep up with the much taller Danior Matriarch. "It isn't as if the girl is such a prize in herself," she was panting. "I *mean* so ignorant, so clumsy...

This last made the Jaran Matriarch Trishien look up from her reading. Sunlight caught the lenses worked into her mask, fiery eyes in a cool face. "I'd like to see *you* fall downstairs even once without breaking your neck, much less make a habit of it."

"So she has a brilliant future as a tumbler," snapped Karidia, coming to a breathless stop before Adiraina. "Is it *really* possible that this girl is a pure-blooded Knorth? I *mean*, all the Knorth ladies died here over thirty years *ago* except for the child Tieri and we all know what became of *her*."

Adiraina's hand closed convulsively on the letter which she had been stitching. "It wasn't Tieri's fault that her lord brother went directly from the White Hills into exile, without her. Aerulan had saved her from the assassins by hiding her in the empty halls. I tried to do the same when I concealed her in the Ghost Walks for twelve long years and told no one, not even this council, not until she died in the moon garden, bearing an illegitimate child to an unknown father, to her utter disgrace. She was sister-kin to me, the daughter of Telarien, the granddaughter of my dear, dead Kinzi. But here it ends. We will not speak of her or her bastard again."

There was a moment's embarrassed silence, even the truculent Karidia looking abashed. By the opposite window, Cattila's Ear had dropped a stitch. Adiraina released her cloth letter and removed the needle from her thumb.

"As for this girl's mother," she said, with an abrupt return to her usual calm manner, "all I know is that she was pure Knorth and a potent Shanir, as members of that house so often were. Remember, my own gift is to sense bloodlines by touch—back a hundred generations, if necessary."

"So you keep reminding us," Karidia grumbled. "Worth your eyes, was it? All right, all right: we *don't* know if developing the blood-sight caused your blindness; they just happened at the same time. A fat lot of good either does us now, anyway. Without the mother's name, we wouldn't know how to bring the daughter into sister-kinship even if we wanted to. And the darkling taint? You're sure that's in this uncouth brat too?"

"Regrettably, yes."

"So, we have here a purebred Shanir Knorth who probably knows who her mother was, but won't tell us. She also refuses to say where she's been for the past nineteen-odd years. Given the taint, it could have been in Perimal Darkling itself. And you once even said that she and the Highlord could be twins except, of course, that he's at least ten years older than she is. I ask you! What are we supposed to do with a mystery like that?"

"We crack it," said the Ardeth Matriarch tartly, "or we crack her. What else do you think we've been trying to do this past winter? We *have* to know what we're dealing with."

"Make her drop the mask?" said Yolindra. "How indelicate!"

"Yes," said Trishien dryly, "especially since we forced her to wear it in the first place."

"I see now why you turned her over to Kallystine," said Dianthe, as she swept past yet again. "If you want to learn the worst about anyone, dear Kally will bring it out."

"I resent that!" yelped Karidia, and took off in pursuit.

Yolindra's chime of laughter broke as the sound of hoof-beats below made her glance down into the Forecourt. "Brenwyr," she said.

The others glanced at each other, momentarily united by the unease which the Iron Matriarch seemed to create these days.

"And she's wearing that horrid skirt again."

Trishien grinned. "Jealous, Yo? But I forgot: unlike some of us, you enjoy being hobbled. Never mind. I'm sure she'll change before coming up here rather than offend you or scare the children. At least, she's insisted that our young Knorth be properly clothed, which is just as well considering that her brother didn't make any provisions for her at all."

"Only you would call those old rags proper clothing," the Edirr Matriarch retorted with a sniff. "Still, I suppose they are better than that awful pink dress she arrived in."

Dianthe had come to stand beside Adiraina, scarcely breathing hard at all despite her brisk walk. *Ah, to be ninety again*, thought the blind matriarch. She felt her friend's hand on her shoulder. The fingers spoke to her with quick, deft changes of pressure.

Seriously, what does the Highlord think of his sister in Kallystine's tender care? It can't be what he intended when he sent her here.

Adiraina put her thin hand over Dianthe's. *It wasn't. He thought his steward Rowan would take charge of her.*

A Highborn girl alone in a Kendar garrison? Ridiculous!

So I said, and snatched her out of the steward's hands. Rowan must have told him that, but he doesn't know about dear Kallystine, anymore than he seems to have known that he should provide his sister with suitable clothes, quarters, and guards. So we have her quite to ourselves.

"Hmmmm." Dianthe's fingers drummed briefly. *At least until the Highlord comes home. 'Point of law,' as Trishien would say: custom may put her in our hands, but she's still Knorth. Be careful, old friend. About those clothes, though. Why did Brenwyr insist that she wear them? You do realize whose they were, don't you?*

Adiraina sighed. *Yes, I do. Having a Knorth in the halls again seems to have set all the old ghosts walking, as it were. For me, Kinzi Kin-singer; for Brenwyr, in a more literal sense, young Aerulan.*

But this girl is so very different, Dianthe's fingers protested. *She's Knorth too, of course, and young, but so gawky, so maladroit...*

You've forgotten what young Knorth are like.

Dianthe considered this rather blankly. "You're right," she said. "It's been so long." *If this girl follows the way of her house, she'll grow to be a beauty.* The fingers paused a moment. *I wonder if Kallystine realizes that...* "What is it?"

Adiraina had suddenly stiffened. "Someone in the Halls has just experienced a berserker episode."

"I warned you!" Karidia burst out. "This comes of using Shanir powers and breeding for them. Oh yes, Ardeth, you and Kinzi did, admit it or not. Manipulating bloodlines, creating monsters...and now that precious Iron Matriarch of yours has blown up in someone's face!"

"It wasn't Brenwyr," said Adiraina, shaken. "I don't know who it was."

The matriarchs looked at each other. Berserker Highborn were Shanir with a strong affinity to the Third Face of God, That-Which-Destroys. Adolescent girls sometimes passed through a mock-berserker phase, but the genuine thing was not taken lightly by anyone remotely interested in a quiet life.

"Well, someone's got to find out," said Karidia, and went. The others were still discussing possibilities when she returned, hauling with her the young sewing teacher.

"It was that wretched Knorth," she announced, almost with satisfaction. "Tell them, girl."

The instructress told her story, stammering to find herself with such an august audience.

"I never said a-anything about using knot stitches as a code!" she wailed, clutching her shredded sampler. "That's a third circle secret. She shouldn't have known about it herself, much less mentioned it in front of the children. *And* she sang them Jamethiel's lament, a-all about obedience and Honor's Paradox...

"The trouble with that young lady," remarked Trishien after the instructress had burst into tears and been dismissed, "is that she isn't used to people who can think."

"Of course not!" snapped Karidia. "At that age, it's indecent! Honor's Paradox, indeed. As if anyone in that classroom was ready to learn about that, or perhaps ever will be. *And* the knot-stitch code. That wretched girl has nosed out another of our mysteries, without being sworn to keep quiet about it."

"You can't have it both ways," said Trishien reasonably. "We haven't trusted her with the secrets of the Women's World, so she learns what she can and owes nothing to us. Excuse me." Her hand had written something in a spiky script. She read the short message and signed an acknowledgment in her own rounded letters. "A weather note from Kirien: Mount Alban reports increased weirding. The College thinks a storm is on the way. What a pity," she added, musing, "that this Jameth was born a Knorth. The Jaran would know what to do with a mind like that."

The Coman Matriarch flushed. "H-how *dare* you think of a purebred Knorth in those terms! You stick to corrupting your own women, you...you scrolls-worm! And as for your precious Kirien..."

"*Karidia!*"

The collective voice and will of the other matriarchs brought her to a dead halt, a bit dazed, as if she had run full-tilt into a wall.

"Remember where and what you are," said Adiraina sternly. "Behave."

"None of us have been quite normal, I think, since that girl arrived," remarked Dianthe. "Haven't you noticed? She makes people forget themselves. I wish, though, that the sewing teacher hadn't slapped her. Have we really made the Highlord's sister so vulnerable?"

Karidia snorted, rallying. "Before you start thinking of that girl as helpless, you'd better look at this."

She held out the sampler which she had appropriated from her young kinswoman. They all regarded it at first with bewilderment, then with growing apprehension as Adiraina took it, spread it out on her lap, and examined the slashes by touch. Each of her fingers fitted into one.

"Oh dear," she said. "Oh *dear.*"

III

Jame's first thought, as she pitched forward down the spiral stair, was an echo of the instructress's: "Oh no. Not again."

Then she gave a shout to warn anyone who might be on the steps below her, curled up, and rolled. The trick was to keep all extremities tucked well in and let the heavy velvet of her gown act as padding as she caromed down the stair's stony throat. It worked, as it had all too often over that long winter, until her hem caught on a broken tread. Suddenly checked, she crashed down full length at the foot of the steps and lay there for a moment, thoroughly shaken. Then, in a language which, hopefully, no one else at Gothregor understood, she began to swear.

"*What* was that?" voices exclaimed above. "Lady Jameth, are you all right?"

They were probably wondering if she had finally managed to break her neck. Here came one of them now, hopping down the steps to find out.

Jame struggled to rise, in furious contention with the tight under and voluminous overskirt. Dammit, she was *not* going to be found tied up in knots, like some poorly wrapped package. Her foot tangled in the damaged hem, ripping it more, as she floundered upright.

The lady on the stair bent to peer around its newel. No broken body huddled on the floor below. She descended to the arcade which extended around the Forecourt, under the classrooms. No one there either. Crossing the gallery, she examined the sweep of the court. Nothing.

"Vanished again," she called to her friends above.

When she had hopped laboriously back up the stairs, Jame emerged from a niche under them, shaking dust from her skirts. The sound of renewed lessons rolled down to her, the sewing

teacher's voice shrilling above the others in praise of obedience, self-restraint, endurance, and silence, as if by sheer volume she could obliterate the past few minutes. Jame wondered what precious, petty secret she had stumbled across this
time, to have made that little idiot panic so badly. Well, not an
idiot, exactly—only willfully ignorant, like so many others in
these halls.

Come to that, her own response hadn't been particularly
brilliant.

She regarded her black-gloved hands with disgust. The
nails looked almost demure in repose beneath their ripped-out
fingertips—a secret of her own which she bitterly regretted
having at last betrayed. The first time those retractile ivory
claws had made their appearance, in her seventh year, they
had gotten her thrown out of her Haunted Lands home. A
fine joke it would be if the same thing happened here, and
perhaps no more than she deserved.

In the meantime, though, what next? Back to her room in
the Caineron compound to repair her damaged clothes? Although no needlewoman, she usually wasn't as inept as she
had been in the sewing class. Indeed, certain individuals in
the past had found her very nimble-fingered, although not at
skills which the ladies here would appreciate. She wouldn't
have made such a mess this afternoon if she hadn't been worried about Jorin.

The Royal Gold ounce cub had been taken away from her
on her arrival at Gothregor, after Kallystine had made a fuss.
Jame had missed him terribly, especially on cold nights when
she was used to having him crawl into bed with her, a warm,
purring lump who usually by morning had appropriated both
blankets and pillow. Even so, they hadn't been entirely separated. Blind from birth, Jorin used Jame's eyes to see; likewise, she was slowly learning how to share his other four senses.
As a result, when he went for his daily run in the outer ward
she, in a way, accompanied him. He should be out enjoying
himself now. Perhaps the link between them was simply weak

today, but what if the ounce was ill or hurt? She had been trying to contact him when she had inadvertently sewn her fingers together.

Worry again directed her: Jame found herself turning left onto the northern leg of the gallery, toward the inner ward and the subterranean stables where Jorin had spent the winter.

This section of the arcade and the apartments opening off of it belonged to the Brandan. A randon cadet and her captain stood by the main entrance, both wearing the dress grays and scarlet shoulder-embroidery of their house. Although each compound was considered sovereign territory with its own small garrison, bemused guards had allowed Jame to explore all of them but one. She slowed, remembering her rebuff on the Randir threshold by its smiling, cold-eyed captain, whose name she had never been able to learn.

The Brandan captain looked up. Close-cut sandy hair, one brow broken by an old scar, flattened nose—a stranger.

Ah. This must be the Brandan's day to rotate the guard, new cadets coming down with their officer from the randon college at Tentir, the old either returning there or going on to the Southern Host. Would these two let her pass? The cadet looked uncertain, but the captain crossed low-held wrists in the salute of Kendar to Highborn, curiosity in her good-natured, bright blue eyes.

Jame passed with a nod, feeling suddenly shy. Who was she to receive tribute from a randon officer? Ganth Gray Lord's daughter, yes, but she hadn't known that until a few months ago. The last Knorth lady, clothed in rotting velvet...Behind the mask, what was she becoming? Who had she ever, really, been?

Abruptly, she felt the touch of Jorin's senses. The surface under his paws was hard—stone, not packed earth—and he was running. The air smelled of stone too. At the end of the long gallery, a Kendar maid leaped aside with a shriek, her armload of clean linen flying. Through the blizzard of white sheets hurtled a silver-gilt form. Blind Jorin had apparently gotten this far by ricocheting off walls and was headed for another one when Jame saw him. Instantly, he straightened out, came pelting down the hall, and leaped into her arms. Struck in the chest by forty pounds of rapidly moving ounce, Jame went over backward. The Brandan captain loomed above her. Someone was shouting that the cat had attacked her.

"He did not!" she gasped, clutching Jorin.

"I can see that, lady," said the captain, amused, as the ounce hid his sleek head under Jame's arm. "Damned funny behavior for a full-grown hunting ounce, though."

"He is not full-grown...well, not quite...and he doesn't know he's an ounce. A tabby cat named Boo raised him."

"Ah. Well, that explains everything."

Someone shoved the captain aside. Jame saw riding boots, a brown, divided skirt, a heavy coat with inserts of braided leather, and a masked face. Although she had never met this lady before, there was only one person whom she could be: Brenwyr, the Iron Matriarch.

What Brenwyr saw were Jame's torn clothes. Brown eyes widened, then flared red. The impact of her sudden fury seemed to pick Jame up off the floor and nail her against the arcade's inner wall. She slid sideways in a water-flowing evasion, snatched up both of her skirts and ran, Jorin pelting after her.

Afterward, she supposed that they must have bolted right through the Caineron compound and into the derelict halls beyond, where the women of numerous minor houses had once lived. What brought her up at last, hard, was a wall which she had apparently also tried to run straight through. At least the tapestry had muted the collision. It hung before her now, frayed and faded but still wonderfully wrought: a moon garden full of pale blooms, seen through an open door.

Sanctuary, she thought, still half-dazed; then, as Jorin climbed into her arms chirping anxiously, *What in Perimal's name happened?*

But she already knew. When Ganth had realized with the appearance of her claws that she was Shanir, he had driven her out with just such a blast of mad rage. That time, she hadn't stopped running until she was across the Barrier into Perimal Darkling.

Trinity. That was another secret which she hoped these women never learned. Yet she had sung that song to those children, as if to remind both them and herself that there was more to their world than needlework. To that little sewing teacher, though, it had been only a tale of ancient days. Few knew or guessed that Gerridon, Master of Knorth, had indeed gained a semblance of that immortality for which he had betrayed his people, through the souls which the Dream-Weaver had reaped for him and the slower passage of time in Perimal Darkling. There in his monstrous house he still dwelt, deeper in shadow with each captured soul which he devoured, yet desperate for more as their number dwindled and darkness crept closer to claiming him as its own.

And there Jame had also lived, from the time of her flight from the Haunted Lands keep until two years ago.

That was hard to believe now.

Half her life had passed in those dark halls, yet most of it was a blur, like the fading images of a bad dream. Had she been made to forget, or willed it to protect herself? Sometimes she wondered: Had it even, really, happened?

When she had finally stumbled back to her old home two years ago, she had remembered nothing of the decade since her expulsion. Since then, fragmentary memories had begun to return, like snatches of an old, dark song: practicing the combat *kantirs* of the Senethar on the green-veined floor of the Master's great hall under the eyes of massed Knorth death banners; learning how to read the master runes in a pale book, in a library whose volumes slithered, whispering, on the shelves; dancing the Great Dance as her namesake had before her under the instruction of golden-eyed shadows; realizing at last with horror that she was being trained to take the Dream-Weaver's place.

Only afterward had she learned that this last was no coincidence.

Gerridon needed someone to reap souls for him, to keep him both immortal and human despite the shadows' hunger. Whatever the Women's World thought, his sister-consort had only been his tool, not understanding the evil which he had asked her to commit until too late. Her fall had not been complete, and in the end she had redeemed herself. Still, she had paid a terrible price. So massive an abuse of power had opened a rift in her nature to the chaos beyond, so that toward the end all souls which she touched were caught in the vortex and sucked down, irretrievably. Before that final stage, however, Gerridon had sent her to the exiled Ganth Gray Lord specifically to breed her own successor. Jame was the child whom he had wanted, or so her Senethari Tirandys had told her. No one had counted on twins. Likewise, Gerridon hadn't expected Tirandys to teach the new Jamethiel honor as well as the Senethar. When the night of her investment came, she had slashed the hand held out to her between the red ribbons of a bridal couch, taken the Book Bound in Pale Leather, and fled back across the barrier into Rathillien.

Thus, she had come again to the Haunted Lands keep, stripped of her memory, searching for the twin brother who had stood by while their father had driven her out but whom she still loved, almost as the other half of her soul. But everyone there was dead, slain by the Master in his search for her—everyone except Tori.

Her efforts to find him had taken the next two years, including a sojourn as an apprentice thief in the wonderful, god-ridden city of Tai-tastigon.

Now here she was at last, in their ancestral home, with a twin brother who turned out to be not only Highlord but (thanks to the slower passage of time in the Master's house) a decade her senior. Or rather, here she was without him. Judging from his continued absence, he wished that she had stayed lost. So did Jame, in a way, but she was Kencyr. She belonged with her people. It had crossed her mind not half an hour before that she might be on the verge of a second expulsion. If she was driven out again, this time from the heart of the Kencyrath, where was there left to go?

The image rose in her memory of a snowfield high in the Ebonbane, splitting open, thundering down into the maw of the chasm hidden beneath.

Why had she suddenly remembered that?

Ah. Over the tapestry was a wooden frieze depicting big cats at play—Arrin-ken, actually, third of the three people, that made up the Kencyrath, once its judges. On the night of the Fall, many of them had been blinded with burning coals and then slain in the Master's hall, where their flayed skins still lay as trophies on his cold hearth. The rest had fled to Rathillien. A thousand years ago, though, they had withdrawn into the wilds. The carver, therefore, had never seen one. Jame had. In the Ebonbane, on the chasm's edge, Immalai the Silent had laid bare all the shadows which years in the Master's House had bred in her:

Child, you have perverted the Great Dance as your namesake did before you. You have also usurped a priest's authority and misused a master rune. We conclude that you are indeed a darkling, in training if not in blood, reckless to the point of madness...

Under his silent voice in her mind had spoken all the Arrin-ken in their distant retreats, a woven chorus of power, judging her.

But in the end she had passed judgment on herself. She had indeed done all those things and perhaps more besides, which she had now forgotten. She could have blamed the darkness bred into her or the training forced on her, neither her fault. She could even have blamed her Shanir blood, which had made the rest possible. Instead, she had chosen to take responsibility for her own actions, to jump into the abyss and die, if that was required.

It wasn't. Immalai had overridden the others, suspending judgment.

An unfallen darkling, innocent, but not ignorant...

It was something, Jame supposed, to embody a paradox which could make even an Arrin-ken pause. Despite all the dark things she had been taught, despite some of the truly stupid things she had done, she hadn't yet fallen from honor. So, be damned if she was going to let anyone drive her over the edge of anything, if she wasn't prepared to go.

Nor was she ready to surrender Jorin. Jame looked back the way she had come, out of doors hanging askew down a long corridor half-sunk into dusty twilight. The guards might try to follow her. She didn't think much of their chances, though, in this wilderness of empty halls which, thanks to a winter of ceaseless exploration, she probably knew better than any of them did. No, no one would take Jorin away from her tonight, unless she tripped over a search party. Best, though, to keep moving.

She pushed aside the tapestry. Behind it was a door, and through that, under the grim shadow of the Ghost Walks, the moon garden itself.

Tall, windowless walls surrounded it. Pale comfrey sheltered against its northern end, three feet high with drooping, bell-shaped flowers on racemes as curved as a scorpion's tail. Then there were yarrow with their lacy, silver-gray foliage, white self-heal, wild heart's-ease already hanging their heads against the coming night, and a dozen other flowering herbs, all pure white. A small brook cut across the southern end of the garden, emerging from a tunnel under the outer wall and plunging under ground near the inner to join the fortress's subterranean water system. Beyond it, against the south wall, the delicate fiddlehead scrolls of young ferns arched up through the last, sheltered crust of snow. All the white flowers glowed slightly in the dusk (except the yarrow, still in tight bud), and white moths danced over them, wings luminous with pollen.

Jorin plunged into the deep grass with an excited bleat.

Jame followed more slowly. She was tempted to spend the night as she sometimes had in the past, escaping Kallystine,

but didn't want to bring her bad dreams here. The garden had
a dreaming quality of its own, haunted not so much by a ghost
as by the half-forgotten memory of one. Against the south
wall hung a tattered death banner. A gentle, barely discernible
face gazed out of it, the texture of the wall behind showing
through its weatherworn threads. It was a Knorth face, Jame
thought, but she didn't know whose, much less why it had
been exiled here while the rest of the family banners hung in
state in the old keep. No, she would leave the garden and its
lady in peace tonight. Bending, she picked a spray of white
primrose. A light shake caused its buds to spring open and the
pollen within to luminescence. Surrounded by a nimbus of
eager moths and followed by a reluctant ounce, she entered
the Ghost Walks.

Once the Knorth had occupied these mural apartments
from the northern gate to the eastern, but they had been a
dwindling house long before the massacre. On that spring
night, the northeast drum tower had been large enough to house
them all. A door in the herb garden's corner opened immediately into the kitchen. The family's guard had occupied the
ground level, where they had slept through the slaughter taking place over their heads—inexplicably, some had thought
afterward, but Jame suspected the expert use of poppy dust.

She was less certain about the Shadow Guild's claim to
invisibility. Its members were said to wear clothes made from
the fibers of the transparent *mere* plant, earned garment by
garment as apprentices. Journeymen went on to a knife tempered in *mere* sap. Masters of the Guild acquired *mere* tattoos,
bit by bit covering every inch of their bodies, including eye-
balls, and as far into every orifice as the dye needles would
reach. The Grand Master was said to be totally invisible, able
to walk through walls, and quite insane from *mere* poisoning—
if one believed that such an unlikely thing as *mere* existed.

A stair spiraled upward along the curve of the tower. The
second floor, divided into apartments circling a hall, had been
occupied by the family itself. Jame went through the silent

rooms, the primrose wand dimly lighting her way. In the central hall she paused, looking about at the moldering rugs, the dusty furniture, the cold fire-pit. From the dark corners came a furtive rustling, instantly stilled. Jorin's nose twitched at the sharp smell of mouse.

"They were all here, you know," she said softly to him. "Mothers, daughters, aunts, nieces, cousins—the last dozen or so purebred Knorth women left on Rathillien, even those who had contracted out to other houses. It was their first family gathering after the thaws. They were up late, waiting for their men to come home. Ganth had gone off to hunt a rathorn, you see."

The ounce gave an uneasy, questioning chirp, as if he really did see. Perhaps he had plucked the image out of her mind of those eerie, armored beasts.

"That's right. Like the mare I killed in the Anarchies. Like that white, death's-head foal of hers who's probably still after my blood—small blame to him, even if it was a mercy killing."

All winter Jame had been hunting too, not for a slayer but for the slain. The dead could sometimes touch the living. Hadn't her brother carried the bones of a child all the way from Kithorn to the Cataracts and been helped more than once by her ghost? Hadn't she herself played tag-you're-dead in Penari's Maze with its very bad-tempered, very deceased architect?

These walks were also said to have their ghost: a Knorth girl named Tieri, killed in the massacre, whose body had never been found. The unburnt dead always return, it was said. For years, lights and sounds had been reported in these dusty halls but never investigated, on orders of the Ardeth Matriarch, who had virtually ruled the Women's Halls during the Knorth's long exile. Finally, the disturbances had stopped. Jame's own prowlings had been in part a bone-hunt, as boys used to steal off to haunted Kithorn to retrieve relics of its slaughtered garrison for the pyre. They saw this as a test of nerve, as well as a service to the dead. Jame simply wanted to touch the family she had never known. Here in the Walks, though, there was no point of contact—not even with those faded bloodstains on the floor where, perhaps, her great-grandmother Kinzi, the last Knorth Matriarch, had died.

Nonetheless, when Jame regained the stairs, she again climbed.

The entire third floor had been reserved for the Gray Lord's use. It all looked gray enough now with dust and dusk, a desolation of public rooms serving as antechambers to the Highlord's apartment. Standing on the threshold of his bedchamber, Jame reflected that it had really been the Highlord's reaction which had sealed the tragedy.

Ganth had assumed that the Seven Kings of Bashti had commissioned the assassins. That still made a certain amount of sense. Collectively, the Bashtiri of the Central Lands hired more Kencyr troops than anyone except Krothen of Kothifir, and were always complaining that the Kencyr code of honor unduly restricted the orders which their mercenaries would obey. They might have reasoned that if they could eliminate the family which held the Kencyrath to its old, honorable ways, they could make contracts more to their taste with the surviving houses.

But there sense and sanity alike had ended for the Gray Lord. He had marched down into the White Hills where all seven kings were engaged in one of their usually bloodless squabbles and had attacked without parley, although his Host was not only greatly outnumbered but faced with the kings' Kencyr mercenaries as well. The end, after three bloody days, had been a stalemate and exile for the handful of surviving Knorth.

The Bashtiri kings still swore that they hadn't sent the killers.

It all seemed impossibly remote to Jame, like a tale told of ancient days. Yet the people she had known at the keep in the Haunted Lands had lived through this, even if Ganth had forbidden them to tell his children about it. If they had, though,

would that have made it seem more real? Perhaps the imper-
sonal past never did. Perhaps that was why nothing in the
Ghost Walks touched her.

At least, so Jame thought as she turned to leave. A gust
of wind blew through the broken windows behind her. It
came again, harder, to rustle dry leaves across the floor, to
lift and plait the tattered ribbons of arrases against the wall.
The age-blurred hunting scenes shifted, and shifted again in
the dimming light, dream images tumbling through the indistinct forms of leaf and bough, hunter and hunted. Gray,
gray not a forest at all but a city street, deep-shadowed, down
which dead leaves blew. One of the shadows moved. It was
crawling toward her, flat on the ground, like a spreading stain.
The leaves rattled over it. Its fingers slid, elongated, over
the cobblestones, and seemed to clutch them to pull itself
forward. Then it raised its head.

"Are you thinking of me, butcher of children?" Jame heard
her own voice demand harshly, and knew that she was backing away. "Why can't you leave me alone?"

Something caught her behind the knees. Her hands leaped
out to grab the window frame, to prevent her from tumbling
backward out of the tower. Across the room, another gust of
wind combed out the shreds of tapestry.

Jame sat down with a thump on the low windowsill. Sweet
Trinity. If her nightmares were going to pursue her into waking life, she was in deep trouble. Anyway, that particular ghost
didn't even belong here. Bane was one of *her* dead, not
Gothregor's—assuming that the Tastigon mob had finally managed to kill him.

Another attempt at mercy, another bloody mess...

Most people would say that a man who mutilated children
for sport didn't deserve even that much. But they didn't understand. Neither did Jame, entirely. He had threatened,
tempted, and ultimately saved her when the mob had come to
take him to the Mercy Seat to be flayed alive for the one murder in a score which he hadn't committed. Even then, he

couldn't die without his soul, which he had given for safe-keeping to the Kencyr priest Ishtier. Ishtier in turn had treacherously used it to create the Lower Town Monster, which fed on children through their soul-cast shadows. With Bane on the Mercy Seat, under the knife, Jame had tried to destroy the demon Monster, to free his soul so that he could die. By then, though, the mob had been after her too, and she'd had to flee Tai-tastigon without knowing if she had succeeded. The alternative hardly made for pleasant dreams. It helped somewhat that Ishtier had paid for his betrayal with madness, but not much. In his warped way, Bane had been a friend—and blood-kin. Jame was sure of that, with or without proof. As much Ganth's son by a Kendar mistress as she was his daughter by...

No. Don't even think it.

She had been careless before. There were women here, she suspected, who could pluck the very thoughts out of one's head. Ancestors only knew what would happen if they learned who her mother was. Luckily, they had decided that her own full name must be Jameth, the alternative never having occurred to any of them. She hid behind their mistake as she did behind the mask which they had forced her to wear. But hiding had only brought a stalemate. Now circumstances had forced her a little into the light, and she couldn't decide whether to advance or retreat again.

Jame sighed. So much at Gothregor confused her. She wished she could talk to Marc about it, but the big Kendar was still with the Host at Kothifir, enjoying his first rest in ninety-odd years. Not that he could advise her about the intricacies of the Women's World, of course, but problems tended to unravel before his tranquil common sense.

What are you hiding from, lass? he would probably ask now. *Wear that mask long enough and you'll forget what your own face looks like.*

Small loss that would be.

Even so, which will you choose—the face or the mask?

The Women's World prized the freedom which masks gave them to conceal their feelings from men, to live their lives hidden as they did within these halls in the mysteries of sister-kinship; but they hadn't chosen to share that life with Jame.

She remembered the children's taunt: "Seeker, seeker..." that damned game so much like blind man's buff, played with the eyeless mask. The blind seeker must catch someone, correctly guess her name, and then assume it while the mask passed to a new face and a new seeker groped for her lost identity among her jeering peers.

I'm groping now, thought Jame with a sigh.

The face or the mask, oh bother. Marc's "simple" questions never had simple answers.

There was a face at Gothregor, though, which the Women's World apparently hoped to recreate beneath the mask which they had made her wear.

Well, why not? This seemed to be a night for ghost stalking.

"C'mon, kitten," she said to the ounce. "Let's go visit Aerulan."

IV

Light and shadow interwove in the room where the Lady Kallystine sat at her evening adornment. Candles burned everywhere, their flames reflected in endless succession by mirrors lining the walls. All the fiery sparks danced restlessly: no amount of silken hangings, drawn however close, could shut out the fitful breath of the south wind called the Tishooo, which had risen within the past half hour. In the farther reaches of the large chamber, black-clad Kendar maids moved silently, ceaselessly, among the banks of candles, relighting those which the wind had extinguished. They had no need to approach their lady's dressing table, however: the candles there had a trick, after a moment's hesitation, of rekindling themselves.

By their light, Kallystine admired her reflection. Here in her own chambers, she wore no mask but a delicate lacework of leaf gold, dusted as lightly on her face as the iridescence on a jewel-jaw's wing. Carmine brought a warm glow to high cheekbones and full lips. Powdered sapphire traced the veins of throat and snowy breast. Her personal maid, a young Kendar-Highborn half-breed, was brushing her long, black hair with slow strokes. Kallystine basked in the sensation, watching herself in the mirror through half-closed eyes. She was twenty-five years old, at the height of her power, and used to getting everything she wanted. What she wanted most at the moment, however, seemed perversely to have abstracted itself.

"Would it be too much to inquire," she asked the room at large, in her most languid voice, "if the Lady Jameth has yet been found? Can it really be that every spare guard is searching?"

"No, my lady; yes, my lady."

No expression colored the handmaid's voice or face. A winter in M'lady's service had taught her to keep her thoughts to herself. Kallystine noted the tone. She picked up a long, handsome braid of hair from the table, ran it through her fingers once or twice, then carelessly tossed it to the maid.

"Here. I shan't need this after all," she said, and smiled to see the girl receive back her own hair as woodenly as she had hacked it off earlier, so that her mistress could experiment with it as a fall. It was a Highborn's duty continually to remind others who held the power. Her father, Lord Caineron, had taught her that.

He had also commanded that she reduce the Knorth Jameth to a similar state of submission. "Break her into pieces," his last correspondence had abruptly concluded, "then grind them into powder."

Kallystine wondered what the creature had done, to make her father so angry. As always, she had tried to carry out his orders, with little success. Oh, the girl obeyed her, but with such cool reserve that Kallystine hadn't been able so much as to scratch her composure. Worse, despite the matriarchs' apparent indifference, she had found herself hesitant to use her usual, more direct methods: after all, the wretched girl *was* a Highborn Knorth, and a strangely intimidating one at that. Oh, it had been maddening.

Ah, but now, finally, she had something to work with.

"Describe to me again that deplorable episode in the classroom," she said, selecting a candied tadpole from an alabaster bowl.

The handmaid again described in a perfectly flat voice all that the Caineron spies had been able to learn. However, no amount of coaxing or threats had induced the little girl who had been closest to say what she had seen, the moment before the instructress's sampler had fallen to shreds. She was an Ardeth, and the Ardeth Matriarch had sworn her to silence.

That blind bitch, thought Kallystine, biting off the tadpole's head. Why should she queen it here at Gothregor, over the

Highlord's own consort? As for the cool way Adiraina had dismissed her plan to occupy the old Knorth quarters—

"Oh, no, my dear. That would hardly be appropriate."

Impossible, explaining to her father why she hadn't carried out that particular order regardless. Hard enough to understand it herself, or the Women's World at all, kept as she was at its lowest level—more of Adiraina's work, surely, as though she couldn't be trusted with their stupid little secrets!

(Not that Father wouldn't probably find them fascinating. If he *should* ask, well, the first rule of the Women's World was obedience, wasn't it?)

Secrets...

The Knorth's hands and those perpetual gloves, hiding (oh, delicious thought) what monstrous deformity?

Kallystine's attention focused sharply on her reflection. Was that a wrinkle? No, of course not. Just the same, her skin had been more radiant two years ago, when she had first become Torisen's limited-term consort. She knew that he had consented only to stave off her father, but she had still managed to dazzle him. It had seemed inevitable that he would agree to a half-Caineron heir. Now, however, that contract had almost expired. She still didn't doubt her charms, but in order for them to work he had to be *here*. Somehow, it was that wretched Jameth's fault that he wasn't. But the man had to come home soon, and she must prepare for that day.

Kallystine's mirror reflected most of the room behind her, including a basin set on a tripod. She regarded it with discontent. The matriarchs (those meddling cows!) had forbidden her to experiment directly on the Highlord, but Great-aunt Rawneth had suggested an alternative. If only it worked, she could at least greet Torisen on his return with the same fresh complexion that had captivated him against his will two years ago. The potion lacked only the proper activating agent, which Great-aunt said she must discover for herself. The Kendar had proved useless. As for her half-breed servant...

"Show me your hand."

Stony-faced, the maid obeyed. Her right hand was oddly withered, with blue, protruding veins, discolored spots, and swollen joints, the result of repeated immersions. What a pity that its lost youth had not proved transferable to the next person who had used the basin. Science was *such* a imprecise art.

Kallystine repeated these observations out loud, adding over her shoulder, "Make a note of that."

In the dark corner by the bed, knitting needles began to click.

Ah, thought Kallystine suddenly, but what if she were to use a pureblooded Highborn—the purest in Gothregor, by all accounts? That would be poetic revenge indeed, to make the one pay who was responsible for this long winter of lost opportunities; and afterward, given those omnipresent black gloves, who would ever know?

The Tishooo caught its breath. Hangings swayed backward out the first story windows, then in again as the wind exhaled—"Whoo!"—extinguishing a quarter of the candles. Maids hastily relit them. The room seemed surrounded by walls of moving air, as cut off by the growing storm as by the Caineron guards. Tonight, this was like a corner of Restormir, sovereign, inviolate, where a child of the house might amuse herself as she chose. So thought Kallystine, smiling at her reflection with half-closed eyes as she savored the other two pieces of information that she had gained tonight: a story and a fact which to her was the most exciting news of all: someone had actually slapped the Knorth Jameth, and gotten away with it.

Muted voices sounded by the door.

"...tripped right over one of our search parties," a guard was saying. "No, we didn't see the ounce."

What a pity, thought Kallystine. She'd had such amusing plans for that cat. Still, one shouldn't be greedy.

"Lady Jameth," she said sweetly, turning. "How kind of you to pay this visit."

The Knorth stood motionless, a slender, dark form surrounded by candles. Her skirt spread out around her, its lower
edge merging with the room's shadows, its folds concealing
her gloved hands.

"Leave us," said Kallystine to her servants.

They went, all but the indistinct figure by the bed and the
handmaid, who slipped aside at the door and remained in the
room, concealed by a hanging, the severed braid in her withered right hand, the frozen expression still on her face.

Kallystine had risen and was slowly, languidly, circling the
Knorth. Her train, iridescent as a peacock's tail, wound around
the other's plum-dark skirt. The jewels in her hair mocked the
other's archaic simplicity.

"So," she said, regarding the Knorth's dusty hem. "You've
been for a stroll in the abandoned halls, perhaps even in the
Ghost Walks? Gone to visit the scene of past familial glories, hmmmm? What a pity the future will hold so few of
them, but then there are so few of you Knorth left, aren't
there?"

The answer to this apparently being self-evident, the Knorth
didn't reply. Like the handmaid, she had learned to say as
little to M'lady as possible.

"Well, perhaps there's one more of you than you think,"
Kallystine snapped, annoyed enough to play her main card
before she had intended.

The other's poise broke. "What do you mean? Who else
could there be?"

"Ah, someone in the shadows," said Kallystine, still circling, beginning again to enjoy herself. "Have you ever heard
of a girl named Tieri?"

"The ghost in the Walks?"

"That childish story. Properly fooled we all were by it,
too. Well, it seems that Aerulan hid the brat in the empty
halls, where the Ardeth Matriarch later found her. A ghost
she may be now, but she lived for twelve years after the massacre. The last Knorth lady, an Ardeth prisoner in her own

halls—much good it did that blind hag in the end. Tieri died, you see. In the moon garden. Giving birth to a bastard."

"Poor Tieri."

"Rather pity yourself. She was your father's youngest full sister, your aunt."

"So the child was my first cousin—or is it still alive?"

"Who *cares*? The point is that there is, or was, a Knorth bastard. Three of you left, my dear, and one a, a *thing*, that calls into serious question whether you yourself will breed true. I needn't tell you how damaging even the whisper of this could be to your prospects. But the secret needn't go outside this room, if we stay friends." Unexpectedly, her voice grew husky. She reached to touch the other's hair. "Such very, very good friends…"

The Knorth pivoted away. Her hair slid like black water over Kallystine's white hand. Her heavy skirt, swinging, clipped the tripod, splashing some of the basin's contents on the floor. Oblivious, they stared at each other. The wind died between them. In the corner, for a moment, the knitting needles were still.

Kallystine sighed and withdrew her hand. "Then again," she murmured, "perhaps the other way is better. We needn't disagree, my dear, not if you serve me well. As a gesture of our understanding, perhaps you will help me with a pet project." She faced the Knorth across the basin, smiling again with a sleepy, almost benign malice. "Such a small thing, my dear. Just stir this mixture for me. With your bare hand."

The girl stared at her. "Why on earth should I?"

A noise drew their attention downward. The ounce Jorin had emerged from under his mistress's full outer skirt to sniff at the puddle on the floor. Now he was scratching around it.

"Ah," said Kallystine. "I wonder. Is it true that ounces have special glands which produce the most exquisite perfume? Shall we find out?"

"Ah oooo!" said the wind, and sucked the drapes out the embrasures into the night. The candle flames leaped and died.

In the sudden, rushing darkness which followed, a strong hand grabbed Kallystine by the hair and thrust her downward into icy liquid. She reared back, sputtering, clawing at her eyes. Her face felt strange.

Then the candles on the dressing table flickered back to life and she saw herself in the mirror.

M'lady Kallystine began to scream.

V

Adiraina still sat by the window, alone now in the falling night. The breeze off the Snowthorns had turned to a rising wind that lapped around her until she felt as if she hovered in it, perilously balanced.

It had taken her a long time to regain even so much poise as this. The old should be used to death's imminence, but tonight had brought back the memory of too many struck down too soon: strong Kinzi, sweet-faced Aerulan, Tieri...

She had almost put that sad child out of her mind, until now. Growing up alone in the Ghost Walks where so many had died, herself the only ghost... Had that long concealment really been necessary? What if she, Adiraina, had actually been punishing the girl for having survived when Kinzi had not?

No, *no*, NO.

"I didn't have a choice," she had protested to Dianthe, when at last the secret had to be told. *"You remember what those times were like. Ganth's madness had thrown us all into chaos, defenseless. The assassins might have returned if they had known that any Knorth women had survived."*

"I can understand not telling the lords," Dianthe had agreed, *"then or later. Tieri was the last of her house, a prize—except that without her lord to give assent, any child of hers would have been a bastard. The Kencyrath was in trouble enough without that. But couldn't you at least have told us?"*

Not without knowing who had sent the assassins in the first place; and with Tieri dead, Adiraina hadn't wanted to know at all, when the answer might destroy what was left of her world. What did it matter if the blood price for the slain went unpaid when no Knorth were left to collect?

But now the Knorth had returned, brother and sister, Ganth's children.

And if someone still wanted all the women of that house dead?

They can't, she told herself. *Not after all these years.* Anyway, too many secrets had been kept too long. She daren't betray them now. Long awaited footsteps sounded on the stair. Silk rustled. So, Brenwyr had changed out of "that horrid skirt" but not, from the length of her stride, into the traditional tight under-gown.

"Greetings, Brandan," Adiraina said formally.

"Greetings, Ardeth."

A hand touched her shoulder. *Grandmother-kin,* said the fingers, with that special emphasis that indicated an embrace. "Sorry I'm so late," the Iron Matriarch added out loud. "I meant to attend the council meeting this afternoon but, well, something happened."

"So I heard. You finally met the Knorth. I have said all along that you should, but not quite like that. Do you feel better now, dear?"

"Of course," said Brenwyr, irritably. "Why shouldn't I?"

"You know perfectly well. You flared, my dear. A perfect example of a mature berserker episode, the sort that always gives you such terrible headaches afterward. That's your touch of Knorth blood again, I'm afraid, the quarter that dear Kinzi gave you. Oddly enough, just before you someone else flared whom I never suspected before of berserker tendencies but should have, given her bloodlines: Jameth."

"Aerulan never flared."

"Dear Aerulan had none of the family curses. All in all, she was the most atypical Knorth I've ever met. But this isn't Aerulan."

"God's claws, don't you think I know that?"

"I have occasionally wondered. My dear, are you quite sure you know what you are doing?"

"No!" Her boots rang on the ironwood floor as she began to pace restlessly back and forth. "Sometimes I think I'm going out of my mind altogether—a proper Knorth response, eh? After I killed..."

"My dear!"

"All right, grandmother-kin. After my mother died, all the self-control I have, I learned from you. I know what it cost you, too."

Adiraina dismissed this with a graceful gesture, even as the memory of Brenwyr's most recent flare sent a stab of pain through her head. Linked by her own Shanir traits to That-Which-Preserves, she knew that she had been lucky to survive her fosterling's childhood, much less her agonizing adolescence.

Brenwyr must have been watching her closely. "It seems that I can't help but hurt what I love best. Ancestors know, I loved Aerulan—but she's been ashes on the wind for thirty-four years! I was barely more than a child then. Since, I've honored a dozen contracts, borne four sons, managed my lord brother's keep, and become a matriarch on the council. You know the name they call me behind my back. Where has that iron discipline been this past winter? All I can think about is Aerulan, about ransoming her banner out of that cold hall, away from the moldering dead. Now. Before anything else can happen."

"Has Lord Brandan spoken to Torisen again about that?"

"He says he won't, that the Highlord doesn't understand, that the issue is too delicate to force. I ask you!"

"He might be right. I've often thought that Torisen Black Lord doesn't know our customs as well as he should, or is likely to with no Knorth Matriarch to instruct him. It occurs to me, though, that eventually there may be one here again."

"This girl Jameth? That's absurd!"

"No. I would say that it's inevitable. Who else is there? It's a disturbing thought, though, considering the example which she has already set for our younger sisters. Do you know what that child said when I told her to keep quiet about what she had seen in the classroom? 'Why?' Oh, she'll obey, but still...!"

"Are questions really so dangerous?"

"Now, my dear. You *know* they are."

"Why? All right, all right: it doesn't matter. After the massacre, though, didn't the Randir Matriarch swear that there would never be a Knorth Matriarch here again?"

Adiraina shifted uneasily. "What a foolish thing for dear Rawneth to have said. I'm sure she's long since thought better of it. It doesn't matter anyway, as long as no Randir Highborn are in residence here and Jameth has been forbidden to enter their compound—but perhaps I shouldn't depend on that: the Knorth are so unpredictable, so hard to manage! Why, even Torisen, quiet as he is, has given Cousin Adric some uneasy moments."

Despite herself, Brenwyr smiled. "*Does* Lord Ardeth try to manage the Highlord?"

"Of course. And yet, and yet, sometimes, late at night, I wonder. This impulse, this almost compulsion to control these two young people... Do we find them so threatening because they remind us of what the Kencyrath once was like, and perhaps must be again if we are ever to fulfill the purpose for which we were created?"

"To defeat Perimal Darkling? Do you really think we ever will?"

"Ancestors only know," said Adiraina, and paused.

Before the Fall, her ancestors *had* thought they knew. Of course the shadows would be defeated, as soon as the three aspects of their god deigned to manifest themselves in the three Shanir known collectively as the Tyr-ridan. Earlier matriarchs had tried to speed that day by mating together potent Shanir. Whether they should have done so, especially within the bounds of blood-kinship, was still hotly debated. One such match had produced those dire twins, Gerridon and Jamethiel Dream-weaver, who in turn had been bred together with no issue except, perhaps, the Fall itself. Nonetheless, some matriarchs believed that in general their predecessors had the right idea.

Adiraina winced, remembering Karidia's taunt: "...*manipulating bloodlines, creating monsters...*" True, she *had* suggested the blood-cross which had produced Brenwyr, but really...!

"This much I do believe:" she said, "unless our god has forsaken us utterly, someday the Tyr-ridan *will* come, and then we all will face the ultimate test."

The wind veered, bringing with it a distant, enraged shriek and the sound of shattering glass.

"Someone must have annoyed Kallystine again," Brenwyr remarked sourly.

"I do believe that you are right, although I've never heard her break one of her precious mirrors before. Amazing, the way sound carries tonight. Earlier, I thought I heard the Knorth. 'Butcher of children,' she was crying, if that can be right. 'Butcher of children!' It sounded almost like an evocation."

Brenwyr had come to stand beside her. "The Tishooo plays strange tricks. I thought I heard Aerulan calling my name, over and over, the night she died. Speaking of evocations, do you know where I met the Knorth this afternoon? In the arcade, just where Aerulan fell. There she was, in a heap on the floor with a cat in her arms and a torn skirt—Aerulan's skirt..."

Adiraina groped for the younger woman's hand and clutched it. "You mustn't ill-wish that girl," she said urgently. "You *know* how dangerous that can be! My dear, my dear, remember your discipline: forget what you can't help. We both must. It was all over so long ago."

"Thirty-four years ago tonight." The bitter twist in her smile was as audible as broken bones grating. "Why, grandmotherkin, don't tell me *you* forgot. This is the anniversary of Aerulan's death."

VI

The moment the candles blew out, Jame whisked herself through a window into the night, as handily as anyone could whose legs were practically bound together by a tight underskirt. Jorin scrambled after her. They paused outside, listening to the commotion behind them.

"Now, that's a very excitable lady," said Jame to the ounce, "and not a very bright one. She thinks that you're a civet. Perfumes. Huh."

The screams resolved themselves into words. "You'll pay for this!" Kallystine was shrieking. "I'll see that you pay, you stinking Knorth!"

"Trinity," said Jame, as glass shattered in the room which she had just left, and again and again. "*All* her mirrors? Why? Let's just keep out of her way for awhile, eh, kitten?"

They went like shadows through the interconnected courtyards which separated the main hall blocks, a dark, gliding figure and a Royal Gold ounce cub, silver-gilt with traces of its winter coat. Over black mountains to the west, the sky had shaded to a deep indigo spangled with stars. The wind whooped around them, swirling Jame's skirt until she was obliged to hold it down with both hands. It was turning into a boisterous night, full of vast uproar. As a rule, the Tishooo only visited the Riverland when the priests weren't paying adequate attention to the weather. Its name in Nekrien meant "The Old Man"—an odd title, given its prankish nature. When it wasn't chasing its own tail or snatching up loose slates or plunging down chimneys, it was said to carry off unwanted babies and to turn shadows inside out.

Here was the Forecourt and across it, the old Knorth keep. Actually, the keep's lowest level long preceded the Kencyrath's tenure in this valley, or even that of the Hathiri. The ruins of ancient Merikit hill forts lined the Silver, many of them, as here, worked into the foundations of later buildings.

Inside, all was pitch black, heavy with the smell of cold stone and old cloth. Jame closed the door, groped for a box of candles on a shelf and lit one—cautiously, as she'd had chancy luck with fire ever since using its master rune the previous autumn, accidentally setting fire to a blizzard. The flickering light revealed a large, low-beamed hall. Faces stared out of the shadows against the walls, stirring restlessly in the wind that soughed under the door—death banners, row after row of them, woven of threads from the clothes in which each had died. These were her ancestors, such as had escaped the Fall into this new world, such as hadn't suffered exile with Ganth. All had the distinctive Knorth features—silver-gray eyes under arched brows; high, sharp cheekbones; obstinate chins— to which were often added the hard lines of arrogance and cruelty, it being the privilege of the Kendar weavers to portray the dead as they saw fit, yes, even to that wild, sidelong stare or those fingertips gnawed to white bone.

Who *were* all these people, anyway? Jame knew some names from old songs, but not to which banners they belonged. Her people, lost in time, receding. When their names, at last, were forgotten by all, would their faces crumble away as already the oldest here had done?

...past familial glories, a dying house...

But some were more recently dead than others. On the far west wall, flanking the door to the inner ward, hung the banners of those slain that terrible night in the Ghost Walks. Above a strong-jawed, older woman who might be Kinzi was the tapestry which Jame had come to see, the only one there close to her own age. She raised her candle in salute.

"Hello, Aerulan."

On first seeing that bright face with its whimsical smile, no one thought, "This is a death banner," but rather, "This is someone I would like to meet." It came as a shock a moment later to realize what that thin red line across Aerulan's neck represented. She was so plainly someone meant to love and be loved, not to bleed to death with a slit throat in the arms of the girl who would later become the Brandan Matriarch. Now it seemed that she had died leading the assassins away from where the child Tieri had lain hidden. That should have made her even more real to Jame. It didn't. Oh, this was hopeless, trying all winter to reach across a gap years deep, full of pyrrhic ash. The burnt dead *were* dead, and that was that.

She was about to turn away, sighing, when something about the banner caught her attention. As a rule, one only noticed Aerulan's face. Now, however, something about the dead girl's clothes, the cut of her tight-laced bodice…Jame felt a jolt of recognition. It wasn't, of course, the same dress which she now wore—Aerulan's russet gown had been teased apart thread by bloodstained thread to make the weft of this tapestry—but the style was as distinctive as its owner's teasing smile:

Do you know me yet?

Jame's sudden grin mirrored that on the face above her, more closely than she knew. "Walking all winter in your shoes, standing here now in your damned swaddling shift, I'd better, hadn't I? Well met at last, cousin."

The door to the Forecourt opened. A blast of wind extinguished Jame's candle.

"I tell you, I saw a light under the sill," said a dark figure in the doorway, to someone behind her. "Where d'you say that box of candles was?"

Jame shrank backward in the rustling darkness, silently cursing. Betrayed by fire again. They would hear her if she opened the door to the inner ward, assuming it wasn't locked. She edged northward along the wall to the spiral stair in the corner, hitched up her skirts, and scrambled upward with Jorin bounding on ahead. Candlelight danced over the steps at her heels. On the second floor landing, she paused to listen and learn that the people below were indeed Caineron guards, seeking the Knorth runaway.

They were climbing the stair.

Quick, quick—up to the lofty third-story chamber where the High Council met in the jeweled light of stained glass windows, up again into the northwest tower which Jame had never visited before, it having been so hideously cold here in winter. At the top of the stairs was an unlocked door. She slipped inside and closed it softly behind her. Her ear against its inner panels, she heard heavy feet mount the steps. The door started to open.

"Wait!" a guard called from the council chamber below. "That's Gothregor up there. Leave it be, for honor's sake, and help me search down here."

The door closed. Feet descended.

"Whew," Jame said, very softly, to Jorin. Then she turned.

The room was almost as dark as the hall below, except for what light seeped around its shutters as the wind rattled them impatiently. Jame groped over to the western window. When she unlatched it, the shutters flew open in her face and the Tishooo rushed in, exulting: *So there you are!*

Seventy feet below lay the grassy expanse of the inner ward, surrounded by the fortress's massive outer wall. Lights shone in the mural rooms opposite where her brother's Kendar were making themselves snug against the night. From this height, she could see over the battlements to the pale glimmer of Chantrie's ruins on the river's far bank. Jame wished that she had known about this vantage point when Lord Caineron had passed. As it was, she had spent the day keeping well out of sight, trusting Caldane no more than the Knorth garrison had. After all, the lord of Restormir had strong reasons, personal as well as dynastic, for wanting to get his hands on her again.

Thinking about Caineron reminded her of Graykin, his bastard son and erstwhile spy. At the Cataracts, though, she had accidentally bound Gray—something which only established Highborn males were supposed to do. There would be serious trouble if word got out about that, but nothing compared to the furor if anyone learned that she had also entrusted this Southron half-breed with the Book Bound in Pale Leather.

The Book, the Ivory Knife, and the Serpent-skin Cloak—those three objects of great if ambiguous power, kept by the Master in Perimal Darkling after the Fall. No one knew what roles they might play in the final conflict, only that each was necessary. Now at last two of them had come to Rathillien. The Knife lay hidden in Jame's room here at Gothregor, sullenly eating a hole in her mattress with its malign presence. As for the pale Book with its collection of master runes, what a poor guardian she had proved of that. In Tai-tastigon, both the Sirdan Theocandi and the priest Ishtier had coveted the deadly tome and been destroyed by their brief possession of it. At the Cataracts, with Caldane on her heels, she'd had to entrust it to Graykin.

No word had come of it or him since.

In her experience, that damned Book could usually look after itself, using whomever it pleased to do whatever it wanted.

As for Graykin, though, sooner or later Caineron would realize that his son had changed sides. Perhaps he had already. Perhaps that was why Jame had felt so uneasy these last three days since Caldane's passing and why now, when thinking about Gray, she found herself leaning out the window to look northward, toward the Caineron stronghold, Restormir. Her bond with the Southron was only of the mind, not the blood, but still it twitched at her attention like a string tied to a broken tooth.

What was she doing at Gothregor anyway? Playing dolly dress-up, demonstrating incompetence at things she had no wish to learn, wasting time when she had urgent business elsewhere... Damn Graykin anyway, and damn her too. Trapped behind a seeker's mask, searching for a name that would let her survive among her own people, how could she even defend herself, much less someone dependent on her?

Jame shivered. So this was what helplessness felt like: a cold draft up the spine, a premonition: *Find a way to fight back, soon, or be destroyed. Something is coming.*

"What?" she asked the breathing night.

No answer, no defense?

Other ladies would look for that from their kinsmen and guards. She was cut off from her brother's Kendar and her family was dead except for Tori—accidentally, wasn't it?

Could she really have other surviving kin within the degree of blood—a first cousin, in fact, accidentally a bastard?

Illegitimacy shouldn't exist among the Highborn, whose ladies usually controlled conception at will and grimly honored the terms of any contract to which their lord bound them. She remembered Lyra, Caineron's young daughter, contracted to Prince Odalian of Karkinor and longing for the child she would never dare have without her father's consent. To misbreed as Tieri had was black disgrace, dishonoring both mother and child. Now Kallystine claimed that it also called into doubt the constancy of all Tieri's female blood-kin.

No one had mentioned this last, personal application to Jame before or, she suspected, to Torisen. Either the lords didn't care, or knowledge of Tieri's disgrace was very restricted, perhaps to the matriarchs. Odd. Odder still that they would tell Kallystine, whom no one trusted. Perhaps they hadn't, directly. Everyone knew that when the council had met today, Cattila's Ear had listened in. Jame knew through Jorin's senses that there had been three people in Kallystine's room when they had left it: M'lady herself, her maid, and a stranger with an almost familiar, earthy smell, like the inside of a potting shed. Perhaps that had been the mysterious Ear, who some claimed was not even a Kencyr, admitted only at Cattila's insistence. Whatever she was, though, perhaps she had been carrying tales.

One way or another, a great secret had fallen into enemy hands.

How damaging was it, though, really? Brought up by Kendar, Jame didn't share M'lady's revulsion at illegitimacy. If Tieri's misfortune got her off the breeding books, she didn't care if people expected her to litter kittens. Unfortunately, as long as the issue was legitimate, most lords probably wouldn't care.

Regarding the Highlord, though, when—if—Tori found out
about the Knorth Bastard, how would he react? Kendar had
raised him too. He was still said to feel more at home among
the randon at Kothifir than here in his father's stronghold.
Strange to think of the Highlord of the Kencyrath as an outsider. In some ways, she and he were still much alike. Old
songs claimed that, living or dead, twins occupied corners in
each other's soul. Jame could almost believe that, asleep if
not awake: all winter she'd had the recurrent dream of seeking
her brother up and down Rathillien, as once she had sought
him through the bleak rooms of the Haunted Lands keep. On
Spring Eve, she had even dreamt that she had tracked him
down at last, only to have her dream twist into the nightmares
that had haunted her sleep ever since.

Jame hugged herself, shivering. Think of something else.

She turned away from the window to survey the room.
Starlight revealed it to be circular, containing two chairs, a
worktable, and a fireplace down whose throat the wind whistled
off-key. On the mantle was a branched candlestick with wax
guttered to the sockets. Behind that stood a pitted bronze
mirror, placed to throw back candlelight and, incidentally, a
distorted image of the room. In it, she seemed to be wearing a
black coat much like Tori's and almost his thin, handsome
face, but so haggard…

…*looking like the unburnt dead…*

The faint, uncanny echo of her thoughts made her start;
however, she was still alone in this cold tower room.

Rumor said that Tori sometimes stayed awake for weeks
on end. Well, if he was losing sleep because of her, it served
him right. He should never have stranded her here. She stuck
out her tongue at the reflection.

The surrounding walls were lined with shelves full of parchment scrolls. A second door opened off the south wall. Outside was a narrow platform and a catwalk swaying through
dizzy space to the southwest tower of the keep which housed
sleeping quarters. Now, where had she learned that? Then

Jame remembered, and knew why the guard had called these
upper reaches "Gothregor": it was customary to identify a lord,
his possessions, and his chambers by the name of his fortress.

This was Tori's study.

The ladies of the halls speculated endlessly over the
Highlord's refusal to reoccupy the Ghost Walks. Most saw
it as a slap at M'lady Kallystine's ambitions, or an evasion
of her company. However, faced with this austere bivouac
at the very top of her brother's ancestral keep, Jame wondered if in truth he loathed everything that had been his
father's. What had his life with Ganth Gray Lord been like
after her expulsion and before his own departure, under
mysterious circumstances, at the age of fifteen? Twin or
not, Tori was no longer the child she remembered. Nameless boy under Lord Ardeth's protection, young commander
of the Southern Host, Highlord of the Kencyrath, he had
lived a lifetime since their childhood together, and a life
uncommonly private for someone born to power. Look at
this chamber. There was hardly room here for his servant
Burr, much less for the retinue which his position would
seem to demand. Knorth poverty only explained part of it.
The Caineron guards had been right to respect such determined privacy. So should she.

But at the door she heard M'lady's guards still below.

Damn. She would have to wait them out. The thought
of inactivity, however brief, reminded her that, like her
brother, she hadn't slept in several nights. His chair, set before the cold fireplace, looked dangerously comfortable. She
sat down on the floor, her back to a bookcase. Jorin flopped
across her knees.

I need a bigger lap or a smaller cat, she thought, bemused,
and, despite herself, fell asleep.

Interim I
Kothifir Encampment: 54th of Spring

"What do you mean," demanded Lord Ardeth, "'Something is coming'?"

Torisen Black Lord stopped short in his restless pacing, startled and annoyed to find that he had spoken out loud. What *had* he meant? The words had simply risen in his mind, out of a formless but growing apprehension. Dammit, lack of sleep was no excuse to lose control.

Turning, he tripped over a footstool.

Damn.

During his tenure as commander of the Southern Host, these lodgings had been sparsely furnished, each piece elegant and useful, with room in between to pace. Pereden, his successor, had redecorated according to his own tastes: gaudy, pretentious, and cluttered. Dead as he was, that wretched boy would break Torisen's neck yet—turnabout fair play, perhaps.

The leavings of that other, worthless life seemed suddenly to press in on him. He had to get away, out into the desert dark, to prowl alone through the remaining hours of this interminable night...

Ardeth stood in his way. "My boy, you mustn't."

"Thal's balls, Blackie," Harn Grip-hard growled from the table, crumbling the report which he had been pretending to read. "Your enemies already think you're half crazy. Wander around tonight looking like the unburnt dead and they'll be sure. Remember what day this is: thirty-four years ago your father ran mad as a gelded rathorn and most of us ran after him, all the way to death in the White Hills. No one in the Hosts, north or south, has forgotten that. No one ever will."

"Oh, really!" Ardeth protested—against the expression, not the facts. "Still, your behavior since the Cataracts *has* cost you much of the credit you gained there. This continued refusal to sleep, merely for fear of dreams..."

"Who told you that? Was it Burr, spying on me again?"

"No."

Torisen ran thin, scarred hands through his dark hair, gripping it briefly to remind himself with pain. Burr had been Ardeth's agent years ago, openly, when he himself had been a nameless boy in the old lord's service. Now Burr served him. After the events leading up to the Cataracts, everyone must know that he often avoided sleep, if not why. His three oldest friends, here in this room, knew full well that the pattern went back years.

"All right," said Ardeth soothingly. "We'll discuss that another time. But as for your refusal to make certain necessary decisions...listen to me: you *must* form an alliance with some house strong enough to protect your interests. If you're too fastidious to bargain with your own bloodlines, use your sister's. The girl *has* to be contracted out for the best advantage you can obtain. Oh, if only my son Pereden were alive to offer for her...!

"My boy, what's the matter?"

Torisen had turned sharply away.

He was remembering what it had felt like, in his tent by the Cataracts, to break Pereden's neck. Then he'd had to go into the Wastes with Ardeth to hunt for the bones of his "hero" son, knowing all the time that Harn had reduced them to ashes on a common pyre at Hurlen. Damn Pereden anyway, that vain, spoiled boy who had led the Southern Host against the vastly larger Waster Horde, against orders, in a stupid attempt to prove himself a better commander than Torisen had been. Captured, he had changed sides, seduced by the promise that the Horde would make him Highlord. And all because he thought that Torisen had stolen Ardeth's love.

Fathers and sons. How did any of them manage not to murder each other?

Pereden would have used the shame of his treachery to destroy Ardeth, if Torisen hadn't killed him first.

Right. Try explaining that *to a grief-stricken father.*

Torisen stepped out onto the balcony and leaned on the rail. The Host's permanent encampment formed a city at the foot of the escarpment, with Kothifir on the cliff-top above. To the south, over the garrison's roofs, he could see the Wastes, a line drawn flat on the horizon, black beneath, star-fretted above—*his* land, which Ganth had never even seen.

Still, the Gray Lord's shadow fell over him. Maybe he would never escape it as long as he claimed the Highlord's power, as he had his father's ring and battle-sword, now hanging from a belt-loop at his side. Songs said that Kin-Slayer made its rightful owner all but invincible. For Torisen, however, it had remained sullenly inert, as if it knew how Ganth had died, cursing his runaway son, disowning him. Ironic, if the only thing he *had* inherited from Ganth was his insanity. He could feel the tug of it now. Somewhere, something was about to happen.

No. Think of something else.

He turned restlessly back into the room, trying not to chafe under the anxious regard of his friends. An aimless step brought him up short before another of Pereden's prize possessions: a full-length mirror in an ornate golden frame. He stared blankly at the shadow which fell mask-like across the reflection of his face, feeling empty with fatigue. Hounded day after day by the lords, haunted night after night by dreams...

The face in the mirror stuck its tongue out at him.

Torisen recoiled, then controlled himself, furious. She was four hundred leagues away, wasn't she? He had seen to that.

But all winter, the moment his eyes had closed, he had felt her hunting him as relentlessly as she had as a child, playing hide and seek. She had almost caught him too, on Spring's Eve.

It was a dream, he reminded himself, scowling defiantly into the mirror. *Only a damn dream—wasn't it?*

It had, at least, been seven weeks ago, too long even for him to stay awake. Since then, when the need for sleep had overwhelmed him, he had hidden from her in the one place to which he thought she would never willingly return. In his dreams, reduced again to childhood, he had huddled miserably in the dark, cold hall of the Haunted Lands keep, hearing the tentative rustle in the shadows of dead Kendar returning to what, for a haunt, passed for life, hearing those other slow, dragging footsteps descending the stair from the battlements where his father had died but refused to stay dead, the mad mutter in the stairwell growing closer, more distinct night after night...

He hadn't bolted the stair door. Did he dare rise to do it? Jame would, if she were here. No one stood up to Ganth but her. She was so strong. He could stand anything, if only that door were bolted, but he wouldn't run out to find her. He *wouldn't*. He would stay here, with Ganth's madness fumbling at the door, mumbling through the cracks:

"It's all her fault, boy. She is *strong. She has power. You've got to destroy her, boy, before she destroys you...*

"Drink, lord," said Burr.

Torisen looked down at the cup of mulled wine which his servant and old friend had thrust into his hands. His cold fingers curled around it, the lace-work of white scars grateful for its warmth. Had he spoken out loud again? A fortnight awake, dreams bleeding into reality—he had starved himself of sleep often enough to know the signs. Dammit, why couldn't he master them?

Control. Must keep control...

He raised the cup to drink, then in the mirror saw Ardeth's eyes on him. The wine smelled peculiar. A shudder went through him, followed by rage.

"Traitors!" he heard himself say in a harsh voice not his own. "You eat my bread and yet you conspire to betray me. You, and you, and you...

Burr's plain face had gone stiff. Without a word, he took
back the cup and drank deeply from it, his mud-brown eyes
locked on the Highlord's silver-gray. He blinked. Ardeth
took the half-empty cup from him before he could drop it.
Harn threw a burly arm around his sagging frame to swing
him around to a seat by the table, growling over his shoulder:
"Blackie, you damn fool."

Torisen Black Lord stared, beginning to tremble. "I—it
wasn't...

The rage had gone as abruptly as it had seized him—but
he wasn't a berserker, to flare like that, or to speak those words
with that voice. All, all had been Ganth's, born of that obsession with betrayal which had driven some of his loyal followers to suicide and the rest to contrive his son's escape from the
Haunted Land's keep. Those Kendar had ransomed Torisen
out of darkness with their lives and honor.

*Listen: hear them now in the shadows of the hall, bereft of honor
and life, rustling, rustling...*

"No. I refuse to dream this."

He turned his back and stepped out again onto the balcony, to grip the rail, to master his shaking hands. Even now,
she was seeking him, but he wouldn't hide again in the dream
of that terrible hall, where madness fumbled at an unlocked
door. He would stay awake—for the rest of his life if necessary.

Wait it out, just wait it out...

Part II

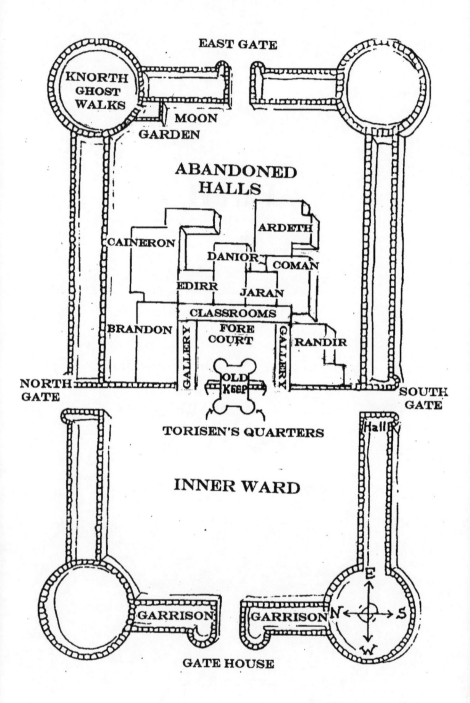

Gothregor: 54th – 55th of Spring
I

The dream began as it always did: Jame was searching for Tori.

She was angry with him for letting their father drive her out, but she still had to find him because…because she had something for him. Ganth's ring and sword. The ring was on her finger; the sword, ill-omened Kin-Slayer, in her hand.

The sword worried her. It had broken in their father's hand, but now it was whole again, except for the hilt emblem. Under the cracked crest something moved, dark and wet: fleshless lips that muttered endlessly in their father's voice; sharp teeth that gnawed at her hand. She couldn't let go, though, until Tori took the sword out of her grasp. But when he did, he didn't notice how it had hurt her. He didn't care. So she didn't warn him about the mad, mumbling voice or the hungry teeth.

Then she was searching for Tori again because he had sent her away, and now he was hiding from her, as if this were some silly game.

On Spring Eve she at last found him, standing at the edge of the Southern Wastes, his back to her. He was holding Kin-Slayer and listening to the voice. Unnoticed, blood ran down the sword's blade from his hand, where the teeth did their silent, malicious work.

She called his name: "Brother."

"I refuse to dream this!" he snapped, and walked rapidly away.

"Come back!" she cried after him. "You can't run away from me forever!"

But he had already disappeared into the blowing sand.

No, not sand but dry leaves, hitting her face with furtive, brittle taps. Before her lay a gray city street, lined with decaying houses. Something dark crawled over the broken cobblestones toward her, its shadowy fingers delicately probing the rubble as it came. Behind shut doors, children were whimpering in terror. The Lower Town Monster, not destroyed after all, whispered a voice on the wind. Her voice, from another place, another dream.

The gibbous moon emerged, white and cold. Not sand or leaves, but snow, hiding the summits of Mounts Timor and Tinnibin as they loomed above her. She was in the Blue Pass of the Ebonbane, facing east toward Tai-tastigon. Something was crawling toward her like a shadow cast on the snow. Then it raised its head, and she recognized Bane's features.

The wrong brother had answered her.

Turn. Flee. If only she could escape back into the waking world, leave him here where he belonged, nightmare creature that he had become…

"You can't run from me forever," whispered the darkness behind her, mockingly. *"Blood binds…"*

The moon waxed, waned, and then waxed again, the snow melting under its pale light. The shadow-thing that pursued her sank into the green of spring, but still it came on, sometimes crawling, sometimes wrapped around some wild creature which it caught and rode until the soul was eaten out of it. One stag lasted a week before falling to pieces before the horrified Grindarks who were hunting it. On it came, down the trade road beside the Ever-Quick, through the Oseen Hills, over the toes of the Snowthorns, into the Riverland, and finally to the gates of Gothregor itself, to break its long fast and then to hunt…

Jame woke with a gasp. Slowly, the tower room redefined itself around her, Jorin's grunt of protest at the sudden tightening of her arms changing back to a drowsy purr. Calm down, calm…

Those damned dreams again. Bad enough that they repeated themselves every time exhaustion forced her to sleep. Worse, that each repetition ended with a new installment, as if the pursuit really was drawing nearer. But, after all, they were only dreams.

All right: she *did* resent the way that Tori had treated her. It hadn't been easy to restore Ganth's sword and ring to him. Some of the things she had done, some of the places she had been, would have startled him considerably, if he had bothered to ask. He never had. Of course, Marc could tell him, but Tori disliked spies so much that she didn't think he would seek information behind her back. Fine, then: let him stay ignorant; but she really should have told him that Kin-Slayer had been re-forged in Perimal Darkling.

As for Bane, the Lower Town Monster might have been constructed around his soul but it had never (to the best of her knowledge) had his guiding intelligence. *Blood binds?* That made no sense either. Tori was the blood-binder, not she, not that, with his terror of the Shanir, he would ever admit such a thing even to himself.

Blood—its taste when Bane's farewell kiss had nearly bitten through her lower lip, the hidden scar which her tongue could still trace...

That had been real enough.

As for the rest, it would be different if she were a far-seer. Never mind that her thoughts had actually crossed Bane's at least twice in Tai-tastigon, or that her mental distance from Tori had seemed to diminish greatly since they had both been exposed to wyrm's venom the previous winter. That wasn't farseeing. She had never far-seen anything in her life, dammit, and she wasn't going to start now.

But still the last image of this latest dream lingered: in the Brandan night nursery, a shadowy form creeping up the side of a child's cot to break a long fast? Bane always liked little boys.

Ah, it was no use. Dream or not, Caineron patrols or not, she had to see for herself that her brother's house was safe.

Down in the Forecourt again, Jame cut across toward the Brandan compound with Jorin trotting at her heels. A bright, gibbous moon had just cleared the mountains to the east. Near midnight, then. Her shadow fluttered on the grass in the boisterous wind, as though at any moment it might shred and blow away. Shadows *had* become detached before, along with the souls which cast them. That, after all, was what the Lower Town Monster had been, while Bane had walked shadowless in the noonday sun. Then too, the Sirdan Theocandi had sent his soul abroad at night as the assassin Shadow Thief.

But neither he nor Bane had had to contend with the Tishooo, which was romping along with Jame, snatching at her hem like a playful dog.

"Stop that!" she cried.

"Whooo…?" said the wind, and swept up under her full outer skirt, inverting it.

Jame found herself cocooned in heavy velvet, blinded, entangled. As she struggled to free herself, she heard a whistle— shrill, excited, and very, very close. Jorin was growling. Then someone yelped, as though in surprise or pain. The taste of blood again—in the cat's mouth, not her own. Jame clawed the gown away from her face.

No Jorin, nothing but an empty courtyard full of wind.

Where, there, ancestors be praised: a glimmer of silver fur in the shadows, a very upset ounce slinking toward her across the grass. Catching him, she pried something out of his jaws. It felt like coarse cloth. However, except for a corner stained with blood, she couldn't see either it or her own hand, which the rest of it covered.

Sweet Trinity. Could this be *mere*?

Jame stood holding the scrap of invisible cloth against the wind's tug, feeling suddenly chilled.

"Kitten, let's get under cover. Fast."

Strangely, no guard was on duty at the entrance to the Brandan quarters. Jame crossed the arcade where, earlier, she had encountered the Iron Matriarch, and entered the compound proper. Still no guards or anyone else, although she could hear whistling in the distance.

The nursery was on the second floor, at the heart of the compound. The door stood half open, warm firelight spilling out of it. Jame slipped inside. It was a large, L-shaped room with many cots in it, all empty, as far as she could see. Nonetheless, fires were lit on the several hearths. *Someone* must be here. Jame stole silently between the rows of small beds toward where the room bent to the right. The hearth-fires danced uneasily as she passed.

The fire at the far end of the ell, however, had burnt down to tinkling embers. At one side of it sat a comfortable chair, empty. At the other was a cot, in which something moved sleepily. Bending over it, barely visible in the gloom, was a shadowy form. Jame could see the wall through it. It raised its head and looked at her out of eyes like the wells of night. The tenebrous planes of its face shifted. It was smiling at her. Jame went back a step, nearly stepping on Jorin as he scuttled under a bed. Then she saw that those shadowy fingers were resting in the creases of the child's blanket, inches from its sleeping face.

She heard herself say, hoarsely, "Don't you *dare!*"

Footsteps sounded on the nursery tiles behind her. She turned just as the Brandan captain rounded the corner and stopped short, clearly startled to see her. For an instant, Jame was also disconcerted: she thought she had seen something flicker aside between her and the sandy-haired Kendar, but nothing was there now except a stray shadow on the floor.

The captain advanced, scarred brow knitted in a frown. "Lady, what are you doing here at this time of night? Did you know that every Caineron in the halls is searching for you?"

Obviously, she hadn't yet seen the thing by the cot. She also didn't notice the shadow on the floor until her own, cast ahead of her by the room's outer fires, fell across it. Then she gave a sudden gasp and crashed to her knees. Her own shadow seemed to be floundering in that other darkness. As the two locked in unequal combat, she pitched forward and lay writhing on the floor.

"Get out!" she cried to Jame through clenched teeth. "Run!"
What in Perimal's name...? Was this somehow Bane's
doing?

But even as Jame turned to look back at the cot, where the
child had woken and was beginning to cry, an all too solid arm
slid around her neck from behind. It jerked her off balance. A
flash of steel...She barely got her own right arm up in time,
the edge of her hand against the other's wrist, holding back
sharp death for an endless moment.

Abruptly, she was released and flung sideways, almost on
top of the stricken Kendar. Shadow hands were sliding over
the woman's throat and face, fumbling at her eyes, while she
tried futilely to tear them off. In another moment she would
blind herself. Jame grabbed her wrists.

Above them, a shrill whistle began as if in triumph, but
ended with a breathy explosion. Still gripping the Kendar,
Jame twisted about to peer up over her shoulder. Something
indistinct loomed over them—man-shaped, she thought, but
somehow she couldn't focus on it. All that showed clearly
were wild eyes without a face, a knife poised in midair, and
below it a skinny, bare wrist, marked by Jorin's teeth.

For a moment, she thought that the assassin wanted them
to "see" their killer, or rather to rub in that they couldn't. Then
she realized that, just as he had caught her seconds before, so
now he himself was caught. A shadowy something stood behind him, its indistinct arm around his neck, and its ghost of a
hand grasping his knife hand at the wrist.

M'lady, whispered darkness. *Have you noticed? Every time
we meet, someone bleeds.*

The shadow hand tightened on the other's wrist. It drew
the knife across some six inches below the terrified eyes, cutting slowly, cutting deep. The assassin jerked. Blood spurted,
painting his neck, his chest. His breathing changed to a desperate wheeze as his trachea was severed, but without his
soul he couldn't die. Jame flinched aside as his shadow fell
away from the Brandan captain and scrabbled past her. The

moment it reattached itself, the stricken assassin crumpled, twitched, and lay still, defined against the floor by the spreading pool of his own blood.

The shadowy thing that was Bane rose from the corpse like black smoke off a pyre. It bent its head against the ceiling and spread wide its sooty arms. Out of that towering charnel cloud, the glimmer that might be eyes stooped over Jame, no, bowed ironically, then melted into the upper shadows, leaving behind only the ghost of a mocking whisper: *Later...*

Jame gave a long, shuddering sigh. Later? Trust Bane never to do anything direct.

She released the Kendar's wrists. The woman huddled on the floor with her face hidden in the crook of her arm, clammy-skinned and shaking, but with her shadow still intact. No soul damage there. Perhaps the assassin's shadow-casting technique was limited to incapacitating his prey. Although it was screaming with fright, the child also appeared unhurt when Jame rose hastily to check it. As she scooped bedding off a nearby cot, Jorin crept out from under it.

"Some help you are," she told him.

After piling the blankets on the randon to combat shock, she gingerly turned over the sprawling figure. It no longer cast a shadow. So, Bane had broken his fast after all. Really, this *mere* cloth was amazing: only where it was soaked with blood could she see it clearly. She stripped off the other's sodden hood and stared down at the waxy face of a boy not more than fourteen years old.

"He's an apprentice in the Bashtiri Shadow Guild," said the captain behind her. She had sat up, clutching the blankets around her. Her teeth rattled together as if with the cold and her square, scratched face was haggard, but she came of hardy Kendar stock and had trained in a tough discipline.

"What's he doing here?"

"At a guess, trying to earn his journeyman's *mere*-tempered knife by fulfilling the contract which someone took out on the Knorth women, thirty-four years ago. I had kin on duty here

that night. Bloody hell. Why didn't someone anticipate this?"
She tried to stand up and failed, cursing. "Everything is upside down tonight. None of my cadets are where they should
be. There's always some confusion, settling in a new garrison,
but this…! I should have realized that it wasn't just the other
house guards ragging us."

Jame rose, the hood a flicker in her hand. "Well, he's dead
now."

"He probably didn't come alone. There are usually thirteen shadows in a casting. Lady, I'm not sure we can protect
you. Run. Hide. Trinity knows, you're good enough at that.
The Caineron have been taking your name in vain from one
end of the halls to the other, all evening."

The click of footsteps made them both start, but it was only
the child's attendant, a Kendar maid, come back from whatever
errand had drawn her away. She was outraged to find her charge
shrieking itself apoplectic in the presence of two apparently
indifferent adults, but then she saw the far end of the room
awash in blood and showed signs of waxing hysterical herself.

"Don't!" said Jame, Highborn to Kendar.

The girl stopped with her mouth open. It stayed that way
while she listened to the message which Jame wanted her to
convey to the Brandan guardroom, in hopes that at least the
watch officer would be on duty. She left still looking as if
someone had hit her between the eyes with a board.

"You need help," Jame said defensively, meeting the
captain's eye, "and someone's got to be told that there are
foxes loose in the hen-house again. C'mon on, kitten."

"Lady, where are you going?"

Jame paused at the door, tucking the hood into her belt.
Where indeed? To run, to hide? No. There was blood on
the floor of her brother's house and blood in her veins, swift
and hot after the winter's chill as she had never thought to
feel it again.

"To warn the other house guards; then, perhaps, to hunt
foxes."

II

Brenwyr stalked through the midnight halls in one of her blackest moods. Talking to Adiraina usually calmed her, but not tonight, on the anniversary of Aerulan's death. It didn't help that during this short walk back to the Brandan quarters she had been stopped three times by Caineron patrols, on the last occasion nearly clouting the Caineron captain for daring to question her own presence, abroad so late. That entire house seemed to have run mad tonight, from Lady Kallystine on down—and no, dammit, she would *not* give them permission to search the Brandan compound.

As Adiraina had guessed, Brenwyr still had a splintering headache. Thirty-four years ago tonight, she had suffered an even worse one, brought on by a row that afternoon with Aerulan. No. The argument had been entirely one-sided, caused by her stupid jealousy over Aerulan's kindness to her cousin Tieri—a mere child, for God's sake! Aerulan had only laughed, and Brenwyr had stormed off. That night, the Tishooo had brought her Aerulan's voice, calling, calling, but she had heard it through such a haze of pain that she hadn't believed it was real, until too late.

It's my fault she died, the Iron Matriarch thought savagely, for perhaps the millionth time. *I ill-wished her, that afternoon— in a filthy temper, not meaning it, but it stuck, and it killed her.*

Not even Adiraina knew about that.

Sometimes, Brenwyr almost consoled herself remembering how the assassin had shrunk back as he felt her curse strike home: "*Shadow, by a shadow be exposed*"—whatever that had meant. More to him, obviously, than to her, as was often the case. No, that yellow-eyed bastard wouldn't soon forget the Brandan Maledight. But blood prices weren't paid by words, however blighting, nor the dead brought back by remorse. Because of her, Aerulan was both dead and unavenged.

Thus raging at herself, she entered the Brandan compound, and there, coming down the arcade toward her through slanting bars of moonlight, was Aerulan.

Someone whistled—a thin, high, excited note—and then something seized the slim figure from behind.

It was all going to happen again, thought Brenwyr, frozen in sick horror, and she for her sins must witness it, over and over and over...

But this time Aerulan had a moment's warning from the ounce trotting at her side. She grabbed the invisible something which had her around the throat and bent sharply forward. An indistinct form shot over her head. Bright steel clattered on the flagstones at Brenwyr's feet. Hobbled by her tight underskirt, the girl toppled forward to land on something that fought back. The two, visible and otherwise, were rolling about the arcade, pounced indiscriminately by the cat, when Brenwyr finally realized what she was seeing. She snatched up the assassin's knife and ran forward.

The Knorth saw her coming. "No!" she cried.

Brenwyr hesitated, then struck almost at random with the hilt. "What in Perimal's name do you mean, 'No'?" she demanded as the Knorth shoved her stunned attacker aside.

"If he's dead, he can't answer questions. Besides, look." She pulled off the *mere* hood. Underneath was the face of a surprisingly young, blond boy. "I'd like to know who's sending children to cut my throat, and why."

"Children, eh?" Brenwyr tried desperately to wrench her mind away from the past, to focus on this stranger in Aerulan's clothes whom she had spent the winter refusing to meet. "And just how old are you, girl?"

The other snorted, a most un-Aerulan-like sound. "Older than this fellow, anyway, and better trained, for all that thrashing around just now. Still, he would have had me cold if he hadn't expected an easy kill. This damned dress!"

She hiked up her outer skirt, ripped open the under-gown's side seam, and began to tear long strips off of it as the wind tried playfully to twitch them out of her grasp.

Over three decades preserving those clothes, carrying them to each new house where a contract sent her, clinging to them for comfort in each strange bed, to the last moment, until a stranger's footstep stopped at her door...

Rip, rip, rip...

Berserker heat flared in Brenwyr's blood, kindling red in her eyes, until the other's voice hit her like cold water in the face:

"Lady, for pity's sake, *not now.*"

Impostor, usurper, destroyer...

No. *She* had made the Knorth wear these clothes. *She* had pretended that Aerulan again walked these halls, always just out of sight so as not to imperil the illusion. Delusion. Obsession.

"*Name a thing,*" Adiraina had told her, "*and you gain power over it.*"

What a fool the Iron Matriarch had been to believe that. But now, in this moment of hard-won freedom, Brenwyr heard her own hoarse voice say, "Do what you must."

"Good!" said the Knorth, and bound the unconscious boy with Aerulan's dismemberments. Where he lay, in the shadow of the arcade's waist-high wall, the white fabric showed up against the *mere* as though it were wrapped around empty space. "Two down," she said, rising, "eleven to go— oh!"

A burly figure had suddenly appeared outside the arcade, thrown an arm around her waist, and scooped her out into the Forecourt.

"Greetings again, Matriarch," said the Caineron captain affably. "I thought I heard familiar voices. It seems that we won't have to impose on your hospitality after all. Lady Jameth, M'lady Kallystine would like a word with you."

The Knorth started to protest.

"Shhh," said the captain and put her hand over the girl's mouth. "Remember the fourth duty of silence. Malie, take that cat back to the stable. Good night, Matriarch."

She strode back across the courtyard with the Knorth, still uttering muffled protests, tucked under her arm. A cadet snatched the ounce as he tried to follow and bore him off in the opposite direction, too well bred to bite or scratch but with all four legs stuck up in the most awkward angles he could manage.

This joint abduction took place too quickly for Brenwyr to protest; but then again, she thought, watching them go, why should she? The Knorth was a Caineron responsibility. Let them guard her. Brenwyr's duty lay here, with this trespasser in the Brandan domain.

"*Two down, eleven to go*," the Knorth had said. Thirteen what?

But her mind slid off the thought. The wind blew, the moon shone—and she stood at the very spot where Aerulan had fallen, with an assassin of the Bashtiri Shadow Guild at her feet. When this fellow opened his eyes, perhaps they would be yellow, like those of Aerulan's killer. Perhaps...perhaps she would wait and see...

III

It was her own fault, Jame thought, as she sat a virtual prisoner in the Caineron's second floor guardroom.

Of course, since Ganth's fall the Caineron had tended to treat all surviving Knorth as only temporary inconveniences. That Caldane hadn't seized power yet said more about Torisen's unexpected qualities as a leader than about any slackening of Caineron ambition. Jame realized now, though, that she hadn't helped by letting Kallystine treat her all winter as a servant. No wonder these Kendar showed her so little respect.

Worse, they had brushed aside her talk of assassins as pure hysteria. What else could one expect from the crazy Knorth? Not even the *mere* hood of the dead boy had impressed them, looking as it did only like a blood-soaked scrap of cloth. The Caineron captain had dismissed it with a glance: "That time of month, is it?"—as if some suspicion of hers had been confirmed.

Jame had seen no point, after that, in mentioning Bane.

At least the Brandan Matriarch knew about the assassin in the arcade. Even if she didn't realize that his brethren were abroad tonight, surely she would have her guard deal with the one they had captured. How frustrating that Jame hadn't been able to tell Brenwyr about her captain, incapacitated in the night nursery. Of course, the Kendar maid knew. Perhaps even now the alarm was spreading, but so far she heard no sound of it.

Meanwhile, the Caineron ten-commands sent out to search for the Knorth runaway began to check back in. The first report came from the Brandan compound. The Caineron still hadn't been permitted to enter there, but a Brandan guard on the northern perimeter spoke of cadets lured away from their posts, locked on the wrong side of doors, tripped by wires, and in general victimized by tricks ranging from the silly to the malicious. Several Kendar had been slightly injured and a maid had been knocked unconscious by a tumble downstairs. It was all a damn mess, the guard had said in disgust, like an exercise in disruption or an assault by boggles.

"At least we've put a stop to that," the Caineron captain remarked, and shot a glance at Jame.

But it didn't stop.

"Lights, moving in the Ghost Walks," reported a ten-commander. "Wills-o'-the-wisp, like the old days when the Ardeth kept us out. This time, we investigated. Nothing. Ruin and shadows."

Shadows also figured in the next reports, coming mostly from the Edirr compound but spreading southward into the Danior. They seemed to be creeping everywhere, terrorizing whomever they met but as yet doing little harm. The only things which kept them out were bright lights or the wind, which had begun a restless prowl of its own inside the halls.

They're looking for me, Jame thought.

If she hadn't been in odd places all night, dodging Kallystine, the assassins would have run her down long ago. Now they were trying to flush her out. If she really was the only one at risk tonight, perhaps she had better stay in this brightly lit room, away from shadows of all sorts. Let Bane hunt the hunters, if he chose. Thanks to the Caineron, she was out of the game, safe.

But still her gloved fingertips drummed on the chair's arm, quieted themselves, and drummed again.

The captain was also beginning to lose patience. Word had come earlier that, in a final act of defiance, M'lady's servant had hanged herself with her own braid. Oddly enough, though, Kallystine seemed to blame the Knorth Jameth for all the evening's misadventures. On first hearing of Jame's capture, she had furiously demanded that the truant be delivered to her quarters, along with any instruments of torture which her guards might have on hand. The captain had blandly suggested that M'lady meet her errant charge here, on more neutral ground. This, however, Kallystine had so far refused to do. It wasn't clear to Jame who would win in such a tug-o'-war, randon Kendar or lord's daughter, training or raw power. She felt like a bone between two dogs.

Meanwhile, the captain's latest, carefully worded message had as yet gone unanswered. "What," she grumbled, "no more threats to tell daddy? Our runner must've fallen into a hole somewhere. Cadet, go see."

But it was no hole down which the messenger had tumbled.

"I found her at the foot of the privy stair, and another of those damned trip-wires at the top," the second runner reported, white-faced. "She's dead."

The captain turned on Jame with an oath, but the runner caught her sleeve, fingers leaving bloody prints.

"Ran, it wasn't the fall. Someone cut her throat."

Just then, the Tishooo found the guardroom. It flowed in past the captain and cadet, making the candle flames dance, stirring the arrases. These latter surrounded the room, enlivening it with their bright depictions of randon life, stitched in their off-duty hours by generations of Caineron guards. The hangings served the practical purpose of stopping drafts and, like most Kendar work, were peculiarly effective. Thus the Tishooo found itself trapped behind them. Jame marked its approach by the rippling of the tapestries until it slid out between two of them to tweak at her skirt.

Come out and play, it might have been saying. *Come out and play*.

The room had filled with sharp orders and activity, the prisoner forgotten. Jame slipped between the tapestries, edged her way behind them to the door, and darted out into the hall, still unobserved.

If she was the prime target, why this other slaying? From what she had heard, the Shadow Guild considered it unprofessional to kill without a fee. However, given the age of these would-be assassins, perhaps this was more than the settlement of an old contract: perhaps this was a blooding mission. If so, each of the thirteen might intend to claim a kill tonight in a kind of limited open season on Gothregor. Still, wouldn't they want to be sure of her before announcing their presence too openly? Logically, yes; but despite all their advantages, these were boys, off the leash for perhaps the first time, running wild. While she had sat safe in the Caineron guardroom, one of them had lost patience and bagged a cadet, not realizing how quickly the body would be found.

Damn. She had to do something about this after all.

What she did first was to descend to the ground-floor cubbyhole which Kallystine had assigned to her. If these brats liked sharp toys, she had one too—except that someone had beaten her to it. The tiny room had been torn apart. The Ivory Knife was gone.

DAMN.

Objects of power certainly fell into and out of her hands with unnerving frequency. Worse, if the Shadow Guild *was* behind this ransacking (and how unlike it to stoop to theft), it meant that someone had told the assassins exactly which out-of-the-way broom closet was hers.

Betrayal.

She remembered Ganth raving about it in the Haunted Lands keep, on those nights when no one slept. The stupid Caineron, the scheming Ardeth, the ambitious Randir, the whole bloody web of friends and foes who had entangled his house in such ruin. Now, thirty-four years later, who out of that snarled past wanted his daughter dead?

She could stay here, where the hunters had already searched, or flee into the empty halls as Tieri had...

Run. Hide...

No. Since when had she let good sense dictate to her, or hesitated to act, however stupidly?

"I'm losing myself," she said out-loud to the stranger who stood, fragmented, in a broken mirror. "I'm half lost already."

Then stop hiding, lass, she could almost hear her friend Marc say. *Take off the mask.*

Well, yes: Although the matriarchs had forced it on her, she had used it quite literally as a way not to face life in the Women's Halls. Behind it, she had pretended to be someone else, a nameless seeker lost in a game whose rules no one would explain. But she *had* been told, repeatedly, that the girl behind the mask was ignorant, clumsy, and altogether hopeless. If that was true, the assassins' work was as good as done.

Why should she make things easy for them?

Jame dropped the mask. The face in the shattered mirror looked back at her, one brow raised and the other askew. Wise Marc. So there she was after all, cockeyed as ever. Time to gird up what was left of Aerulan's skirt, braid her hair, and get on with it—quickly, before good sense returned.

Out again in the hall, she paused to listen. The Caineron quarter was beginning to seethe. The guards' harried effort to find her would be nothing compared to the cold ferocity with which they would seek their comrade's blood-price. They were a self-absorbed house, though, intent on private vengeance; so far, no general alarm had been raised. Good enough, for her present purposes.

She drew a deep breath and let it out in a loud, long whistle. The single note hung in the air like an exclamation mark, as it had in the Forecourt and again in the arcade.

Here she is! Jame was almost sure it signaled. *Here, here, here!*

No answer. Had the killer already left the compound?

No. There came the reply, from some distance to the east, a warbling, inquisitive note which might have been dismissed as a trick of the wind.

Where? it trilled. *Where?*

Here! Jame whistled again, peering down the corridor toward where moonlight flooded into it through a set of arched windows.

The question came again, closer and more complex, as if demanding further information.

A shadow started across the moon-washed flagstones, then hesitated. Jame could almost see the boyish, *mere*-clad figure who cast it. Because her night vision was almost certainly better than his, she stepped into the light to give him a good look. With a muffled exclamation, the shadow darted toward her. She turned and ran, quick footsteps close behind her.

Among these intruders' disadvantages was not only their night vision but also their age: what boy could resist a really good game of hare-and-hounds? Now, to whistle up the rest of the pack and then, and then... Well, she would think of something.

The assassins had apparently looked for her first in her own room, then fanned out to search the Ghost Walks, the Brandan compound, and the Caineron. Now most of them seemed to be moving southward. Consequently, Jame raced in that direction, through the dark corridors of the Edirr and Danior, hearing first the excited whistle of her pursuer, then answering signals ahead. Each trill seemed to convey complex information—more than she could decipher on short notice. Instead, she concentrated on pinpointing the position of each whistler, down what hall, around what corner, up what stair. In her mind's eye, she saw a complete floor plan of the halls, in far more detail than anyone could who hadn't once been obliged to memorize an entire city. She used her training now to slip past the assassins ahead as they tried to intercept her, once cutting it so close that she heard two of them collide on her heels.

From the locked doors which she passed, Jame concluded that the inmates of the halls had finally realized that something was afoot. So much the better, if it kept them out of her way. Unfortunately, the closed doors also impeded the Tishooo, which was soon left behind. A pity, since she had hoped it would make shadow-casting too risky, as it apparently had in the arcade.

At least seven of the pack were on her heels by the time she was halfway through the Danior compound. She was wondering, rather breathlessly, where the rest were and what to do with the ones she had when ahead voices warned her that she was about to run into a guard patrol.

One cadet dead tonight was more than enough.

She swerved aside and plunged down a stair into the sublevels, whistling to draw her deadly tail after her. Below, she went on as quickly as she could through the unlighted passageways, forced now to rely entirely on memory to avoid running into walls.

At the end of this long corridor should be the entrance to the subterranean levels of the Jaran compound. Jame was so sure of this that she ran into the closed door at a brisk trot, nose first. It took her a dazed moment to remember that there was indeed a door between the Danior and Jaran compounds, but she had never before found it shut, much less locked. Extending a nail through the tip of a ruined glove, she began to pick the lock.

The door swung open. On the threshold, in torchlight, stood a tall woman with eyes full of reflected fire: Trishien, the Jaran Matriarch.

"Er…" said Jame, hastily putting her hands behind her back. "Hello."

"Good evening," said the scholar matriarch, as calmly as if every day she opened her cellar door to a Highlord's sister dressed in rags. "Is there, perhaps, a problem?"

"A bit of one, yes. Shadow Guild assassins are after me."

"Ah. You had better come inside, then. With the relocking of this door, the Jaran and Ardeth compounds will be fully secured." She smiled faintly at Jame's surprise. "Like me, many Jaran ladies are scrollswomen, and so are many retired randon. Our guards listen to us, and we listen to the Ardeth Shanir when they have nightmares."

The offer of sanctuary was tempting. A shadow might slip under a door, but if the assassin who cast it couldn't follow, surely it could do little harm. Never mind that the *mere*-tat-tooed masters of the Guild could reputedly walk through solid walls. These were only apprentices. Nonetheless, if she was right, there were at least ten more bloodings to prevent.

"Somehow, Matriarch, I've got to draw them off. All of them, including the three or four more who must be in the Coman or Randir quarters, if they aren't here. There isn't time to backtrack, either. I've got to cut through your compound."

"I—see. Child, are you quite sure you know what you're doing?"

"Very seldom," said Jame with a sigh. "Tonight, maybe. Lady, please. I—I can't explain it, but somehow this sort of thing is my job, my responsibility."

"I see," said the Jaran Matriarch again, after a pause. "In that case, it would be more dangerous to get in your way tonight than in theirs. This corridor leads straight under the compound. We will clear it."

She departed with her escort, taking the torches with her. Jame waited in the dark, wondering how far a shadow might be cast in absolute darkness, if at all. Side doors closed, farther and farther away: the Jaran, sealing off the passage. For a moment, she wished very much that Trishien hadn't taken her at her word. Maybe it *was* mad to claim such a task. If there had been anyone else to deal with the situation—but no: somehow, there never was.

A glimmer appeared at the other end of the hall down which she had come—one, two, three, seven wills-o'-the-wisp, as the Caineron guard had described them. As the ghost lights bobbed closer, Jame felt her spirits bob up with them. Insane or not, this was still much, much better than practicing knot-stitches.

"Calli-calli-catch-me-if-you-can!" she shouted down the hall, spun, and darted away.

Swift feet followed.

IV

"Put more wood on the fire," Karidia ordered.

"Lady, th-there isn't any more," stammered a voice behind her.

The Coman Matriarch whipped about, skirt belling, to glare at the group huddled around the fire-pit in the middle of the great hall. Forty-eight frightened eyes stared back at her—the entire Highborn population of the Coman compound, most under the age of thirteen.

"You," she snapped at one of the few adults. "Go fetch a chair to break up."

"Y-yes, Matriarch," quavered the woman, but didn't move.

All the room's furniture was pushed up against its walls, well beyond the faltering ring of firelight. The first duty might be obedience, but no maxim had the strength to drive anyone here back into the dark tonight.

Karidia snorted, but didn't insist. She wasn't about to admit that nothing would get her to cross that stretch of shadowy floor either.

Even less would she acknowledge any flaw in her handling of the night's events. When word had come that the Ardeth Shanir foresaw imminent danger, Karidia had refused to listen. *She* knew how the Ardeth Matriarch schemed to make those precious freaks of hers seem important. Hadn't Adiraina even claimed that all matriarchs and lords must *be* Shanir, even if most of the latter, incredibly, didn't know it? How *dare* she make reference to Karidia's own mock-berserk fits in adolescence? When the Coman captain had protested Karidia's dismissal of the Shanir alarm, she had told the Kendar to go help the Ardeth herself, if she was so concerned, and to take her precious guard with her. *Now.*

Reluctantly, the Kendar had obeyed.

The disturbance had started almost immediately afterward. First, there had been that unearthly racket in the hallways—shouts, whistles, wails, and a sound like a dozen cats being boiled alive. Then the pounding had begun on doors. Objects flew. People were literally thrown out of bed. And in the midst of this were the shadows, sliding over floors and walls, terrifying the inmates, throwing those whom they touched into convulsions. In short order, the entire Highborn segment of the household had been roused, driven out of their rooms and herded into the great hall, from which they were now afraid to stir.

"Listen," said someone by the pit. "It's stopped."

The uproar had been continuing in far corners of the compound, moving systematically from room to room, seeming to grow more violent as the invaders had run out of places to search. Now, however, the loudest sound was the wind as it threw itself against the hall's shuttered windows and rattled the smoke-trap above the pit. It had been considered bad luck to shut out the Tishooo, Karidia remembered, ever since the Knorth ladies had died in their snug quarters while the wind howled futilely outside.

A fine time to think of *that*.

"Look!" said the same voice again.

Three shadows had come into the hall. They lay on the floor, man-shaped, but cast by no readily-seen forms. Karidia quickly circled to stand between them and the women huddled by there. She thought she could almost hear the intruders, almost understand their whispered council, although she would furiously have denied that it was her own Shanir gift which allowed her to do so.

"That settles it," one of them was saying in Bashti. "She isn't here. Now what?"

"Go on hunting. D'you want to tell the Guild Master that we failed?"

All three shadows on the floor wavered, as if touched with sudden cold.

"'S not fair!'" burst out the third angrily. "A place this farking large, the prey not where we were told to look, nor yet this farking book we were supposed to steal, and then the Master's got to screw up even our blooding by limiting who else we *can* kill. You're in dead trouble for scragging that cadet, mate."

"Damned trick of the light," muttered the first. "Her eyes *did* look red."

"*And* she was too farking young, meat-brain. We were told to look for a matriarch."

"It's *got* to be a test of wits," the second protested. "*Any* eye will be red, if you pop it out properly."

"Farking right," said the third. "My turn to try."

His shadow slid over the flags toward Karidia. She stood her ground, glaring.

"You foulmouthed little boy," she said.

The ghost of a chuckle answered her—or was it only the rustle of dust on stone? The wind continued futilely to batter against the shutters, but here in the still hall motes of grit were rattling out of corners, out of cracks. First to its knees, then to its feet, a form compounded of dust and darkness rose between stalker and prey. It cast no shadow. Rather, it *was* a shadow, upright, aware. It turned toward Karidia. Why, the impudent thing: it was *bowing* to her.

Something long and limp twitched feebly in its hand. Turning back to the three intruders, it held the thing up by the hair. It was like the flayed skin of a shadow, all essence sucked out of it but for that last flicker which kept it, horribly, alive. Its throat had been cut. Its captor slid a tenebrous finger into this slash and slowly drew it downward, ripping. The shadow-skin jerked. A long sliver of it came away in the other's hand and was tossed into the dying flames of the fire-pit, where it kindled with a thin shriek and was consumed. In that sudden blaze of light, Karidia saw the three assassins clearly, transfixed. Obviously, it had never occurred to them that someday they might encounter shadows more frightening than their own.

For some time, Karidia had been dimly aware of a disturbance going on more or less under her feet. She was still surprised, though, when the flagstone on which she stood began
to tilt and she was obliged to hop quickly to one side. The
counterbalanced stone overturned with a crash as a ragged
figure scrambled up the stair beneath from the cellar.

"Shit on a half-shell," it said, stopping dead on the top
step and regarding the shadow-man with dismay. "It must be
'later.'"

The shadowy figure dropped what was left of its victim on
the floor (where that agonized face, sinking into the grain, was
afterward found to have left a permanent image), bowed again
as if to say, "The stage is yours," and melted back into the
cracks.

By now, Karidia had recognized the errant Knorth—not
by her face, which the matriarch had never before seen naked,
but by the gloves and tattered remains of Aerulan's gown.

"*Well!*" she said, in a tone of high, moral outrage.

The Knorth gave her a quick, rueful look.

Footsteps rang on the steps behind her. She bolted up into
the hall, turned, and kicked the first of her pursuers back into
the arms of his fellows.

The three assassins above converged on her.

Not since the Fall had it been customary to teach Highborn
women the Senethar; consequently, the Coman by the fire had
never before seen one of their own fight, much less against
invisible opponents. The effect was both startling and spectacular, a death-dance tracing its *kantirs* across the floor between firelight and shadow, fierce and beautiful. On the hall's
far side, the Knorth lunged for the door and threw it open.
The wind swept in around her in a triumphant whoop.

"Alli-alli-all-after-me!" she cried over her shoulder, and
plunged out into the night, closely pursued.

The younger girls burst into applause.

"Quiet!" snapped Karidia. She stalked over and slammed
the door.

No mask. Not even the vestige of one.

"Shameless," the Coman Matriarch muttered to herself. "Utterly shameless."

V

The Tishooo had grown in strength over the past hour. Now it was snatching up slates, casting down chimneys, and generally wreaking gleeful havoc in the upper air.

Jame skimmed along on its wings. She had come out on the south side of the Coman near its eastern end and had turned right because a gust of wind had pushed her that way. Before her lay a series of interconnected courtyards leading toward the Randir compound and the Forecourt. It suited her to be outside, where the Tishooo blew too hard for her pursuers to try their shadow-casting tricks. Let the bastards catch her if they could. Over the wind's roar she heard the brazen bellow of a horn as someone finally sounded the alarm. With luck, it was the Brandan captain, the only person she had met all night who might know what she should do next.

The Randir loomed before her. She dodged right into the covered passageway that separated it from the western end of the Coman. Ahead lay the Forecourt, with the old keep in its midst and the Brandan compound on the far side. Running feet echoed in the passage behind her. Then she was out under open sky again, racing over grass. Ahead, the Brandan horn boomed again, at last drawing together its scattered garrison. Presumably, the captured assassin was also on his reluctant way to that muster.

In that, however, she was wrong. As if by thinking of him she had conjured up his ghost, the blond boy's pale face rose in the arcade, disembodied. White ribbons fluttered down— the last of the petticoat bonds. Then he was over the low wall and coming at her. How in Perimal's name had he gotten loose? She had relieved him of both his knife and hood, although not managing to hang on to either herself. That blade in his hand— not steel: ivory. Sweet Trinity, he'd had it all the time, before she had known that it was stolen and had thought to search him for it: The Ivory Knife, whose least scratch meant death. Jame swerved wildly, and her foot slipped on the new grass. The blond assassin loomed over her. This close, in bright moonlight, she could see him as a flaw in the rushing air, the Knife white in his *mere*-gloved hand. He had her cold—but he had stopped to stare in disbelief at the Knife, then at her unmasked face, then back.

Jame kicked his feet out from under him. As he fell, the Knife flew out of his grasp to land a dozen feet away. Of the three aspects carved on its pommel—hag, lady, and maiden— the third smiled back at her with a face so nearly her own. Under it, the grass began to die.

She scrambled after it, but it seemed to leap out from under her hand, kicked by a *mere*-shod foot. Damnation. At least one of the other ten had overtaken her. She rolled to her feet to find herself ringed by black shadows on the pewter-gray grass.

At least, when still attached, their shadows were no more dangerous than her own; but there were eleven of them now, ten armed. She thought they would try to make a quick end of her. After all, this was no private place, and the alarm continued to blare out overhead. But it had been too long and frustrating a hunt to end so tamely.

"Mousie," breathed one, and darted at her.

She didn't see his knife flash until the last moment. Cloth ripped. Damn again. She'd forgotten that she wasn't wearing her knife-fighter's *d'hen* with its reinforced sleeve. Air wavered as the boy dodged back.

"Mousie," whispered someone behind her.

Whipping around, she felt a line like fire across her shoulder and saw the fabric darken. First blood.

"Mousie, mousie, mou…"

Jame turned toward that last mocking whisper, caught the assassin's knife hand as it flashed past, and jerked him into a fire-leaping elbow strike to the chin.

"Tag!" she said.

His head snapped back and his hood flew off. The next moment he was airborne as she used earth-moving leverage to hurl him into the colleague who had just started his run at her.

Cat-and-mouse became free-for-all. The assassins hadn't trained for this sort of scuffle and couldn't see each other any better than Jame could, to judge from the curses and collisions. The latter, as much as wind blowing and water-flowing, helped her to glide through their confusion. Nonetheless, she knew that her luck was wearing as thin as Aerulan's dress. The Ivory Knife had disappeared, picked up or kicked into deeper shadows. With or without it, they must try to kill her quickly now. The horn had stopped blowing. Each garrison would secure its own compound before converging here, but they would come soon.

Then she saw dark figures in the Randir arcade, silent and motionless, watching her. How long had they been there? Why didn't they help? Who were they, anyway—Randir, or some other house guard answering the alarm, struck dumb at the sight of the mad Knorth capering in the moonlight? How their eyes glowed. Couldn't they at least see the heads of the two assassins whom she had unmasked, bobbing about apparently on their own? Maybe, if she could snatch off a few more hoods...

At that moment, the Tishooo intervened. It had been careening around the courtyard, indiscriminately trying to brain people with flying shingles; but suddenly it indulged in a violent updraft, taking with it torn grass, bits of Aerulan's dress, and nine hoods.

In the moment of windless calm which followed, Jame saw three shadows streak across the grass toward her. She leaped back—not quite in time. One of them clipped the shadow cast by her left arm, and her whole left side went numb. She staggered, but it was the assassins who fell as their shadows collided on the spot where hers had lain. Other boys, darting forward, tripped over their *mere*-clad colleagues and went down in a heap of swearing heads. Turning, fighting to keep her balance, Jame found herself face-to-face with the only assassin between her and the keep door. Stripped of his anonymity along with his hood, he looked very young and very scared.

"Move!" she snapped at him.

He moved.

She lurched past, threw open the door and pitched head first into the dark interior. The Tishooo, returning belatedly with a roar, slammed the door shut behind her. She pulled herself to her feet, hanging onto the door handle. Extending a nail, she fumbled about inside the ancient lock. The bolt creaked home just as a weight hit the outer panels. The door was made of well-seasoned ironwood, proof even against a battering ram, but the lock was old and rusty. It wouldn't hold long.

It wouldn't have to, thought Jame, leaning against the door. Surely now those guards in the arcade would realize that something was wrong and come to the rescue.

The door shuddered again and again. Something inside the lock groaned. Dammit, where were...

They weren't coming.

Jame knew that as suddenly and surely as she had that the assassins had been told exactly where to find her room. She kept forgetting that someone in Gothregor wanted her dead.

So. There wouldn't be any rescue after all. Well, there seldom was.

She pushed herself away from the door, groped for a candle, and lit it. Stumbling, she crossed the death-banner hall to the door which would have opened into the inner ward, except that a lock which would take more time than she had to pick secured it. She made for the northwest spiral stair, saluting Aerulan as she passed.

Her left foot hit the risers as she climbed, but she could only tell because she kept tripping. She was tempted to slam her left hand into the wall to try to wake it. The Bashtiri had made her a prisoner in her own body, as surely as if she had been stricken with apoplexy.

Below, the door crashed open.

On all fours, Jame scrambled up into the third-story chamber of the High Council. Ah, this was no use: they could run her down with ease now, however high she climbed.

Don't panic, she told herself, pausing to gulp down air. *Think. If they have tricks, so do you, and knowledge, and the will to use it.*

The judgment of the Arrin-ken came back to her: *Child, you have perverted the Great Dance and misused a master rune, a darkling in training if not in blood, reckless to the point of madness...*

"Shut up," she muttered, hearing the slur in her voice from a half-frozen mouth, hating it. "Shut up, shut up! You ran away, left us all to make our *own* judgments. I'll do whatever I damn well have to, to survive."

And yet—and yet—they had given her an idea.

In the middle of the chamber stood a massive ebony table. Jame dripped wax on the western end of it and fixed the burning candle upright in it. Then she clambered up to stand on the smooth, black surface. Those gorgeous stained glass windows soared up thirty feet all around her with moonlight streaming through them. Three of the walls displayed the crests of the nine major houses, separated by stone tracery. On the fourth, facing eastward, was a map of Rathillien, jewel-colored even in this light, if with subtler hues.

A thin breath of air had followed her up the stair to ruffle the candle's flame, but now the breeze abruptly died. They had closed the lower door. Stealthy footsteps sounded in the stairwell behind her, climbing slowly, cautiously. Jame smiled. At least she had finally taught them to respect their prey, and so bought herself a few precious minutes.

She cleared her mind.

What she needed was a certain master rune; but no one could carry any of them for long in memory and she didn't have the Book Bound in Pale Leather for reference. She thought, though, that given its nature she might be able to reconstruct this one from the Senetha's more esoteric *kantirs*. If only she could have danced them, but not in this lead-footed state. Instead, she stood there, filling her mind with their airy movements as her body would have traced them, waiting for the rune to emerge from the dance.

A face floated up the dark stairwell, looking first wary, then confused. Whatever the assassin had expected, it wasn't this motionless figure standing on a table with its back to him, black against the amber gold of the map's Southern Wastes. Nonetheless, he ascended to the hall. Ten pale faces came hesitantly after him, splitting to right and left, blocking the entrances to all four towers, surrounding their prey. A moment's uncertainty followed, with a rapid exchange of glances.

This wasn't the hunt which they had been led to expect— a soft kill like the others here thirty-odd years ago and the glory of closing the Guild's second-oldest contract. Through all their minds were running other stories, told of the only open contract older than this, which also involved a Kencyr Highborn, if of a different house. How many of their fellows had vanished utterly over the years while trying to close that account? The Guild shouldn't have accepted a second contract against the Kencyrath, however lucrative. It would never take a third.

Then they tensed, thinking that their prey had begun to move; but it was only her hair, stirring slightly about her face and shoulders. Loose strands of it flexed in the air. The braid started to unravel, as if combed out by invisible fingers. A slashed sleeve suddenly flared wide. The ribbons of her skirt began to plait themselves about her bare legs. It looked for all the world as if she stood in a rising wind, but at the other end of the table, the candle flame rose without a tremor in the still air.

The blond boy made a strange sound in his throat, turned, and bolted down the stair. They heard his feet slap on the steps in panic-stricken flight.

With a sharp gesture, the oldest stopped the others from
following. He had to signal twice more, though, before their
shadow-souls detached and flowed—across the floor, up the
table legs, onto its top…

Jame didn't notice. Her mind was full of a great wind, on
which her soul balanced precariously like a fledgling on the storm
blast. To this stage the dance had come. She hadn't yet the skill
to pursue it further, or the immediate need. The master rune
had come to her piece by piece in patterns drawn on the air. She
wouldn't be able to hold it long, though. Her thoughts plummeted to earth. She found that all this time she had been staring
blindly up at the stained glass map, at the spot where the artisan
had depicted a storm of black wings over the mountains of
Nekrien. How appropriate: the Witch King of that southern
land was said to have ruled the winds for more than a thousand
years. Still looking up at the map, she brought the rune hovering to the tip of her tongue, wrapped in the words which would
unbind it. Then, because the last time, in the Ebonbane, the
result had exceeded expectations, she barely whispered:

"*Wind, blow.*"

There was a frozen moment, then a gigantic inhalation outside. The windows exploded, jewel-bright slivers scything
outward. Ten wisps of darkness were snatched off the table
and sucked, wailing, into the night. Inside, ten bodies crumpled
to the floor. The Tishooo kept inhaling. Jame dropped flat
and clung to the tabletop as half of the roof disappeared with
a death shriek of timber. The wind roared up through the gap.
Shapes like great, soft-winged bats swarmed up the four stair-
wells from the lower hall, pale faces flashing past, white hands
flailing, as the death banners took flight. The air was full of
them, caught in the swift, upward spiral of the wind, a storm
of ancestors ascending.

One of the ancient tapestries had snagged on the corner
of the table, held by a disintegrating weft while its upper warp
strings flew bare. They seemed to be weaving into a new shape
in midair, or rather weaving *around* something. String ligaments

gave form to the shadow of an arm, a shoulder, and a face with the deep glimmer of eyes. Bane looked at her through the web of another man's death. The threads of his mouth shifted. He was smiling at her.

Then his head tilted back as he followed the other banners' flight, and the smile died.

These were the honorable dead. He had staked everything on death restoring his own lost honor, squandered in games of cruelty and despair. That gamble might have won, if not for Ishtier's treachery and Jame's bungling. How much did he blame her for that failure? Why was he here now, if not to collect his own blood-price? Some of the threads had worked free of the corner. They streamed up between shadow fingers as he reached for her.

"Don't!" she cried.

A moment later, without thinking, she had grabbed for that phantom hand as the rest of the anchoring weft gave way, but caught only a tangle of flying threads. The thing that had given them shape was gone, sucked upward with the rest of the dead into the beating darkness.

Beating?

Jame twisted to peer upward. Her own loosened, flying hair half-obscured her view, but through it she thought she saw the air above the keep full of vast black wings flailing against the moon. In their midst, far up, an old man fell and fell, never to reach the ground.

Then the man, the wings, and the wind all vanished, as suddenly as if some door in heaven had slammed shut.

Jame lay still for a moment, hardly believing that it was over—but what in Perimal's name had she seen, there, above the keep? It *must* have been an afterimage, brought on by staring too long and hard at what flew above the mountains of Nekrien on the map.

Oh, hell. The map. The windows. She sat up to gaze in dismay at the broken traceries, empty of glass, and the hole in the roof, with a few banners snagged on the shattered beams.

Tori was not going to be pleased.

Then she heard voices below, speaking softly in Kens. At last, the guard had begun to take an interest, unless these were the strangers with glowing eyes whom she had seen in the Randir arcade, come to see how the Shadow Guild had fared. Jame slid hastily down off the table, noting that her foot could almost feel the floor although otherwise her left side remained numb. She located the first assassin by falling over him. He was dead. So were the other nine. That surprised her: she had thought that they couldn't die when separated from their shadow-souls, but this separation had apparently been so abrupt that not one of them had survived the shock. Worse, none of them had the Ivory Knife. Also missing was the blond boy.

A Brandan cadet paused on the final turning of the stair, clearly startled to find the missing Knorth in such a place. More guards of her house came up behind her. Their captain staggered up the steps after them, leaning heavily on a cadet.

"Some fox hunt," she muttered, as disconcerted guards stumbled about the chamber, tripping over invisible bodies. Then she caught sight of Jame's bare face, and quickly looked away.

All winter, people had been lecturing Jame about the impropriety of going unmasked, but she had never really understood how they felt—until now.

"What took you so long?" she demanded, her voice sharp with sudden embarrassment.

The cadet had helped her captain over to the ebony table and left her leaning against it. "Lady," she said, still not looking at Jame, speaking very low, "it was a right mess. That maid you sent for help managed to knock herself silly falling downstairs. It took me nearly an hour to haul myself down to the guardroom."

"And then you had them sound the alarm."

"Yes. Trinity!" Her gaze, turning upward, had seen the moon through shattered rafters. "D'you always have this drastic an effect on architecture?"

"Fairly often," said Jame with a sigh, remembering the state in which she had left Tai-tastigon and a certain palace in Karkinaroth. "But what about Brenwyr? Why didn't she raise the alarm much earlier?"

The captain didn't know. Jame remembered her last glimpse of the Iron Matriarch, standing motionless over the captured assassin, that strange red light simmering in her eyes. Had Brenwyr moved at all until the alarm had broken in on her, just before Jame's arrival in the Forecourt?

An irate voice sounded in the lower hall, then in the echoing throat of the southeast stairwell. The Caineron captain. Damn.

"Look," Jame said hastily to the Brandan. "Are you sure there are always thirteen assassins in a casting? I only count one dead in the nursery, ten here, and a twelfth who, I think, ran away."

"For a blooding, the thirteenth would be a guild master." This time she did look at Jame, sharply. "D'you mean to say that he's still on the loose?"

The Caineron captain stalked into the hall, her cadet guards trailing cautiously after her. "So, lady, here you are at last," she said to Jame. "The next time you're scared by a little wind, try to show some gumption instead of scuttling off."

Jame opened her mouth, then shut it again.

The captain had already turned away with a startled oath, having just seen the pile of naked, white bodies which the Brandan cadets had begun to collect and strip.

Let her think what she liked. Explanations would hardly help.

Suddenly, Jame felt the hair prickle on her scalp. Brenwyr stood at the mouth of the northwest tower, staring at her with eyes as red as a cat's by firelight. Sweet Trinity, now what?

"Pardon, lady," someone mumbled at her elbow.

The next moment, two Caineron cadets had seized her arms, in the manner of hastily securing a fugitive. The reason was Kallystine, who had just entered the chamber.

*Her guard must think it worth their lives to let me slip away
again*, Jame thought, watching Caldane's daughter sweep
across the floor toward her as if they were the only two people
in the room.

Instead of her usual daring mask, Kallystine wore a heavy
veil, which her rapid progress flattened against her hidden features. Jame stared. Those lines of cheek and chin of which
M'lady was so proud—could they possibly be sagging?

"Lady," she blurted out, "what's happened to your face?"

Kallystine slapped her.

Jame saw the blow coming, with something in the other's
hand that flashed cold in the moon light; but the cadets' grip
held her fast, so that she could neither block nor dodge. It
struck her numb left cheek, hard enough to jolt back her head.
She heard the others gasp. Belatedly, the cadets released her
and backed away, looking shocked.

"There," said Kallystine's honeyed voice, the smile audible
in it. "Now you also know what it feels like, to lose face."

Jame touched her cheek. There was still no sensation in it,
but to her fingertips it felt odd, like a mask of soft leather with
a great tear in it. Through the tear, she felt something hard
and wet. Then she knew. That flash in Kallystine's hand had
been the blade of a razor-ring. The wetness was blood; the
hard thing under her finger tips, her own cheekbone, laid bare.

As that afternoon a slap had made her berserker blood
flare, so it did now. Jame fought it. Her nails were out, sheathed
in the palms of her clenched fists, and everyone was backing
away. Not long ago, she had spoken a master rune. Now she
again felt the power rise, seeking a half-remembered form—
something from the last pages of the Book, to rip apart the
senses of all who heard it, to rupture ears and burst eyes. It
clawed its way up her throat like a live thing as she struggled
to master it, half-succeeding at the last moment. Still, it burst
out with terrible, wordless force.

The first thing the Kendar heard afterward, when their
ears stopped ringing, was Kallystine's babbled complaints and

orders. When their eyes had cleared sufficiently and the worst nosebleeds had been checked, a Caineron guard bundled her lady off to her quarters with far less ceremony than she was accustomed to.

The Brandan Matriarch sat on a step with her head on her hands.

The Knorth had disappeared.

"Oh, no," said a voice among the remaining Caineron. "Not again."

VI

This time, however, there was a trail of blood.

A still-shaken group of cadets followed it up the north-west tower stair to the apartment called Gothregor and there lost it, in the middle of the Highlord's small study. They looked behind chairs, out windows, under the table, and up the chimney, without success. Then someone remembered the catwalk to the other tower and, for her pains, was sent across to check.

"Nothing," she reported back, bright green with height-sickness, and lost her dinner behind the Highlord's chair.

Nonetheless, it was decided that the Knorth must also have crossed over and then gone down the southwest stair, while no one below had been in a fit state to notice. In that case, she could be anywhere in the greater fortress by now. The cadets were dispatched to search there, with orders from the Caineron captain not to tell anyone anything. When she included the Brandan cadets in this charge, their captain raised her brows, but didn't comment until they had gone.

"Two *are* missing," she said, as the Caineron tossed *mere* clothing over the bodies, temporarily concealing them. "One is almost certainly a guild master."

"No need to cause more panic. They'll be long gone by now."

"They came back after all these years, apparently as soon as word reached them that a young Knorth was in these halls again and spring weather permitted travel. They don't give up that easily."

"Look," said the Caineron impatiently. "It will be dawn soon. *Mere* or not, they aren't day hunters. By night, we'll have that wretched girl in our hands again, bound and gagged, if necessary, and the halls totally secured."

"As, perhaps, they should have been ever since she arrived."

The Caineron shook her head like a baited bear. She knew she had handled this badly, but be damned if she would admit it. "How could we guess that the contract was still active, thirty-odd years later? I know, I know: they've been after the so-called Randir Heir longer than that, but this is different. Anyway, the brat has scuttled again. If we can't find her, on our home ground, how d'you think the Guild will?"

"Gone back into hiding, yes. And hurt. With all due respect, how could your lady have been so *stupid*? We may have war over this."

"Over what?" asked the young Danior captain, emerging from the stairwell with her Edirr counterpart on her heels. "Trinity! Old Man Tishooo really took a dislike to this place, didn't he?"

"Never mind that damned wind," snapped the Coman captain, coming in with the Ardeth. "What in Perimal's name was that cry? *That's* what scared my ladies out of the few wits they had left."

"You're lucky," said the Ardeth soberly. "It reduced our Shanir to convulsions." She glanced at Brenwyr's huddled figure on the stair, and shot the Brandan captain a questioning look.

The latter replied with a flick of her hand: *I don't know.*

The Jaran captain had arrived during this exchange. "Well," she said, surveying the damage. "I see that someone got in the Knorth's way after all."

"Don't be an idiot!" the Caineron almost shouted. "A freak wind did this! Don't you farking know what the Tishooo is like?"

"All right, all right," said the Jaran pacifically. "Just tell me this, then: whose blood is that, on the floor?"

The Caineron shuffled her feet. If it had been left to her, the others would never have known. As it was, the Brandan told them.

The randon looked at each other with dismay. There hadn't been anything like this in the Women's Halls since the quarrel between Kinzi and the Randir Matriarch Rawneth, and even that hadn't come to blows, if only because the Shadow Guild had struck first.

"At least it's only a lady," said the Coman. "Think how much worse it would be if this had happened to someone important."

"Right," the Danior said dryly. "It's only the Highlord's sister, his sole surviving blood-kin. Quiet as the man is, I don't see him letting this pass without comment. You were right," she said to the Brandan. "This could mean war."

"Not necessarily."

They all turned at the sound of this new voice. The Randir captain had entered the chamber some time during the past few minutes and stood in the shadows, hidden by her dress grays, listening. Now she came forward, half out of darkness. Moonlight caught the thin gold lines embroidered on her shoulder and the white teeth of a smile which never quite reached her eyes.

"If the damage is repaired before the Highlord returns, how much complaint can he make, even if the girl is so ill-bred as to tell him? At the Priests' College, we have a healer so powerful that he once nearly restored life to a sheepskin coat. Shall I send to Wilden for him?"

The Brandan's brows rose again. "A Randir, prescribing for a Knorth? Shouldn't we at least consult Rowan, Torisen's steward? After all, this did happen in the old Knorth keep, not in the halls."

"Keep or not," said the Caineron, glowering, "the matriarchs made me responsible for the brat, and the only other death tonight in the halls was one of my own cadets. This is *my* business. Hell, yes: send for the healer! Should we risk civil war over a scratched face?"

The Brandan touched the marks around her own eyes, made with her own nails in the night nursery.

"There's something else you should see."

For a moment, it seemed that the Caineron would stop her, but then she stepped aside with poor grace. In an apparently empty corner, the Brandan bent to flick something away. A pale, tangled patch appeared, seeming to float a foot off the floor. In it was a confusion of thin arms, parts of two torsos, and a boy's head, lolling, dead eyes wide open in disbelief.

"Damnation," said the Jaran softly, after a moment. "They came back. And I was right: someone *did* get in the Knorth's way."

The others paid no attention to that. Taking the Caineron at her word that the missing Knorth was her responsibility, they disbanded in haste, each to secure her own compound against the two intruders still at large.

The Brandan stayed to help her matriarch. This time, Brenwyr rose at a touch on her shoulder. Blood had run down from her ears and red-flecked eyes, like scarlet tears.

"Save your questions," she said harshly. "I can't hear them anyway. And if you're staring at me, don't."

Descending step by blind step to the lower hall, she put up her hand to confirm what she had seen earlier. Among the night's other casualties were all the death banners on the west wall. Aerulan was gone.

A maledight curse—half pure malison, half prophesy—began to form below the level of Brenwyr's conscious mind. She felt it quicken, as always not knowing what shape it would take. Then it rose like a sickness which must be spat out or swallowed back. All the darkness of that long winter, all the misery and madness… She spat:

"*Roofless and rootless, blood and bone, cursed be and cast out!*"

No light, no relief, no sound, even, of her own voice in her stricken silence.

"Oh, Aerulan!" she cried.

The captain led her away.

VII

Brenwyr's words carried, as such curses do, until they reached the one for whom they were intended. Four flights up, a sigh answered them:

"'*Roofless and rootless*'? The same to you, Brandan. '*Cursed be.*'"

The door leading from the tower out onto the platform of the catwalk had been left open. Now it swung back. No one had stopped to think that a flat door is not going to lie absolutely flush with a curved wall. The jagged hole in the council chamber roof gaped beneath. Jame had heard every word spoken there. In fact, she had felt inclined to tumble down on the captains' heads, if they didn't shut up soon and go away. Oh Trinity, was this faintness only shock, or had Kallystine doctored her blade?

They *had* gone, cursing her.

She stumbled back into her brother's study and collapsed into his chair. Senethar techniques had stopped the bleeding. Similar measures to control pain hadn't yet been necessary, but soon would be as the numbness wore off. Her front teeth felt loose from half-swallowing a master rune, and her throat raw. As for her cheek, the pulse there was already beginning to throb. She touched it gingerly. No doubt about it: M'lady Kallystine had done her a serious mischief. Sweet Trinity, talk about losing face...

But she needn't. The Randir captain had spoken of someone who might set all right. A healer from Wilden. A priest.

There was the rub.

No Kencyr liked or trusted his own priests, anymore than he did the god whom they served. Both were ignored as much as possible by the rest of the Kencyrath, except when a house wanted to get rid of a Shanir boy. The unforeseen result was

that the Priests' College had accumulated most of the curative Shanir, who tended to mature too late for their families to
realize what they were throwing away. Lords sometimes bar-
gained to get their healers back, but they never really regained
control of them. Being a novice changed a boy. Being a priest
warped him utterly.

So, at least, Jame believed, judging by Ishtier.

Moreover, the very thought of deep healing made her skin
crawl. Buried deep in every individual's mind was a soul-image—a metaphor for his or her essence in which illness and
injury were also reflected. Repairing the image healed the body.
A Shanir healer entered the collective soul-scape to do this, in
perhaps the most intimate experience known to the Kencyrath.

Be damned if she was going to let anyone that close to her
now, Jame thought, even if it meant wearing a mask the rest
of her life. It wasn't as if her face had ever amounted to
much, anyway.

Here, her thoughts began to blur, perhaps influenced by
the healing techniques which normally ended in *dwar* sleep,
perhaps by whatever-it-was which Kallystine might have put
on her razor's edge. She slept fitfully for a time, in and out of
dreams. A terror of helplessness kept her from the deeper
reaches of *dwar*, which would have speeded the healing process but which also would have set the scar. Awake or dreaming, she stared up at the warped, bronze mirror over the mantle,
in which her ghostlike image sat in her brother's chair.

More shadowy still was the reflection of the two figures
who stood behind her, backs turned, on a balcony over a moonlit
waste. From a great distance, she seemed to hear their voices.

"...*my boy, it's almost dawn,*" one was saying. "*Don't you
mean to sleep at all?*"

"*I will,*" replied her brother, dogged, "*when the chair behind
me is empty.*"

Dammit, he was blaming her again. Somehow, everything
out of his control must be her fault, as their father Ganth Gray
Lord had taught him.

...Ganth's hoarse, mad voice dripping poison in her brother's ear: "*You were all right until* she *came back, your darkling half...*"

"Father, no!" she protested thickly, rousing. "*You* drove me out, into shadows. It isn't fair to blame me. It..."

"*...'s no good whining,*" someone else seemed to answer her.

Jame cringed back again in the chair. That voice, with its pretended sophistication, its underlying power and cruelty, which she had last heard as a prisoner in his tent at the Cataracts...Caldane, Lord Caineron. The reflected scene behind her had darkened into a different prison, where torchlight glowered on dank stonewalls.

Sounds answered Caldane: the rustle of befouled straw, harsh breathing, mumbled words.

"*Done enough to you already? Oh no. You betrayed me, Gricki. No one does that, least of all my own misbegotten bastard. I'll find a use for you yet—in a few days, when I've thought of something special.*"

"No!" Jame cried again, struggling against the grip of nightmare to rise and turn. "Caldane, don't you dare..."

But the effort made her wits whirl. She thought, dazed, that she must have fallen, but didn't remember hitting the ground. Her angle of vision was...odd. Askew. Instead of Restormir's dungeon, she glimpsed Gothregor across the Silver, shadowy ruins, and the blond boy-assassin, looking terrified. Then, very, very close, a pair of yellow eyes glittered down at her, with no face behind them. Not just *mere* clothes, but *mere* tattooing—the mark of a guild master. Invisible lips drew back from rotten teeth.

"*You were sent to find a pale book,*" tongue and ulcerated throat said harshly from midair. "*Instead, you bring me this strange knife.*" Trinity. She must be seeing him through the eyes of the Maiden, the third face carved on the pommel of the Ivory Knife. "*You were sent to kill a girl. Instead, you tell me that all your brothers are dead. That is unsatisfactory. Oh, I'm so glad that you agree, boy, because this isn't over yet...*"

No, not yet. Not alive, not dead either. Just lost, bewildered, and very, very frightened.

Brothers, where are you? Where am I? What happened to us? There was a great wind, full of wings, and in its midst the Old Man snatched us up. Flying, flying, falling ah! Dead branches against the moon, catching us, but we cannot catch them. Where are my hands?

On an ironwood floor, beside an ebony table, growing cold, growing stiff...

No. Here. Not dead but not alive either.

The other is here too, snagged out of the air by the tree's bleached fingers, a darkness that flows down the white wood, stronger than we are, older and more cruel, a shadow with hungry, silver eyes. Run, hide!

...but we are growing cold and stiff.

"You can't run from me forever," it whispers, smiling. *"Blood binds."*

Jame sprang to her feet. For a moment, the suddenness of her rise struck her blind. *Dreams,* she thought, breathing hard, forcing herself to stand still. *Nothing but damned dreams...*

"No," said Torisen's half-choked voice. "I refuse to dream this!"

Her eyes cleared. She was staring directly into the bronze mirror and a warped version of her own face seemed to stare back at her in horror. It had the same Knorth features, at least, even the blood across one high cheekbone. But it wasn't her.

"Tori?" she whispered. "Tori, wait!"

A hasty step forward had turned into a lunge as her legs failed her, and his image had recoiled. She clung to the mantle for support, her breath clouding the cold bronze.

"Dammit, where are you? Come to me, brother. Come!"

The metal cleared. Reflected in it, behind her, she saw the tower room and Torisen's chair, over which her shadow lay. No. Something sat there, spun of nightmares, silver-eyed. It rose, smiling. The wrong brother had answered, her darkling shadow-bane…

Run. Hide.

Images blurred into a nightmare of flight. Underfoot, stairs, ironwood floors, grass, flagstones, get away get away get away… A stab of pain brought Jame up short. She blinked and found herself, breathless, in the ruins of her tiny room in the Caineron quarter. She sat abruptly on the bed and was enveloped in down from the slashed mattress.

Sweet Trinity, was this another dream? *Not with feathers in it*, she thought, sneezing. *Nothing so innocent.* As for the rest…

…Torisen and Ardeth on the balcony; Caineron and Graykin; the Ivory Knife in a guild master's invisible hand; the souls of the boy-assassins hunted by Bane; *Blood binds…*

All phantasms of a possibly drugged mind? Perhaps. Earlier, she had refused to believe that she might far-see anything—what did she want with another Shanir curse?—but these images rang all too true, all but the last. Bane was *not* her shadow. Darkling she might be, but unfallen, her soul and honor still her own.

Besides, the bastard was up a tree somewhere, breakfasting on nasty little boys. What would *their* souls taste like— sticky fingers and snot?

But then, if not Bane, what had her brother seen, to react with such horror? The room's broken mirror told her, over and over in a dozen shattered planes. Oh God.

Another flare of pain. Sensation was returning in ragged waves, in between which she hastily applied the appropriate technique. Ironic, that she had learned it here at Gothregor. Because of childbirth, the Women's World knew more ways to control pain than even her Senethari, Tirandys, had been able to teach her.

Then she looked again, and saw by her reflection to her surprise that she was wearing travel clothes—black boots and pants, black knife-fighter's *d'hen* jacket with its tight right sleeve and full, reinforced left—with no memory of having put them on.

Roofless and rootless...

So, she hadn't come back here to hide. Well, they would have found her eventually anyway, wherever in Gothregor she had gone to earth. Then there would have been a forced healing as subtle as a rape and a lunatic's confinement, with Kallystine gloating through the keyhole. And all that time, Graykin would have been in Caldane's hands where service to her had landed him, because she did believe that part of her dreams, if nothing else.

So she was running: North, to Caldane's Restormir, to the rescue, if she could manage it with a face that could start a war?

Blood and bone...

At least, Tori would never believe what he had far-seen in his mirror. She wondered bitterly if he would even remember it, having seen him wipe far more important things completely out of his mind when they touched on the Shanir.

As for the rest of the Kencyrath, if it disliked unmasked females so much, it need never look on her face again. In her hand was a strip of clean linen, ripped from the hem of a spare underskirt. She wrapped it around her head, over the bridge of her nose and across both cheekbones, binding up the injury. A half-mask covered the whole neatly—not that it made her a proper lady, she thought, scowling at her visored image in the broken glass, any more than skirts had made her Aerulan. Damn all mirrors, anyway. No more trying to see herself as others wished her to be, no more useless reflections.

She left the room without a backward glance.

The compound seemed abandoned, except around Kallystine's quarters. At a guess, the Caineron guard had searched their own territory while she had slept in Tori's chair and were now out combing the rest of Gothregor for her. The other compounds proved to be locked tight and fully garrisoned. Jame therefore had no trouble raiding the communal kitchen for provisions or making her way westward through the empty corridors north of the Brandan.

From the top of the wall that separated the Women's World from the inner ward, she saw her brother's scar-faced steward Rowan arguing with the hall guards at the gate, demanding information and entry, getting neither, while the fortress's regular garrison gathered behind her.

No one noticed the slight, dark-clad figure who slipped down off the wall into the shadows on their left and then walked around behind them toward the subterranean stable. The thieves of Tai-tastigon could have taught the Shadow Guild something about passing unseen through a crowd. That the Knorth Kendar failed to notice the same figure a few minutes later, going in the opposite direction with an ounce trotting beside it, reflected more poorly on their powers of observation, but it was a very confusing night.

The post-rider, dispatched in haste for the Priests' College, nearly trampled someone under the North Gate. Swearing, she wrenched her horse to one side and thundered past.

Fifty miles to Wilden. Four hours riding flat out with a remount at Falkirr, Jame thought, watching the messenger plunge down through the steep middle ward and across the broad outer. The healer priest could return just as quickly, if he hurried. She and Jorin were getting out none too soon. They followed the rider down through the wards to the curtain wall and the northern barbican, passing out under the latter unchallenged into the apple orchard beyond.

Overhead, the gibbous moon shone bright at zenith while the stars sank into the deep blue of a predawn sky. The air was giddy with apple blossoms. Looking up through their white glimmer at Gothregor's looming darkness, Jame experienced a moment of bleak clarity.

What she did next, she had to do, for honor's sake as much as for her servant's life; but it would end her chance of acceptance by the Kencyrath in any role which it had been prepared to offer her. So this was the end of the long, bleak winter, turned into empty spring. Driven from the heart, where was there left to go?

Cursed be and cast...

Stop it, stop it. Brenwyr's curse buzzed in her mind like bees in the night's carcass. What would Marc say, if only he were here to ask?

Perhaps, again, "*Stop hiding. Follow honor and forget the rest.*" Wise, wise Marc.

Dawn birds were chirping sleepily as they left the orchard, bound northward for Restormir, forty leagues away.

Interim II
Kothifir Encampment: 55th of Spring

"My boy, it's almost dawn," said Lord Ardeth. "Don't you mean to sleep at all?"

"I will, when the chair behind me is empty."

Torisen saw the old lord's worried look. The chair in question *was* empty, now that Harn had reluctantly left to do the rounds of the watch. He knew that. And yet...and yet...moments ago, something *had* sat down in it.

Think of something else. Burr.

"I hope," he said, "that there was nothing worse in that wine than a sedative."

Ardeth shrugged. "An infusion of black nightshade never hurt any Highborn. The dose wasn't measured for a Kendar, though. You should never have made him drink it."

Torisen winced. He should have asked about the wine's composition earlier, too. Pieces of the night kept slipping away from him. He forced himself to half-turn, his back still toward the empty chair. His servant slumped on the other side of the table, his head in a pool of wine as red as spilt blood. He touched Burr's broad shoulder. The bond between them told him that the Kendar only slept, but was beginning to breathe with difficulty. Face down in narcotic wine...

Torisen carefully turned the man's head to one side, clearing nose and mouth. His hands had begun to shake again. Sixteen years together, through a dozen hells not even counting Urakarn, and he had almost let Burr quietly suffocate within arm's reach.

"You and your damned drugs," he said to Ardeth unsteadily. "Have you ever tried to live without them?"

"Why should I? My boy, can't I persuade you..."

"No!"

Ardeth's pharmacopoeia might do no harm in itself—after all, Highborn were almost impossible to poison—but it could rob Torisen of the few defenses which his lack of sleep had left him. The old terror returned like a hand closing on his throat: not only to dream such horrible things but to be trapped in one of his nightmares, unable to wake. This whole night had begun to feel that way, but dawn was almost here.

Hold on, just hold on...

He found himself again in front of Pereden's ornate mirror. His pale face seemed to float in the glass, black coat and hair casting almost no reflection. The room behind him was dim, lit only by gray light seeping through unshuttered windows. At his back was a chair—his, he realized, from his tower room at Gothregor—and in it sat an indistinct form. He must be dreaming, but he couldn't wake...

Movement in the back shadows of the mirror: the ghostly reflection of the Wolver Grimly entering the commander's quarters in Kothifir, stopping short.

"I smell blood," he said.

Torisen looked blankly down at his left hand, at red running along the white scars on his palm. His grip on Kin-Slayer had cracked the hilt emblem.

Ardeth came forward at once, fussing. "Let me see." He took Torisen's thin, elegant hand and turned it palm up. "You are so hard on yourself, my boy. More scars..."

"That's enough," said Torisen thickly, detaching the other's grip with a strength that made the old lord blink. "That's more than enough."

"My boy...?"

"I'm not. That was Pereden, and he's dead. Remember?" He jerked the emerald signet ring off his left hand and held it up. "I'm Ganth Gray Lord's son, former commander of the Southern Host, present Highlord of the Kencyrath, and I will *not* be condescended to or spied on. *Understand?*"

Ardeth fell back a step.

"My lord," he said, shaken. "I understand that you are tired and ill. I will leave you to rest." With a formal salute he departed, deliberately not glancing at the Wolver who remained crouched in the shadows, on guard.

Torisen looked at Ganth's ring for a moment, then slipped it onto a finger of his right hand. Was this how Pereden had felt, trying to exorcize his pain by inflicting it on others? In another moment, he would have accomplished that wretched boy's revenge by telling Ardeth the truth about his son, after all he had done to protect the old man from it. Torisen put both hands over his face, heedless of the blood which still trickled down between his fingers.

Sweet Trinity. He *must* be going mad.

"And whose fault is that?" Ganth's voice asked. *"You were all right until she came back, your darkling half. Now you will never be right again until she is…"*

What? wondered the Wolver Grimly, ears twitching.

But Torisen's hands had slid from his eyes to cover his mouth, stopping the words. The fur slowly rose down Grimly's spine. Did his friend know that he had been speaking out-loud? The "darkling half" must be Tori's newfound sister, whom Grimly had met at the Cataracts the previous winter and liked very much.

Until she is what?

In turning away from Ardeth, the Highlord had brought himself again face to face with the mirror. Now he froze, staring into it. All Grimly could see was Torisen's reflection, a smear of blood down one cheek from his cut hand. The Highborn made a half-choked sound:

"No. I refuse to dream this. I refuse…No!"

"Don't!" yelped the Wolver.

Too late. Kin-Slayer was out of its sheath, hissing through the air. Glass shattered. Grimly threw the unconscious Burr to the floor and shielded him with his body as razor-edged shards scythed overhead. Wood shrieked. Clay dust filled the air. For an endless moment, Grimly was sneezing too hard to wonder what had happened. Then he looked up. The mirror had disintegrated. So had the foot-thick wall behind it where blade and brick had met. A shaft of gray dawn light lanced through the ragged hole into the dusty murk of the room. Outside, dogs had begun to howl.

"Son of a bitch," said Grimly reverently. "You finally made the damn thing work. Tori, where are you?"

Dust began to settle. The room was empty except for the Wolver and Burr's sprawling figure. Below, hooves rang on stone. Grimly leaned out the ragged hole in time to see Torisen bareback on Storm, his quarter-blood Whinno-hir, bolting out of the courtyard, Kin-Slayer still naked in his hand.

Grimly remembered the old songs. You didn't unsheathe a battle-blade, especially that one, unless you meant to kill someone.

You will never be right again until she is...

Dead?

"Oh, no," said the Wolver. "Oh, Tori, no." He dropped to all fours and ran out of the room yelping, "Tori, Tori, wait for me!"

Part III

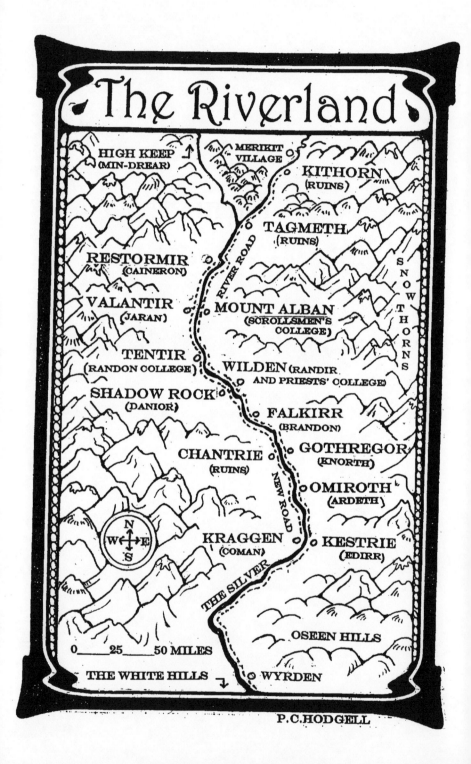

The Riverland: 55th – 58th of Spring
I

The Riverland stretched out along the upper reaches of the Silver, bracketed by the Snowthorn Mountains—a rugged country, over two hundred miles long but scarcely ten across at its widest. The Silver was the frontier between those two giants of the Central Lands, Bashti and Hathir. At the height of their power, a thousand years ago, they had built rival fortresses up the length of the river from the Cataracts to Kithorn. Supplying the northern garrisons had always been difficult, however. After a massive earthquake disrupted the Silver from end to end, destroying all travel on it, they had given up and ceded their mountain keeps to the Kencyrath in exchange for military aid. Kencyr troops had served as mercenaries in the Central Lands ever since, the Riverland having proved too poor to support them either.

Meager strips of arable land surrounded Gothregor, most of them lying fallow. Thanks to Torisen's long absence with the bulk of his troops, it would be a thin harvest for the Knorth garrison and a worse winter. Black cattle grazed between the furrows. A bull stamped at the smell of strangers, but more to be feared were the horns of the cow suckling her calf behind him.

Beyond, the land was almost untouched except for the ancient River Road running along the Silver's east bank and the New Road occasionally glimpsed through trees on the west. To leave either was said to be dangerous. No reliable map existed of the reaches between the keeps—because all cartographers were incompetent, the lords said. The scrollsmen themselves simply couldn't agree on details, leaving some to complain in disgust that the terrain must differ for each traveler who crossed it.

Nonetheless, not wishing to be overtaken, two fugitives followed a hunter's path about a quarter of a mile up the mountainside with trees above them and a sweep of wild flowers below. So far, though, no one had passed by on the River Road, coming or going. *Odd,* thought Jame. Maybe the priests weren't going to send their precious healer after all

Morning slid into afternoon. The sun was in decline when they came to a brook plunging down through trees into the steep meadow below. While Jorin lapped avidly, Jame sat back on her heels with a sigh, feeling the pull of tired muscles. A winter of roaming halls had ill-prepared her to tackle mountains. Still, she should grow accustomed to it quickly. The same, alas, could not be said for Kallystine's handiwork. Gingerly, she touched her face. Beneath the mask, her cheek felt swollen and hot. At least it didn't hurt, the numbness of the assassin's touch having long since merged into her own pain control. It was hard, though, to keep the wits clear during such a sustained effort. Lulled by the stream's voice, she let her senses drift.

The day turned luminous around her. High overhead, snow blew off the western peaks in sparkling veils. Below, set against the darkness of pine forests, panicles of meadow grass floated in a golden shimmer. Down on the valley floor, birds flew up in a wave along the River Road, as if disturbed by someone passing by, northward bound. White wings gleamed in the upper air.

"Wah!" said Jorin, and dropped a half-eaten fish in her lap.

The sight reminded Jame that her own last meal had been sometime the previous day. However, she wasn't hungry. Damn Kallystine anyway, if this light-headedness was in part her fault. It was difficult to poison or infect a Highborn, but M'lady could be counted on to have tried her best.

Wait a minute. Those disturbed birds. *Had* someone passed by below?

She didn't think so, but couldn't be sure. At least, no one could have seen her as she knelt behind this waving screen of grass. Anyway, it was time to move on—higher up the slope, if she couldn't trust herself within sight of the road. She drank deep; splashing icy water on her flushed face below the mask, then rose and left the path for the trees above, Jorin bounding on ahead.

They found themselves in a forest of straight, pale trunks, floored with silver-edged ferns, roofed by spring foliage. Unseen doves were calling at a distance. A breath of air ruffled frond and leaf.

It was beautiful, Jame thought, but in an odd way it reminded her of the Anarchies or the Heart of the Woods at Hurlen—both areas of native power, intolerant of any alien presence. Marc had told her that his old home was much like that too—but Kithorn Keep lay nearly sixty leagues to the north, in Merikit hands. Here, she was still in the heart of the Riverland, which the Kencyr lords had claimed as their own for a thousand years.

Roofless and rootless...

Now, there was a thought not without irony: suppose the Kencyrath itself had none too secure a grip on this land which it called home? After all, her people were alien to this world despite their long sojourn here. What if it saw them as invaders, as unwelcome as Perimal Darkling had been to the entire series of overlapping universes which made up the Chain of Creation? What had the Earth Wife of Peshtar called her and Marc?

"Stepchildren, if even that."

The loamy smell of the forest reminded her of Mother Ragga's low-beamed lodge and of the Earth Wife herself, that fat, old woman stuck together like a jackdaw's nest. On the floor of her house had been a map composed of dirt and rocks brought from all over Rathillien. By pressing her ear to this ridge or that hollow, she could hear what was happening on a mountain or in a valley half a world away. Listening to Marc's little bag of Kithorn soil, she had even heard the weightless feet of his long-dead sister running across the keep's abandoned courtyard.

Kithorn, from whose ruined battlements Torisen had seen the Burnt Man hunt a kin-slayer with his pack of Burning Ones. Now some claimed to have heard the latter in the Riverland itself. Easy enough, safe within Kencyr walls, to dismiss them as bogies to frighten Merikit children. Not so here, under green leaves. Presumably, the Wilden priests should keep such things off Kencyr territory, including Old Man Tishooo from the south and weirding from the north. Patently, they had not.

This land is unguarded, Jame thought with a sudden shiver. *Anything can happen here.*

The light changed as the sun set. All shadows merged into a misty twilight, with a gilt glimmer edging each leaf. One by one, the birds fell silent. The wood seemed to hold its breath, then let it out in a long sigh as the wind passed between the trees. So like the Anarchies, but there she had been protected by the Earth Wife's *imu* medallion, which now lay shattered in the hollow at the Heart of the Woods near the Cataracts. A shiver slid down her spine. They were absolutely alone, and yet they were being watched.

Jorin's ears pricked. The faintest of sighs, somewhere above...

Pale faces stared down at them through the foliage; white hands hovered as though in precarious benediction. The Knorth death banners hung there in rows on twig and bough, arranged just as they had been in the lower hall of the old keep. A breath of wind stirred them, so that for a moment the dead seemed to move restlessly in their tapestry webs. Then all was still again.

"Old Man, Old Man," said Jame softly, admiring the Tishooo's parting prank.

She could see, though, that for some of the banners this had been no joke: those too old for such a flight hung in shivering knots of warp threads, the identifying woof stripped away. Who would remember those Knorth dead now? Would Torisen know what names to chant on Autumn Eve to the empty places where their banners had hung?

"There are fewer of us left than I realized," said Jame to Jorin.

But as always she only looked for one, there, on the western side of this airy gallery. The familiar face smiled ruefully down at her through the fading light.

"Hello again, cousin," she said to it.

All the banners would eventually have to be rescued like so many treed cats, but only Aerulan was her immediate concern. How to get her down, though? Her banner hung on a small branch some thirty feet up, nothing between it and the ground but slick bark and air.

Hmmm…Treed cats. Cats climbed trees. With claws.

Jame looked at her hands. She loathed even the sight of the ivory nails beneath those black gloves, the most obvious of her Shanir traits and the source of so much past grief. Moreover, she had been taught that to use them in any way whatsoever strengthened her bond to the third face of God: Regonereth, That-Which-Destroys. As when faced with a locked door at Gothregor, however, practicality won.

"Right," she said, stripping off her gloves and tucking them into her belt. "Here goes."

Soon she was well off the ground and climbing. How much farther? Tilting back her head to look, she saw Aerulan about ten feet above her…no, closer: the branch was bending, the banner's cord slipping.

"Aerulan, no!" she cried up at it. "Don't jump!"

The death banner plunged down on top of her. She scrabbled at its blinding folds with one hand, trying to hang on with the other, but the impact had jarred her loose. The next moment, she was slithering down the trunk with bark shredding under her nails, then in the air, falling, crashing through the silvery undergrowth, hitting the ground.

Darkness.

Well, that's it, thought Jame, *I'm dead.*

Then she realized that the tapestry still covered her face. Pushing it aside, she found herself nose-to-nose with an anxious ounce.

Rolled up, the banner made a long, surprisingly heavy bundle, which Jame slung across her back by its cord, shifting the food sack's strap so that the latter rode on her hip. She always seemed to be carrying around relics of the dead—although not as ostentatiously as her brother who, the previous fall, had ridden all the way to the Cataracts with the bones of Marc's sister in his saddlebag. Maybe no one could escape the past, but most people didn't get stuck with such tangible fragments of it. Still, this time Jame was glad of the company.

By now, dusk was falling. The air thickened with shadows which cloaked the color of the forest and hid whatever paths might run through it. With difficulty, Jame chewed a handful of dried fruit while Jorin grumbled over cheese rinds. Then she curled up among the roots of an oak and fell into a troubled sleep, the death banner spread over her for warmth, the ounce in her arms.

Dwar sleep would have been natural now. By fleeing the healer, she had tacitly decided to live with the face which Kallystine had given her. Still, every time the velvet dark yawned, she jerked back from it, half into the waking world. Confusedly, she remembered the last time she had fled injured, southward from her old home, the poison of a haunt's bite already at work in her savaged arm.

Poison: *Had* Kallystine's blade been tainted?

Betrayal: Who had sent the shadow assassins after her?

The moon rose, on the wane toward the quarter, faintly aglow through night mist in a cage of white branches. Dead wood against the lunar disc, white on white…she had dreamed of such a thing, sitting in her brother's chair. Darkness had flowed down those pale limbs, was there still, leaning against the trunk. No. That was only the last of the tree's bark. Where it had peeled away at eye level, however, two points of light glimmered mockingly.

Luminous moss, she told herself. *It feeds on decay.*

However, moss seldom has a face.

Out of the shadows, Bane smiled at her.

She knew she should be frightened, but Aerulan held her. Their eyes met over her head, Bane's silver-gray and Aerulan's too, like her own. It was, after all, a family trait. The shadow-man sketched an ironic bow, as if to say:

"*If not now, later. I can wait.*"

The patches of light that had been his eyes seemed to blink. Then they fluttered away. Not moss. Moths.

"Later, what?" she cried after him. "Dammit, Bane, you're my b…"

But the word died on her lips. She had evoked him by it before, but did he truly know that they were half-siblings? She had only guessed it herself during her last confrontation with Ishtier, after the mob had taken Bane off to the Mercy Seat.

"*He trusted you!*" she had shouted at the priest. "*Because you brought his mother, the Gray Lord's mistress, down out of the Haunted Lands, because he thought—and you let him think—that you were his father. But Ganth Gray Lord was alive when you deserted him, wasn't he? You've betrayed not only Bane but your lord as well. Coward, lack-faith, renegade…*"

"*And who are you to pronounce sentence on me?*" the skull-faced priest had spat at her. "*Thief, whore, outcast…*"

"*The lord you betrayed was my father, the man consigned by you to torture on the Mercy Seat, my half-brother, and I—I am Jamethiel Priest's-Bane…*"

"…WHO SHALL YET BE THY DOOM."

Somehow, for the second time, she had caused the God-voice which never lies to speak through the false priest's mouth, against his will. The boom of it filled her head. What had it called her?

"CHAMPION, FRATRICIDE, TYR-RIDAN."

…no, no, no…

Then memory merged into nightmare as she slid uneasily back into sleep.

In the grip of his god, Ishtier had lost control of his temple. The power, set loose, spiraled outward, spreading fire and madness. Everything was burning—houses, people, the very air.

In Judgment Square, the holocaust wind blew away piles of
ash—all that remained of the mob that had stormed the
Thieves' Guild palace in search of Dally's murderer. On the
Mercy Seat sat a figure, charred black, the greasy smoke still
seeping out of fissures in its skin. Its cinder-lump of a head
was cocked as if listening

From the hills about the immolated city came a yelping
cry: *"Wha, wha, wha?"*

"HA!" boomed back the answer—and the thing on the
Mercy Seat, the Burnt Man, rose to summon his pack of the
burning damned so that they might hunt down one more to
join their number, while the fratricide's blood trail was still
fresh...

"No!" Jame gasped, waking with a start

Aerulan's death banner, wrapped warmly about her, was
covered with a dusting of snow which the wan sun had already begun to melt.

It was morning.

II

The haze of the previous day lingered, turning the sky the color of thin milk with the sun a dim opal afloat in it. By the latter at her back, seen intermittently through leaves, Jame knew that they were still going north. Soon high clouds swallowed it, however, and she was no longer certain.

The forest floor had leveled off. Upper foliage and undergrowth made the mountains' contours difficult to guess. At first, Jame thought that this wouldn't present a problem: after all, they had only to turn left and keep going eventually to hit the River Road. At some point between Gothregor and Falkirr, though, the Silver bent sharply westward, and then again before Wilden. To miss either turn would set them adrift in the folds of the hills. Ganth was said to have gotten lost within a mile of Gothregor on the night of the massacre. The Tishooo had brought him the screams, but he hadn't been able to find his way home until dawn. She was much farther into the wilderness now than he had been then.

They came out of the trees at last, opposite the rock face of a cliff crowned with flowering laurel. A self-important brook chattered over stones at its foot. Jame stopped in dismay. She had expected a clear path ahead with the mountain slope falling away to the left. They must have overshot the first turn. They were lost.

Then she focused on the cliff face opposite. Stronger sunlight would have thrown its details into greater relief, but even so she thought she could trace an image: the front of a house, so low set that it seemed half-sunken into the ground. Carved on its walls were a series of ovals with circles in them—that crude, face-like symbol of ancient power known as the *imu*. Serpentine forms in stone rioted up the jambs and over the lintel.

It looked exactly like the Earth Wife's lodge in Peshtar. When Jame took a step toward it, however, its details changed with her new perspective, becoming merely those of a weathered rock face. She had been thinking about Mother Ragga only a moment ago. Her imagination must have supplied the rest. When she retreated, however, there it was again—but not exactly as it had been before: now, the rock slab of a door stood ajar.

It had been obvious in Peshtar that Mother Ragga had special talents. Beyond her far hearing, the *imu* medallion which her half-feral girl had given Jame had the power to strip the skin from the face of a darkling changer and to protect her in the Anarchies. However, Jame had only thought of the Earth Wife herself as a local wise-woman. To find the image of her lodge here in the wilderness was unsettling. She didn't think she would investigate that door, or wait to see what might emerge from it.

Anyway, the sight of the busy stream on its threshold had given her an idea. This world might have some odd aquatic conditions, from the great Chaos Maw, a whirlpool miles across on the edge of the Eastern Sea, to patches of dead water off the Cape of the Lost where ships sank like bricks; but one natural principle usually applied: water descends. Eventually, this brook should lead them to the Silver.

They followed it well into the afternoon as it wound downhill in a series of rapids, strengthened by freshets. On its bank, Jorin surprised a woodchuck still groggy with its winter's sleep and made quick work of it. Cheese rinds, it seemed, were not enough. At last, through a break in the trees, Jame saw a sprawling mass of stone below, which she at first took for a natural formation. It wasn't. They had come out above and slightly north of Falkirr, the Brandan keep.

Jame had met Brant, Lord Brandan, at a memorial feast given by her brother after the battle at the Cataracts.

"The High Council needs to see you," Tori had said, *"to reassure themselves that, despite your bloodlines, you're only a pawn, not some dangerous new player entering their game of lineage and power."*

Since many people believed that she had appeared on the edge of the Escarpment with a flash and a loud bang, Jame supposed that reassurances were in order. Nonetheless, the dinner had been a disaster. She'd had to sit there in that hideous pink dress, not permitted to eat, drink, or (ancestors forbid) talk, while the lords had discussed her as if she were a prize filly about to turn brood mare; and Torisen's responses had grown more and more curt as he realized, apparently for the first time, what they were both in for.

He might at least have been grateful, Jame thought, that (thanks to her) Lord Caineron had been off in his tent "not quite feeling in touch with things" and that none of those present had identified her hastily procured gown as having formerly belonged to an overweight Hurlen streetwalker.

About the only thing Jame had to be thankful for during that endless dinner had been Lord Brandan's consideration. Not that he had ever spoken to her directly—that would have been the height of bad manners—but his remarks to the others had shown a respect for her feelings quite startling in that context. Of course, he could intend to press his own strong claim for her first contract: thirty-four years ago, he had begun to pay the enormous price demanded by Ganth for Aerulan's contract in perpetuity.

Be that as it may, the dip of his banner told her that Brandan hadn't yet returned from Kothifir.

Then too, she and his sister Brenwyr had parted damning each other.

Cursed be and cast out...

She was out of Gothregor, all right, but cast how far? Under that kind of a malison, did one ever stop running?

No. She wouldn't think about that now. She would *not...*

They started down toward the Silver, quickly losing sight of Falkirr behind trees. The brook, now a tumultuous young river, tumbled beside them over stone ledges and around large, flat slabs. Curiously, when the latter diverted the water's course, the direct route was marked across their white surfaces as though some giant had flicked them with dripping hair. Along the wet lines, cracks had formed.

A scurfy little pine was using these fissures to cross the rock, its gnarled roots probing blindly ahead with the concentration of a mountaineer negotiating a sheer cliff-face. It looked like the desperate sort of shrub that finds itself seeded in shade, on the thinnest of soil, which now was using the first chance offered to escape. At the rock's edge it paused, roots like many jointed, arthritic toes flexing stiffly in the air; then it toppled over into the stream and was swept away, tumbling crown over root.

It occurred to Jame that she had just witnessed her first case of arboreal drift.

"Wha," said a voice behind her, barely audible above the water's roar. "Wha wha…"

For a moment, Jame froze. Then she hastily withdrew into the south bank trees, pulling Jorin with her.

No, it wasn't the Burning Ones of her dream but something almost as bad. Two men had emerged upstream on the water's far side—a Randir officer and a priest. The latter, very upset, was yapping questions at the former. The words carried imperfectly to the hidden listeners:

Why had the randon allowed her to escape? Did he realize *where* they were? Brandan…trespassing! What would he say? *Where* were the dogs? *Wha wha wha…*

Jame shrank back. They must be hunting her. But how in Perimal's name had they known she was no longer at Gothregor, much less anywhere near here?

"*Woo! Woo!*"—baying now, deep-throated, bone rattling.

Jorin began to growl, his fur rising in her grip.

Three hounds had come out of the trees opposite, straining on their leashes. Two were tall, black-coated lymers—loosely muzzled tracking dogs which seemed already to have caught the scent. Dwarfing them was the third, a steel-gray Molocar bitch, four feet high at the shoulder, of a battle breed whose jaws could shatter tempered spear-shafts. It was she who bayed, like a great bell tolling war. Hindered by the lymers and unhelped by the rest of the company (which kept well clear), the handler awkwardly tried to strap an iron muzzle on her. The Molocar flung it away and, with a contemptuous, sideways snap, crushed his skull. Baying, she plunged across the stream in a storm of spray, pursued by the freed lymers and Randirs' alarmed shouts.

Jorin bolted, with Jame a step behind. They cut westward through the trees, hoping to drown their scent in shallows downstream; but when they emerged below on a rocky overhang, the current beneath ran too fierce to risk. Damnation. They would have to make for Falkirr. From what the priest had said, the Brandan garrison wouldn't welcome Randir hunters on their land—but neither would they let her go her way after the intruders had been chased off.

As she hesitated, loath even now to give up her freedom, movement caught her eye. Down the rapids came a tall, golden willow.

At first, remembering the scrub pine, Jame thought that this much larger tree had also been swept away by the spring runoff. Then she saw that, ever so cautiously, it was walking down the steps. The bulk of its roots formed a fibrous mass which cushioned its descent. Pulling it along were its long fringe roots. The caps of the latter glistened with some kind of secretion which ate into whatever it touched, giving the tree innumerable toeholds. Its crown swayed with each step. Wands and narrow, shining leaves undulated like curtains of gold in the last direct sunlight of the day.

Something came crashing through the woods toward her. To her surprise, out of the undergrowth burst not one of the dogs but a young man.

He stopped short, panting, staring at her with wild, pale eyes set in a thin, white face. His hair was also white: A Shanir, wearing the brown robe of an acolyte.

"Highlord?" he whispered.

"No!" said Jame, remembering even as she spoke how on the battlefield at the Cataracts she had been repeatedly mistaken for her brother.

With a moan, the Shanir fell to his knees and began to beat his head against the stone. For a moment, Jame simply stared. She had never before seen someone deliberately try to brain himself. Then realization dawned.

"*You're* the one they're after!" she exclaimed. "Here, now: stop that!"

When he didn't, she seized his shoulders and forced him back on his heels. He swayed in her grasp, blinking blood out of unfocused eyes.

"You owe me no debt," he mumbled, "if you aren't willing to pay."

Sweet Trinity, now what? She ought to run, to leave this fugitive priestling to his own people—if he survived the dogs.

"Give me your robe," she snapped.

When he only gaped at her, she seized the shoulders of his garment and hauled it off over his head. He sprawled forward as it came free. For a moment she stared down at his emaciated back, the prominent ribs crisscrossed with welts. Then she jerked him to his feet and shoved him toward the curtain of golden leaves swaying past the cliff's edge.

"Get aboard. Try to find a dead branch to hang onto and watch out for those wands. It may not care for passengers. Move!"

Some of the glaze left his eyes and the corner of his mouth twitched. "Yes, sir."

"You too," said Jame to Jorin. "Go."

The hounds were in the woods, the two lymers perforce running silent, the Molocar bell-mouthed on the Shanir's trail. Jame backtracked some fifty feet, then darted off at a right angle due south, dragging the robe. Plunging down a steep slope with stones turning underfoot, clutching at bushes to slow her descent, she looked back to see Jorin bounding over shrubbery after her. Try telling a cat to do anything...!

At that moment, still looking backward, she collided with someone, hard, and fell. They rolled down the slope, tangled blind in the gown, bouncing over rocks and grappling ineffectually with each other. At the bottom, she kicked free. The garment floundered back, seeming to wrestle with itself, and produced a tousled blond head, apparently without a body.

"Right," Jame breathed to herself.

She should have guessed what had frightened the birds along the River Road the previous day, passing by unseen. At least the blade which the young assassin waved nervously in her face was steel, not ivory. His whistled summons wobbling shrilly, again and again; but if the Guild Master heard, he didn't respond. After all, this was still supposed to be a ritual blooding.

"Right," said Jame again, louder.

"P-please," the boy stammered in accented Kens. "Please!" *Don't let me fail*, he was really begging. *Let me make this kill.* Journeyman thief stared at apprentice assassin. "Please? *Please?* You want it, you earn it!"

The boy lunged, desperate, inept. Hindered by Aerulan's banner slung across her back and the food sack on her hip, she still caught his blade with ease in her *d'hen's* full, reinforced sleeve and whipped it away. A water-flowing move sent him head over heels after it, into a cloud-of-thorn bush. There he floundered, *mere* cloth ripping on barbs sharper than the blade after which he frantically groped, pale skin turning red.

"*Dammit!*" said Jame, exasperated. "Didn't your precious master teach you *anything?*"

Jorin had been slinking around them, chirping anxiously at the copper smell of blood. When a muzzled lymer erupted from the undergrowth behind him, he rose on his toes and bounced into the hound's face through sheer fright. The beast retreated, trying to shake him off, uttering muffled yelps as feline claws raked his eyes.

Down the slope charged the second lymer, the Molocar bitch roaring on his heels like an avalanche.

With a cry to Jorin to follow, Jame bolted toward the stream. She heard the assassin thrash panic-stricken in the thorns, where he hadn't the sense to lie still, then his scream, cut short by the crunch of jaws.

She burst out on a cliff's lip. The river curved beneath in a gorge, its northward course obscured by an opposite rock spur crowned with undergrowth.

Where was that willow? The air had thickened with twilight, all edges blurring, all colors melting in a molten haze. Downstream to the west, nothing. How fast could the damn thing travel, anyway? When she turned again to look eastward, the tree loomed over her like a shimmering hillock. An upper branch swooped over her head. Its trailing leafage swung into her. She found herself tangled up in it, off her feet, off the cliff. Golden leaves flattened against her eyes; supple wands fumbled about her throat.

Something crashed though them, knocking her free. Jorin. Falling, she grabbed for the ounce but caught a bough instead and clung to it for a moment, breathless. Then she scrambled inward to throw her arms around the trunk as to a mast, just out of the wands' hissing reach, as the tree swayed again like a ship in stormy seas. Looking down, she saw that the pale Shanir clung to a section of trunk well below her while Jorin balanced on a branch near him, wailing. Below, the burnished bole plunged down to the writhing serpent's knot of its roots.

Someone had scored the golden bark at eye-level—to mark this tree for spring harvest? Such resilient wood must be much prized. It would probably long since have been cut if the Riverland weren't so stripped of workers. Small wonder, then, that when the sap had begun to run, so had the tree, hell-bent on escape. The creek bed must simply have provided the easiest route.

The willow's draperies swung forward, then back, far enough to give Jame a glimpse ahead. She saw the Silver a bare sixty feet away, and something else, much closer.

"Oh, my God," she breathed, and then shouted in warning to those beneath her, "Low bridge!"

The willow swayed forward again, more violently, gaining momentum. Its upper wands cracked against the water's surface like whips. It reared back, trunk groaning, foliage a golden blur, over and down.

The second forward swing had nearly dislodged Jame, who had only kept her grip by wrapping her legs around the trunk and sinking her nails into its sensitive bark. When the upper boughs crashed over backward, she was pinned beneath them, under water whose coldness shocked out her breath.

The trunk quivered against her like a bent bow, its water-laden foliage keeping its crown submerged. The bridge which spanned the creek's mouth, carrying the River Road on its back, must be overhead by now. Yes. Here came the swift current of the Silver, striking her from the right, nearly plucking her loose. Above, the water glowed with the molten light of the sky, willow wands streaming black against it. Below, leaves shone gold against the pebbled darkness of the riverbed.

Don't panic! she told herself, fighting the desperate compulsion to breathe. *It* can't *stay bent like this for long...!*

Under those pebbles seemed to be a pattern as if of overlapping shields. A trick of light and water? They *couldn't* be rising and falling as though with some monstrous, slow respiration.

Then suddenly she was flying upward, through water, through leaves, through air, flung by the tree's recoil across the river—straight into the boughs of a giant white cedar which leaned out from the opposite bank.

Her impression afterward was that the evergreen had carefully rolled her from branch to branch down to the ground. At least, that was where she found herself an unguessed-at time later, sitting on a bed of pine needles, looking at her hands. Half-frozen fingers stung as sensation returned to them and the nails ached. The stitching at the gloves' tips had been ripped out.

A slope of feathery ferns stretched from the river's edge up to a band of sumac, a wide swath of churned earth cut through it by the willow's passage. Something was coming down toward her under the fronds. Jorin's head popped up, all long neck, pricked ears, and wide, anxious eyes. The moment she saw him, he gave an excited bleat and bounded down to her. She hugged him, noting that his silver-gilt fur was barely damp. Presumably, the lower section of the willow's trunk had remained in an arch above the water. Her own god might not give a damn about her, but something in the universe apparently looked after cats and idiots.

Speaking of the latter, where was that pale, young man?

They found him a few minutes later, in some difficulty. Dismounting from the willow, he had stepped into its muddy wake and as now being slowly carried off by the sumac as it took advantage of the disturbed earth to seek sunnier slopes.

"I had no idea that the Riverland could be so lively," said Jame, regarding him across the crawling belt of trees. "Not taking root, are you?"

"I-it's more a case of the roots taking me. I sank in a-and they wrapped around my ankles."

He tottered, waving thin arms to keep his balance, a half-naked scarecrow, all bones and pale skin with a preternaturally white thatch of hair.

A Shanir. A priestling. She ought to let him drift on with the arboreal tide until his own people fished him out—but if she had understood correctly, what debt could her brother owe such flotsam as this which he hadn't been willing to pay?

Jame sighed. "Hold on a minute."

The hillside was studded with large rocks, some of which had been thrust aside by the willow and were now slowly sinking in its wake. The sumacs' runners snaked around them. Jame began to thread her way through the maze of slender trunks, jumping from stone to stone. Forgetting Aerulan's extra width on her back, she became wedged between close-set trees and freed herself by pricking their thin bark. As they recoiled, the runners of the whole clump writhed like serpents in the earth. The Shanir bit back a cry of pain.

"I'd come to think," said Jame sourly, "that my house had first claim to any situation this absurd. Who are you, priest-bait, to trespass?"

The pale young man flushed.

"Kindrie," he blurted out defiantly. "My name is Kindrie."

III

The moment he had spoken, Kindrie felt the heat in his face
chill with dismay. Anonymity had been his last defense. But
then he had felt perilously off balance ever since encounter-
ing this masked stranger, in a way which had nothing to do
with subsequently being tossed into a tree, swept across a
river, and dumped in a bog. His first impression that he had
run into the Highlord was, of course, ridiculous. Somewhere,
though, he *had* met this peculiar boy before, under alarming
circumstances.

"Kindrie," the other repeated, as if he too were fishing for
memories. "I've heard of you. You were with the Kencyr
Host at the Cataracts. What in Perimal's name are you doing
here?"

"Sinking."

"Uh yes." The stranger glanced down at the rock on which
he stood. "So am I, if not quite as fast. Look, I think I can
pull you up here with me, and then it's an easy jump to the far
side. Give me your hand."

Kindrie hesitated. Under the split tips of the other's glove,
something glowered bone-white. Reluctantly, he reached out,
and was caught in a grip like sheathed ice.

The shock of it made his senses lurch.

Cold. So cold and dark.

Overhead, not the canopy of sumac leaves but far, far
up, a fire-broken roof with verdigris lightning lacing the sky's
greater darkness above. Beneath, a vast hall, paved with
stone whose green veins pulsed cold with each sullen, silent
flash. Death banners lined its walls, rank after rank. Threadbare hands clutched together tattered clothing; slashed, disintegrating faces regarded him slyly askance, snickering
against cold stone.

Got you now, healer...

Ancestors preserve him. The touch of those bare finger-tips had plunged him straight into the other's soul but he hadn't the strength to deal with an image so complex, so foul. He hadn't the courage. He must get out. Now.

The flash of something white...

CRACK.

He found himself lying on the ground a dozen feet beyond the willow's wake, staring up at cracks of twilight between black oak leaves. His jaw throbbed. The stranger was staring at him, fists still clenched but forgotten.

"Sweet Trinity. I can't have hit you *that* hard."

Kindrie struggled up on an elbow. He saw that he had not only been knocked across a clearing but clean out of his boots, which the sumac had kept.

"You didn't," he said confusedly. "That is, you did, but..." How to explain the tremendous power of that soul-image to protect itself, or his own involuntary response, as though to a lightning strike? "God, you've got strong defenses!"

"I should hope so. Touch me like that again, priest, and I'll knock you half way to the Cataracts!"

"I am *not* a priest and what's the matter with your face?"

They stared at each other.

"You're the healer that the Priests' College was sending to Gothregor."

"And you're the mad girl I was sent to heal."

"Mad? God's claws, I begin to think so! Here I am, on the run from a Wilden healer, and he runs bang into me. Likewise an incompetent assassin, a wandering death banner, a shadow demon, a Randir search party, and a walking tree. What *is* this place—the crossroad of the worlds?"

Kindrie didn't know what she was raving about, or care. It was the rising level of her voice which scared him. "Oh, please!" he cried. "We aren't far from the river. They'll hear you!"

That sobered her instantly. "I doubt they'll guess that we
forded by tree, but still..." She hesitated, then said grudgingly,
"It will be dark soon. You can make camp with me tonight, if
you like, as far from here as possible."

Kindrie's impulse was to run until he dropped, away from
both his pursuers and this unnatural female; but daylight *was*
fading rapidly, and this wilderness terrified him. He gave a
small, reluctant nod.

"All right, then," said the other, and jumped to solid ground.

The ounce had been waiting with growing impatience
on the far side of the drifting grove. He didn't attempt to
cross, however, until his mistress turned to look at him—
no, at the tricky path which he must negotiate. Kindrie
suddenly realized that the beast was blind, that he was using the girl's eyes to see his way. He was *bound* to her. Of
all the damning things which Kindrie had been told at Wilden
about the Highlord's sister, no one had mentioned that, like
Kindrie himself, she was Shanir. Above the willow's path,
they struck the west bank's New Road and followed it northward until a ravine opening above it provided shelter sufficient to hide a fire.

While Kindrie held thin hands out to the small blaze which
she had kindled, the Knorth draped her sodden jacket over a
nearby rock. Then, to his surprise, she unrolled a death banner and also spread it out to dry, its gently smiling face turned
toward the warmth. It seemed to watch them benignly as they
sat on opposite sides of the fire, regarding each other warily
over the flames and eating winter-shriveled apples. The ounce,
offered cheese, scratched the ground around it and trotted
purposefully off into the dark. Watching the cat's mistress
gingerly chew her own dinner, Kindrie remembered the host
of disfigured dead in her soul-image and shivered.

"I heard about you at the Cataracts," she said, so suddenly
that he jumped. "You grew up in the Priests' College at Wilden,
but ran away to serve first Lord Caineron and then Ardeth.
You were free. Why did you go back?"

"It wasn't my idea," snapped Kindrie, despite his resolve
to keep quiet. "Tending the wounded, I-I overtired myself
and collapsed. When I woke, I was back at Wilden. It seems
that Ardeth's people didn't know what else to do, with their
lord off bone-hunting in the Southern Wastes and a sick healer
on their hands."

"And Ardeth let you stay there all winter?"

Kindrie winced. "H-he had other concerns, I suppose.
His dead son Pereden, your brother, and Kothifir is so far
away…"

"Awkward to apply pressure at a distance, I agree, but
still…! And Tori had nothing to say about this either?"

"The Highlord owes me no debts if he isn't willing to pay!"

"Proud," she said, considering him, "and devious, to imply
and deny a debt in the same breath. Whatever he owes you,
priestling, he owes. But that's his business. So. Winter passes,
a call comes to Wilden for a healer, and you take the opportunity to bolt."

For a moment, she was silent, absently combing out tangled
hair with long, black-sheathed fingers. One hand stole to her
injured cheek.

Don't ask me to heal you, he silently pled. *Don't, for both
our sakes!*

The hand dropped

"So. You're free again. What next?"

"I don't know."

From that terrible waking in Wilden the previous winter,
he had fled to the most secret corner of his soul-image to hide,
to wait for the rescue which had never come. Three years ago,
the priests would have left him alone, mistaking his blank stare
for that of the halfwit which they had always believed him to
be. Now they knew better. Was it only yesterday that they
had finally tricked him into emerging? And then, and then…

Yes, he was out of their hands, but free? Not after what
they had done to him. Perhaps never again.

"Stop that!"

He blinked, surprised to find the Knorth kneeling in front of him, gripping his clenched fists through the protection of the food sack. His head hurt.

"God's teeth and toenails. I've never met anyone so determined to beat in his own brains. What is wrong with you?"

"Leave me alone!"

He wrenched free, lashed out at her clumsily, and fell on his face as she slipped aside.

"Leave me alone," he said again, his voice muffled, and began to cry.

"Sweet Trinity," he heard her mutter. "And I thought *I* was a mess." A moment later, she dropped her still-damp jacket over his bare shoulders.

Kindness, he thought. *If I accept that, I'll break down completely.*

He rolled over to look up at the Knorth. "How does your brother feel," he said, "about you being Shanir?"

Silver flared in the gray eyes above him. Kindrie flinched, guessing too late that the ability to mind-bond with an ounce might be the least of the other's Shanir attributes. If her powers were great, however, so was her control. Silver tarnished to gray.

"What do *you* think?" she said flatly, and returned to her side of the fire.

Kindrie answered her silently, in the darkness behind his squeezed shut eyes: *I think it may kill him.*

FRATRICIDE.

The God-voice had broken its silence of over two thousand years to call the Highlord's sister that, or so the priest with the skull-like face and the maimed hand had told Kindrie yesterday. Kindrie hadn't disbelieved it—how could one doubt the Voice of God when it burned its way like acid out of some unwilling throat?—but now...!

On the march to the Cataracts, Torisen had fallen into one of his mysterious nightmares and no one had been able to wake him from it. At Ardeth's insistence, Kindrie had entered the Highlord's sleeping mind to try to help. There he had stumbled across the soul-image of the blighted house with the vast death banner hall which he now realized had not been Torisen's at all but his sister's. It had apparently been poisoning the sleeping man. Kindrie had exorcised it, but he didn't trust his power to banish such a thing indefinitely. Given Torisen's violent antipathy to all Shanir, he might have been stricken by the mere knowledge that his sister was one. That prejudice, after all, was what prevented him from honoring his debts to Kindrie. Those he might shrug off, but not a sister's claims. And then…and then…

"*She will destroy him*," that death's-head Ishtier had hissed, leaning close, breathing the dregs of his winter-long sickness into Kindrie's face, "*unless you render her harmless, shall we say? Yes, you, boy. No one else has been able to get close enough. But a healer's touch, ah, nothing comes closer than that.*"

B-but he *was* a healer. How could he ever hurt someone the way he himself had been hurt?

"*Just a little change in your soul-image, boy. It was clever of you to choose the Priests' College itself as the external metaphor of your soul. My colleagues thought they had you locked up here, mind as well as body. They didn't know about that image hidden within an image, that secret garden where Lady Rawneth confined you most of your childhood when the rest of us thought you lack-witted. But now m'lady has traded that secret to me. I could destroy your pathetic little bolthole—uproot the comfrey and heart's-ease, sow the ground with salt. Instead, I will give you a chance to regain it. We have taught you how to read soul-images, boy. Read the Knorth's to learn where she has hidden the thing which she stole from me, and then deal with her as she deserves, or you will never be at peace again.*"

Then they had sent him out with an escort of priests and Randir guards, bound for Gothregor, so confident he was broken that they hadn't bothered to watch him. What that skull-faced Ishtier had done to him was obscene, but so was what the priest wanted him to do. So he had run—straight into the very person he had been trying to avoid just as she, for some reason, had been fleeing him.

In his mind, he was still running. The outer dimension
of his soul was that long corridor which spiraled down into
the subterranean Priests' College, past dim classrooms where
masters had beaten him, past dank dormitories where he had
learned all shades of violation but one. None of that had
mattered, though, while his inner spirit remained a refuge,
inviolate. Behind one of the imagined doors was the secret
room where the Randir Matriarch had confined him, as a lesser
woman might have locked a child in a dark closet. Where he
had gotten the idea for the moon garden which had transformed Rawneth's prison into a sanctuary and the source of
his strength, he didn't know. He might gladly have stayed
there forever, even after his jailer stopped bothering to lock
him in. However, three years ago he had overheard angry
voices outside the door of his secret soul, saying that a Knorth
was Highlord again.

"But I'm part Knorth too," he had said, blinking at the astonished priests.

Now Ishtier had hidden that door, and he was trapped in
the outer dimension of his soul, in that corridor with its stale
stench of warped, wasted lives down which he endlessly ran,
pursued by the fear that to save Torisen he might have to do
the terrible thing demanded of him, beating his fists against
locked door after door as he passed, searching for the one that
opened into peace.

Let me in, let me in, let me in...

IV

The priestling had begun feebly to strike his head again, although he was asleep. Jame tossed aside all the rocks within his reach, then picked up the empty food sack. At least she had guessed right there: only direct contact with the Shanir triggered that horror which she had felt in the sumac grove, as if she were being turned inside out. Like most people, she had no idea what her own soul-image was, nor did she care to, when a mere touch of it left such a foulness in her mind, like the foretaste of vomit.

You've lived in ignorance so far, she told herself. *This is no time to stop.*

Scattered provisions rolled about underfoot. Apples, dried fruit, cheese.

Blind Jorin had never had much luck hunting prey which she couldn't see, except when the Arrin-ken Immalai had helped him. She would keep these despised rinds against his return, hoping that he at least wouldn't get lost.

Their meager rations regathered, Jame sat down again on her side of the fire, took a small sewing kit from an inner pocket of her *d'hen*, and began awkwardly to stitch up her split gloves, while still wearing them. A quarter inch at the tips, however, she left open. Marc had suggested that once. Only an idiot would forgo any advantage now, the cost be damned.

Nonetheless, her bare nails must never touch that damn Shanir again.

Jame swore as the needle slipped, pricking her finger.

The Old Blood, she thought sourly, licking a drop of it. *The God-chosen, the Shanir.*

How could one hate what one oneself was? Easily. Look at Torisen—except he didn't know he was a Shanir blood-binder and far-seer. Look at this healer, then, who kept trying to hurt himself. As far back as the Cataracts, hadn't he worked himself into a coma trying to help the wounded?

Help...

Sore as her face still was, she no longer felt that trace of heat which could either have been infection or Kallystine's parting gift. Could that be the healer's work? She could ask him to do more. Even now, she didn't have to be scarred for life...

No. He was priest-trained and she was Priest's-bane.

"Your name is an omen in itself," Marc had once said. *"Servants of God, any god, will be bad luck to you, and you to them."*

True enough. She remembered Ishtier, gibbering, trying to gnaw off the hand with which he had touched the Book Bound in Pale Leather. Some people deserved all the bad luck they got.

Did this young man, though? Her brother would hardly tell her what debt he owed to another Shanir. He had let one thing slip, though: Kindrie had a Knorth grandmother. Tori hadn't asked her name. The very idea must have made his skin crawl, as it did Jame's now—not that such distant, bone-kinship could matter much. If it had, prejudice aside, Tori would have extended the protection of their house to the healer long ago.

But with Tori hiding in Kothifir, Kindrie was her problem. Left on his own, he would surely be recaptured by the priests, whom he would tell about her. Every day that folk assumed she was still hiding in Gothregor increased her chance of success at Restormir.

To travel with a priest, though, past Wilden...

Wha ooo, said the wind, keening down the ravine, making the little fire dance. *Wha wha oooo...*

No. It wasn't those others, flame-mouthed Merikit avengers of the dead, on her trail from Tai-tastigon.

Fratricide.

No.

The wind died and the fire sank. Jame sat beside it, waiting for her heart to stop pounding. It seemed to her, though, that she could still hear fragments of sound—*singing*—close by. Trinity. Could their pursuers have camped almost on top of them?

Thinking that they were probably at the mouth of the ravine, just off the road, she climbed to the pine coppice above. With the stars overcast and the moon not yet risen, it was too dark under the trees even for her excellent night-vision. Oh, for Jorin's keen nose and ears, although her use of both had been limited recently. She crept forward through crusts of sheltered snow toward the rocky beak which overhung the road, then lay flat on an aromatic bed of needles at the edge of the trees to wait for her eyes to adjust.

The only sound now was the wind soughing through the branches overhead. The only light came from below. Down the New Road drifted faintly glowing forms which Jame recognized as ghost-walkers, man-shaped patches of weirding mist which were said to precede a weirdingstorm. She herself had never seen weirding before, but had heard of its strange properties. Travelers caught in it had been known to emerge hundreds of miles away, if at all. Singers claimed that the ghost-walkers were those whom the mist had trapped, doomed to wander forever in its clammy clutch like the souls of the unburnt dead.

The wind momentarily died. The ghostly procession drifted to a stop.

In that lull, Jame smelled the unmistakable reek of human sweat.

A sudden, rasping snore made her jump nearly out of her boots. It ended with a loud snort. Not a dozen feet away, a dark shape which she had taken for a boulder rose, stretched, and scratched itself. It was a large, naked Merikit, a senior of his tribe to judge by the profusion of his braids, but so smeared with charcoal as to be almost one with the night. At his bare feet was a small, ceremonial fire, set but not lit. He muttered rapidly through the chant which she had heard before, as if his unintended nap had made him lose his place, then in ringing tones addressed the final lines to the fire, which made no discernible response. Satisfied nonetheless, the big man shouldered his sack with a grunt and scrambled down to the road. The wind had picked up again, the ghost-walkers resuming their southward drift. Catching up with one, he disappeared into it.

Jame blinked. Was she dreaming? In the morning, she might think so, unless...In among the fire's pale kindling was a cinder shaped like a charred, human finger bone.

Proof, she thought, and pocketed it.

V

Morning dawned gray and chill, the fifty-seventh of spring, three days before Summer Eve.

"I had such a strange dream last night," said Jame, sleepily, to Aerulan.

As usual, her cousin didn't answer, but her warm arms gave a questioning hug.

"Well, first there was this hairy, naked man, covered with charcoal as if he'd fallen into a fire. He turned. His face had been burnt off and his eyes had boiled away. Then his charred flesh crumbled and his black bones clattered down at my feet. A cold wind scattered fragments of skin like black moths. I couldn't get the taste of them off my lips. But then I forgot about that, because there was something behind me. Such a chill darkness, big as a mountain, eyes like caverns...No. Like the empty sockets of an Arrin-ken blinded with live coals in the Master's hall, somehow escaped alive. The whole Snowthorn range was one huge, crouching cat, and I was under its paw.

"*In the Ebonbane, by the chasm, you escaped my judgment*, it said in my mind. So cold. So desperately bitter, like a winter wind flecked with burning. *But* these *mountains are mine.*

"I wanted to argue as I did with Immalai, to say that I act only as I must to survive with honor, with precious little help from any of his kind...

"But Graykin kept distracting me. All this time, you see, I could hear him whimpering. I know he's in desperate trouble and that it's my duty to get him out, but he nags and nags and nags until I could hit him! At least, though, he's still alive...

"Oh. I forgot: you aren't, are you?"

Remembering that, she woke, to the warm embrace of Aerulan's death banner and an aching sense of loss.

There are so few of us left…

Sometime during the night, Jorin had crept under the tapestry and now slept curled up as close to her as he could, his head tucked under her chin. Stroking him, she noted by the tight swell of his stomach that he had eaten well. Her hand disturbed a strange scent on his fur, musky and wild, like the Arrin-ken Immalai but with a faint reek of singed hair.

The burnt cat…had that been a dream, or the brush of her sleeping mind against Jorin's as the blind taught the blind to hunt? An Arrin-ken might well help a "little brother"—it had happened before—but not all those great, immortal beasts were as well disposed toward her as Immalai had been, nor was she still in his territory. More than one voice in that chorus by the Ebonbane chasm had wanted her to jump.

Jorin began to growl in his sleep.

"Hey!" said Jame.

The ounce snapped at her. She lay very still with his teeth through the collar of her woolen shirt, his breath hot against her throat. His eyes, seen aslant, looked as black as holes in rotten ice.

"Heyyyy," she said again, half crooning.

Jorin shivered, let go, and began apologetically to lick her chin. His tongue was very rough.

"Kitten," she said, fending him off, "you've been in bad company."

Throughout this, the Shanir hadn't stirred although his pale eyes were open. When urged, he sat up listlessly. Was this despair, or an inward turning so complete that it left no attention to spare? Goosebumps marched unheeded up his thin arms. She pulled off her outer shirt with its torn collar and put it on him, taking care to touch his bare skin only with her gloves. Linen undershirt and flash-blade's *d'hen* would do for her. The latter, especially, she had no intention of putting aside while the master assassin might still be after her, slight protection as it would be against the Ivory Knife.

As for her dreams, Graykin's crying had at least convinced her that if she arrived at Restormir with a healer in tow, so much the better. Luckily, getting Kindrie to return the way he had come proved easy: when she turned him left onto the New Road and gave him a push, he stumbled northward without seeming to notice which way he went, or to care.

Patches of mist still drifted down the valley, but without the ghost-walkers' definition. Had that been a dream too? In Jame's pocket, though, was the odd-shaped cinder. She would keep it, she thought, to remind herself that in this wilderness the strangest of things might be real.

By day, at least, her sense of Bane and the blind Arrin-ken waned. After all, they were both Kencyr, as alien to this world as she herself, even if the latter marked this whole mountain range for his own, as Immalai had the Ebonbane or the lords this valley. The land might not be theirs to claim. Anyway, thought Jame, the burnt cat probably didn't even exist. Dreams had played tricks on her before.

So had her imagination, come to that, and so it might be now: throughout the day, she kept catching half-glimpses of the Earth Wife's lodge. Never again did it appear as clearly as it had on the cliff-face. An arrangement of leaves, or bark, or shadow seen askance would merely suggest its carved lintel or *imu*-decked walls, gone when regarded directly. It was only her nerves, Jame decided. How likely was it, after all, that a house should be keeping pace with her through this wilderness? In that case, though, she wished her imagination were less vivid: with each imagined glimpse, that shadowed door had crept farther open.

For the most part, the roadway was set well back from the river so that trees and undergrowth hid it from the opposite bank. Nonetheless, Jame would again have sought a higher, more obscure path if she hadn't been traveling with someone whose boots had been eaten the previous day by a grove of trees. Presumably, the healer could repair his own injuries. That didn't prevent him from sustaining them first, though,

nor did it help that he paid no attention where he was stepping. Regarding the trail of bloody footprints behind them,
Jame wondered if she would have the heart to drag him all the
way to Restormir.

The New Road connected Kraggen, Shadow Rock, Valantir,
and Restormir, the home keeps respectively of the Coman,
Danior, Jaran, and Caineron. Shadow Rock, sister keep to
Wilden, couldn't be far ahead. The east bank was already
stripped of trees by Randir foragers and scored with erosion.
Still, because of the Shanir's shambling pace they were forced
at nightfall to made camp short of the Danior fortress.

Kindrie fell asleep at once, wrapped in Aerulan's banner.
Jame sat up to tend the fire and wait for Jorin, who had again
scorned the cheese rinds and slipped away when her back was
turned. If he learned more self-reliance, she told herself, that
was good, regardless of who taught him.

The thought of such dark instruction reminded her of Bane.

"*For such a clever person,*" he had said to her, moments before the mob had come to get him, "*you are remarkably ignorant. What a pity I shall never have the chance to educate you.*"

He might try yet.

Memories: his shadowy figure watching from an upper window as the half-flayed body of a child was pulled from the
River Tone below. Later: "*There's a rumor that since you joined the
Thieves' Guild, Bane has given up young boys.*" Later still, Bane at
the Res aB'tyrr, extolling the freedom of the abyss while his
bullies held the inn's staff captive: "*The weight of honor twists
us,*" he had said. "*Better to let it go, to fall away from all restraint,
that is the course for you, as for me.*"

"*I don't understand you at all!*" she had cried, and he had
answered with that slow, secret smile of his:

"*You know me as well as you know yourself.*"

Wind ruffled the horse-chestnuts above the hollow where
they had camped. Rising sap traced the leaves' primary veins
with faint luminescence, so that each defined its movements
in the dark by a ghostly, seven-fingered dance.

"Ssssaaa…" breathed the wind, and the trees fluttered their innumerable hands. "Sssssaaaaa…"

—or was that "*Thaaaa…?*"

No.

Thoughts of the Burning Ones, Bane, or the blind Arrin-ken were all dangerous, apt like the smell of blood to draw that which she most feared.

Jame leaned forward to put more wood on the fire. Across the sinking flames, she looked directly into the cool silver of Bane's eyes.

He lay stretched out on the ground, propped lazily on an elbow. Firelight caught the dark bronze of scale armor made of last season's oak leaves. They rustled as he breathed.

"*Thaaaaa…*" sighed something under the trees which was not the wind.

The half-burnt sticks of the fire scattered as something thrust up through them. Jame stared at what, for an instant, she took to be an overbalanced log. But logs don't have fingers, charred black as these were, and logs don't grab wrists. It jerked her hand downward. She could feel the heat of the quickening flames through her glove, as well as the crushing pressure of the Burnt Man's grip. Kin-slayers were his special prey, and this time she was without Aerulan's protection. Her fingertips began to smolder. She remembered the story of a Merikit fratricide who had been pulled through a campfire into the ground beneath. All his companions could save had been a boot, with his foot still in it.

Bane watched, expressionless now, his eyes reflecting only fire. Had none of his dubious humanity survived? Was he now purely the demon which Ishtier had sought to create? But he had crossed the running water of the Silver, as no demon could have done. Perhaps he could still be reached.

"Your choice, b-brother."

An absolute stillness came over the figure opposite. He hadn't known, hadn't even guessed, but Jame could feel the conviction of it sink in, as it had with her in the Tastigon temple. For a moment, they stared at each other. Then he threw back his head and began silently to laugh.

The chestnuts cast up their hands—*aahhhh!*—as a gust of wind swept into the hollow, fanning flames, rattling dry leaves. Fragments of Bane's armor whirled into the fire. The chestnuts beat at the ascending sparks. Jame was still braced against the Burnt Man's pull, with fiery tongues leaping up toward her sleeve. Bane continued to laugh, even as the wind began to scatter him like autumn's memory.

"Choose, dammit!"

His laughter died. He looked at her, expressionless again, and then leaned forward. Between the flares of firelight, his face dissolved into shadow, but she could read his lips:

"...*my choice, then: no blood-price, sister*..."

At his touch, the charred thing gripping her wrist crumbled and a quick leap of flame kindled the remains of his leaf shell. Suddenly released, Jame caught only the glimpse of a man-shape in flames, rising, as she went over backward.

"Ssssaaa..." said the wind, and departed with leaf ash on its breath.

Beyond the fire, no one watched.

Sweet Trinity, thought Jame, sitting up, dazed. *Did I fall asleep after all?*

But her wrist still hurt. On the black leather of the glove were the ashy prints of four fingers and a thumb.

VI

Jorin trotted back into camp just before dawn, smelling of nothing worse than catmint and bringing the conciliatory gift of a dead vole.

Day broke, with no visible sunrise. Clouds cut short the mountains, pushed along by a steady wind from the north. White birds ghosted southward under the overcast and deer drifted after them across the upper meadows, in and out of clouds. At some point, morning became afternoon. Day had begun almost imperceptibly to wane when veils of luminous mist came sailing down the valley, some low enough to brush along its floor.

"That's weirding," said Kindrie nervously. "You don't want to touch it."

A bank drifted past, leaving empty a bush which a moment before had been raucous with quarreling blue jays.

"Uh, right," said Jame.

She was glad that the healer was taking notice again, if only because his sleepwalker's pace had driven her half wild. Graykin's crying had haunted her dreams again last night, as forlorn as that of a lost child. Time was running out. Therefore, when Kindrie stumbled back toward somnambulance, she ruthlessly prodded him awake again with questions.

"You told the Highlord that you had a Knorth grandmother. What was her name?"

"Telarien, I think," he said vaguely.

"You *think*?" she demanded, silently swearing: the name meant nothing to her.

Kindrie flushed. "Lady Rawneth said that once, when she didn't know I could hear her."

Now, *that* name made Jame's eyebrows rise under her mask. Rawneth: the Randir Matriarch, Kallystine's great-aunt, the so-called Witch of Wilden. High company for a lowly acolyte.

"Did she name anyone else? Mother, father, family cat?"

"No! You aren't supposed to have any kin at all when you're a b-b…"

"A bastard?"

Kindrie turned and limped hastily away, the tips of his ears scarlet through the white thatch of his hair.

Hmmmm, thought Jame, following him. That was the second case of bastardy she had heard about in the past four days, among a people who rarely misbred. Wouldn't it be curious if *he* were Tieri's unfortunate child, the Knorth Bastard? But no: one maternal grandmother didn't make a Knorth. Fortunately. The last thing she wanted, less even than a semi-demonic half-brother, was a priestling first cousin.

Still, she wondered briefly who Tieri's mother had been.

Ugh. Tori was right: better not to know. Change the topic.

To her own surprise, she heard herself ask, "What can you tell me about the God-voice?"

The Shanir turned and stared at her. "Why should you ask about *that?*"

Why indeed? Because sometime, since Ishtier had passed on the Voice's judgment to her in Tai-tastigon, she had heard something like it again. Recently. But what and where?

"All right," she said, dodging his question, "this is what I do know: it's the Voice of God—supposedly; it speaks through whomever it pleases, often in riddles; it never lies. What else, priest?"

"I am *not* a priest!"

"D'you mean, then, that you don't know anything?"

"I bet I know more than you do!" Kindrie snapped

That might even be true, he thought. Locked in the garden of his soul, listening at the door, he had eavesdropped not only on Rawneth but on the priests as they discussed secrets which they never dreamed he overheard, much less understood. Suddenly, he couldn't bear that this hateful Knorth should think him as stupid as the Priests' College had.

"Of course," he said, trying to sound superior, "we've always had indirect contact with our god through the Shanir. Oracles, maledights, berserkers..."

"Healers?"

"Er, yes, I suppose. But the first time the God-voice spoke was on this world, just after the Fall. The Arrin-ken had made Glendar Highlord in place of his brother Gerridon, Master of Knorth. The priests dissented. They claimed that all the lords had failed in their duty by letting such a disaster happen and that we should start afresh on Rathillien, as a hierocracy."

"Ancestors forbid!"

"It might not have been so bad a thing. Whatever the priests are like now, on other threshold worlds they used the power of the temples to help the Shanir defend our people. They were champions."

"Ha!"

"You've got to understand," he heard himself plead, as if defending his tormentors somehow made bearable when they had done to him. "Once it was a noble thing to be a priest. They performed a vital service, without which we would long since have been destroyed. Then came the Fall and flight to this world, with the lords blaming all Shanir, hieratic and secular, because Gerridon and the Dream-weaver were of the Old Blood. Worse, every other time we've had to retreat, we've found the Kencyr temples waiting for us on the next threshold world. This time, for some reason, their construction was incomplete. So the priests found themselves not only under attack by the High Council, which had always wanted them out of politics, but also cut off from the full power of their god. How were they supposed to defend themselves?"

"Apparently, by trying to replace the Highlord with a High Priest. You people have never lacked nerve."

"*My* people...! Well, nerve was no defense against the Voice, which spoke for the first time through the High Priest to denounce his ambitions, destroying him in the process. The College thinks that since this world's temples were never finished, the god-power found a different channel—one that, for a time, actually listened and gave judgments wrapped in riddles, which the Arrin-ken tried to solve. Then came one that they couldn't: *'Fear the One, await the Three, seek the Four.'*"

"Oh, that's helpful," said Jame. "Nearly everything in the Kencyrath comes in threes: The faces of God, the Tyr-ridan, the three times three major houses and temples."

The One might conceivably be Gerridon, she thought, under pressure to become the Voice of Perimal Darkling, darkness articulate, as the Tyr-ridan might ultimately become that of the Three-Faced God.

"But what on earth," she wondered out loud, "comes in fours?"

"That's the big mystery. The Arrin-ken set out to solve it two thousand years ago, and haven't been heard from since. Neither has the Voice, until recently."

"I thought they left out of disgust with the Highborn."

"That was part of it. The God-voice offered an excuse to decamp, but they also took it as an order. Two thousand years without justice...I wish they would come back."

Someday, Immalai had said, *someone will call us. It might even be you.*

Jame thought of the blind Arrin-ken, and shivered. Some judgments were best deferred.

"The One, the Three, and the Four," she repeated. "What comes in fours, besides the Senetha and Senethar?"

"The elements," Kindrie suggested. "The seasons, the phases of the moon from full to dark, the fingers on Lord Ishtier's left hand..."

"*What?*"

He flinched away, as if from a blow.

"Look, I apologize for shouting more or less in your ear, but what in Perimal's name do you know about that forsworn renegade, Ishtier?"

"L-lord Ishtier has been at the Priests' College all winter, ever since the mission returned from Tai-tastigon with him. H-he was ill until recently. D-did you say 'renegade?'"

"Sweet Trinity, yes. Don't the other priests know?"

They don't, Jame thought, reading Kindrie's confused expression. Ishtier must have regained sufficient wits to lie to them. The mind boggled at that. The loss of honor was in itself so unthinkable that one forgot how dangerous a thorough rogue like Ishtier could be.

Kindrie regarded her askance. "Did you, *er*, abstract something from Lord Ishtier?"

"Steal it, d'you mean? No. He, *er*, abstracted something from me. The last I saw of him, he was trying to gnaw off his own hand after having touched this thing, which must be how he lost the finger. A pity he stopped short of the elbow. Sweet Trinity. You said that the God-voice spoke again recently, for the first time since the Arrin-ken left. Was that through Ishtier in Tai-tastigon?"

From his expression, she knew that it had been. Oh, lord. Now she was really in the dunghill, neck deep. What the Voice had said to her was alarming enough, without whatever frills Ishtier might add. The other priests must think that, in her, they had a real monster on their hands, against whom all measures were justified.

But was it really their god who had spoken through the renegade priest after so long a silence? Where *had* she heard something like the Voice since, not obviously, perhaps, but in its under-notes? If the Tastigon oracle proved false, what happened to its dire prophecies then?

Eh, this was hopeless. After all, Ishtier had accepted the Voice as genuine, and he was the poor goop through whom it had chosen to speak.

Stop clutching at straws, she told herself. *Whatever is, is, and you've got to live with it.*

But oh, lord—FRATRICIDE...and TYR-RIDAN.

It began to rain.

VII

Cold drops stung Jame's face, while Kindrie hunched thin shoulders under the rain-darkening cloth of his borrowed shirt. Only Jorin seemed unperturbed. He was taking this wretched weather unexpectedly well, Jame thought as she watched him trot on ahead. Some ounces enjoyed getting wet, but the blind Royal Gold had hated water ever since his breeder had tried to drown him as a kitten.

Strange. He didn't even look damp now.

When he returned, grumbling, at her call, she found that his coat was quite dry. So was the road ahead, and the leaves of trees a dozen feet away weren't dripping. The rain, it seemed, was exclusively for her benefit.

It came down harder, laced with hail. No. With tiny, green frogs.

"Do you mind?" she demanded, extracting a wriggling froglet from deep inside her shirt. It clung to her finger tip with anxious toes.

"Geep, *geep*, *GEEP!*" cried a growing chorus, doing agitated push-ups on her shoulders; but if they were trying to tell her something, Jame wasn't interested.

"Will you *stop* that?" she shouted up at the roiling clouds

The shower of frogs stopped. A moment later, rain began again—in a circle around them.

"This place has the damnedest weather," Jame muttered, flicking off her clothes and proceeding, carefully, over the lively ground, with Jorin bouncing like a wound-up toy at her heels

Kindrie stared after her. She *was* mad—and so was he, to be following her. His experience with Highborn women was limited to the Randir, whom he thought abominable, but at least they didn't wander about the countryside being rained on by frogs.

Why was he still in this lunatic's company? The last thing he remembered, before that suddenly silent bush, was challenging the Knorth about her Shanir blood. Then had followed the long nightmare of running, running... No. Walking, stumbling how far? His feet throbbed and he felt a sickening fatigue alien to his healer's nature. Where in all the names of God were they?

The naked slopes across the river were ominously familiar. So was the roof of a watch tower glimpsed ahead over trees on the west bank.

"That's Shadow Rock," he said in a stifled voice. "Wilden... You've lured me back to Wilden!"

He turned and fled, blindly, blundering, only to trip and crash down on the New Road's hard stones.

"Steady," said the Knorth, over him. "What *is* all this? Surely you realized that we were going north."

"No! I-I didn't notice."

"Huh. I should have let you go on sleepwalking. Listen: we're going farther north still, all the way to Restormir."

"*Restormir!* Why?"

"Because a friend of mine has fallen into Lord Caineron's hands. He needs rescuing. He'll need a healer too, if dear Caldane starts on him."

As simple, as insane as that.

For a moment Kindrie lay speechless, shaken like a cage by his own heartbeat.

Only someone who had never seen Restormir would propose such a thing. He remembered his brief time there the previous autumn, after his initial flight from Wilden, when he had taken service with the first Highborn he had met, needing protection from the priests, naively hoping it would lead to contact with the lord whom he really wished to serve, not knowing that Torisen and Caineron were mortal enemies. He had tried to help the Highlord anyway, and Caineron had repaid him for it. Remembering that, Kindrie shook even harder. His back still bore the marks of the corrector's scourge, because he couldn't forget.

No one had come to his rescue then, anymore than over this past winter.

Torisen couldn't have, he told himself. Either time. Otherwise, it would have been the natural thing for a Knorth to do—as it was now? No. Not for a female, however well-born. Yet this unnatural creature would have led him in a daze all the way to Restormir.

She sat on her heels two paces away, regarding him scornfully, expecting him to refuse. That stung. Dammit, wasn't he part Knorth too?

"All right," he heard himself say.

"You're sure?"

"*Yes!*"

He rose, stiffly. Flesh and bone, but he ached, with a sudden copper taste in his mouth. His nose had started to bleed. That shouldn't be. He was a healer, whose first subject was his own body—except that he was shut out of his own soul-image. He could still enter the soul-scapes of others to help as far as his limited strength allowed, but as for healing himself… Frail as he had always been, for the first time he tasted his own mortality.

No. Don't think about that. Don't think.

Stiff-shouldered, trying not to snuffle, he limped past the Knorth toward the two places which he least wished ever to see again.

Jame rose and followed him, frowning. Pleased as she was that the healer had decided to go, she didn't understand why. In the last few minutes, she had watched him flip through a dozen emotions, frantically, like a gambler with a losing hand. This bravado probably wouldn't last long either.

Priests! she thought. You couldn't depend on them for anything.

They were close to Shadow Rock now, the home keep of Hollens, Lord Danior. Although only a bone relative, Cousin Holly was the closest kin Torisen had on the High Council and therefore his heir presumptive—not that the young man relished that distinction. Lord of the poorest house in the Riverland, he could barely maintain his own council seat, much less hope to occupy the Highlord's for long, should Torisen's death put him there.

Jame had met him at the Cataracts' dinner party. A nice boy, she had thought, if rather too much in awe of her brother.

More of Shadow Rock came into view. The original keep had only been a Bashtiri outpost, built to keep an eye on the much larger Hathiri fortress across the river. The Danior had marginally expanded it, limited by the defile which it occupied under the shadow of a balanced rock which someday would probably smash it flat. Today, its lord absent in Kothifir, it looked abandoned—the outer gate locked and all its windows tight-shuttered except for one high up in the watch tower, which stood open.

Out of this last, a little girl leaned to peer across the river. Then someone pulled her back in and closed the shutter, quickly but quietly.

So, people in hiding garrisoned Shadow Rock after all. From what?

They rounded a corner and, for the first time, saw Wilden on the opposite bank.

It filled a valley much larger than its sister keep's, widened farther by quarry-work which had left sheer surrounding walls of live granite. These the low clouds cut short. Judging from a distant rumble, the overcast also hid a considerable water-fall at the valley's upper end. Streams plunged down on either side of Wilden between the mountains' granite flanks and the inner walls of the fortress. Wilden itself angled down the valley's floor, presenting tier after jagged tier of its internal structure, tower after terrace after tower. Between the trap-ezoidal jaws of its double outer walls, it looked like a mouth full of sharp, ragged teeth. The streams had been dammed before it to form a brimming moat. From this, runoff driveled down the steep outer ward toward the curtain wall that sealed off the valley, toward the River Road and the Silver below.

As they crept past, Jame saw that the doors of the upper gatehouse stood open. Through them, white glimmered in the premature twilight: the ruins of the hill fort around which Wilden had been built, carefully preserved on a tiny hillock in an inner courtyard like white bones cradled in Randir jaws.

The Priests' College was somewhere in there too.

"Is there a temple in the College?" she asked Kindrie.

"Of course not. That much raw power would burn out the novices' minds."

"But they *are* drawing power in, from Tai-tastigon and beyond. I can feel it. A cesspool of divinity...How many priests in residence, priestling?"

"I am *not*...Nine of the first rank, when I left. Maybe a score of others, as well as acolytes and novices. Oh, my God. Look."

Although it had stopped raining, heavy clouds roofed Wilden's valley in a ponderous eddy. The hub of their slow circling was the fortress's farthest tower, whose heights they obscured. Above that hidden summit, a sulfurous yellow light grew, glowering down through the wrack's thinner patches. It spread. The moat reflected its progress, then the rivulets, then the Silver itself. The water smoked sullenly in its wake.

"The weather around here may be peculiar," said Jame softly, "but this is getting downright spooky. What in Perimal's name have we walked into?"

"Lady Rawneth is conjuring," the Shanir said in a taut voice.

Jame stared at the approaching light. As Kindrie had said, Kencyr power came indirectly from their god through the temples and the Shanir. This felt different. She knew that some of Rathillien's so-called magics were accessible to anyone who knew the proper formulae, while others required the catalyst of faith. The latter was impossible for the average Kencyr, compelled to believe solely in his own absent god. However, she herself had accomplished two acts of it in Tai-tastigon, saving one native godling and killing another, through her faith in the truth of her own research. That had been nothing, though, compared to the natural forces unleashed here.

"But what do the priests think of Rawneth conjuring on their doorstep?"

"Knowledge is knowledge," said Kindrie, as if quoting hieratic dogma. "Besides, s-sometimes they trade information. She told Lord Ishtier h-how she kept me locked in my own soul-image m-most of my childhood."

"*What?*"

"Her revenge, she called it, although I never knew for what. S-sometimes she let me out, when she wanted s-someone to try her spells on who wasn't apt to die of them."

Jame remembered Ishtier's experiment with Bane's soul which had resulted in the Lower Town Monster. Perhaps it hadn't been as freakish as she had supposed—except that Ishtier had been trying to break the Kencyrath's monotheism by creating a genuine god.

I bet he hasn't shared that *bit of failed research with his peers*, she thought.

Kindrie started. "What was *that?*"

Something very close and, for the sound of it, very large, had just said, "*Quonk!*"

Out of the corner of her eye, Jame saw a green lump flash by in the river. That wailing, honking roar drifted back upstream, sounding quite distraught: "*Quoooooonk...!*"

If the unknown lump had been upset, however, Kindrie was beside himself.

"She's really done it!" he babbled. "W-we've got to get away from here! It will do whatever she commands a-and then it will please itself..."

Jame caught his arm. "What are you talking about?"

"A demon! Ishtier told her how to conjure it. That was the price he paid to learn how to bar me from my soul-image."

"*Quonk!*" boomed that strange voice again, this time with an air of self-encouragement. "*Quok, quok, quok...*"

Each grunting "*quok*" sounded closer than the last. Jame could have sworn that it had somehow gotten ahead of them again. However, she wasn't as scared as Kindrie. For one thing, she'd had some practical experience with demons; for another, it was hard to take one seriously which talked to itself, much less in that tone. The Shanir was right, though: this was no place to linger.

However, their way was barred by a pool of rainwater collected in a dip of the road. Something huge was rising out of it. Two bulging eyes emerged first, round as soup plates and about the same size, with slit pupils and irises each like a golden lattice crossing a rose-colored ground. An expanse of bright green forehead followed, then a broad snout circled by an even broader mouth. The snowy vocal sac inflated like a lesser moon,

"*QUONK!*" said this apparition, eyeing the white-haired healer with evident satisfaction,

Kindrie fainted,

Jame, on the other hand, nearly jumped into the pool to throw her arms around that vast, green neck—not that they would have reached,

"Why, Gorgo, you've grown!"

Gorgo, formerly the Lugubrious, switched his goggle-eyed gaze to her, and immediately looked apprehensive. The previous year, Jame's own experiments with the so-called gods of Tai-tastigon had first gotten him killed and then resurrected in his current (although much smaller) shape. Neither, obviously, was an experience which Gorgo would soon forget,

"...*quonk*..." he said feebly, gulping,

Another sound came out of his closed mouth. It sounded suspiciously like muffled cursing. Gorgo yawned, wide, wider, like a toad beginning its molt, and there, snuggled in the pit of his throat, was a human face,

"I *hate* it when he does that," said Loogan. "'*Quonk!*' What a sound, *and* it nearly blows out my eardrums."

Jame stared at the Tastigon priest. "Sweet Trinity. Did Gorgo swallow you, or are you wearing him?"

"I don't know *what's* going on," said Loogan crossly. "We were both in the temple, preparing for the evening rites, when *this* happened. In fact, if I squint, I can still see the sanctuary. I don't think we're really here at all—wherever 'here' is."

Gorgo gurgled,

"Ah. He says we've been sent to fetch someone—that fellow on the ground, I think. A lady wants him."

"Sorry. He's under my protection."

"Oh. Well, that's that. Overreached herself, she did, trying to snag us in the first place. We're already slipping free, none too soon."

Gorgo's attention had strayed to a flight of dragonflies hovering about a nearby clump of reeds. He turned his massive head. Loogan's tongue shot out—all three feet of it—and snapped an insect out of the air,

"Gaaah!" he said, around a mouthful of shimmering wings. "I *hate* this. We're going home. Now. Before he finds out that it's the m-a-t-i-n-g season."

"Loogan, wait! Is everyone all right in Tai-tastigon?"

"Hardly everyone. Men-dalis has got troubles, but I expect you'll hear about that sooner or later. All your friends at the Res aB'tyrr are fine. Goodbye."

"*Wait!* What happened to Bane?"

"Believe me, you don't want to know."

As he spoke, the priest's round face had been fading. Only his voice now emerged from Gorgo's throat, as if from a growing distance: "Bye-bye, duckie. Keep your feet dr…"

Gorgo's mouth still gaped wide open, frozen in what appeared to be astonishment. An iridescent sheen had come over him,

"*Quo…?*" he said tentatively, and burst with a faint pop, like a soap bubble,

All that remained was the puddle, with a rumpled dragonfly floating in the middle of it,

VIII

Loogan and Gorgo weren't the only ones who had disappeared. So had Kindrie and Jorin. The healer must have woken in time to hear Jame conversing familiarly with a "demon" and bolted, the ounce scampering after him.

Damnation.

Wet weather had somehow allowed the Wilden Witch to snatch an Old Pantheon rain god and his priest in the midst of their ritual lavations. She hadn't been able to hold them, but with that sort of power she was bound to try again, this time maybe conjuring something less ambitious but more effective— like a real demon. And it would be after Kindrie, whom Jame had just sworn to protect.

"It never rains," as Loogan might say, *"without drowning some-one."*

At least the tracks of both Shanir and ounce showed clearly in the soft earth, heading upward from the road. Jame followed at a trot. Overhead, the clouds went from gray to black, edged by that unearthly yellow light which still spread out from the towers of Wilden. The weirding mist trailed down in darkening veils.

At first, Jame thought that the diminishing light was to blame when the prints of Kindrie's bare feet seemed to distort. She crouched, peering. No. The outer toes *did* splay at right angles to elongated feet, with indentations at the end of each toe that suggested claws.

Something ran after the Shanir, treading in his footprints step by step.

As she rose to follow, the back of her head seemed to explode.

Ancestors be praised for long hair was her first dazed thought thereafter. Once again, the thick, coiled braid under her cap had saved her skull from fracture or worse.

Then she became aware of weight, pinning her to the ground, and of cool air, moving across her face. Someone had removed her mask. She rather thought, too, that she was being sat on.

All she saw at first, though, through cautious, slitted eyes, was the nearly empty food sack bobbing over her. Withered apples flew out of it as if by themselves. Above and behind it hovered angry eyes without a face—bloodshot whites, yellow irises, hardly ever blinking. When they did, the pressure on her eased and the food bag sagged, as if for a moment her assailant became the shadow after which his guild was named.

The empty sack went flying. Crooked, yellow teeth bared at her in a snarl, which she smashed with a handy rock.

Free. On her feet. Running, closely pursued.

Tripped by a root, Jame turned her stumble into a lunge for the nearest sapling, bearing it down with her weight, then rolling off to let it whip back. Yellow eyes hastily shut. The slender trunk passed between where they had been. She tried to rise, but a freezing numbness had seized her legs. The assassin's shadow swarmed up her body, ending in two very real if invisible hands about her throat. Yellow eyes glared down at her, unblinking.

"Where is it?" a thick tongue hissed in midair, like an adder in a cage of rotten ivory, spitting blood and fragments of broken teeth in her face. "The book, you witch, the Book Bound in Pale Leather. Where?"

"I-I don't have it." Sweet Trinity, who had told him about that? Marc, Graykin, Kindrie…"Ishtier?"

The grip on her throat tightened. "That priest-spawn! What has he told you, bitch? What?"

What *could* Ishtier have told her, except perhaps how he had forced a master assassin to attempt theft for him? If the guilds of the Central Lands were like their eastern counterparts, the Bashti thieves would howl over this.

Broken teeth sneered. "Bluffing, weren't you? As if a whore's-daughter ever knew anything."

White flashed. The Ivory Knife. Oh lord, where had he found to hide that?

"Guild Master," she heard herself croak. "I know this much: why the blooding at Gothregor failed."

The Knife hesitated. Her neck felt cold, where the blade so nearly touched it.

"Why, bint?"

"The 'prentices were unprepared and under trained."

He slapped her, hard, across her injured cheek. "One of them gave you that, at least."

"No," said Jame, through sudden pain, tasting blood.

"Then not. Kencyr are too stupid to lie. Under-trained, how?"

"Not enough fighting experience." Amazing, how she found herself reporting as a journeyman to a master, if of different disciplines. "Too much dependence on shadow-casting techniques, under adverse conditions."

"Unprepared for what?"

"Partly, for me."

He struck again, harder. She almost lunged upward into the sharp ivory, a risk she might have taken with any other knife.

"Why don't you put that thing away, master, and try your own luck with me?"

He gave a sharp bark of laughter. "I tested your sort thirty-four years ago, sow. Soft throats and soft kills—except for the one who led me such a chase and the other one who cursed. Red-eyed whore...!"

A red-eyed maledight...

"Brenwyr?" Jame said, stupidly

"*That* was the name. Unprepared for what else, slut?"

"For Old Man Tishooo, who blew away their souls, and for a shadow-demon named Bane, who fed on them. In fact," she added, carefully, "if you were to look above you now..."

He laughed again, harshly. "Kencyr never lie, but 'if' cuts no bread."

"This time," said Jame, "it does."

Bane dropped on the assassin out of a tree, like a coat of shadows. The guild master gasped. His frantic efforts to shrug off his tenebrous assailant became the jerky movements of a man being clothed against his will. His shoulders twitched as the other settled over them. His arms stretched and his hands flexed into gloves of living shadow. The Ivory Knife wobbled in his loosened grip, directly over Jame's face.

"Watch it!" she said.

Bane looked down at her. What Jame saw was the shadowy mask of his features, through which the assassin's eyes stared wildly. What he saw, for the first time, was her injured face, freshly bloodied. His grip on the guild master tightened. The man shrieked, and dropped the Ivory Knife.

"Eeee!" said Jame.

How she managed it, she never knew. A moment later, though, Jame found herself sprawling a dozen feet from where the Knife quivered upright in the sod, the grass dying around it.

Something unseen was blundering away through the trees, trailing a thin wail as much of rage as fear. The master assassin had bolted. Now there was a mount which would need some taming, even for such a rider. With luck, they would break each other's necks, Jame thought sourly, wiping her face. So much for Kindrie's first aid.

Sweet Trinity. Kindrie.

She snatched up the Ivory Knife and ran back the way she had come. Here was the clearing where the assassin had jumped her, her mask, cap, and linen bandage laying where he had dropped them. Beyond, those curious, composite footprints led on upslope. She followed, toward the sound of raised voices.

IX

"It's weirding up something fierce, Ten," the cadet on point
called back, a plaintive, disembodied voice out of the dark,
dripping forest. Muffled thunder rolled down the valley like a
boulder wrapped in flannel. "And I think it's going to rain
again."

"We should have turned back two days ago, when the
ghost-walkers passed," the tall cadet in Five's rear-guard position muttered. "All patrols should, when it starts to weird
up like this."

His voice carried, as he meant it to. The new ten-commander turned to look back at him over the seven intervening
heads.

"Standing orders," he muttered defiantly, but his eyes fell.

Brier Iron-thorn could almost smell the slow burn of
his resentment. Before her arrival at the college, a new
Knorth cadet with a battlefield appointment, he had been
provisional Ten.

In fact, none of the young cadets looked happy. All but
one of them Riverland bred, of old Knorth stock, they had
come to Tentir that spring thinking themselves the cream of
its new crop, only to find how hard it was to serve the Highlord
in a college dominated by his enemies. Worse, older cadets
looked down on them both for having missed the great blooding at the Cataracts and for taking the place of friends killed
there. Then, in the crowning insult, they had been put under
the command of an upstart Southie of Caineron *yondri* stock.

To Brier, their discontent looked like the pout of spoiled
children.

How old were they? Fifteen? Sixteen? At their age, she
had already been in the field with the Southern Host for years,
first with her mother, then on her own after Rose Iron-thorn's

death in the Wastes after the debacle at Urakarn. Life was hard for the many Kendar who had lost their natural lord and must seek a new one. Nicknamed *yondri-gon* or threshold-dwellers, they could serve a house for generations before its master deigned to take them into regular service, especially if that house was the Caineron and its lord Caldane, who deliberately swelled his ranks with the desperate displaced who would do anything to gain his favor. Two years ago, when she had turned seventeen, he had at last given Brier her chance as a randon candidate—if she passed his private initiation.

The cadets, watching, were suddenly still. Under the helm of mahogany hair, the Southie's expression hadn't changed: as always, that hard, handsome face might have been carved from teak and those green eyes from the same malachite as the stud in her left earlobe. But for a moment the cadets had seen something there which had frightened them very much indeed.

Brier turned away. "Point, wait there. We're coming down to you."

Near mutiny returned to the ranks. "Down" meant farther south. Their assignment had been to check out the rumor of a naked Merikit seen near the college—just another dirt job for the Knorth rookies, they had thought, as well as an oblique insult to their new leader, since only Caineron hunted Merikit for sport and were said to treat them no better than wild animals when they caught one. This Merikit would, of course, long since have gone, assuming he had existed in the first place. They had expected to cover their assigned territory in time for supper. Instead, Iron-thorn had led them out of it, southward.

Now it was dusk two days later, under dark trees and a weirding overcast, with no food, no Merikit, and the prospect of more rain.

They were long overdue at Tentir. Commandant Sheth, no friend to the Knorth, could have their token scarves for this as it was. Had that, perhaps, been his purpose in assigning them to a former Caineron? What *was* the Southie playing at, anyway?

It would not have reassured them that Brier herself didn't
know. She only sensed that something was tugging her. It felt
like her new bond to the Highlord, but how could that be when
he was still in Kothifir, over four hundred leagues away? Normally, Torisen's grip on his Kendar was so light-handed that
her former mates dismissed it scornfully as limp. But how
could Brier know what he might be capable of? The Knorth
were so different from the Caineron, upon whom all her previous experience was based.

Different, and mad.

She had been brought up to believe that, too. Hadn't Ganth
Gray Lord's insanity infected the entire Host, leading to its
near massacre in the White Hills? Didn't his son sometimes
shun sleep until his wits half turned? What was she to think
of a Highborn who at the Cataracts had offered her sanctuary
from Lord Caineron's wrath as if he actually cared what happened to her? That show of concern was only the Knorth
glamour, she told herself, useful for binding gullible randon
like Harn Grip-hard as tightly as blood could have done. Her
own decision to change houses had been based entirely on
ambition, since she could now never hope for advancement
under the Caineron. She would use Knorth influence and the
Knorth would use her ability. Pure self-interest, on both sides.
It was mad to think that Highborn and Kendar could deal with
each other on any other basis.

And madness was contagious.

Is that what pulls me southward? she wondered. *Have I
gone mad too?*

The scout suddenly reappeared, with an urgent gesture for
silence. Whatever he had found, though, defied his ability to
describe by sign. Brier cut short his efforts with a brusque
Show me, then followed him down to the edge of the trees,
the squad close on their heels.

They emerged under black clouds so low here that they
seemed to tangle in the branches overhead. An unearthly yellow light filtered down through them. Below, the river's pale

breath was slowly flooding the valley to the height of the low-est trees. Between roof and floor of mist lay a slope strewn with large boulders, knee deep in grass, across which veils of weirding silently drifted. It was this middle ground to which the scout pointed.

A Randir ten-command was playing hide-and-seek among the boulders—if "play" was the right word for that silent, fur-tive activity. The strange cadets seemed almost to slither through the grass, supple as serpents, long-skulled heads and many-jointed hands weaving as though in quest for a scent. Flushed from cover, a white-haired Shanir stumbled into the open. The seekers surrounded him. They began to play him back and forth, still in that unnerving silence, as he floun-dered with exhaustion in their midst.

It was no affair of hers, Brier told herself. As a Caineron, the first lesson she had learned was to mind her own business.

The Shanir tripped and fell. The Randir crouched in a circle around him. One drew a fingertip delicately down his cheek, leaving a thin, red line.

"Stop that!" Brier Iron-thorn roared.

Her own cadets jumped, then nervously followed as she strode down the slope. Below, ten pale, blank faces turned toward her, ten pairs of ghost-lit, glimmering eyes, but still no one spoke.

"What in Perimal's name d'you think you're doing?" she demanded of them, then stopped short.

A Randir captain had stepped between her and the group crouching around the fallen Shanir. Brier blinked. She didn't recognize any of the ten-command, but this gaunt woman was a Tentir instructor, currently posted to the Gothregor Women's Halls and still wearing her dress grays with gold-striped shoul-der embroidery. What in hell was she doing here?

"Minding our own business, cadet," said the captain, smil-ing. The other Randir rose and silently ranged themselves be-hind her, still surrounding the Shanir. "We suggest that you do the same."

Brier blinked again. To hear her unspoken thoughts answered was unnerving. Worse, she suddenly realized that whatever was going on here, she couldn't just walk away from it.
The rules she had followed as a Caineron no longer seemed to
apply, but how was a Knorth supposed to react? For the first
time in her life, she didn't know what to do,

"Randir business, on Danior land, with someone under
Knorth protection. Interesting."

The new voice made them all turn sharply. A slim, dark-
clad figure stood on top of a white boulder, looking down at
them. For a moment, impossibly, Brier thought it was Torisen
Black Lord. Then she saw the other's mask. She had indeed
been drawn southward by her bond to the Knorth, she realized, but not to the Highlord,

"Don't move, Kindrie," said Torisen's mad sister. "I think
you've landed in a nest of bogles."

X

Jame had immediately recognized the Randir captain from Gothregor, or at least her semblance. That the woman herself should be here was quite possible: Wilden was her home keep, after all; and, given their crawling pace, she could easily have beaten the fugitives to it—but in such company?

From the boulder's height, Jame could see Kindrie's track beaten through the tall grass as he had fled from cover to cover. The ten Randir cadets, however, had left no trails at all, while their officer still stood as if by chance in the Shanir's footsteps, her own feet sunk into them to the ankles. It was too dark to see if, like Bane, she cast no shadow. If she *was* the demon whom Lady Rawneth had conjured, that would explain the ten others as bogles, mindless projections of her power. Yes: *if.*

"'Knorth protection,'" the randon repeated, smiling up at Jame. "Now, who are you, girl, to confer that?"

One point to me, thought Jame.

The real captain had never seen her dressed like this, but she would have guessed after that slip about the Knorth. A demon concentrated the worst attributes of its host soul, without always gaining its knowledge. Unfortunately, she didn't know the Randir's true name either, which would have helped if this creature was indeed constructed around her soul the way the Lower Town Monster had been around Bane's.

The other's smile peeled back into a broad grin, baring very white, distinctly human teeth whose incisors had been chipped to form points, so recently that they still bled. Behind her, ten faces broke into empty smiles, luminous eyes devoid of pupil, iris, and life.

The glowing eyes of the strange cadets in the Randir arcade at Gothregor...these?

"Why don't you come down and play, little girl?" crooned their captain. "Or shall we amuse ourselves elsewhere?"

As one, the ten turned their gleaming gaze on Kindrie.

The dark randon on the upper slope moved as if to protest, but checked herself. What in Perimal's name were Knorth cadets doing here anyway, Jame wondered, distracting her at such a moment?

"Your mistress won't thank you for hurting this boy," she said quickly to the face smiling up at her. "She must want him back alive."

"But not necessarily intact. Healers are such fun."

White hands reached out toward Kindrie. Long nails rattled together over him like thorns in a winter wind. Where they brushed his skin, red lines appeared and began to drip.

That did it.

For some time, thunder had been grumbling closer. Now the yellow light above flared briefly, as lightning gave an oddly muffled crack. To destroy a demon, Ishtier had once told her, you needed first its true name and then lots of fire or water. True, she didn't know what to call the creature gloating up at her, but by God, maybe she could still wipe that damn grin off its face. No time to conjure up the proper master rune, but Gorgo still owed her at least one favor.

"All right," she said to the lowering sky, "*Now.*"

A raindrop struck her upturned face, then another and another, hard. One moment she could see all the way upslope, where the red-haired Kendar had barked an order at her command and was starting down with the cadets scrambling into formation behind her. The next second, the rain had drawn a hissing, gray veil across everything. A wail of protest came from the grass below where Jorin lay hidden.

Something was climbing the rock. For a moment, Jame looked into a face from which all features had been washed except the sharp-toothed grin. Fingers webbed with melting flesh groped for her. She launched herself over the creature's head, as much through water as air, to land hard on the flattened grass beyond. Wet fur brushed against her, chirping anxiously. Jorin. She stumbled toward where she had last seen Kindrie. There he was, a pale, huddled blur on the ground, ringed by cloud-of-thorn brambles. She slashed through them with the Ivory Knife and hauled the Shanir out.

Suddenly, the air around them changed. A glowing mist so dense that Jame couldn't see or hear anything at all replaced the rain. She tightened her grip on Kindrie's arm while a frightened ounce pressed so close that he stood on her foot. Those two points of contact were all she could feel. Beyond them, all of Rathillien might have melted into chaos.

Then Jame realized what had happened: under cover of the storm, a bank of weirding had swept down on them.

Sweet Trinity, now what? Weird-walking had occasionally been practiced in the past, with mixed results. A walker might cover great distances, but he also might end up one place and his feet another. Still, the naked Merikit had risked it. This mist-bank was traveling southward. Would it roll past or was it already taking them with it? Since Jame neither wanted to stay where she was nor find herself at the Cataracts, much less both places simultaneously, she stumbled on in the direction which she had been going, hoping it was northward, dragging Kindrie and Jorin with her.

Time seemed to dissolve along with everything else. Past and future melted into a present that stretched on and on until it was hard to imagine anything but mist.

Then, between one step and the next, the world returned.

The mist rolled away southward, leaving them under a dusky sky fretted with stars, on the crest of a ridge. Some distance below, stretching from the river bank back until the western hills swallowed it, was the largest fortress Jame had ever seen. Actually, it looked more like a city with many walled districts. A castle keep built on a towering mound dominated the whole, separated from it, moat-like, by the split waters of a tributary rushing down to join the Silver.

Jame only had a moment to stare, though, before someone behind her gave a startled exclamation. She and Jorin leaped aside as a number of people plunged out of the retreating mist, hanging on to each other. The lot of them tumbled off the ridge, taking Kindrie with them, to fetch up in a pine spinney a little way down the slope. Jame was left facing the dark cadet, who had emerged last and least precipitously from the mist.

"If it's any consolation," she said to the Kendar, glancing at the muddle below as it began to sort itself out with dolorous cries, "the one on the bottom is a healer. Who *are* you people, anyway, and where have we all landed?"

The tall randon was staring down at the mass of buildings, in patent disbelief.

"Restormir," she said softly. "*Restormir.*"

Interim III
The River Road: 58th of Spring

Something bad was coming.

The Wolver Grimly had sensed it all day in the prickling of his fur. He had seen it, too, in the animals he had passed—roe deer standing in tight knots in meadows by the River Road, wild cats wailing in the hills, field mice, snakes and even worms crawling out of their holes onto the road's surface.

He knew from the procession of ghost-walkers which had drifted past two nights ago that serious weirding was on the way. Worse, a really bad weirdingstrom could trigger earthquakes, the mere thought of which made the fur down his spine rise.

His mount jibbed, snatching for its bit as Grimly fumbled with the reins. Wolvers seldom rode, nor did any horse care to be ridden by them. Damn. There went a stirrup. He scrabbled for it, not realizing until the reins slipped through his paws that in his bone-deep fatigue he had reverted to wolver shape. The horse squealed, bounced sideways, and threw its rider into a convenient thorn bush. As Grimly extricated himself, swearing, it bolted back the way they had come. On foot again, dammit—falling behind, and he the only one on the right trail.

As far as anyone else knew, Torisen had simply disappeared after charging out of the courtyard in Kothifir.

"*You don't see me,*" he had said to the guard at the gate, and the man hadn't. Quite possibly, he would never see anything again.

Simultaneously, a kind of selective blindness had raced through the entire encampment. Grimly hadn't understood how that could happen until he had heard shaken men comparing it to the effect of Ganth's madness on the Northern Host thirty-four years ago. That was something out of an old song to Grimly. He had never imagined that Ganth's son might also have such power over his followers, much less be ruthless enough to use it.

However, in the faces of Ardeth, Harn, and Burr (groggy, but recovering), he had seen that this was what they feared. They had decided to keep as much from the Highlord's enemies as possible, while they themselves set out to find him. Harn and Burr thought he had disappeared into the back streets of Kothifir. Ardeth was sure that he had fled into the Wastes, as he had done once before, and proposed to search for him there.

Listening, Grimly had realized that none of Torisen's friends expected to recover him sane. What chance did Tori stand against such a consensus? Far less than he deserved, the Wolver had thought, so he hadn't told them about Kin-Slayer or the distant, endangered sister. Instead, he had claimed that the upcoming Summer Eve rites required his presence at home in the Grimly Holt—which happened to be just over half way to the Riverland by the River Road. Harn and Burr hadn't thought much of him for that, but he told himself that he didn't care as long as it kept them looking for Tori in the wrong direction.

He had wondered if he himself might be wrong, though, when the first three post stations on the way to Hurlen reported that the Highlord hadn't passed them. Then again, no one had seen him ride out of the encampment in any direction whatsoever. At the fourth station, a hundred miles east of Kothifir, Kendar spoke of hearing someone gallop past, but not being able to see who it was. The fifth station recognized Storm; the sixth, finally, identified his rider.

Grimly had begun to worry about Storm. The quarter-blood Whinno-hir had unusual stamina, but this pace would eventually kill even him. Sleep-starved, fleeing nightmares, Torisen had ridden a horse to death once before, on his mad dash into the Wastes four years ago. It would upset him horribly if he did it again. Halfway to the Cataracts, however, Grimly found the black stallion, exhausted but safe, at a post

station. Torisen had gone on by post horse. Grimly couldn't
run down a succession of fresh mounts so he too, reluctantly,
had taken to the saddle.

That had been two days ago. Now it was dusk, the fifty-
eighth of spring, and he was close enough to home to smell it.
The road rolled northward over gentle hills. To the left lay
a wild meadow with nightjars skimming over it and luminous
mist collecting in its hollows. To the right ran the Silver, swift
and chuckling. Glowing witchweed bent in its margin. Grimly
found himself trotting, eager despite his fatigue. From the top
of the next rise, he would be able to see home. Here was the
hill's crest. Ahead, the main road swung to the right, following the river's curve, while a spur of it ran straight on into the
lowering shadows of the Grimly Holt.

Just short of the fork, a dark-clad figure trudged northward, leading a lame post horse. Grimly recognized the black
coat, dusty and travel stained as it now was. He also caught
the cold gleam of Kin-Slayer.

"Tori!"

The Highlord plodded on, unheeding. When the Wolver
caught up with him, he blinked as if just waking and regarded
his friend without surprise.

"Oh. Hello, Grimly. Going home for Summer Eve?"

Bloodshot eyes, disheveled hair, four days' growth of beard,
and yet that unassuming elegance clung to the Highborn, which
Grimly thought he would probably still possess halfway through
his own cremation. What unnerved the Wolver, though, was
that dead calm tone.

"Er actually, Tori, I was trying to catch up with you."

"Really? That's kind, but I don't know what good you can
do. Better, perhaps, that you should go home. That's it, isn't
it, just ahead?"

"Yes," said Grimly.

He glanced surreptitiously at Torisen's nearest hand, his
left, which held the post horse on a loose rein. It seemed to
have nearly recovered from the cut which Kin-Slayer's

cracked emblem had given it. Kencyr could shrug off much
worse than that, he reminded himself. A Highborn, especially a Knorth, could look as haggard as a haunt and yet
keep going days after a more sensible person would have
dropped dead.

"Yes," he said again, more confidently. "That's the Grimly
Holt."

"Good. When I blink, I see something so different—a
huge fortress with seven, no, eight walled districts surrounding a tower on a high mound. Restormir? But that's ridiculous. I'm all muddled, Grimly."

"That's lack of sleep," said the Wolver, beginning to be
frightened again.

Tori *never* spoke about such things. He was an intensely
private person, whose secrets the Wolver had no wish to know.
Now they might both have been caught in the same nightmare, where barriers fell and anything might happen.

Then he caught sight of Torisen's right hand, which still
gripped Kin-Slayer's hilt. It was swollen, especially around
the emerald signet ring which appeared to be almost sunken
into the finger wearing it. Burst blisters showed around the
edge of the white-knuckled grip. Red lines radiated out from
them. Only the worst neglect could have brought such infection to a Kencyr—such as clutching the hilt of that malignant
sword constantly for four days?

"Tori, come home with me. Please. You can rest there.
The whole pack will keep watch over you."

"And what will they protect me from, when I don't know
myself? You see, that's what I'm going back to the Riverland
to find out. Either my Shanir twin is doing this to me, as
Father claims, or I've gone mad."

Father? Grimly thought, confused. *Twin?*

"All right," he said, trying to match his friend's calm. "We'll
find out when we get there. In the meantime, though, why
don't you at least sheathe the sword?"

"Oh, I can't do that. Not until it kills someone."

Grimly was staring at him, speechless, when crows swarmed above the Holt in a black, raucous mob. Their uproar masked the oncoming rumble until it was almost underfoot. Then the earth began to quiver like a piece of fresh-killed beef, making Torisen stagger and Grimly crouch low. The lame horse threw up its head, jerking free, and plunged off the road into a patch of mist. It didn't come out the other side.

"Oh no," said Grimly, as the rumble faded. "That's weirding. Tori, listen to me: the wolvers' keep will protect us if we can reach it before the weirdingstrom hits. You've *got* to come with me now, if you don't want to be swept all the way back to the Cataracts, if not beyond. Tori, please!"

Torisen blinked. "It looks so much like Restormir," he said in wonder. "Caldane will just have arrived home. We mustn't go there, Grimly."

"We won't," said the Wolver, taking his arm. "I promise. Now come along. We're almost home."

Part IV

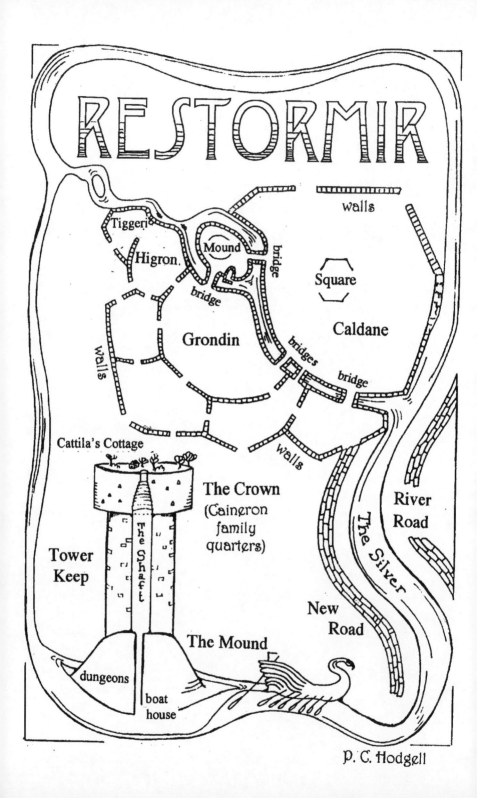

RESTORMIR

walls

Tiggeri

Mound

bridge

Higron

Square

bridge

Grondin

Caldane

bridges

walls

bridge

walls

Cattila's Cottage

The Crown
(Caineron
family
quarters)

River
Road

Tower
Keep

The Shaft

The Silver

New
Road

The Mound

dungeons

boat
house

P. C. Hodgell

Restormir: 58th of Spring
I

"Look," said Jame, for the dozenth time. "Why don't you all just go home? We'll be fine."

The answer came back with the same dogged patience as on each previous occasion: "Lady, I can't leave you here. You must see that."

Jame sighed. In fact, she understood the Kendar's dilemma perfectly well. To abandon the Highlord's sister on the doorstep of his archenemy was unthinkable—but to linger put his cadets at risk.

The latter huddled together on the southern slope of the ridge, six male and three female, where they all had taken refuge from sharp Caineron eyes. Only one, a cadet named Rue, was shorter than Jame, although the Kendar girl outweighed the Highborn by a good thirty pounds. The biggest, five-leader Vant, almost matched his tall ten-commander. All were armed for the hunt with long knives and short, elk horn bows, which the rain had rendered useless. Size and weaponry notwithstanding, to Jame they looked as bedraggled as a parcel of Molocar pups.

"For ancestors' sake, get them away!" she said to their leader, dropping her voice. "They aren't ready for this."

Brier Iron-thorn stared at her. *And you are?* A Highborn girl, sequestered and cosseted all her life—but this one spoke so disconcertingly, as if from her own store of experience. Brier had meant to respond slowly and firmly, as one does to a child or a half-wit. Instead, she found herself protesting:

"Lady, if only you would tell me what you intend to do!"

Jame hesitated. The cadet would think she was crazy but, dammit, this stalemate was wasting time. "All right," she said, and told her.

Brier blinked, twice. The Knorth *was* mad. Kendar at the Cataracts had whispered it when she had suddenly appeared in the middle of the battle and afterward been confined by the Highlord to the inner chamber of his tent until he could discreetly bundle her home by closed litter. *How sad,* the Caineron had said to each other, smiling.

"Don't interfere, cadet," the escaped lunatic said, looking hard at her. "This is honor—and obligation."

For a long moment, Kendar regarded Highborn without expression, then made a brusque gesture of acknowledgment. "Honor is honor, and obligation is unarguable. I can't stop you, lady, so I'll have to go with you."

"Lady," Vant burst out, "you should know: Ten is a Caineron herself."

"Was!" Rue snapped.

Ah, thought Jame. She had wondered why this tall cadet sounded so familiar. Confined to her brother's tent at the Cataracts, she had perforce overheard him outside, binding new Kendar to his service. One of them had spoken in just such a voice, rich but nearly inflectionless, a Caineron schooled to concealment.

"*Raiding another house's Kendar,*" Harn Grip-hard had said afterward to Torisen. "*You won't hear the end of this in a hurry.*"

"*It can't be helped. I'll be damned if I'll let Caldane ruin someone like that—for her mother's sake, if nothing else.*"

"*Huh. Old debts aside, you've snatched a real prize. M'lord Caineron is going to be furious.*"

Jame's curiosity had set Jorin's whiskers twitching then, as it did again now. One thing at least was obvious: after Graykin and herself, the last person who should visit Restormir uninvited was this erstwhile Caineron. She said as much.

"Nonetheless," the Kendar replied, in a voice like ironwood.

"...in trouble enough as it is," Vant was protesting to the other cadets in a low, urgent voice. "The Highlord won't thank us for encouraging this, this..."

He felt the eyes of the Highlord's sister on him, and stuttered to a halt. What word was there, anyway, both diplomatic and strong enough to describe so absurd a predicament? He lived to serve the Highborn, of course. Any ambitious Kendar did. But they in turn should behave as befit both their dignity and his. He had sneered at the Southie Ten at every opportunity. Now, however, he resented that she so obviously was not up to the situation.

"We're already days overdue at Tentir," he argued doggedly, not meeting anyone's eyes. "D'you *want* to make the Commandant a present of our scarves?"

"If Ten goes," said Rue stubbornly, "so should we."

"No!" said Brier and Jame simultaneously.

"I agree with Rue," another cadet said, with a wriggle that might have been deference to his superiors or a digging in of heels. "If we stay behind, that's what people will remember about us for the rest of our lives. Anyway, think what an opportunity this is! We didn't have a chance to prove ourselves at the Cataracts, but a raid on Restormir—they'll talk about that at Tentir for the next fifty years!"

"Oh, at least," said Jame dryly. "Especially if you get skinned alive in the process. D'you really want to risk a blooding like that?"

"Well, lady, you know what they say: true tests are sent, not sought."

Brier and Jame looked at each other. Both knew that maxim's corollary: refuse such a test and risk never being sent another. Put that way, it would be as serious to interfere with such a matter as with honor itself.

Nonetheless, Vant made one last try. "Ten, I'm warning you. This may not ruin us,"—not if *he* could help it, anyway—"but it certainly will you."

"In that case," said Brier Iron-thorn, rising and towering over him so that, big as he was, he shrank from her, "you have something to look forward to, don't you?"

II

Half an hour later, a ten-command in close formation trotted toward Restormir as if eager to take shelter for the night. Innumerable stars, except to the far north, where darkness blotted them out, lighted their way. A faint grinding noise came from that direction, and the earth occasionally shivered underfoot.

More strangeness on the way, Jame thought.

She stepped on the heel of the cadet in front of her and would have fallen if hands hadn't caught her. Brier had tucked her in the middle of the formation, where her dark clothes rendered her almost invisible. By contrast, Kindrie's white hair shone in the front rank like a beacon. The cadets on either side gripped his arms tightly, as though to hustle along a prisoner, when in fact they were supporting most of his weight so that his bare feet hardly touched the ground.

They came to a small, half-built compound on the tributary's southern bank, at the fortress's western end, which belonged to Tiggeri, Caineron's youngest established son, still in Kothifir in disfavor.

"Not too deep, I hope," Jame had said. *"Not if you intend to pass yourselves off as his retainers."*

"Tiggeri's practical jokes never quite bury him, lady, but sometimes he makes his Kendar very nervous. If on their way home they found this healer wandering, they would bring him along as a peace offering to M'lord."

A peace offering. Jame glanced at Kindrie again, this time with a twinge of unease. The Shanir had served Caldane briefly. She had heard that they had parted with no love lost. Perhaps Restormir was dangerous for him too—but he was a healer, dammit. What risk, ultimately, could he run? Anyway, too late for second thoughts: here was the gate, and now they were through it into Tiggeri's compound, unchallenged.

Only the rathorn crest stitched in white on their black to-ken scarves marked them as Knorth. Easy enough to fold the needlework inward and to turn the scarf knot to the front in the style which Tiggeri favored. Jame had been afraid at first that Iron-thorn would balk at this stratagem, which her own knowledge as a former Caineron had suggested. Something about the big Kendar made subterfuge seem impossible. How-ever, she had apparently decided that on this mad night any-thing might happen—not that "anything" included lying about their identity if directly challenged.

It was a relief, therefore, to find Tiggeri's compound virtu-ally empty. His people must still be with him in Kothifir, where perhaps he had managed to stay by design. Only established since the previous summer, he and his retainers still lived in half-constructed quarters which would have been cruelly cold that winter. Still, huge piles of fire wood showed that they would rather have kept these stark lodgings than give up the morsel of independence which their lord had granted them. How important it was to be established, given permission to bind Kendar in one's own right.

If he ever found out about Graykin, Tori would have a fit.

The squad slowed, for the first time hearing the sound of the greater fortress as it lapped about this silent compound. Ahead loomed the castle keep on its high hill. The lower, older portion of the tower was dark, but on top of that like some fantastic crown sat the family quarters. There all win-dows stood open and lit. Snatches of song and laughter fell from them, disjointed by the height, and the quarters below gave back echoes, laugh for broken laugh, cry for cry.

"Passwords!"

The challenge fell suddenly on them from a guard-box perched on top of the wall which they were approaching. Under the box, sputtering torches bracketed the closed gate leading to the next compound.

"Passwords!" the guard demanded again, with a curious, high-pitched giggle. "C'mon. *You* know!"

"I *don't* know," Brier shouted back. "We just got here."

"Atta girl." The gate creaked open. "'I-don't-know.' Tomorrow's watchwords, if you're interested, are 'I-don't-care.'"

Brier waved the squad through. "Are you drunk?" she demanded of the guard, who was now leaning perilously far out of the box to watch them pass.

"*I'm* not. *They* are." With a giddy sweep of his arm, he indicated the lit windows of the keep high above. "Five days and five nights, ever since M'lord got home. All the sons are up there too, except yours. Think what fun you're missing, cadet! If Kencyr weren't so hard to poison, we'd all be dead by now. What've y'got there?"

He was peering down at Kindrie, trying to focus.

"Something M'lord lost awhile ago."

"His Shanir toy, is it? Good, good. That Southron plaything he brought back with him won't last the night. Distract 'im, thassa idea. We've had about all the fun here we can stand."

He gagged briefly, but there was nothing in his stomach to bring up, nor had there been, probably, for the better part of five days. They heard him begin to giggle again as they pressed on, his voice a shaky echo of his master's, carousing in the high keep above.

That shrill titter followed them all the way through the quarter belonging to Higron, Caldane's sixth established son. They heard it in raucous guard-halls, in shadowy side streets, in the darkened bedrooms of children, once even burbling in a rain barrel where a burly Kendar was trying to drown himself.

Jame fell in beside Iron-thorn, a nervous Jorin trotting close at her heels. "You know," she said, "this isn't particularly funny. I had no idea that the bond between Highborn and Kendar could work this way."

"A lord's health always affects his people, lady, depending on how tightly he grips them. All the Caineron hold very tight. Then too, excessive wine can complicate matters."

Jame shot her a sidelong glance. "You feel it too, don't you?"

"I'm sworn to your brother now, lady," the other said stiffly. "But my family has been Caineron *yondri* for generations. I feel enough to remember why I seldom drink."

They were approaching the gate of Grondin, Caldane's oldest son and the frequent butt of Tiggeri's practical jokes. Once, Brier could have judged to a hair how matters stood between the brothers. Not now. But to reach Caldane's citadel they must pass this way.

Grondin's district was the largest in Restormir except for M'lord's on the far side of the river. Two bridges spanned the latter, the farther to the east, leading to Caldane's general compound; the closer to the north, connecting by a side door to the castle mound itself. Brier proposed to use this latter route, if she could get her squad past Grondin's watchmen.

This proved easy.

Once the guard had locked the gate behind them, however, he gleefully whistled up his cronies to harry the "Tiggie" cadets like so many stray dogs.

Brier hurried her squad on. Tiggeri notwithstanding, she had seen Grondin drunk. To fall into his people's hands just now would be more than unpleasant. Damn. It sounded as if the entire district was rousing to join in the fun. Drunken haloos echoed from street to street to mark the twisting course of the chase.

"We're going in a circle," said the Knorth.

Brier almost demanded how she knew, but then glimpsed the tower looming over rooftops to her right. She had only been in Restormir briefly two years ago and never in this quarter, which was laid out with as little foresight as everything else that Grondin did. Moreover, her sense of direction was even worse than her head for heights. Perhaps this narrow way cut back to the main thoroughfare. No. Windowless walls rose on three sides, close and dank. A dead end.

The uproar approached. Torchlight washed across the blind alley's mouth. Then someone seemingly overhead cried:

"Haloo-loo-loo! *This* way!"

Torchlight withdrew as the hunt followed that insistent voice, now crying in the upper distance:

"Kalli-kalli-catch-'em-if-you-can!"

Brier's relief was short-lived, however; when she turned back to her small command, the Knorth was gone.

She might have asked herself, *where?* Only a drainpipe to the roof broke that blank expanse of discolored brick. Instead, all she could think was that the girl had bolted. Knorth or Caineron, all Highborn were alike after all.

However, nothing her superiors did diminished her own responsibility. She must get these cadets safely away.

At the alley's mouth they turned left—toward the relative safety of Higron's gigglers, Brier thought. But soon afterward she realized that she had gotten turned completely around when they came to a wall with the sound of swift water beyond it. Left again and here was the eastern bridge leading to Caldane's compound.

"Well, it isn't exactly the back door," said the Knorth, breathless at her elbow, "but I take it we can still reach the citadel by this route. You didn't think I'd run out, did you? Sweet Trinity. You did. Cadet, listen: you can expect some fairly strange behavior from me, off and on, but never that. Understand?"

The Kendar simply stared at her.

"Right," said Jame. "I'll just have to prove myself as we go, won't I?"

And she would, she swore to herself, just as she had to Marc—but not by telling this wooden-faced cadet how she had spent the last half hour scrambling about on the roof tops with a death banner slung across her back, playing hare-and-hounds for the third time that week.

"After you," she said, indicating the bridge with a sweep of her hand.

Water plunged under the span, snow-fed, raging between the close-set walls of the two compounds. The noise made ears ring. On the far side, after they had slipped through Caldane's gate and closed it behind them against the river's roar, Jame repeated the question which she had tried to ask half way across.

"You must have lived in this quarter when you served at Restormir. How well d'they know you here?"

"Well enough," said the cadet shortly. "It can't be helped." She gave Jame a sharp look. "How did you know I'd done a home tour?"

"I, er, must have heard it somewhere," Jame said, embarrassed.

In fact, she had overheard it from inside the Highlord's tent.

"*Ancestors know what that Kendar did to make Caldane so angry,*" Torisen had said and paused—in question, Jame had thought.

The quality of Harn's silence in response, however, had said as plainly as words, *There are some things Highborn shouldn't ask.*

"Odd that there's no guard here," she said, hastily changing the topic and backing up for a look at the sentry box perched over the gate.

Her foot hit a trip-wire. She went over backward, nearly landing on Jorin, who sprang aside with an affronted exclamation. Affront turned to a terrified squawk at a tremendous crash. Shards of crockery flew out of the shadows.

"Clumsy lot, you cadets," said a calm voice overhead.

A gray-haired man sat on the edge of the box. Propped against its corner support, legs dangling, he looked more like a discarded puppet than the veteran randon officer which his token scarf declared him to be.

"Well, well," he said, smiling down at the big Kendar. "Welcome back to Restormir, Brier Iron-thorn."

Brier answered in a language which Jame didn't understand, but the man interrupted her.

"Use common Kens, child," he said gently. "You don't have a right to Caineron battle-speech anymore."

"As you say, Randon Quick-foot. Are you going to raise the guard?"

"I just did, or tried to," he said, with a curious roll of his head toward the makeshift alarm. "Why are you here?"

"Private business, ran. Nothing that should endanger the Caineron or Restormir, as far as I can see."

She wouldn't have come, Jame realized, if she had thought that it did. It wasn't easy, after all, to change the allegiance of generations.

"Fair enough," said Randon Quick-foot. "You're hardly the one for whom the watch was set, anyway. Most of our people are out chasing reports of Merikit at large in the valley. No one here has forgotten Kithorn."

"That was our mission too, randon, out of Tentir. We were about to call it off due to serious weirding."

"Weirding." His eyes flickered in his slack face. "Not that too. Still, our randon can go to earth, the Merikit way. Away from Restormir, their wits should at least be clear enough for that."

"Yes, randon. Without help."

The officer's mouth twisted in acknowledgment of some point which Jame didn't catch. "True, child, true. 'Help' can be costly. Advice is cheaper, so I'll offer you that, for old time's sake: whatever your business, stay out of M'lord's way. He's initiating a randon candidate tonight."

"I...see. Good-bye, Ran Quick-foot, and thank you."

"That was quite a crash," said Jame as they went on. "Why aren't we up to our necks in guards by now—and what was wrong with your friend?"

"My friend, lady? Yes, I suppose he was. He's been chewing black-root. A bit of it keeps the head clear. More leads to progressive paralysis, like a series of self-induced strokes. Five days of it...At best, he'll never be quick-footed again."

"And that's what's happening to randon all over this compound tonight? For a toad like Caldane?"

"No, lady. For the same reasons you invoked earlier: honor and obligation."

One of the cadets gave a startled exclamation, and Jame turned quickly to find a stranger in their midst. By her clothes, she was a common Kendar, perhaps a baker. She had come up behind the squad and then, because her pace was faster, walked straight into their ranks. Eyes wide but unseeing, she passed between Jame and Brier. They stared after her. She was walking on her toes, as if lifted by the scruff of the neck and hauled forward.

More sleepwalkers overtook and bore them along, as if caught in waters running rapidly downhill. All flowed into Restormir's main square. The large, open space was already full of people—men, women, and children—moving in unison as if to the steps of some strange dance. If one turned, all did; if another gestured, a thousand hands followed suit. Expressions crossed their sleeping faces like windflaws over water: anger, arrogance, and something very like fear. Some were mouthing words, others mumbling them, so that a low murmur filled the square from side to side.

"Wait here," whispered the Knorth.

Before Brier could stop her, she had slipped into the crowd and begun to winnow through it, apparently in search of the most articulate sleep-talker. No one paid any attention to her. Nonetheless, the walkers were becoming more agitated. Now it looked as if each one of them was circling something, or someone. The Knorth walked backward in front of a large Kendar, face to face, perhaps the better to hear him. A thousand hands swung in a sudden, vicious slap, but only one struck home.

Brier swore. Ducking into the crowd, she snatched the Highborn out from under the Kendar's feet while he and a thousand others went on kicking thin air. Back on the square's edge, she propped her against a wall.

"Did you hear that cry?" the latter asked, dazed.

"No, lady. You didn't make a sound." Brier's attention sharpened. "You're bleeding. Healer...."

"No!" The Knorth straightened, hastily drawing a sleeve across her face. "Don't fuss. I'm all right."

In the square, the sleepers stumbled and for a moment fought to regain their balance, again on tiptoe. The sight of all those windmilling arms would have been funny, if not for the sudden terror on their faces.

"It's never been this bad before," Brier muttered. "Never. What in Perimal's name is M'lord drinking?"

"It may be as much a matter of what he drank," said the Knorth under her breath. "*Damn.* C'mon, then."

III

Jame was still silently cursing herself as they left the square. It seemed that the bond between lord and Kendar was so cruelly tight here that those poor people, reduced to near stupor by Caldane's excesses, were unconsciously mirroring his actions and mumbling his thoughts. If so, under all his bully bluster Caldane was scared sick about something. And he was taking it out on that poor bastard whose cry she had so distinctly heard, if no one else had. It was Graykin whom Caldane was abusing, she was almost certain…because he couldn't get his hands on the Southron's new mistress? Could all this somehow be the result of that little trick which she had played on Caldane in his tent at the Cataracts?

They were drawing near the two arms of the river that surrounded the castle mound like a moat. More Kendar drifted past them, but no one tried again to raise the alarm. Two randon sprawled at the gateposts of the moat bridge. One watched them approach but didn't speak, perhaps because she no longer could. The other was dead. Brier saluted both.

"This way," she said, and led her small command over the bridge and around to a lesser door which opened directly into the mound.

Inside, they descended a ramp of weeping stone, lined with doors. The dank, mildewed air made Jame's nose twitch and Jorin sneeze. At its foot the decline sank into black water, lapping against weed-crusted lintels.

"Here," said the Kendar, and put her shoulder to the last unsubmerged door.

The shriek of its rusted hinges made Jame flinch, but no guard appeared. Beyond, a corridor lined with more stout doors stretched out ahead of them, its far end curving out of sight. The Kendar looked at Jame expectantly. All she remembered from her dream about Graykin's prison, though, was this stink of decay and Caldane's voice echoing off stone walls.

There was no sound of M'lord now, as surely there would be if he were still kicking Graykin around a cell. Had she been wrong, or were they both somewhere else?

"We'll have to search," she said. "How big is this place?"

"On this level, perhaps two hundred cells, opening off a series of concentric corridors like this one. You pass from one hall to the next through short passageways which double as guardrooms. There are at least a dozen levels above this, extending up into the mound. Below, who knows."

Oh, lord. "We'll have to separate, then."

"Lady, are you sure?"

Jame sighed. "Hardly ever, about anything."

But she didn't call off the hunt, to the cadets' delight and their commander's disgust. The latter sent the former off in pairs, herself going with Rue. That left the two Highborn. Kindrie hadn't spoken since his encounter with the bogles. Jame wondered if he was having second thoughts—much good they would do anyone now.

Jorin was snuffing around the corridor. Unfortunately, he had never met Graykin, nor did Jame still have any of the spy's clothes. But she remembered their slightly sour smell. The ounce sneezed twice, then trotted off down the hall. She followed, Kindrie trailing after her.

They went down one curving hall after another, cutting between them by way of the numbered doors, moving toward the core. The whole dungeon seemed to be empty. Caldane must have cleaned it out the previous winter and not yet gotten around to restocking it with prisoners or guards. Cadets began to call back and forth to each other, as if this were all a game. Brier Iron-thorn must be having a fit. But they were out of Jame's way for the moment, which was what she had intended in splitting them up. The fewer to witness her first meeting with Graykin, the better.

However, the cell to which Jorin led them was empty.

Damnation, Jame thought, standing in the middle of it. Now what?

Of course, there was that thread of contact which had first warned her, back in Gothregor, that her servant was in trouble. She hadn't touched it since. After all, sharing awareness with Jorin was one thing, but with this scruffy little half-breed whom she barely knew? Ugh.

Don't be so damn squeamish, she told herself sharply. *Why did you come, if not to rescue him?* The image of Graykin's thin face rose in her mind's eye. *Where are you?* she silently asked it. *What do you see? What do you feel?*

Pain. Intense, obscene, wrenching at shoulders as though to tear the flesh off of them, dragging the skin up around the throat...Hard to breathe. Underfoot, nothing, down and down and down...But to the side, two faces staring, a young Kendar in the background, sick-eyed, eclipsed by Caineron's full moon gloat:

"*...told you I would think of something special. Now dance, puppet, dance....*

Oh god, his fat hands on the wires, jerking them....

Far below, down in the dungeons among the rats, someone screamed.

Jame woke to the echo, cracking off the stonewalls around her. She was curled up in a ball on the floor. Her throat hurt.

Kindrie and Jorin had backed away from her into the far corner.

"Backlash," said the healer hoarsely. "Whoever this man is, he's bound to you, isn't he? *Isn't he?*"

Before she could answer, Brier Iron-thorn came swiftly into the cell, very large and controlled, prepared to be very dangerous. The sheer force of her presence brought Jame lurching to her feet.

"S-scream?" she stammered, in response to the Kendar's sharp question. "What scream? Oh"—remembering the echoes—"*that* scream."

Now she's going to think I'm a fool, as well as mad. But Graykin...

"He's not here anymore," she said, not very coherently. "Caldane has him up in the tower."

A buzz of excitement rose from the hall, where more cadets had arrived in time to overheard her.

"I *can't* take you up there," said Jame desperately. "Any of you. This isn't hide-and-seek in the dark anymore. This is Highborn against Kendar...and if these innocents don't know what that means, Brier Iron-thorn, I'll bet my boots you do. Think! Torisen doesn't know where we are. If Caldane gets his hands on any of us, he can do anything he wants, and get away with it!"

"Are you going on, lady?"

"I have to."

"Then so do we."

Jame ran a distraught hand through her hair, forgetting that it was under a cap. "My brother is going to skin us all. You know that, don't you? Oh, hell. Caldane will probably beat him to it, anyway."

IV

The heart of Restormir proved to be hollow. At the bottom were the flooded levels of the dungeon, a black, noisome well in which floated debris and drowned rats. The innermost of the concentric halls overlooked it, ring on ring of them connected by iron stairs, extending upward to the top of the mound.

The Knorth raiders climbed out of the prison pit as though into a different although no less deserted world, over a stained alabaster rim into a court paved with white marble across which dried leaves rattled. All around reared up the inner walls of Caldane's tower keep. On the court level, tall glass doors opened into reception halls, in whose dusty depths a wealth of mirrors and diamantine panels gave back the soft glow of stolen sunlight.

Jame caught her breath. For a moment, she had thought that the rooms were full of motionless giants. Now, however, she saw that they were gilded statues, multiplied by reflection. Portly figures, arrogant faces...they all looked like Caldane, larger than life, striking various heroic poses.

Snatches of discordant music and laughter echoed hollowly down the throat of the tower. The man himself was above in the Crown—carousing with how many of his kin? The Caineron was the largest house in the Kencyrath, and Caldane easily the most prolific lord. Aside from his numerous progeny, there must be several hundred Caineron Highborn, not that all lived at Restormir, much less in this tower. Of those who did, hopefully many besides Tiggeri had elected to stay in Kothifir.

Shouts above, and a jeering chant: "Go, go, go...!"

A golden shower rained down, mostly into the pit but some spattering the rim and the last cadet over it. He and the others hastily drew back. Either someone had a phenomenal bladder, Jame thought, or how much water, from what height, equaled how many Caineron? No equation came to mind.

The cadets stared upward, eyes widening with their own calculations.

Ancestors be praised, thought Jame. *Now they understand.*

As if in answer, their gaze returned expectantly to her. Innocents these children might be, but not cowards.

Their commander had been watching her throughout, stone-faced as if to say: *This madness begins and ends with you.*

True, but not very helpful.

A regal stair swept up around the inner walls, fit for the ascension of kings although strewn with a winter's dirt. Jame began to climb, Jorin bouncing on ahead, the others following close behind.

Balconies studded the walls seemingly at random, decked with winter-worn finery—here a torn banner of silver and gold, there cat bone chimes clattering in the errant breeze. Inside, one glimpsed quarters left in disarray, presumably, by the Cainerons' hasty departure for the Cataracts the previous winter. Overhead, the Crown cantilevered out in nine tiers around the top of the shaft, leaving some twenty feet at the center open to the night sky. Stars shone there, eclipsed by small, swift shapes and one larger than they, which hung slowly swaying.

Jame was leaning over the balustrade, trying to see what the latter was, when a harsh sound made her turn quickly. One of the cadets had doubled up on the steps, down which he would have surely rolled if Brier Iron-thorn hadn't stopped him.

"Height-sickness," said the Kendar tersely, steadying the boy.

For a moment, Jame was puzzled. A hundred feet to the courtyard, as much again to the floor of the pit…. Not bad. Then again, the only height that bothered her was from the back of a tall horse. Kendar, however, were prone to acrophobia.

So was Caldane.

"Why would a man afraid of heights live at the top of a tower?" she wondered out-loud.

"M'lord? If he thought that fear was common knowledge, he'd spit blood. Besides, the Crown was his father's work."

Of course, thought Jame. No one as vain as Caldane would admit any weakness, to others or to himself—nor, from what she had heard, would the Caineron Matriarch let him fall short of his father's measure.

Then she recoiled. Blackness like a piece of flapping cloth had swooped in front of her face and hovered there on furry wings. Wide, quizzical eyes in a velvet fox-mask; delicate, cupped ears; a long, flat brush...

"*Quipp?*" said the foxkin, and dove inside her jacket.

"Healer, get down here," Iron-thorn said, impatient, preoccupied; then, as an afterthought: "Ignore it, lady. It's harmless."

Easy for her to say. Jame wriggled, trying to reach the furry body as it clambered up the curve of her ribs toward the spine.

Kindrie bent over the cadet.

"Can you help him?"

"*Quipp!*" said the foxkin in Jame's ear, and scuttled back down her collar.

"With the nausea, yes; not with the vertigo. His entire soul-scape is reeling." The healer himself suddenly staggered, his bare foot sliding off the step. The Kendar caught his arm.

"Don't tell me it's contagious," said Jame sarcastically, but she was perplexed: a Shanir healer should draw more stability than that from his own soul-image.

Ah. The foxkin had gotten into her *d'hen* sleeve—the full left one, fortunately. She shook it gingerly. A darkness with luminous eyes gathered at the cuff, then shot off. Jorin nearly sprang over the balustrade after it.

"Life out here is just too exciting," said Jame. "Let's go inside."

They had almost run out of staircase, anyway. It ended in
a landing under the first of the nine tiers, with a door opening
into what had been the old keep's ramparts. Now, off the
main corridor, the level was divided into tiny rooms which
probably housed the Crown's Kendar servants. If so, however, none were there now.

Feet tramped overhead. Objects thudded. Then there
was a crash, an oath, and a sound like the spring migration of
the bison, fading into the distance.

"What on earth is above us?" Jame asked.

"Kitchens," said ten-commander and healer simultaneously.

"I forgot that you both were here before. How well d'you
know the layout?"

"Not very…" they began, and stopped short, eyeing each
other warily.

"M'lord insisted that I stay within earshot," said Kindrie.

"And I was only crown-side once, lady." The bronze planes
of the Kendar's face seemed to clamp shut on the words.

Whatever happened between her and Caldane, happened there,
Jame thought, warning herself, *That's her business. Just this once,
mind your own.*

They found a minor flight of stairs and mounted it cautiously.

The room into which they emerged was indeed a kitchen,
given over primarily to stewing. Fireplaces lined the walls, each
with a waist-high, three-legged cauldron sitting in it. The nearest
was full of water, in which bobbed whole carrots, discolored pars-
nips, and onions still in their outer skins. Other pots and pans
hung from the low rafters, except for those piled dirty on the floor.
Parsley, figs, and raisins were strewn about an overturned chop-
ping block. Grapes rolled underfoot. The strong licorice smell of
half-crushed anise and fennel rose from a mortar.

"Hotchpotch, or an attempt at it," said Jame, drawing on
memories of the kitchen at the Res aB'tyrr, and remembering
that she hadn't eaten all day. This broth really needed some
meat, though—mutton, or pheasant, or chicken.

From out in the hall came a rapidly approaching storm of feet, cries, and clucking. A white hen ran past the door, closely pursued by a dozen Highborn men in their finest if rather soiled clothes, brandishing knives, cleavers, and slotted spoons. No one glanced into the stewry—fortunately, because the sight and sound of them had frozen the cadets open-mouthed where they stood. Peering cautiously around the door's edge, Jame saw the pursuit plunge off down the curving hall, on its second lap of the tower. From somewhere above came a muffled chant:

"*Food, food, food...!*"

Then Jame realized that the door opposite had opened and someone was leaning out of it, just as she was from hers, to stare after the vanishing hunt. A girl, maybe sixteen, wearing a tight, pearl-strewn bodice and a flame-colored skirt....

Behind masks, their eyes met.

"Why, lady!" the younger Highborn gasped.

Jame plunged across the corridor and shoved the girl back into what proved to be a pantry.

"Stay!" she snapped over her shoulder at the startled Kendar and slammed the door in their faces.

Surrounded by strings of onions, garlic, and mandrake, she faced this young Highborn whom she had first met in the royal apartments of a Karkinoran palace, the nominal consort of its prince.

"Well, Lyra. Now what?"

Caldane's daughter stared at her. "It *is* you! Oh, how splendid! Maybe now things will start happening again!"

"'Things'? *What* 'things'?"

"*Anything!* It's been so dull here, since Karkinaroth and the Cataracts. We did have fun on that barge ride in between, didn't we?"

"You did, anyway," said Jame, remembering their flight after the prince's death and the collapse of his palace. She had never considered what effect all that excitement might have had on a girl like Lyra, whom she had always thought the model of filial obedience, and not really bright besides.

"Oh, yes!"—with great enthusiasm, plunging immediately to despair—"but just look at me now, reduced to scrounging food like a…a menial! At the palace, I at least had Gricki to fetch for me. And that's another thing! If that wretched Southron has done something wrong, *I* should punish him, not Father. He was *my* servant, after all. It isn't fair!"

"Er…" said Jame. "Did you know that Graykin is in my service now?"

"Oh, *that's* all right, then," said Lyra, beaming at her. "We're sisters, or as good as. In that case, *you* should be punishing him."

"I've got to find him first."

"He's up in Father's private quarters." Her expression changed suddenly. "I heard him scream. No one should have to scream like that. Come on. I'll take you to him."

"Well, I'll be damned. That is, er, splendid. Lead on."

She threw open the door. The cadets jumped back, looking startled, curious, and vaguely disappointed. They had, she realized, been expecting a royal catfight. She introduced Lyra to them but not to Brier Iron-thorn, whose expression stopped her. Clearly, Caineron foibles didn't amuse the big Kendar.

Blast the woman, Jame thought. *She turns everything into a test, and I keep failing.*

"*Awk!*" said the hen, and dodged between her feet into the pantry.

"Stop!" cried the pursuing Highborn, rounding the hall's curve.

"Inside!" hissed Lyra.

The Knorth all piled into the pantry, slammed the door shut, and tipped a flour bin over in front of it. Fists beat on its outer panels. From the hall rose a vengeful, hungry cry:

"Give us back our chicken!"

Too drunk to realize what they've seen, Jame thought, backing away from the door. *That's something, anyway*—she turned to met Iron-thorn's stony look—*but not enough.*

"Back here!" Lyra called.

She had retreated to the far wall and now ducked out of sight through a low door, concealed behind a massive bin mounted on rollers. Jame and Jorin followed, emerging in a dark, intramural passage.

"Gran told me about this," Lyra whispered with a giggle. "Father has no idea it's here."

The cadets entered hastily, shoving Kindrie in ahead of them. Their officers, Ten and Five, pulled the bin back over the entrance just as the outer door gave way. They heard confusion beyond the wall, a protesting squawk, and the sound of triumphant retreat.

Lyra tugged Jame's sleeve. "This way."

V

It was very dark between the walls of Restormir, with air as stale as the husks of memory. Sometimes the passage expanded as though into unseen rooms; sometimes it contracted so that one must pass along it edgewise, scraping. The stone brain within that proud Crown might have been half consumed by earwigs, so full of tunnels and blind pockets did it seem.

Jame spat out a clot of spider web, with the distinct impression that she had swallowed its occupant. Forgetting the extra width of Aerulan's banner across her back, she had almost gotten stuck more than once. All she could see was the slightly blacker patch which, presumably, was Lyra, rustling ahead of her. The patch rose. A moment later her foot hit a step. She climbed the invisible stair after her guide, the others on her heels.

Six more flights, almost to the top of the Crown.

From ahead, ever closer, came a stone-muffled chant: "FOOD, *food*, FOOD!" until the walls seemed to vibrate with it. Opening off the stair shaft was a sort of blind gallery, broached with many peepholes through which spears of red light lanced. Below lay Caldane's great hall.

It was two tiers high, its roof supported by stone columns carved in the likeness of tree trunks. Fireplaces roared down one side, making the air before them ripple with heat and the cold walls sweat. Opposite, tall, arched windows stood open to the darkness of the shaft. Between, a hundred Highborn men sat at table, chanting and banging flagons.

"*Food*, FOOD, *FOOD!*"

Empty plates bounced. So did the heads of those who had passed out.

Masked, skirted figures ran between the long boards, carrying wine ewers with which they tried to keep full the flailing cups—not women but young, Highborn boys, Jame saw, as one was suddenly tripped and jerked beneath a table. The men on either side leaned drunkenly down to watch. Above the salt, Caldane's six established sons roared approval. Down in the compounds, their followers must be shouting themselves bloody raw.

All this for one pot of inedible soup, Jame thought. *Maybe that will teach Caldane not to incapacitate his entire Kendar staff.*

—or maybe not: M'lord was not the sort to admit mistakes, much less learn from them.

The man himself lounged in a golden chair on a dais at the upper end of the hall, wrapped in a peacock-blue robe, negligently holding a wine glass. Unlike his flushed, sweating followers, he looked sleek and smug. Sated. Now and again, he glanced out the windows, at something which Jame couldn't see. She recognized that cream-fed smirk, though. It had been on his fat face when he had held her captive in his tent at the Cataracts, and in Kallystine's voice after M'lady had slapped her.

Kindrie had been watching through a different hole. When he turned toward Jame, the spot of light moving from faded eye to pale cheek to white hair, she wondered if he had also seen such a smile, that night at Tentir.

"Are we too late?" he asked in a husky voice, and she knew that he had.

This time, Graykin's pain come to her muted through barriers warily half raised. Worse, though, was that choking hold on her/his throat, through which breath barely wheezed.

"He isn't dead," she said, gulping air, realizing that even so she might not have answered the healer's question.

They climbed again, up to the ninth tier. At the stair's head, Lyra cautiously opened a panel and slipped through. A moment later, she had swung it wide and was beckoning them into Lord Caineron's private quarters.

Jame stopped short on the threshold. For a moment, she was back in her room at Gothregor, staring at her fragmented features in a broken mirror. But these mirrors were whole and the face reflected in them visored, retreating. From behind came a muffled exclamation as her booted heel came down on Kindrie's bare toes.

This is ridiculous, she thought, and entered.

Easy to see where Kallystine had gotten the idea for her chambers at Gothregor, pale reflection that they were of this mirrored wilderness where wall reflected wall and room melted into room. Rich hangings and curious statuary marched off in all directions, over inlaid floors strewn ankle deep with rare furs. A haze of incense drifted under the low, mirrored ceiling. In the midst of such bewildering opulence floated the cadets' faces, seen from every angle as they stared about them.

"We mustn't separate," Jame said, and found that she spoke to reflections.

Had Lyra led them into a trap? Did Caldane know reflective magic? There was a bricked-up house in Tai-tastigon where the owner's first wife had wandered inside one mirror after another for twenty years, searching for the reflection of an open door…

Then Jame looked again, harder. Since when had she been so tall, so busty? All the mirrors were subtly distorted. Caldane *did* practice magic, but only to reshape his own portly image. Between these flattering glasses and those heroic statues in the reception halls below, perhaps he had well and truly convinced himself that illusion was truth.

"Here I am." "Where are you?" reflected faces whispered, turning to look in the wrong direction, echo answering echo. "Five? Ten?"

Iron-thorn's dark visage and the Shanir's pallor moved silently among the silvered planes, caught for a moment and then gone.

"Gricki?" Lyra's light voice called off in the distance. "Gricki!"

The floor vibrated with the clamor from the hall below, muted by stone and fur. Mirrors seemed to ripple in their frames. So very hot and close….

Statuary like the death-molds of men and women, cruelly al-
tered; wolver pelts and mock Arrin-ken; a two-headed ape, stuffed;
a great green parrot nailed to its perch, alive; potbellied bronze
burners, belching clouds of incense to make the mind reel; Caldane's
smell of rich perfume underlain with stale sweat, to make the stom-
ach seethe...

A vast bed, and under its counterpane, face covered, a still
form.

"G-Graykin?"

But no. What strange figure was this, its body laid open
and velvet coils of intestine spilling out, liver and lights strewn
about the bed like stuffed toys? A doll, designed to be nightly
disemboweled...and it had her face.

Jame threw the cover back over it.

Standing almost on her foot, Jorin sniffed and cowered.
She smelled it too: the faint stench of burned flesh. The ounce
slinking unhappily on her heels, she followed her nose.

Ahead, she thought she saw Graykin's face, oddly stiff
and distorted. Another damned reflection, but this time it was
that of a death banner, which she tracked from mirror to mirror back to a small room illuminated like a shrine by innumerable candles. Brier Iron-thorn stood staring at the tapestry,
oblivious to the overturned incense pots at her feet whose hot
coals were singeing the pelts of mottled leather which covered the floor.

"Genjar," she said, without turning.

Jame regarded that sharp face, caught forever by Kendar
weavers in a sneer which the wavering smoke turned almost
into a snarl. So this was Caldane's favorite son, who had led
the Southern Host to slaughter at Urakarn, where a young
Torisen had been taken prisoner and tortured. Hadn't there
been some mystery about Genjar's death afterward?

"A damned strange way to commit suicide," she had heard somebody say.

Caldane had never forgiven Tori, although for what, exactly, no one seemed to know.

Iron-thorn was staring at the tapestry face with that particular woodenness which, for her, indicated strong emotion.

"Surely you were too young to have served at Urakarn," Jame said involuntarily.

"I was. My mother wasn't. She died escaping."

With that, the Kendar turned abruptly on her heel and stalked away.

Oh, lord. What have I put my foot in now? Jame wondered.

The pelts still smoldered in spots, between blue and black markings which looked almost deliberate. Jame had no objection to burning Caldane's roof over his head, except that she was under it too. She beat out the coals with gloved hands. The hides hadn't been entirely scraped bare, as she had thought at first. Each still had a mop of black, braided hair....

Jame rose abruptly and backed to the door where Jorin waited, having refused to enter. She had been standing on the flayed, tattooed skins of Merikit hill men.

Outside, the stink of burning grew stronger.

"Here!" Lyra was calling. "Here! Oh, hurry!"

Jame arrived last, still following her nose, to find her way blocked by the broad backs of the cadets. Water-flowing between them, she emerged in the cooler air of a balcony overhanging the shaft. To one side was a small furnace, sullenly aglow, in a litter of tools, bits of wire, and hooks. Several feet away, a Kendar stood on the very edge of the abyss, looking down. In his hand, forgotten, he held an awl from which wisps of rank smoke still rose.

"Well, candidate," said Brier Iron-thorn.

The man looked up. He was very young, hardly more than a boy, and would have been handsome if not for his haggard face and bloodshot eyes.

"Well, cadet," he said, with a rictus smile. "Is Tentir worth M'lord's price?"

"I refused to pay."

He blinked, refocusing. "So you did," with a sneer that didn't quite stick. "Went the soft way through the little

High-lord, didn't you? Solved Honor's Paradox by turning your back on it." He glanced again over the edge and swayed, gulping.

Not just height-sickness, Jame thought, going forward a step, stopped by Iron-thorn's back-flung, restraining hand. *A grisly hangover. Caldane, you son of a…*

"It *is* a paradox, isn't it?" the boy said, with a cracked laugh. "Where does obedience end and personal honor begin? Nowhere, M'lord wanted me to say. Obedience *is* honor. Then he ordered me to do *that.*" He gestured helplessly toward the shaft, realized that he still held the awl, and threw it away. "I was drunk. I did his bidding. And it broke the bond between us. No more lord. No more honor."

"And now?"

"Why," he said, again with that terrible smile. "I redeem honor, of course. I was only waiting for a witness."

With that, he stepped over the edge and fell without a sound.

"My God!" said Jame, and started forward; but Brier stood in her way.

"Better not to look, lady."

Jame slipped around her. "Honestly, Ten, I probably have a better head for heights than you do…

From below, the figure hanging in the shaft had seemed only a blot against the stars. From here above, it appeared violently foreshortened, the thin, naked body dwindling to invisible feet, the whole swaying fish-pale in the light spilling from Caldane's hall. Peaks rose from each shoulder where hooks took the body's weight, stretching the skin upward. More flesh hooks pierced ears, and wrists, and knees, to make the puppet dance. Oh, Graykin….

Jame struggled to breathe, to stay calm. *It won't help to flare. Caldane is right below us, looking out his window at his toy, smiling—it won't help anyone if I flare…*

Someone touched her shoulder. She felt the berserker rage leap down her nerve-ends, through flesh and fabric, lightning in search of the ground. In its sudden glare, to her amazement, she saw the white flowers of the tapestry which hung outside Gothregor's secret garden. The thunderclap made her gasp, but it cleared her head. The rage was gone. She hadn't moved, but Kindrie had been hurled backward into the cadets, two of whom he had knocked down. His white hair stood on end. Ball lightning rolled off his shoulders like hail to bounce crackling on the floor.

"I did warn you, priest," she said, shaken.

"How many casualties d'you want up here?" demanded Iron-thorn. "Behave, lady."

"Y-yes, ran. B-but my friend, he's choking."

A boom had been swung out over the shaft and lowered, with a makeshift puppeteer's crosspiece fixed to it. The two support wires were secured to the former. Control wires ran up through the latter, back ready for the puppet-master's hands. Cadets raised the boom and gingerly swung the dangling figure back over the balcony, wincing with every jolt for fear that it would tear loose. There was little blood: the hooks, inserted red hot, had finished the cauterizing begun by the heated awl. Nor need they have worried about ripping flesh: muscle as well as skin had been pierced. But between shock and near-strangulation by his own drawn-up skin, the Southron was in uncertain shape.

"Help him!" Jame said to Kindrie.

The healer had been hanging back, random sparks still snapping in his hair. "I'm not sure I can," he said unhappily. "He looks enough like a Caineron to be Genjar's younger brother— but he isn't pure Kencyr, is he?"

"He's a Kencyr-Southron half-breed," Lyra chimed in. "His name is Gricki."

"'Gricki,'" muttered Brier, translating the Southron word: "'filth.' D'you mean we've gone through all this for some Southland's mongrel?"

The Knorth shot her an impatient look. "We can't pick and choose with whom to keep faith."

Brier blinked. A Caineron would have laughed at such a
naive statement: there was always some way consonant with
honor to avoid such inconveniences. And yet…and yet…

Values, Caineron and Knorth, shifted under her feet until
with a jolt she landed on something solid: *Keep faith.*

Yes. Perhaps she could make a stand on that.

"Of course I don't object to his bloodlines," Kindrie was
saying to Jame. "Who am I, to do that? But I've never dealt
with a non-Kencyr's soul-image before, assuming he has one.
A-and besides…" He gulped, looking suddenly both miserable and desperate. "L-Lord Ishtier has barred me from my
own. Just now the door behind the tapestry… You almost
smashed through it, almost got me back into my garden. C-
Can't you try again? Please?"

"You mean you can't heal anyone? But you helped that
cadet on the stair!"

"A bit. As much as I dared. Don't you see? I-I can't draw
on my own soul for strength, or retreat into it to heal myself."

"Sweet Trinity," said Jame, blankly.

Back at Wilden, he had told her how the Randir Matriarch
had bartered that knowledge to Ishtier. She should have realized that the priest had made use of it. Instead, she had brought
the healer into this danger blithely assuming that he was, es-
sentially, indestructible. And he had come without complaint,
knowing that he wasn't. Who, therefore, had kept faith with
whom? Just the same, should she try to help him as he asked?
Did she dare?

"I can't," she said, helplessly. "The last person you
should consort with just now is someone who keeps knocking you across rooms by sheer, bloody reflex. Next time, it
will probably be through a wall. Just do what you can, as
quickly as possible. Any minute now, M'lord is going to
miss his plaything."

"We're lucky he didn't see that boy fall," she said in an
undertone to Brier Iron-thorn, as Kindrie gingerly bent over
his charge.

"He was probably expecting it."

"Ugh. Trust Caldane to test Honor's Paradox with the moral equivalent of a meat axe. Does he put all randon candidates through ordeals like this?"

"Only the best—to prove their loyalty to him, he says. And to see how strong their stomachs are. 'That boy' failed. Sometimes, doing counts less than living with the consequences."

Jame regarded her curiously. "If he had given you such an order, cadet, would you have obeyed?"

Green eyes turned to her, malachite set in ironwood.

"That," said the Kendar, "was not my test."

Behind them, someone gave a startled exclamation. They turned in time to see a Caineron Highborn bolt back through the apartment, throwing aside the jeweled slippers which he had apparently been sent to fetch.

"Yours," Ten snapped at five, and was off in pursuit faster than seemed possible for someone so big.

"Right," said Vant with satisfaction, assuming command. "Up gear, Kennies. We're going."

"Where?" Jame asked.

The other cadets hesitated, obviously feeling that this was a good question.

"Er..." said Vant, not looking at her. "Somebody, wrap that Southie up in something."

"Who?" demanded Rue, pugnacious. "In what?"

"*Anything*, dammit! Here." He tore down a silken hanging and threw it at her.

Jame helped bundle up her unconscious servant. He looked awful, marked not only with his fresh injuries but with the blackened eyes and broken teeth of a previous beating, while his bruised ribs stood out like those of a half-starved dog. A hard winter he must have had of it.

"Father will kill me!" Lyra wailed.

"Calm down!" said Jame over her shoulder. "You're probably the only one of us that he won't."

"He will, he will! Listen, they're on the stair! Gran, help!"

With that, she snatched up her hem, betraying no underskirt whatsoever, and fled down the long balcony.

"Follow her!" Jame snapped at the others.

"Er…" said Vant again, to the air above her head. "That isn't such a good idea, lady."

Jame sat back on her heels, regarding him. He was trying to put her in her place, as he saw it, as tactfully as he knew how. She remembered the battle of wills between Kallystine and her captain, Highborn power against randon discipline. "Perhaps your ten-commander could override me," she said, "but not you. Ever. Now go."

Not waiting to see if he obeyed, not needing to, she and Jorin went in search of Brier Iron-thorn, whom they found at the head of the main stairs, outrun by the fleeing Highborn. Nonetheless, Lyra had been premature: no one was yet on the steps. Nearby, multiple reflections gave back the image of the secret passage, open for a hasty exit. The Kendar glanced at her, then past, impatiently, for the cadets.

"I sent them after Lyra," said Jame. "She's run back to Gran—whoever *that* is—so there's another way out of here—presumably."

No need to be told that she had made a mistake.

Brier turned back to the stair, grim-faced. *Trust a Highborn to muck up.* "Then, lady, you had better go with them."

"You're drunk!" said someone at the foot of steps.

"I tell you, I saw them!"

"Didn't." "Did." "Didn't!" "*Did!*"

Now the speakers were coming up, followed by a crowd loudly making bets.

"*Go,*" said the Kendar, with such force that Jame fell back a step, treading on Jorin's toes.

Trinity, but that was power, and in one who had barely begun her training. The feeling almost overwhelmed Jame that it *wasn't* her place to interfere in randon affairs. Tori would hardly think so. Neither would any other Highborn whom she had ever met. But Marc would understand. Very well: If she couldn't coerce, she would blackmail.

"I won't leave," she said, "without you."

Brier gave the Highborn a hard look. She had been prepared to fall into Caldane's hands herself to delay pursuit, to keep faith with her new lord—a bitter but simple choice. A premonition touched her now, though, regarding her lord's sister, that nothing from now on would be so straightforward. Stepping back, she closed the panel leading to the hidden stair.

After you, the ironic sweep of her hand said.

They went quickly back through Caldane's quarters, drunken voices slurring on their heels. At the end of the balcony, a stair spiraled upward. They climbed, petals drifting down the open well to meet them.

VI

The others waited for them on top of the Crown. A grove of dwarf cherry trees hung with lanterns sheltered them to one side. On the other gaped the mouth of the shaft. Foxkin rode its feverish exhalation, light from the hall striking blue on the undersides of their black wings. Drunken argument sounded on the balcony below, then receded.

Jame sighed with relief. Turning, she found an anxious Kindrie at her elbow.

"We shouldn't be here," he said urgently to her in a low voice. "Can't you feel it? This is women's land."

He was shivering—from the cool air, perhaps, after the overheated rooms below, or from the memory of Wilden halls under their matriarch's cold hand.

"Huh," said Jame with a shudder of her own, remembering Gothregor. "Forbidden territory. At least no man will think of this as a hiding place. With luck, they'll decide that their friend really was drunk. We've only got to wait, then sneak back down by the secret stair."

"Here you are at last!" cried Lyra happily, sweeping down on them through a storm of cherry blossoms. "Gran wants to see you!"

Oh, lord. After a winter of Kallystine, Jame was as well acquainted with the Caineron ladies as she ever wanted to be. Moreover, mask aside, she was hardly dressed for a social call. But go she must, or "Gran" might raise the alarm through sheer pique.

Brier Iron-thorn was regarding her without expression, perhaps remembering how she had slipped away earlier to confer with Lyra.

"Oh, all right," she snapped. "Come along, then, if you want."

The Kendar gave her a brief, hard stare and then a curt nod, judgment suspended.

They followed Lyra through the grove, ducking under low branches, half-blinded by falling blossoms. Jame stopped suddenly. Ahead, through a moving screen of petals, she thought she saw familiar low walls, down which *imus* marched, and a door gaping third-quarters open. The Earth Wife's lodge? Here? No. Emerging from the trees, she saw a cottage set as though in a mountaintop garden, covered with climbing roses. As they approached, the whitewashed walls revealed themselves to be marble and the blossoms clustered about the windows rose quartz, aglow with warm light from within. More light spilled out the front door, which stood nearly open as though in invitation.

"Come *on*," said Lyra, tugging her sleeve.

The door opened onto the black and white parquet floor of a surprisingly large hall. On its far side was a fireplace with two high-backed chairs drawn cozily up to it. One had its back turned toward the door. From its hidden depths came the click of knitting needles. In the other chair sat a very old woman shaped like a slightly squashed apple dumpling, dressed in many layers of clothes. Her white hair was wrapped around her head in a twig-thin braid and her round face puckered inward around a mouth that had long since outlived its ability to grow new teeth. A black foxkin perched on the chair back over her. In her gnarled hands was the end of a knitted scarf, which stretched back to the busy needles opposite.

Jame realized that she had been slow-witted. "Greetings, Matriarch," she said, with the appropriate salute.

Age-gummed eyes fixed on her. The toothless mouth mumbled on its own gums, then opened. "So. You're Ganth Gray Lord's girl, are you? Got his temper, I hear. A touch of his madness too, eh? I never did find out if he was ticklish, though—which you aren't, particularly."

Jame blinked. "What?"

The Caineron Matriarch Cattila peered at her, wheezing slightly.

"Go to bed," she said abruptly to Lyra.

"Oh, but Gran…"

"Now, missy. And no eavesdropping, either. I'd know."

"Yes, Gran. You always do. I never have any fun anymore. Good night, sister!"

As Lyra reluctantly departed, Jame wondered if the old woman would also dismiss Brier Iron-thorn. On second thought, she didn't think that Cattila could see the tall Kendar as she stood respectfully in the shadows by the door. But then Jame couldn't see the occupant of the other chair, either. Through Jorin, though, she smelled something vaguely familiar, something loamy?

"Scatterbrained," the Matriarch was muttering. "Just like her mother. Speaking of dams, what's this about you refusing to name yours? Ashamed?"

"No."

This old woman was beginning to rattle Jame. No one in the Women's Halls had questioned her so bluntly. Rudeness was the prerogative of great age, perhaps: Caldane's great-grandmother must be nearly two centuries old and none the duller for it, despite her mumble-gums.

Cattila gave a snort which might have been laughter. "Good. A waste of time, that sort of shame. So's regret, rose blight, and great-grandsons. You've got the air of a Knorth purebred, though, as Adiraina says. Now, Kallystine's mother was Randir, a niece of the Wilden Witch. Bad blood there. Very bad. Just what did darling Kally do to your face?"

How did she know that Kallystine had done anything, three days ago and over forty leagues away? By post-rider, maybe. One could travel that distance in twelve hours with frequent remounts, bringing the Ear's message-scarf—perhaps the very one which the Matriarch's fingers were now reading.

Someone still worked on the other end of it. A lace section, so much faster to knit than straight work, edged toward Cattila's gnarled hands, a message in transit.

Then Jame placed that smell, last encountered in Kallystine's chambers. Cattila's other visitor was the Ear herself.

"Tell me this much, at least," the Matriarch demanded: "Will this business cause trouble between our houses?"

It would be sweet to pay Kallystine back, but Jame hesitated, remembering the Caineron captain's mention of a possible civil war. She kept forgetting the wider stage on which she now acted.

"No," she said slowly. "Not if I can help it."

Cattila grunted. "Just as well. You Knorth wouldn't've stood a chance. You may not anyway, but that's another matter."

Again came that vast grinding noise, closer than before, like mountains shifting in their beds. A shiver passed through the fabric of the tower. Jorin and the foxkin stirred uneasily.

"What *is* that?" Jame said.

The old woman had clutched the scarf to her chest, flinching as if between lightning flash and thunderclap. Her movement jerked into sight the knitter's hands, old and strong, with very dirty nails. The Ear jerked them back, so that for a moment the two of them seemed to be playing tug of war.

"That's a weirdingstrom," said Cattila, glaring at the again invisible Ear. "A bad one. I sent one of my pets to investigate, but she never came back, did she, Precious?"

This last was addressed to the foxkin, who "quipped" unhappily.

Why, she's bound to that creature, Jame realized, *perhaps to the entire colony. So that's how she learned that I'm not ticklish.*

"I've seen patches of weirding," she said. "Is this so much worse?"

"Is a cataract worse than a raindrop? What do they *teach* you girls at Gothregor these days? Listen: the Three-Faced God created the Chain of Creation out of the chaos of Perimal Darkling, yes?"

"Er..." said Jame, startled. She had always understood that the Enemy was an invader from outside the Chain.

"Listen! The Merikit say that this world rests on the back of a great chaos serpent, left over from the beginning. Its mouth is the great maelstrom called the Maw, that drinks the Eastern Sea. Its offspring run like veins under the earth and water. Some call weirding the Serpent's breath. When it passes over the land, the Serpent's brood awakes, and that includes the River Snake, which lies under the Silver. The first time that happened, the Merikit sent down a hero to subdue the monster. They'll be preparing to dispatch another one now, none too soon. Hear that rumble? North of here, the very face of the earth is changing."

Did the old woman really believe such superstition? But then again, was it? As she had traveled the Riverland's wilderness, stranger thoughts had occurred to Jame. What *was* it which she herself seen on the river bottom when the willow had dunked her?

"If there's going to be an earthquake that bad," she said, "not to mention a weirdingstrom, this tower can't be very safe."

"The quake we'll have to risk. Worse, to be caught out in the weirding. The oldest buildings like this will be all right in the storm: they're built on hill-fort ruins, and those ancestors of the Merikit knew how to stay put. But any additions may be swept away. Good riddance, too! A trap and a snare, this valley has been to us all. Without it, we'll have to resettle the border keeps where we should have been all along, guarding against the shadows."

"But what about your Kendar?"

"Safe in the tower, aren't they?"

"Well, no. They're all out sleepwalking in the square."

The old woman stared at her, toothless mouth opening, closing, and opening again. "Well! Got 'em drunk, has he? The lord of this house, not man enough to hold his own hangover. Oh, how could he have been so careless, tonight of all nights?"

"I think," said Jame slowly, "that I know."

She would rather have kept quiet—it would certainly have been safer—but she felt that she owed an explanation to someone. So, haltingly, she told the story: how Caldane had taken her prisoner at the Cataracts, how she had slipped something into the wine which he had offered her and tricked him into drinking, how that "something," mysterious crystals taken from a Builder's house in the Anarchies, had affected M'lord:

"He started to hiccup and then to float, this, with only a canvas roof between him and open sky. He's terrified of heights. Imagine, drifting up and away, higher and higher and higher.... When would he come down again, and how fast? Matriarch, what can I say? He panicked."

"When?" demanded Brier suddenly emerging from the shadows.

"Er, that would have been the thirtieth of winter. He was still 'not quite feeling in touch with things' on the thirty-first, nor probably for some time after that. Why?"

Cattila had been peering at the big Kendar, smacking her gums thoughtfully. "Brier Iron-thingie, isn't it? I never forget a voice."

"But...Matriarch, we've never met."

"We needn't have. I sit in my garden at the shaft's mouth. Nothing goes on below that I don't overhear."

A dull glow kindled in the Kendar's brown face. "Well, then. You know how angry Lord Caineron was with me, how he swore he would never let me either progress in his service or leave it. His grip is very strong. I didn't think anyone could break it."

"But you must have," Jame protested. "At the Cataracts."

"Yes, lady. Now I understand how. He was distracted."

"Meaning he was probably tethered to the floor having hysterics," said Jame. Then her amusement died. "Matriarch, I listened to his Kendar in the square tonight, unconsciously mouthing his hidden thoughts. He tells himself over and over that he's recovered, that it will never happen again—but underneath he's terrified that it will, and he's trying to bury that fear under excess. That's the reason for his carelessness, and for your danger. I'm sorry for the latter, but by God I had cause for what I did and if need be, I'd do it again."

She stopped, defiant, braced for the old woman's wrath.

Cattila had been making noises like a teakettle coming to a boil. "Heh!" she said now, with an explosive venting of stream which made her bob in her chair. "Heh, heh! 'Not quite feeling in touch with things,' eh? Bouncing around the rafters, more likely. Heh, heh, heh! Face like a dinner plate with frogeyes, I beg. Heh, ha, ho hiccupping *hooo!*"

"I'm glad it amuses you," said Jame weakly, as the Caineron Matriarch beat the arm of her chair with a puffball fist and crowed like a cockerel. "I wish it helped."

Cattila snuffled into the end of the message scarf and blew her nose on it to regain self-control. "Maybe it does, girl. It shows again, as with that boy who jumped, that the bond between Caldane and his Kendar can only take so much strain. T'cha. That idiot won't raise a fat finger to protect his people tonight. They must be free, to save themselves."

"But Brier wanted to break away," Jame protested. "The Kendar below don't."

"That's why they've held on this long. If my darling Caldane were to lose control again, though, and push them too far..."

"Many might wrench free despite themselves."

"Or go mad," said Brier Iron-thorn grimly, "or die."

"It would take a genuine, destructive influence to bring that about," Cattila said, no longer laughing. "A nemesis."

Jame gaped at her. *The* Nemesis, of course, was That-Which-Destroys, the third face of Kencyr god. *A* nemesis was a Shanir who didn't quite make the apotheosis, apparently because the other two aspects of the Tyr-ridan, Creation and Preservation, hadn't yet manifested themselves. "Now wait a minute..."

A low rumble interrupted her. "*Queee!*" said the foxkin, and streaked out an open window. Jorin crouched flat, ears back. Below in the compounds, dogs began to howl. Then, ever so slightly, the tower started to sway. Jame staggered. For one appalling moment, she knew exactly what terror Caldane had felt, so high up, with such a distance to fall. Behind her, she heard Brier swear. The swaying stopped. The rumble faded to no more than an echo in the bones.

Cattila had hunched down in her chair, eyes screwed shut. "A nemesis," she repeated. One eye popped open to regard Jame balefully. "If I were you, girl, I'd get on with it."

What could one say to that?

Jame bowed and turned to leave, but on the threshold the matriarch's voice stopped her: "Why, it's for you!" Cattila was holding up the lace section, which had at last reached her fingers. "'Don't walk,'" she read out-loud. "'Run. My turn comes next. You shouldn't have stolen my *imu*.'"

Jame boggled. "*Imu*? Your...?" The earthy smell, the dirty nails, the proclivity to eavesdrop... "M-mother Ragga? Is that you?"

"'Step-mother to you, if that,'" Cattila read, from stitches knit half an hour before. Jame shook her head as though to clear it. To imagine that the Earth Wife's lodge was following her was one thing: but what in Perimal's name was its mistress doing in the service of a matriarch, much less serving as her Ear on the very Council of Matriarchs?

"Earth Wife, listen: I did *not* steal..."

"'Don't talk. Run. Here I come.'"

Jame bolted outside, followed by Brier and no one else. *Dammit*, she thought, stopping, feeling profoundly foolish. Those two old women had really spooked her, and for what? The night seemed normal again, the tower rock steady. Foxkin still flitted nervously around the shaft's mouth, but the dogs had stopped howling. A babble of voices floated up from the hall below: "You're drunk." "I tell you, it moved!" "Didn't." "Did." "*Didn't.*" "DID!"

"Look," said Brier. She was pointing toward the roofline of Cattila's cottage, black against a faint glow beyond. Dawn?

But it was far too early, and in the wrong direction.

They circled the building. From this height, one should have seen the northern reaches of the Silver, a glinting, sinuous ribbon threading back into the dark hills. Instead, a vast river of luminous mist flowed down the valley, filling it from slope to slope. Ruined Tagmeth showed black against it for a moment, as small with distance as a toy, and then was swallowed. Farther back, against a pitch-black sky, peaks emerged like islands in a slowly boiling sea. A continuous grinding noise came from its hidden depths—faint, distant, ominous.

"Is it moon-dark?" the Kendar asked. "Has this world fallen into shadows at last?"

The weirdingstrom must be loosening knots of tension in the ground as it came, Jame thought, sending tremors on ahead of it. As good an explanation as any for the River Snake's writhing.

"It's more a case of Rathillien rising," she said, "which isn't good news for us either. And that tidal wave of mist is coming fast. Damn! If it isn't one thing, it's another. C'mon."

"Take the boat!" Cattila called after them. "God's teeth and toenails, Knorth, Lyra Lack-wit was right: things *do* happen around you!"

VII

The ten-command waited uneasily where it had been left, under drifting petals.

Jame knelt beside Graykin. Difficult, in this light, to see if he had regained any color, but his breathing was more regular than it had been and his skin less clammy to the touch. After all, she reminded herself, he was half-Kencyr; the shock once past, his recovery should be rapid.

"Good work," she said, grudgingly, to Kindrie, who looked startled at the compliment.

As for the cadets, however, the boy taken ill on the stair had been sick again with the tower's movement and several others looked distinctly unwell. Mistrusting their stomachs if not their nerves, Brier stopped them at the stair-head and descended alone, cautiously, into the chambers of her former lord.

The Kendar moved well for someone so large, Jame thought, leaning over the upper rail to listen, but not as quietly as she herself would have done—not that Iron-thorn obviously thought her capable of anything but causing trouble. Odd, to be considered inferior and superior simultaneously. It reminded her, with a painful jolt, how she and Marc had parted without finding a balance between her newfound Highborn blood and his Kendar, after all they had been through together.

Roofless and rootless, how *could* she live among her own people—or anywhere else—without equals, without friends?

Iron-thorn reached the foot of the stair, turned toward the balcony, and froze.

"Well, well, well," said Lord Caineron's voice.

Jame leaned farther over the rail, holding her breath, gesturing urgently for the cadets behind her to keep back. The burnished crown of the Kendar's head was a dozen feet below her. Caldane remained out of sight, but he must be very close.

"Brier Iron-thorn," purred his hated voice. "How kind of you to drop in, just when another randon candidate has, er, dropped out. But I forgot. Pretending to be a Knorth now, aren't you? Not easy, is it, with Caineron blood in your veins? Not possible, I should think. Come, girl: we both know where the real power lies."

His voice had grown thick and deep. Jame's skin crawled. There *was* real power here, stripped to its ruthless core by days of self-indulgence, enough to shake even those of a different lineage. For the first time, she understood how Caldane could have ordered that young man to do what he had done to Graykin and been obeyed.

"Shall we resume where we left off?" Lord Caineron was saying. "Would you like to reapply as a Caineron candidate? Let's see your obedience, girl. ON YOUR KNEES."

Brier Iron-thorn made a choking noise. She crashed down as though the legs had been chopped out from under her.

"Kendar are bound by mind or by blood. Such a handsome woman as you, though, deserves to be bound more pleasurably. By seed…"

Cloth rustled.

This is obscene, Jame thought, and shouted, "Iron-thorn, *move!*"

Brier looked up with a start, and threw herself aside barely in time. Jame landed where she had knelt.

"BOO!" she shouted in Lord Caineron's face.

"Hic!" he said, recoiling.

Jeweled slippers flew off as he thrashed, hiccupping, inches above the floor. Peacock-blue sleeves flapped like broken wings on windmilling arms.

"*Hic!*"

Pudgy hands leaped up to clamp futilely over his mouth. Small eyes boggled over ring-encrusted fingers.

Highborn, thought Jame, and prodded him in the stomach with a long, black-sheathed finger.

"HIC!"

He bobbed helplessly away from her, beginning to tilt sideways. A sudden stench filled the air as fear-twisted bowels let go.

Rotten, stinking Highborn.

Behind her, she heard Brier say hoarsely, "Don't..." but ignored her.

"Make sport of decent Kendar, will you?" she demanded, following Caldane, jabbing at him. "Play God almighty in your high tower, huh? Well, the next time the urge takes you, remember me. And this. And keep looking down."

Caldane looked, and screamed. He was over the balcony rail. Under his feet was nothing but empty space—all the way to the foul waters of the pit some two hundred feet below.

Jame watched, savoring every detail: the gaudy, flailing figure; the inarticulate cries; the loosened, befouled trousers tangling around plump ankles, falling off. She didn't at first recognize her berserker flare, pure, cold, and deadly as it was, like the chill bite of poisoned wine. This wasn't the brute rage which she had previously known. Use had refined it, could refine it further still, she realized, into an instrument of terrible power. Was this intoxication what it felt like to be truly herself, a nemesis? Very well.

Or perhaps not: in Brier's face she saw her enemy's terror reflected and heard his screams echo from other throats in the hall below. Ancestors only knew what was going on among his Kendar, down in the square. Damn all Highborn anyway, herself most of all. What right did any of them have to respect, much less to friendship?

White-knuckled, Brier gripped the rail to anchor herself. Caldane's panic had plunged her into the reeling world of a height-sickness, which she hadn't known she possessed.

I am not *a Caineron,* she told herself, gulping down nausea, clutching at control. *I am* not.

A cold hand caught her chin and turned her head, neck muscles creaking like ironwood in winter's grip. Gray eyes shaded with silver smiled into her own.

"You don't know what you've done," she heard herself croak.

"I seldom do," said that husky voice, burred with destruction. "But I do it anyway. This is what I am, Brier Iron-thorn. Remember that."

The silver stare held her a moment more, then let go as the other turned.

Brier stumbled back a step, catching the rail, braced for nausea. Caldane had begun to turn bare-bottom-up despite frantic efforts to snag him from the balcony below, but the world didn't spin with him. That slim, cold hand had wrenched her free of the Caineron, perhaps forever.

Dammit, Brier thought. She should have been able to do that herself, as she had at the Cataracts...

No. Even there, it seemed, she'd had help. It hadn't been her own strength at all, of which she had been so proud after so many humiliations. Damn all Highborn anyway, who could jerk her about like...like that Southland's bastard, a puppet on strings.

Out in the shaft, the foxkin had found a new playmate.

"Ticklish," said the Knorth, watching. "Good. Now, what's this about a boat?"

VIII

Caldane's boathouse was a chamber hollowed out of the mound at its base, dimly lit by diamantine panels. In the black water of the slip floated a ceremonial barge, some fifty feet long by twelve wide, with six oars to a side, fixed upright at rest. A small head on a long, serpentine neck arched over its prow. Its sides were figured with wings, which swept upward at the stern. Between the wing tips, on the poop, was a raised dais and on this, a throne under a velvet canopy. Ripples of light danced on the ebon waters; shadows lay across the shining gunwales and deck. The entire craft, from avian figurehead to rudder oar, was sheathed in gold.

"Trust Caldane," said Jame, "to gild a swan."

"But what does Lord Caineron do with a boat like this?" a cadet wondered out-loud.

"Sits in it..." said Kindrie.

"...pretending to be Highlord," Jame finished.

The Shanir stared at her. "How did you know that?"

She gestured toward an embroidery worked in silver gilt on the black velvet behind the throne. It looked like a crown, but she had recognized it as a representation of the Kenthiar, a collar of ancient and mysterious origin which supposedly only the true Highlord could wear in safety. All others who donned it risked their necks. Literally.

"He must be mad!" Vant exclaimed. "To put that emblem on a boat like this, on the edge of a river that isn't even navigable...!"

"*What?*"

He shot her a sidelong glance. "Why, lady, *everyone* knows that river travel in the north ended a thousand years ago, after a great weirdingstrom changed the Silver's course from one end to the other. Back then, there were lots of trade cities on both banks of the Central Lands. One night, all the dogs started to make such a racket that orders were given to strangle them. After the din stopped, people could hear the earth growl. A red fog came down the Silver. It kindled lights in the air, and on the water, and under it, like whole weed forests burning."

"Catfish jumped out of the river," another cadet chimed in. To all of them except their Southron ten-commander, obviously, this was an old, favorite story. "Then the water leaped up—whoosh!—like a fountain. It swallowed its islands, jumped its banks, and flooded its cities. Whole populations disappeared—drowned, the survivors thought, although no bodies were ever found."

"Bashti and Hathir never recovered," Vant broke back in, glowering at the cadet, talking fast. "That was when they gave the Riverland to us, because they couldn't bring garrison supplies upriver by barge anymore, because it got so strange here that none of their people would stay anyway, but our priests settled it down..."

"Huh," said Rue. "Not so's you'd notice it. The Merikit say that the River Snake caused it all. Its tail reaches to the Eastern Sea, its heart lies at Hurlen, and its head is under the well at Kithorn keep. When it writhes, the Silver goes mad."

The others laughed.

"Stick to facts, shortie, not singers' fancies," said Vant scornfully. "Or do you Highkeepers really believe that tripe?"

Rue glared up at him. "We border brats face facts every day that would make a Riverlander like you shit in your boots. Anyway, your stories are as much hearsay as mine. Red fogs, jumping catfish, fire under the water—*all* singers' stuff, I bet. All we know for certain is that to this day any boat risking the river north of Hurlen tends to arrive without its crew, if at all, and no bodies are ever found."

Wonderful, thought Jame. Cattila couldn't ask for a neater way to dispose of awkward guests, if that had been her intention. She was a Caineron, after all, and a matriarch.

The rumble began again, closer, louder. Paving stones rippled underfoot; the water in the slip seethed.

On the cadets' upturned faces, Jame saw the same dread which she herself felt, not so much of the unstable earth as of the massive weight poised overhead, mound and tower and crown.

The earth bucked, throwing them all off their feet.

The back wall had split open. Rats swarmed through the fissure from the dungeons, over those Kendar not quick enough to get out of their way. Jorin squawked and bounced like a wound-up toy as they darted across his toes. Oblivious, they plunged past, into the slip, swimming frantically out toward the open river where they would surely drown.

Debris began to fall.

"Get on board!" snapped Brier.

The cadets vaulted down into the barge. Jame was poised to leap after them when, without ceremony, Brier picked her up and tossed her into the boat's stern. She landed awkwardly. Jorin did better despite also having been thrown—the only way to get him onto any boat.

The cadets' first action on boarding was to pitch Caldane's throne over the side and to tear down the canopy with its offending emblem. On the dais, Kindrie struggled to cushion Graykin's limp form with the velvet sway. Jame went to help, for once intending to keep out of the Kendars' way. However, as she watched the cadets plunge about in the waist, she realized that none of them had crewed a barge before or perhaps even been on one. Going down the Tardy to Hurlen, she had pestered those Southron barges with so many questions. Why couldn't she remember any of their answers?

Because you're scared half witless, she told herself, and took a deep breath.

"First," she said, to no one in particular, "we have to cast off."

Brier gave her a black look. "Throw off the front moorings!" she shouted to the cadet nearest the prow, and turned aft to deal with the stern lines herself.

The barge had begun to roll with the water's surge, snub-
bing itself sharply again and again. Left, right, left…

"Wait," said Jame, but the Kendar brushed past her.

"Too damn tight," she grunted, working her thumbs between the two-inch thick port hawser and its cleat.

Rolling to the right again, the heavy rope coming taut…

It parted with a bass twang under the Ivory Knife. Half-
freed aft but not fore, the barge swung its stern with a crash
into the righthand pier, snapping oars, throwing everyone from
their feet except Jame, who hung on to the cleat, hacking at
the slack, starboard hawser. It gave way as Brier lurched to
her feet, staring.

"What…?"

"I do have my uses," said Jame, sheathing the knife. "You
might remember that."

Meanwhile, someone had taken an axe to the prow lines.

The tremor subsided. The barge, freed, rocked uneasily in
its berth. Into that taut silence came the crack of stone overhead, giving way.

Cadets grabbed the surviving oars and half-rowed, half-
poled the boat forward. The slip gave way to a tunnel bearing
left, fed through gates to the right by the river. As darkness
and the current seized them, they heard the crash behind them
of the ceiling giving way.

Something overhead chittered and whirred. They burst
out of the tunnel under a roof of bats in panic-stricken flight.

Jame had a moment to note that they had emerged on
the mound's southeastern side, just short of where the encircling arms of the river moat rejoined. Then the reunited
might of the tributary seized them and they hurtled down it
between Grotley's compound on the right and M'lord's on
the left.

They shot under the bridge which they had crossed earlier,
barely clearing it with their swan's head prow and the
helmsman's crows-nest in the stern. Jame thought she glimpsed
Ran Quick-foot's broken-doll figure. The water beneath glinted

and flashed. Overhead hung a midnight sky tinged with an opalescence not that of dawn.

The roar of the swollen stream redoubled between the high, narrow walls. Over it, though, Jame thought she heard cries. Some of Caldane's people must have woken up— enough, she hoped, to anchor Restormir against the coming storm. As to Caldane himself, the foxkin wouldn't let him float away altogether—worse luck. Still, perhaps this hadn't turned out so badly, she thought, shooting a defiant look up at Brier Iron-thorn in the crows-nest as the Kendar clung to the rudder oar.

Brier was staring up at the wall which bounded M'lord's compound, at the fresh cracks which laced it. The sound coming from the other side was shriller than Jame had at first realized, disturbingly like an echo of Caldane's screams. Ahead, the wall bulged outward, fragments of it tumbling into the water. Suddenly the whole gave way. People fell with the masonry, clinging to it and to each other as though to anchor themselves even as they were dragged down. The barge plowed into them and over. As it plunged past the breached wall, its riders glimpsed a street within, where buildings seethed like kicked ant-nests, as desperate hands clung to walls and doors to stop their lord's tumbling world. The uproar leaped outward at the Knorth. Its madness stared blindly up from the white faces caught in the gold-plated welter of their oars.

Ahead raced the Silver. The barge plunged out into an eddy and was spun around by it, dipping and careening. The white faces in the water disappeared in rapid secession, mouths still agape, as if jerked down. Then the boat shot on its way again, going downstream stern-first.

Bits of barge-lore were coming back to Jame.

"It's no use trying to steer backward," she shouted up at Brier. "Better ship the rudder oar before it gets broken. We need people on the stern with poles to ward off obstacles— not that there are any at the moment," she added, glancing at the broad stretch of river which they had entered after the eddy, "but there will be. Then too, this boat may only have a three- or four-foot draft, but it will ride deeper as we pick up speed, so watch out for shallows that may rip the bottom out of her."

Brier stared down at her from the crows-nest, set high enough to have had a clear view over the canopy before it had been torn down. Spray plastered dark red hair to the strong bones of her face and clothes to the lines of her powerful body. As a figurehead, she was much more impressive than the one on the boat's other end.

"Anything else, lady?"

"Yes," said Jame. "Never, ever spit into the wind."

"You *are* mad!" Kindrie burst out. "D'you realize we're heading back toward Wilden, not to mention Falkirr, Gothregor, and half a dozen other keeps we weird-walked past on the way north? What are we going to *do?*"

What, indeed? At Gothregor, her future had looked bleak enough. Now she was going back, not only with a clear case of Knorth lunacy, but also with a face that could start a war. Then too, there was Graykin. Madness, war, *and* scandal, if word of his bonding got out.

She looked down at the Southron. A scruffy little half-breed, and the Kencyr half of that pure Caineron. At the Cataracts, his desperate need to belong had bridged the gap between them like a spark, surprising both. He was the last person on earth she would have chosen deliberately. And now that she had him, what next, when she couldn't even provide for herself? Perhaps she should break the bond, let him go free...

He began to moan.

"Do something!" she said to Kindrie.

But the healer shook his head. "I've done all I can. His soul-image is odd. He's like a—a ghost, haunting someone else's soul-scape."

"Whose?"

"You should know."

Graykin's eyes fluttered open, then widened as much as his puffy, bruised face would allow. He stared up at Jame, bewildered, close to panic.

"W-who...?"

Her mask confused him, Jame thought. "Do I have to undress?" she demanded, with a sidelong glower at Kindrie's expression. Be damned if she was going to explain that the first time she and Graykin had met, she hadn't been wearing so much as a pleasant expression.

Graykin was still staring. "It *is* you! B-but where are we?"

"In a stolen barge, going down the Silver backwards—which is fairly typical of any rescue I undertake. You might remember that, the next time you need one."

But Graykin had stopped listening. "I w-waited," he stammered. "In Hurlen, all winter, cold and hungry, guarding It, a-and you didn't come. Caineron's agents caught me, dragged me north to Restormir. Caldane t-tortured me, and you didn't come. I could have told him where I hid It, could have bought his favor again, but I didn't tell, I didn't tell and you didn't come!"

His voice had risen to a thin wail.

"Stop that!" said Jame, exasperated, and slapped him.

He crumpled back onto the velvet.

Kindrie bent over his still form. "Why did you do that?" he demanded of Jame; then, in perplexity, "*What* did you do?"

Why and what indeed. It had felt like the edge of a berserker flare, not a tool or intoxication this time but an arrogance, to hurt because she could. And she didn't yet know if she was sorry.

The rumble began again, behind them. Birds rose in flocks from the wooded crest of the east bank, black against the milky haze which now permeated the sky. Jorin scuttled under the velvet swag.

"Why, we're slowing down," someone in the waist exclaimed.

They were. The shore had been sliding by as quickly as a horse might trot; now, walking, a rider would have passed them. The water was rising. It topped the low right bank and spread out over the meadow beyond, a sheet of glass under which grass floated. Ripples from the slowing hull broke it, kindling red witchweed beneath the surface. At the meadow's far edge, trees began ever so gently to sway.

"We've stopped," said someone. "No, we're going backward!"

And so they were. Waves began to slap against their stern. The current had turned, so that the river seemed to be pushing them back toward Restormir and the coming storm.

"The Snake is drinking up the river," Rue said, awed.

More likely the cause was quake-sunken lands to the north, Jame thought.

Beyond the gilded swan's head, the northern sky glowed. Then, around the valley's curve, came the vanguard of the storm: spheres of flickering light, yards wide, and rolling down the Silver toward them.

Jame leaned over the gunwale. "This is the Earth Wife's turn, not yours!" she shouted down at the racing water. "River Snake, River Snake, let us GO!"

The waves subsided. The barge stopped, then began to move southward again as the current turned.

Jame shrugged, shamefaced. "Whatever works," she said.

This may have worked too well. They moved faster and faster, from a walk to a trot to a gallop. Jame clapped a hand to her cap to keep it from blowing off.

"Waah!" said Jorin, under the billowing velvet.

The east bank collapsed, casting down its crest of pine trees like spears. Spray drenched them all. The cadets rowed furiously to keep in the center of the channel—no easy matter without the rudder oar, which Brier had out of its lock to fend off debris. At this pace, thought Jame, they would reach the other keeps much faster than expected, if they didn't come to grief first.

The barge careened around a point.

Ahead, a rocky islet abruptly sank, swallowed whole by a fissure in the riverbed. Water roared into the chasm. The barge swung around its rim. The velvet slid off the dais into the waist, taking with it healer, patient, and bitterly protesting ounce. The same lurch sent Jame reeling toward the side. Something flew in her face. She threw up a hand to ward it off, and found herself gripping the end of a crows-nest guy rope, torn loose from its mooring. The next moment, she was over the gunwale, swinging out above the whirlpool. Water thundered down into it over what looked like stone teeth, into an earthen gullet twisting down out of sight.

"River Snake!" she shouted down into it, her voice swallowed by the roar. "Behave!"

The barge swung and so did she, back onto the dais. Brier stared down first at her, then at the hole in the river, as if unsure which she found more preposterous. The barge plunged on downstream, prow first.

"Better?" Jame shouted up at the Kendar.

Brier had turned to look back. "No."

Behind them, the fissure closed. A great gout of water and red mud vomited up from the riverbed. Its wave hurtled the barge on, out of control.

As the Silver had descended, its gorge had cut deeper and deeper into the mountain granite so that now they were careening down rapids between high cliff walls. Oars smashed on rocks, knocking cadets to the deck. Catfish fell on them. To either side, bewhiskered shapes were leaping as if in flight from the water to the rock face, where some of them stuck and clung. Looking over the side, Jame saw red, mud-stained water, with flashes of white under it—rock slabs, or scales? Were they sliding down the River Snake's back?

The Silver widened as another stream joined it from the right, the confluence a boiling cauldron. Jame thought she glimpsed keep walls up the stream's gorge. The Jarans' Valantir already? Ahead, the river split around a wooded island much larger than the last. They were swept to its left into the narrower channel.

From her vantage point, Brier bellowed down at them, "*Falls!*"

The swan barge leaped out over the first drop as if trying to take wing. The dais fell out from under Jame's feet. The waist seemed to leap up at her. Velvet, cadets, and fish broke her fall. The deck tilted again. This time she didn't leave it, but everything else seemed to, all coming down on top of her. Stunned, she lay on the bottom of the boat, under sodden cloth. Something scraped along the hull on both sides. People were shouting and stepping on her. Then all sounds grew strangely distant.

Something wet tickled her ear. *You're drowning,* said a whiskery voice in her mind. *Get up. This isn't my turn.*

Jame gasped and choked. Her face was under water, pressed down by the masses of wet velvet. The bottom of the barge was awash. Sputtering, she clawed her way free, and found that she had not been alone: beside her lay an enormous catfish, its whiskers rasping against the planks, its thick-lipped mouth agape.

From the other end of the barge, near the prow, Brier Iron-thorn stared at her. "I thought you'd been thrown out," she said.

Everyone else was gaping at her from the shore. The rocks on which the boat was snagged had provided easy steppingstones to the east bank. Brier apparently had stayed behind to gather discarded backpacks, which now dangled in clusters from her big hands.

The barge teetered, groaning. Jame scrambled back onto the dais, fetching up as far astern as she could go. They were balanced again, but precariously. Any moment, the rush of water from behind would dislodge them. Jame didn't dare move to look, but from the way the land fell away before them, she guessed that they were on the edge of at least a twenty-foot drop.

"Get off the boat," said Brier.

The deck shifted slightly forward, making Jame press back against the foot of the crows-nest. "You first," she said.

"Get off," the Kendar repeated, implacable. "*Now.*"

The iron will in her voice almost made Jame obey; but if she did, both barge and cadet would go over the falls, and where would a Southie like Brier ever have learned how to swim?

Dammit, they hadn't time for games. In exasperation and anxiety, she reached for an overriding tone of command such as she had never used before. It rose, compounded of innate Highborn power and something utterly ruthless, like the edge of a master rune.

"COME HERE," she said—and realized with horror, the moment she spoke, whose voice she had unconsciously imitated.

The Kendar's eyes went blank. As in the Crown at Restormir, she started to obey, but then staggered.

"No!" she said hoarsely, and lurched backward.

With a screech, the barge fell.

Jame was thrown off the tilting deck, the catfish flying beside her. She slammed into water as hard as she had half-expected to hit rock. Deep; dark; very, very cold. The weight of Aerulan's banner slung across her back pulled her down. There would be blood in the water if all of this had reopened Kallystine's handiwork. Cold, hard lips pressed briefly against her own. Whiskers tickled. Her thrashing feet hit bottom, kicked off from it. An endless moment later Jame surfaced, sputtering.

Kissed by a catfish. Sweet Trinity, what next?

She yelped as a golden, serpentine neck reared up beside her, then splashed over on its side. The swan figurehead. Other fragments of the barge bobbed up all around her, their gilding too thin to hold them down. This was a small backwater, she saw, blocked off from the Silver's main current by a beaver dam.

But where was Brier?

Near the shore, a dark head broke the surface. The big Kendar was still carrying the cadets' heavy packs, as well as wearing her own.

"They took me straight to the bottom," she was saying to Vant as Jame floundered up on the bank beside her. "From there, I simply walked ashore."

Jame couldn't meet her cold stare. That she, who hated her Highborn blood so much, should have used such a voice on someone like Brier... What difference was there, after all, between her and a pig like Caldane, if they were both capable of such a thing?

"Look!" said cadet, pointing.

The trees on the island stood black against the light growing behind them. Then fingers of luminous mist crept down the stepped falls, tentatively, as if feeling their way. Their tips fumbled around the figurehead, which vanished soundlessly. They groped on toward the shore.

"Climb," said Brier to the cadets. "You too, lady."

The Knorth didn't move. "The Earth Wife wants her *imu*," she said, without turning. "Perhaps she'll settle for me instead."

Brier swore under her breath. This was too much. She grabbed the Highborn's arm and started to swing her into a slap which would knock this latest idiocy out of her with a vengeance.

The blow never fell. Brier's hand was channeled aside in a perfect water flowing move that ended abruptly in an earth moving thumb-lock. Surprise more than pain shocked her into an off-balanced immobility.

"Someone slapped me not long ago," said the Knorth in a distant voice. "Never again."

Brier glared at her sideways, through the wet fringe of her hair. "Then stop asking for it, lady."

She was released so suddenly that she nearly fell into the river. The Knorth was laughing. "Wise Brier-rose. You and Marc should get along splendidly. C'mon."

They scrambled up to join the others on the River Road, fingers of mist combing through the trees after them. Beside the road ran fragments of an ancient wall. Clearly, the same hands had built both, but only the foundations remained of the latter like old, worn teeth fused into their sockets. Beyond them, the land rose in terraced foothills to the base of the cliffs. One towering white rock face stood out from the others. Many windows were cut into it, all dark and shuttered, but on top perched a keep blazing with light.

Mount Alban, the Scrollsmen's College. It must be.

"We've got to take refuge," Jame said, looking up. Underfoot, the earth shivered.

"Lady, you don't go indoors during a quake."

"And you don't stay outside in weirding. Take your choice."

Brier looked down at the mist tendrils that had begun to twine about her boots. "Up," she said to the cadets.

The ruins of a hill fort lay scattered at the cliff's foot, before Mount Alban's main door. Closer at hand was a sturdy wooden building set into the northwest side of the hill. It was locked. Brier and Vant put their shoulders to the door. Looking back, Jame saw mist well up against the broken wall, higher than it now stood, respecting its ancient dimensions, and she remembered what Cattila had said about the resistance of such work to the weirding effect. If they had stayed on the River Road, they might have been perfectly safe.

Mist rolled over the top of the wall which was no longer there. Behind it, mountains high, came the weirdingstrom.

The door suddenly gave way.

Brier rolled to her feet inside, but Vant sprawled, tripping his comrades as they rushed in on his heels. Last over the threshold, Jame hesitated, still looking back. A wizened scrollsman stood beside her—the same, apparently, who had unlocked the door. Now he jerked her back and slammed it, in the very face of the mist.

With a sigh, the weirdingstrom swept over them.

The wooden floor lurched. Dried herbs hanging from the low beams swayed, while down one long wall hundreds of jars rattled on their shelves and many fell off. All the walls groaned. Clay seemed to melt out of their chinks, leaving each board outlined with light. Jame staggered. It felt for all the world as if she stood in the hold of a ship launched into heavy seas.

The old scrollsman had been darting up and down the long wall, catching jars as they fell, bleating with distress at each one missed. Now he stopped, arms full, listening.

"Why, we're adrift," he said.

The next moment he had shoved his burden at the nearest cadet and bolted to the back of the room, where he threw open a door and plunged through it, up stairs. They heard his voice, first in the passageway, then in some echoing open space beyond, shouting:

"We're adrift, everybody, we're adrift! Hurray!"

Interim IV
The Grimly Holt: 59th of Spring

In the northern reaches of Bashti, south of the White Hills, lies a great forest, deep and dark and full of strange things. Men call it the Weald when they speak of it at all. Few enter. Fewer still emerge.

Its eastern corner, the Grimly Holt, is just as feared by ignorant people, although its folk are shy and courteous, much different in manners, if not in blood, from their wild cousins of the deep wood. The wolvers' keep is another of those ancient ruins which line the Silver, this one smaller than most and unreclaimed by later builders. Its walls lie tumbled around the forest floor like so many half-sunken boulders velvet with moss, and a stream runs down the glade which had been its great hall. The loam of countless seasons obscures floor and hearth except where skullcap mushrooms grow along buried veins of ancient mortar mixed with blood.

Tonight, however, the weirding had restored to the keep a ghostly shell of its former self. Glowing mist sculpted itself against low walls long since fallen and pressed down on the thatch of an invisible roof. Wisps trickled in through narrow windows which had admitted no light of sun or moon or star for time out of mind.

This was an opportunity not to be missed.

Since the storm had rolled over them hours ago, the wolvers had been trying to record every detail of their ancient home which the weirding revealed. Long, communal howls slid down the length of beam and stone. Modulated yips described the cunning fit of joints, and hunting scenes carved over the outer lintels, seen in reverse as though from inside a glowing mold. As they sang, the mist pressed closer, taking more clearly the long vanished forms, and misty wraiths drifted down the hall to the sound of music lost in a dream.

The song snarled in snapping argument. There was a small structure attached to the rear wall which none of the singers understood.

"It's a privy," said the Wolver Grimly, and explained.

The word meant nothing in their tongue, so they settled for a description: the hole that all men mark but none claim.

Obviously, thought Grimly, they had never been in Kothifir during an outbreak of dysentery.

In fact, few of his kin ever left the holt at all, or spent much time in man-shape except during adolescence, when each generation in turn discovered that humans have no set mating time. Here on the edge of the great, dark Weald, there were few true humans to imitate in other matters. Torisen's visit the previous winter was still avidly discussed, not only because he was an accepted wolf-friend but because he had marched the entire Kencyr Host through the Holt on a short-cut to the Cataracts.

Only once before in living memory had the forest been so invaded, by a much less courteous party, when King Kruin of Kothifir had descended on it to hunt wolver.

Grimly well remembered his first sight of humankind. Kruin had taken over the old keep as his base camp, never guessing how closely he was watched by his curious, would-be prey. Creeping close to listen, Grimly had heard a court poet declaim *rendish* verse to a bored monarch waiting impatiently for the dawn hunt. But one wolver cub had already been captured in a net of words. The poet had seen but not betrayed him, his vanity revenged for regal yawns.

No other prey was taken. The Holt is a dangerous place in its own right, the deep Weald even more so. Kruin lost most of his party before the wolvers tired of watching men die and led him out. He wasn't pleased to have his royal hunt ruined, but in fairness he offered any wolver who cared to come a place in his court. That "place," most wolvers assumed, would be on his trophy wall. However, the poet's words still sang in Grimly's mind. When he came of age, years later, he took the River Road south and presented himself to Kruin's son and successor, Krothen.

What days those had been, what pleasure and pain.

He had indeed learned *rendish*, from the very poet who had come with Kruin to the Holt. Oh, the intoxication of the words, winding through the rhythms of his native forest...

And oh, the humiliation when his audience had howled back at him with laughter. It wasn't the would-be artist they came to hear, he quickly learned, but the freak with whom the old poet had bought his way back into court favor, as he might have done with a dancing bear or a singing pig. So Grimly had become "the Wild Man of the Woods," a caricature of what he wanted to be, usually drunk in order to stand himself, a sorry thing who had forgotten the dignity of the wolf and not yet learned that of a man.

"Why are you doing this?"

Sharp words, in an exasperated voice, from a young one-hundred commander with haunted eyes and bandaged hands.

Twelve years ago.

Grimly looked down the hall at the black-clad figure sitting hunched on a fallen block: Torisen, his first friend, then barely recovered from Urakarn and marked for death by his Caineron enemies, now the leader of his people.

And still a mystery.

Look at him, rocking back and forth, that damned sword still clutched in his swollen hand and his dark head bent as though listening to it, although the only words came from his own lips, lost under the wild poetry of the wood.

Grimly rubbed his tired eyes. No. They hadn't deceived him: weirding lit the ghostly hall and glowered back from the serpentine patterns forged into Kin-Slayer's blade, but his friend sat in deepening shadows as though they flowed off his black garments like murky waters. At his feet lay fire-scarred stone—

a different floor, a different place. The fur slowly rose down Grimly's spine. Behind him, a new note entered his people's song as they felt their control slip.

"Tori…"

He found himself padding down the hall, then dropping to all fours and creeping. The air seemed to thicken around him. It stank of old burning, and sickness, and fear.

"…a circular hall," Torisen was crooning, in counterpoint to the wolvers' song, "with two recessed windows to the north and south. Broken benches. Collapsed tables. A private dining room on the other side of the open hearth. A scorched door leading up to the battlements, closed but not locked oh God, not locked…

Grimly crept to his friend's feet over grating cinders as Torisen's voice built reality around him detail by detail. The song of his kin faded to the keening of wind through shattered walls. His paws ached on cold stone.

"Tori…?"

The other's rocking stopped, then began again as he hunched lower.

"Shhh…I'm hiding. I said I would never come back here, but I had to. I had to. This is the only place she won't look."

"B-but where are we?"

"Why, in the Haunted Lands keep where I—we—grew up. Oh, I burned down the real one last year, but this is a dream, isn't it? I burned the dead, too, haunts that they had become. Gave them to the pyre. That should have satisfied honor, shouldn't it? But they keep coming back. Listen to them in the shadows. Listen…

The wind keened through the narrow windows, thin and sour with ash, rank soot on the fur, the lips, and the taste of forbidden flesh…

Were those still shapes standing to either side of the embrasures, and those murky points of light, two by two by two—chinks in the wall or unblinking eyes giving back the glow of the sword's malignant blade?

Run. Out of this nightmare, back to his own simple, sane world only feet away, to his own people, crying for him on the wind...

But he couldn't leave his friend.

Shivering, Grimly crouched at Torisen's feet, to bare his teeth at shadows and bite them if he could, caught in a dream which might never end.

Part V

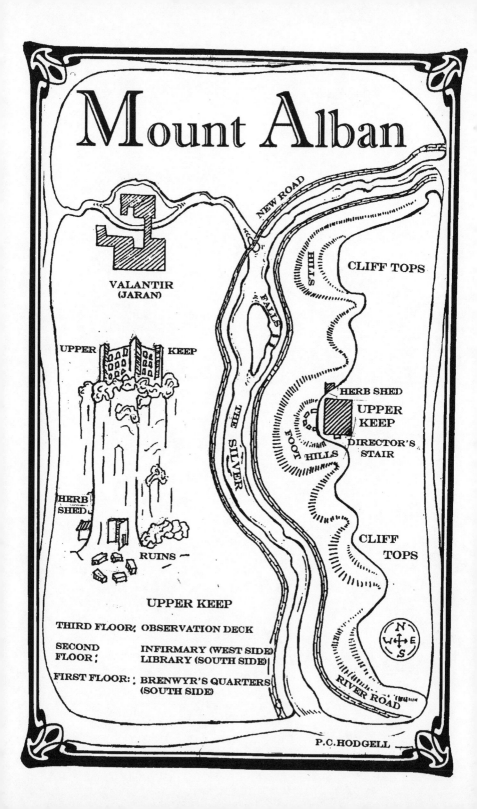

Mount Alban: 59th of Spring
I

Jame paced the infirmary, watched warily by Kindrie and benevolently by Aerulan, laid out to dry over the back of a chair. Having given up begging to be let out, Jorin was curled up on the foot of Graykin's pallet, ostentatiously ignoring everyone. Still, his ears twitched at every tantalizing noise out in the hall. Jame twitched too. Running feet, thumps, curses, all the sounds of departure. But where on earth were they going, and how?

Curtains of oiled cloth across the arched windows had kept out the initial surge of weirding. Now the mist had subsided to a flat, glowing sea, level with the cliff-top, under a ribbed ceiling of clouds which dimly reflected its light. The infirmary had none of the shipboard motion that had almost made Jame seasick in the wooden herb-shed below. Still, the floor did vibrate.

Out in the hall, people were approaching.

"Shift more supplies to the top floor," said a crisp, deep voice. "The entire core of the college is adrift, as well as the upper keep, as the scrollsmen predicted; but we may still lose the lower hall or more if the main door gives way. Has our newest guest been made comfortable? God's teeth, a lady of that stature, to descend on us at a time like this!"

"She was caught out in the storm, Director," said someone soothingly. "It was pure luck that she found our front door at all, swept as far north as she had been, or that the singer sent down to fetch Index heard her escort hammering on it."

Jame frowned. That didn't sound like her own arrival.

Brier Iron-thorn's voice sounded outside. "The cadets have brought up all the supplies they could find, Director. Have you further orders?"

"Not at present, ten-commander."

Footsteps and voices receded down the hall, but the door-knob quivered in Jame's grasp, as though at someone else's touch on the other side.

"Ten!" Vant's voice, approaching. "Captain Hawthorn wants you. Now."

"I see," said Brier, just outside the door. The knob became suddenly inert as she let go of it. "Yes, of course."

"I did warn you," said Vant, smugly.

Two sets of feet retreated down the corridor.

Jame sighed, half-relieved that Brier hadn't entered, half-disappointed. She was still embarrassed by what she had tried to do to the Kendar at the falls. Sweet Trinity, in effect to have used Caldane's voice on someone who equated domination with violation! Iron-thorn's trust in the Knorth had been fragile to begin with. If Jame shattered it, Tori would kill her. He might anyway, on general principles.

But what lady of stature, what Captain Hawthorn, and what had Vant warned Brier about? She wouldn't find out here but she didn't dare go out, either.

Brier wasn't the only person she was avoiding. In the confusion of their arrival, someone had mentioned that Kirien, the Jaran Heir, was also in Mount Alban. He hadn't attended Torisen's memorable dinner at the Cataracts, so Jame hadn't met him. She had heard that he was a scrollsman engaged in studies of the Fall until, coming of age, he took his place as head of the Jaran. The last thing Jame wanted just now was to expose her conduct and damaged face to Highborn criticism.

She found that she was touching her cheek, and jerked her hand down. The impression lingered, however, of a developing scar bad enough to be felt through both mask and gloves. Whatever it had been like after the first injury, the repeated blows to the face which she had taken since couldn't have helped.

Damn.

But she wasn't the only one in trouble here. The Southron hadn't yet retained consciousness. His breathing didn't have the deep regularity of dwar, either; in fact, she could barely hear it.

"He was going to be all right, wasn't he?" she demanded of the healer. "Somehow I could sense that when I touched him, back in Cattila's garden. But not now. What happened? I didn't hit him that hard."

The Shanir sat on the far side of Graykin's pallet, back to the wall, head drooping with fatigue. Her voice jerked him awake.

"I think it has something to do with the bond between you," he said, marshalling his wits. "Why does it mean so much to him?"

"I suppose because he's a bastard, born without a name or a place. I seem to have given him both. He had an identity before we met, though. I'm not totally responsible for who or what he is. I don't even want his service. He's just a stray dog I accidentally picked up."

"You made that pretty clear, when you slapped him."

"Sweet Trinity. What's been the point of this whole expedition, if not his rescue?"—And perhaps to make her forget her own problems. "I've never meant him any harm!"

"Maybe destructive Shanir can't help but destroy, however good their intentions. Maybe innocence isn't enough." He looked up at her askance, through the white fringe of his hair. "If you have this effect on a servant who needs you, what will you do to a brother who fears you?"

"He has no reason to. I love him."

"That makes it worse."

FRATRICIDE, the God-voice had called her. Bane? Or Tori?

Jame looked down at Graykin's still form. "Is he going to die?"

Without thinking, Kindrie reached toward the unconscious man, then stopped. His fingers curled into a fist, which he drew back to cradle against his chest like a broken bird. "Find out for yourself," he muttered, no longer meeting her eyes. "He's your responsibility."

Jame regarded him for a moment with raised eyebrows, then sighed. To date, she had done a poor job of being a Highborn. This was one duty, though, which she could no longer shirk. She knelt and touched Graykin's face gingerly.

A momentary dizziness made her squeeze shut her eyes. In the darkness behind the lids, she felt as if she were falling, except for her fingertips on the Southron's forehead. It felt odd. She blinked away darkness and looked down into a face half-human, half-canine, wholly mongrel, like the dog in the old song after whom she had renamed this wretched boy. Under him, through him, she could see the cold hearthstone on which he lay. A ghost, Kindrie, had called him, haunting someone else's soul-scape. Whose?

Her hand had ivory plates across its back and on up her arm. On her face, the weight of an ivory skull mask. She raised her head with difficulty to look over her shoulder, down the sweep of a vast hall paved with green-veined stone, hung with death banners. Silver Knorth eyes watched her through the bars of their warp threads; the woof on each cheek bunched like an ugly scar.

The Master's hall in Perimal Darkling—her soul-scape?

"No!" Jame cried, leaping to her feet.

The darkness swarmed back, although this time her eyes were wide open.

Got up too fast, she thought, swaying, clutching at composure. Wait for the blood to rise, wait.

Her sight cleared. Kindrie was staring at her open-mouthed. "What happened?"

"I need some air. I'm going for a walk."

At the door, she turned. "All right! I came back for you after all; I've accepted responsibility, and now you can keep watch on that damned cold hearth until your tail freezes off. Satisfied?"

The door slammed. The ounce (who had just gotten through in time) squawked. The Knorth departed, swearing. Graykin's breath deepened into the slow, healing rhythm of dwar.

"B-but what happened?" Kindrie repeated, bewildered, to the silent room.

II

Out in the hall, Jame turned left—away from the direction in which Brier had gone—and stormed off.

All these years of trying to escape her childhood in the Master's House by flight, amnesia, and arson (having left the upper stories in flames behind her) could she still be carrying the image of that foul place in her very soul?

Those disfigured banners, her scarred face.

No, no, no.

"Forget what you can't help," the Women's World taught.

She had smiled at that behind the mask which they had made her wear, thinking, How convenient: what one forgets, one needn't face or try to change.

Now the instructress's voice droned in her mind as it had in that winter-bound classroom, where little girls were taught how to forget some minor thing so that later they might dismiss much greater inconvenient facts.

"Forget, forget."

A minute passed, or perhaps ten.

Jame found herself staring down the crooked stairwell which opened up before her. What had she been thinking about? It was still there, buried none too deeply. Let it lie. Now, where was she?

The upper keep was relatively new in construction and regular in design, built of ironwood and oak. Below it, however, the cave-riddled cliff had long ago been hollowed out and filled with a wooden maze in which all the rooms seemed to be on different levels with ceilings of different heights. Erratic steps connected them, and halls that moved by fits and starts; stairs plunged down dark wells, some slippery with moss, others turned into minor cascades by recent rains.

So much Jame had noted, as she and the others had climbed to the upper keep. Now here she was back at an entrance to those interior regions. Well, why not? With Jorin on her heels, she descended to explore.

Below were the quarters and studies where most of Mount Alban's scholars lived. Signs staked out territories: here the prehistorians, there the epic poets, elsewhere the anthropologists and linguists.

"Serious scholarship in progress," read one notice. "Singers keep out."

"Facts please small minds," declared another.

So the old rivalry between the scrollsmen and the singers still flourished, as it had since the Fall, when the few surviving scrolls had gotten so mixed up that no one knew which was fact and which fantasy. The singers' cherished prerogative, the Lawful Lie, hadn't helped, as their colleagues never failed to point out.

Everything here, though, had an air of abandonment several months old at least. Most of the scrollsmen and singers had marched out with the Host the previous winter and were now enjoying Kothifir's sunny clime. Those left had been the old, the infirm, and the indispensable. After a winter in this dank, drafty chimney of a college, no wonder they were also eager to travel, especially if they could take the dubious comforts of home with them.

The whole thing sounded pretty implausible, though. Did they really expect this massive pile to drift about the countryside, scaring the natives? Still. Not only were the lower windows shuttered but the inner wall was paneled with wood, around which weirding light seeped. The outer rock face should have blocked that out. Was the cliff still there at all? Maybe Mount Alban truly had been cast adrift, like a wooden boat, leaking.

Here was a more recently built stair, cutting down through the chaotic levels with welcome decision. From the depths of the square well came a groaning as of ship's timbers in a heavy sea; and closer at hand, a different sound: quick, light

footsteps descending. Some fifty feet below, a robed figure
scurried across a landing. It was the old scrollsman who had
let them into Mount Alban, bound...where?

"Well, why not?" Jame said to Jorin.

They followed.

The farther down, the more the wood around them protested. At least, Jame thought, the principal supports must be
ironwood, which virtually nothing could break. It wouldn't
even catch fire unless exposed to hot coals for several months,
and then a good-sized beam would burn for generations. The
effect on it of weirding might be another matter. Given the
centuries-old levels through which they were now descending,
the newness of this stair might be more of a protection against
being left behind.

At the stair's foot lay the lower hall. As Kendar had hollowed out the upper reaches of the cliff, so before them Hathiri
masons had enlarged the caverns at ground level into high-
vaulted chambers. Before that, those same caves had been
used by the ancestors of the Merikit, whose fort ruins still lay
on Mount Alban's doorstep.

Jame paused at the foot of the stair, looking left down the
long main hall to the door at its western end. The posts of the
latter loomed some forty feet high and its leaves were secured
by the counter-balanced trunk of a tree. Into the left leaf was
cut a smaller door, cart-sized, and into that, a smaller door
still, the height of a man. Each was outlined with weirding
light, as were the wooden panels to either side.

Across the hall, the door to the herb shed stood open. Out
of it came the chant of an ancient voice. The words became
clearer as Jame approached, if not more comprehensible.

"Loosestrife kills flies," the old man was half-singing.
"Loose lips tell lies. Parsley makes piss; so does a linguist."

A flight of wooden stairs led down to the shed floor. Jame
sat on the fifth step from the bottom, low enough to see into
the room below without venturing down onto its still unsteady
floor. Jorin draped himself across her knees and fell asleep.

Below, the old scrollsman was sorting out the damage done to the wall of herb jars. As Jame watched, he picked leaves out of the glass shards, bundled them together, and put them in new containers, all the time crooning bits of doggerel. These last seemed to consist of herbs' virtues (medicinal, culinary, or otherwise) linked, often in scatological terms, with the names of colleagues, historical facts, or old songs. Which herbs went into which container seemed very important to him, as did the latter's position on the shelves. Jame listened, trying to make sense of it all. The old man's voice rose and fell. Lamps swayed and wood creaked.

A kind of song began to weave in and out of Jame's mind, not words this time but sounds, rising and falling, wild and beautiful. The Wolver Grimly, she thought, half-asleep, serenading her outside the tent at the Cataracts where Torisen kept her a virtual prisoner. Any moment now would come her brother's exasperated cry:

"Grimly, do you mind?"

She jerked awake. No one had shouted. Below, the old man still crooned nonsense; somewhere above and behind her, wolvers still sang.

This is very strange, she thought and rose, pushing Jorin off her lap, to investigate.

The music came from outside Mount Alban's triple front door. Wisps of weirding trickled around jambs and lintel like smoke, but the surface was cool under her gloved hands. Then it grew colder still as a shadow fell outside, as stealthy and massive as an eclipse. Mist and song dissolved into a chill wind blowing through the cracks. Behind her, Jorin began to growl. Jame felt her own hair stir under her cap. Impossible, but she knew the stench born on that dark breath, the exhalation of a tainted land where deformed roots cried as they were wrenched from the ground and the unburnt dead always came crawling back. Incredible to think that once she had thought that loathsome smell only natural, as one does the air into which one is born. Awake or asleep, if she had any sense, she would turn and walk (run) away again, as she had twice before.

Yes, if.

Huh.

The smallest of the three doors opened at a touch into another hall.

It was darker than Mount Alban's had been, lit only by the cold glow of a naked sword. Jame knew that bale-blade. In a moment, she also knew the man clad in dusty-black who sat with his back to her, holding it.

"Tori?"

Her brother stiffened, but didn't turn. "So you've tracked me down after all," he said dully. "No more hide-and-seek. Not from you, not from them. Don't you hear them in the shadows? They're all returning, the Kendar we knew, who ransomed me out of darkness with their souls. Returning, but so horribly changed, and it's all my fault. Listen."

Was she still asleep on the stairs to the herb shed? Had Tori dragged her into one of his nightmares, as he so often had in their childhood?

Scratch, rustle, scrape…the stealthy sounds of the haunts that had been her childhood friends, waking to a nightmare of their own.

"He's here too, you know," said Torisen, whispering now. "Father. Dead on the battlements with three arrows in his chest—no, half-dead on the stair, coming down—can't you hear him? His voice goes on and on, telling me to kill, to kill."

"You tell him," hissed Grimly, "to let go of that damned sword!"

His voice made her start: she hadn't distinguished the Wolver's dark form, crouching at Torisen's feet. Now she looked at her brother's right hand, lit by the hilt which it gripped, and winced. The thin, elegant fingers had swollen to nearly twice their normal size, knuckles and signet ring sunk into puffy flesh, tight skin marked by dark lines radiating out from burst, seeping blisters. She remembered how painfully that sword had blistered her fingers at the Cataracts, and she had only wielded it long enough to get across the battlefield. Tori had obviously been clutching it much, much longer than that.

Torisen put his free hand on the Wolver's head. "Go back to sleep," he said gently. "This isn't your dream. Anyway, I can't sheathe Kin-Slayer until it's killed someone."

Damn, thought Jame, dismayed. *That's a new twist.*

Or was it? Crossing the field at the Cataracts, she had spilled enough blood to glut a dozen swords. Of course, it could also be a thirst which the blade had developed after being reforged in Perimal Darkling. She should have warned Tori about that, or at least about the advantage, and danger, of wearing Ganth's ring on the same hand that wielded his sword.

"Why did you follow me?" he demanded in sudden, almost petulant exasperation. "Don't you see how dangerous we are to each other? I keep thinking that there should only be one of us, but which? Kin-Slayer may have to decide. Father says that you were a mistake, that you're too dangerous to live."

"Damn Father, Kin-Slayer, and the horse they rode in on!"

It came out almost in a shout. The wind faltered, then blew more strongly, the wolvers' voices all but lost on its foul, rushing wings.

"Please!" breathed Grimly, flat to the ground.

"I haven't come all this way," said Jame, trying to speak more softly, sounding half-strangled, "through fire, water, and darkling shadow, to play victim again to that man's madness. Anyway, he's dead. It's your responsibility now. You decide."

"Oh, please. We're losing the song."

"Or should I just drop out of your life again?" She had come up behind him now, wanting to grab those hunched shoulders and shake them, but somehow not daring to touch. "You can't bear to look at my face, can you? It's the price I've already paid for your cowardice. So, dammit, decide!"

Looking down, she saw how unkempt his dark hair was, how threaded with silver. What price had he paid, she suddenly wondered, over that long, bleak winter? What price was he paying still?

His head jerked toward the scorched door which led up to the battlements.

"Listen: he's on the stair. All winter, each night, coming one step farther down, until now. How can I decide anything with him at the door, listening? Listen. His hand is on the latch. He's fumbling with it, muttering. Is it bolted? I-I can't move. I can't."

The door was rattling. It was opening.

Jame threw herself at it, slamming it shut against resistance.

"Dammit, leave him alone!" she cried, and shot the bolt.

She found herself leaning breathlessly against the outside of Mount Alban's smallest front door. What in Perimal's name?

Abruptly, the next larger door swung open, taking the smaller one and Jame with it. She stumbled into the college's main hall, to be grabbed by a furious, white-haired figure. The second door slammed shut behind them, locking, as she was thrown backward against it.

"What do you mean, 'Leave him alone'?" demanded Kindrie. His anger shook him, shook her through his grip on her d'hen. "You're the danger here, not me! I followed you down because I couldn't understand how you could have helped Graykin without manipulating his soul-image, and now I've caught you tampering with your brother's. What did you do to it?"

"I-I don't understand. What soul-image? Whose?"

"The Highlord's! That awful keep in the Haunted Lands. Y-you got into it without even touching him. Don't you realize what harm you may have done to him—and what can a nemesis like you do anyone but harm? You a-and that vile Ishtier. What did you do after you slammed that door in my face? What?"

"B-bolted it, b-but it was only a dream, wasn't it?"

"Dream? Dream? I'll show you how much of a dream that was!"

He dropped her. Jame hadn't realized, until she hit the floor, how far off the ground that slight Shanir had been holding her. He had a Knorth temper, all right, she thought bemusedly, and wondered if it had ever been roused in him before.

Grating sounds came from the shadows. Unable to open the smaller two doors, Kindrie was working the massive counter-weight which secured the double leaves of the largest. Jame looked up. Tendrils of weirding again snaked around all the edges. She scrambled to her feet.

"Kindrie, no!"

The weight sank. Groaning, the tree trunk rose out of its brackets and the enormous doors yawned open. Weirding billowed into the hall.

Kindrie gaped up at it. "But, but, but…"

Jame grabbed his arm and pulled him down the hall with Jorin bounding on ahead. "We'll sort it out later," she said. "Now, run for the main stair, d'you hear? Run!"

She herself made for the steps descending to the herb shed.

"Sir!" she cried down to the swaying lanterns and groaning timber. "Abandon ship: the hall is sinking!"

The old man appeared at the foot of the steps, staring up at her open-mouthed, then darted out of sight.

Jame swore and shot a glance back at the door. Mist rolled down the hall like a tidal wave, but slower and more silent.

A clatter on the steps made her jump. It was the scrollsman scurrying up toward her. At the stair-head, he slammed the door behind him, locked it, and tied a rope to the handle.

"Well?" he demanded, turning to her. "What are you waiting for?"

They ran across the hall, the old man paying the line out behind him, and reached the stair just as the rolling mist engulfed them.

For an endless moment, everything was obscured. Then the weirding lifted.

Jame found herself crouching breathless, one hand locked on Jorin's ruff, the other gripping the edge of a wooden tread with sufficient force to drive splinters under her nails. Kindrie and the old man were clinging to the stair's rails with equal determination, the latter with his eyes screwed tight shut.

The mist formed a ceiling close overhead, but rising. Under it was a hall sculpted of glowing mist—scuffed floor, massive columns, paneled walls like a chamber in the clouds. Opposite, the herb shed's door looked almost black set in such luminescence, as did the rope stretching across the shining floor. The old man pulled in its slack and secured it to the rail.

"There," he said. "That shed is new-built. It should travel with us now, perhaps even longer than the stair does, if the rope holds."

"You mean we'll be trailing it behind us like the...the bait on a troll line?" Jame asked, bemused. Her voice sounded muffled, as had his, both half swallowed by the mist. More glowing details of the hall emerged over them as the white ceiling silently rose. "D'you think we'll catch anything?"

The old scrollsman had already started up the stair.

"Lots of old wood in the lower maze," he was muttering to himself as his head disappeared into the mist. "It won't travel far, whatever happens to the stair. Best to get above."

Abruptly he stopped and ducked back into sight, glaring at Jame. "What in Perimal's name d'you mean, 'we'?"

III

The top floor of Mount Alban's upper keep was an observation deck, open on all sides except for a low wall and the arches which supported the roof. Some two dozen scrollsmen and singers milled excitedly about on it, trying to see something, anything, above the sea of glowing mist which stretched featureless to the horizon under a clouded night sky with a hint of dawn to the east. Every few minutes, someone would cry, "Look!" and there would be a stampede from one side of the tower to the other, back and forth, back and forth.

If this really were a boat, Jame thought, standing well clear, it would long since have capsized.

As the old man had predicted, the new stair had kept them safe through the layer of weirding, which had continued to rise after them sending tendrils of mist before it to lace walls and beams, floors and ceilings. Below, all must now be like the lower hall, ghost-like, its reality left somewhere behind.

Her new acquaintance, Jame discovered, was the mysterious and much sought after Index, his nickname quickly explained as the others crowded around him demanding the location of such diverse information as the history of the late Hathiri empire and the average rate of arboreal drift. Many sources, inconveniently, had gone south for the winter; others were on shelves below in the library. Index had little respect for the latter. Memory, not writing, was the true scholar's way, the title of "scrollsman" notwithstanding. Like most traditional Kencyr, he had probably never learned how to read.

Jame stood beside the southwest corner stairwell, looking warily for the Jaran Heir, ready if necessary to bolt below to the infirmary where she had left Kindrie. What she saw were

Highborn and Kendar so intermixed that it was hard to tell which was which. All dressed in scholars' robes belted over skirts or trousers, worn impartially by men and women. The woolen robes themselves varied in color but not in cut, each having many deep pockets inside and out in which might be stored memoranda or lunch. Some were brightly dyed and elaborately embroidered around collars and cuffs; more a singer's flourish, apparently, than an indication of wealth or race. The singers in general seemed a more flamboyant, mischievous lot. Jame noted that it was two of them, stationed on opposite sides of the tower, whose turn-about cries of "Look!" were making their usually sedate, quite elderly colleagues run back and forth like over-excited children.

Not so the Director, however, who stood as solid as a mountain peak in the center of the deck while his people ebbed and flowed around him, occasionally bouncing off. He, without a doubt, was Kendar, and probably a former randon officer as well, judging by the savage scars about his face. Many took the scrollsman's robe when their fighting days were done. But that tall scholar meekly accepting orders from him looked very like a Highborn. Interesting.

More interesting still was the only other person on the deck under seventy: a young woman, Jame thought, although that cropped hair and profile might as easily belong to a handsome boy. Moreover, he (or she) wore no mask. When Jame had arrived on Index's heels, the other youth had given her a quick, startled look, then turned politely away when Jame had retreated into such shadows as she could find. However, curiosity prevailed.

"Excuse me," she said tentatively, approaching. "Could you tell me what's going on?"

The other turned and smiled. Yes, definitely a woman, a few years older than Jame herself. "Where shall I start? To begin with, we're successfully launched on the crest of a weirdingstrom."

"How can you tell?"

"Observation and deduction." With a sweep of her arm, she indicated the expanse of mist, cloud, and milky night sky. "What do you see—or rather, what don't you?"

Jame surveyed the unmarked cloudscape dubiously, then said, "Ah. The surrounding peaks of the Snowthorns. Left behind?"

"Yes, presumably. How far we'll go, though, no one is sure, or how long it will take to get there. In the past, individuals have been displaced more or less instantaneously as far as the Cataracts."

"You really think that the whole keep is moving?"

"Oh, not all of it. The hill fort ruins should act as our storm anchor, an advantage we have over individual weird-walkers. From what Index reports, we've already left behind the cliff face and the lower hall, as well as half the living quarters."

"The mist level inside is still rising, like water in the hold."

"Hmmm. That could be a problem if it reaches this high, but I expect it will begin to subside before that. This upper keep should travel the farthest, being the most recently built. We think Mount Alban will come apart like a...a puzzle-box, and then back together again as the anchor eventually drags us home from weirding patch to patch when the storm is spent."

Jame reflected that Mount Alban might have an affinity for ruins besides its own, considering how easily the wolvers' keep had snagged it. Perhaps that was how it traveled, from shattered foundation to foundation.

"But what supports us," she wondered out-loud, "if the cliff really has been left behind?"

"The weirding itself, I suppose, and our inner wooden shell. At a guess, we aren't any closer to the ground than when we started. It's all guesswork, though. We've done our research, of course, back to the last really bad storm that changed the course of the Silver for hundreds of miles. The Bashtiri and Hathiri keeps traveled some then, which is one reason why the old empire garrisons were scared out of the Riverland. It seemed likely that the same thing would happen again some day, so we kept that in mind while rebuilding Mount Alban. I gather that the stair to the main hall has come with us. So too has this one."

She gestured over the wall nearest to hand. Looking down, Jame saw an extremely improvised affair clinging precariously to the keep's southern face, disappearing into the mist at the cliff top.

"How far down does it go?"

"Nearly to the ground, with a rope ladder reaching the rest of the way. At the last moment, the Director insisted on the equivalent of a sally port. The point is, though, that no one knows how all this theory will work out in practice. Why, we could even end up stranded in the Southern Wastes. Exciting, isn't it?"

"Very," said Jame wryly.

The scrollswoman had been glancing at her askance. "Pardon me," she said abruptly, "but I have to ask: you are the Highlord's sister, aren't you?"

Jame felt her mouth go dry. Behind her, Index stammered to a halt.

He's overheard, she thought with dismay, but then realized that the old man had simply bogged down in his own material.

"Tansy tea, tansy tea," he was muttering over and over, as if trying to get himself started again.

"'Gerridon's knee,'" she said over her shoulder. She didn't remember hearing that particular nonsense couplet, but must have as she dozed on the stair, and probably a lot more beside.

The old man stared at her. "Tansy tea; Gerridon's knee," he repeated, and was off again, only to be interrupted by another cry of "Look!" and another stampede.

"This is hardly the place for a private conversation," said the young woman. "Let's go below."

Jame's impulse was to bolt down the outside stair and keep going. Instead, she descended with the other, feeling trapped.

"What was that about Gerridon's knee?"

"Oh, just something I heard somewhere." She had apparently stumbled onto another secret, but it wasn't hers to spread, at least not until she knew for certain what it meant.

"Index is a bit eccentric, even for a scrollsman. Most of us here have at least two jobs: one manual and one academic. He tends the herb shed and does research on the Merikit. It's been nearly eighty years, though, since the north was closed to us after the Kithorn massacre. A scrollsman without an active field is like a snake without a tail. So Index started collecting facts about facts: where to find them, who knows what, that sort of thing. It's made him invaluable, and powerful. A word of warning: many scholars exchange information on a barter basis. Index may look as if he's answering questions indiscriminately, but he's keeping close track of debts and credits. At the moment, I suspect he owes you one answer at least."

"I'll try not to waste it," said Jame. Lucky for her that this young scrollswoman apparently didn't play the barter game...unless, like Index, she was keeping score. Just the same, "Er, getting back to what you said before: why should you think that I'm Torisen's sister?"

"You're very much like him. Enough to have given me quite a start when you first came up onto the observation deck. But he's still at Kothifir, as far as I know, whereas Jameth..."

"Jame."

"...whereas Jame is (or was) at Gothregor. Aunt Trishien tells me that the Women's World has been rattled to the back teeth over your disappearance."

Jame remembered the Jaran Matriarch, serenely greeting her on her dash through the Gothregor basements. That was whom this self-possessed young woman reminded her of.

"Aunt?" she repeated tentatively, thinking, I'm missing something here. Who is this person?

"Great-great-aunt, actually."

She opened a door and gestured Jame into a high vaulted room lined with shelves. On them rested such scraps of scroll and manuscript as the scholars had managed to snatch up in their flight from the Master's House on the night of the Fall. A greater treasure saved, however, had been the memories of the scrollsmen and singers themselves, since each of them had memorized a master text to earn his or her robe. That practice still continued. Many of the scholars forced to remain here last winter were those who hadn't yet found someone to whom to pass on their knowledge.

Jorin began to growl. First through his senses, then through her own, Jame smelled something sickly sweet, something rotting.

At the far end of the room, black against the weirding glow of a window, stood a table and a chair. From them, a dark shape rose stiffly and bowed.

"Lordan," said a croaking whisper.

The scrollswoman returned the salute. "Singer Ashe."

Jame had backed up against the closed door. She knew that smell now.

The other was staring at her. "Why, what's the matter?"

"She was savaged...by a haunt...just as I was," said that hoarse voice from the shadows. "But she didn't...die of it."

Jame jerked her hand away from her forearm, which bore the scar marks of human teeth. "How did you know that?"

"Haunts know...what concerns...haunts."

"I'm sorry," said the young woman to Jame. "We've gotten so used to Ashe that it didn't occur to me that she might disturb you."

We're in the room with a talking cadaver, Jame thought, *and I'm not supposed to be disturbed?*

Perhaps she shouldn't have been, though. Everyone had heard about Singer Ashe, who had helped Torisen escape Caineron's trap at Tentir and then had marched south with him and the Host. An infected haunt bite, taken in the White Hills, had killed her three days before anyone had realized how seriously she had been hurt. If not for that, she surely would have died covering Harn Grip-hard's back at the Cataracts.

The battle song she had composed afterward, from the viewpoint of the dead and dying, was something only whispered about in the Women's Halls.

Jame knew all that. Just the same, haunts came from those parts of Rathillien like the Haunted Lands, where Perimal Darkling lay just beneath the surface. Their very nature reflected that shadow realm, where animate and inanimate, life and death, obscenely merged. How could you trust anything that tainted?

Then her mind skipped back to something that Ashe had said.

"The singer called you 'Lordan,'" she said, turning to the young woman. "But isn't that what they call the heir of a house?"

"That's right," said the other, smiling. "I haven't introduced myself, have I? My name is Kirien."

IV

Kirien's smile deepened. The Knorth looked like an illustration of the infinitive, "to boggle."

"But, but, but you can't be! You're a woman!"

"As I told your brother: technically, not until I come of age. Then, nothing in the Law prevents me from taking power, if my house and the Highlord consent. Torisen hasn't agreed yet, but I think he may. As for the Jaran, Uncle Kedan is fed up with playing interim lord and counting the days until he can get back to his own research."

The Knorth shook her head as if to clear it. "I'm confused. If the four duties of a Highborn lady are obedience, self-restraint, endurance, and silence, how does ruling fit in?"

"There's Law," said Kirien lightly, "and then there's custom."

Ashe stirred. Kirien could almost hear her old friend thinking: *Be careful what you say.*

But the Knorth was already working it out.

"If the Law doesn't prevent you from ruling, then maybe it doesn't demand all those other things from any of us. Are you saying that I've half-killed myself all winter trying merely to be conventional? Is that what all those girls in the Women's Halls are doing? In Perimal's name, why?"

"It would take a matriarch to explain that," said Kirien, thinking, Aunt Trishien is right: she does have a mind. "What little I know comes from independent research. I'm not privy to the secrets of the Women's World."

"Those damned secrets!" said the Knorth explosively. "I bet they don't tell this one about law versus custom to the children until they're so trained that they can't imagine any other way of life. I had a sewing teacher like that at Gothregor. Oh, that's clever, to catch them so young. How old d'you

think I would have been before anyone would have told me—
or is that a level of secrecy they would never have let me
reach?"

Kirien thought that she was probably right. It would be
dangerous to the Women's World to have someone so independent possessed of such knowledge, but now she was, with
only half a clue from Kirien. Scholar that she was, the Jaran
Matriarch was not apt to be pleased.

"Aunt warned me that you were a born puzzle-breaker,"
she said ruefully.

The Knorth glowered. "Some things need to be broken."

Ashe stirred again. Kirien would almost have thought the
singer was fidgeting except, of course, that she was dead.

"Not…everything," came that creaking voice. "Not
even…all customs."

The Knorth shot her a baleful look. "You've broken a
whole slew of them," she said in challenge to Kirien.

Kirien shrugged. "I'm Jaran. We have our own customs,
which include not putting girls through the women's school at
Gothregor unless they want to go. The curriculum sounded to
me like a dead bore. Then too, since my Randir mother died
bearing me, I've been suspect breeding stock. The Jaran aren't
much sought after by other houses anyway. We're too uncon-
ventional. So the Matriarchs let me go my own way. That
may change now that my house has chosen me as lordan. But
you're Knorth, with binding customs of your own. Hasn't
anyone told you what they are?"

"The Women's World told me as little as they could about
my house," said the other bitterly. "Not even the names of
the death banners in the old hall, so that I could pay proper
respects to my ancestors. They said it was the Knorth
Matriarch's role to instruct me, but the last one was assas-
sinated thirty-four years ago. That was Kinzi, my great-
grandmother. I have found out a bit, you see, despite the
Women's World."

More than a bit, Kirien thought wryly.

Ignorance is weakness. She understood why the Matriarchs hadn't wanted to strengthen a girl whose bloodlines they
intended to manipulate for their own purposes. In principle,
she didn't believe that people should be used or knowledge
withheld, any more than she believed in the barter game which
her elders so much enjoyed playing. In practice, though, how
safe was it to be totally candid with someone so sharp at drawing inferences, someone who, she sensed, was not being completely open with her?

"What...has your brother...told you?" Ashe abruptly demanded.

"Precious little."

"Perhaps...he has reason."

"Meaning?"

Until now, the Knorth had tried to ignore the haunt singer.
Now they faced each other, one a black outline against the
growing light of dawn, the other black clothed and masked,
two shapes of darkness. Kirien suddenly felt caught between
forces she didn't understand. She noticed that even the ounce
had backed away.

"Ashe," she said uncomfortably, "this is a guest. Don't
you think..."

"Show the Lordan...the knife...which you carry...in your
boot."

Behind the mask, silver eyes blinked. Then thin lips tightened. The Knorth drew a white knife from a boot sheath and
defiantly offered it, hilt first, to Kirien, who took it.

"Why, how odd," she said, examining the blade. "And how
cold."

She was suddenly aware of a dark figure close by on either
side, without having heard either of them move. Ashe's cold
grasp gently but firmly closed around her wrist and drew downward the hand on whose palm she had been about to rest the
knife's point. The Knorth's black-gloved fingers carefully detached the blade from her grip. Then they both stepped back,
and it was possible again to breathe.

The Knorth saluted her with stiff formality. "My thanks for your hospitality, Lordan," she said, her voice very slightly shaking. "I will no longer detain you from your studies."

Then she was gone, the cat slipping out in her shadow, the door closing gently after them.

"I don't understand," said Kirien, "What happened?"

"Describe…that knife," said Ashe.

Kirien looked at her, puzzled, but obediently began the familiar exercise of description: "Item: one weapon, classified knife or dagger; approximately twelve inches long; double edged; composition: ivory."

She faltered, eyes widening.

"Go on," said Ashe.

"Ivory," Kirien repeated, and continued, now quoting, "'carved all of one piece, blade, guard, and pommel; and on that last shall you see the three faces of Regonereth: maiden, lady, hag, and know what you hold by its coldness. The very tooth of death.

"Ashe, that was it, wasn't it? The Ivory Knife, one of the three great objects of power lost in the Fall, whose least scratch means death—and I wanted to see how sharp it was."

V

Out in the hall, Jame leaned against the door, shaking.

You just gave *it to her,* she thought, appalled. *And she was about to test its point. Some guardian you are. Throw the damn thing into the weirding; sink it in an ocean, if you can find one.*

Yes, and into whose hands would it fall then, for there would *be someone else. It was an object of power, like the Book Bound in Pale Leather. It would go where it wished, although it took a millennium to arrive.*

That last thought made Jame almost dizzy. Her life was tangled up in so many things, the scope of which boggled the imagination. Usually, she tried to ignore them. Hard enough, living a day at a time. Eventually, though, she would have to come to grips with them all, or there would be real trouble.

But oh lord, nemesis, fratricide, and Tyr-ridan?

"Are you all right?"

The voice made Jame start. Before her stood a randon whose concerned, pleasantly ugly features gave her a second shock greater than the first.

"Captain!" she gasped, and hastily slipped the knife out of sight in its boot sheath.

The Brandan captain frowned, then also looked amazed as she recognized this masked, boy-clad figure. "Lady? What are you doing here?"

"I might ask the same of you. Shouldn't you be on duty in the Women's Halls at Gothregor?"

"Should, yes, but when my lady Brenwyr needs must leave for Falkirr, blind as she still is, with weirding coming on, how could I or her guard let her go alone?"

Brenwyr. *She must be the "lady of stature" whose arrival had caught the Director so much on the hop. Ask for a matri-*

arch to question and one appears, except that Jame didn't want
so much as to see this particular Highborn, much less demand
answers of her. Still....

"Did you say 'blind'?"

"Aye. It was that shout of yours that did it, lady, if you'll
recall. It shocked her deaf too, but that passed off more
quickly. Not that I blame you for popping off with such a
noise. That was a shocking thing which M'lady Kallystine
did to you."

She was regarding Jame, trying to assess the remaining damage, but the mask thwarted her. Ironic, thought Jame, that if
she had been bare-faced the Kendar would have been too embarrassed to look at all. As it was, the Highborn turned away
first.

"I should pay my respects to the Matriarch, I suppose."

"That's as you decide, lady, of course, but she's none too
pleased with you."

"That I can believe," said Jame ruefully.

After all, the last words the Matriarch had addressed to
her had been a curse. Memory set it rankling again:

Roofless and rootless, blood and bone, cursed be and cast out.

It had never been entirely out of her mind, she realized,
like a burr that sticks and frets. Somehow, being under a Kencyr
roof again made the irritation worse. In Brenwyr, had she
really run afoul of a Shanir maledight? There were old songs
about such people. They usually died young, though, killed by
their families in self-defense, if they didn't wish themselves
dead first. The cursing talent sounded akin to the God-voice,
but with only That-Which-Destroys speaking a frightening
thought. Still, it didn't seem likely that Brenwyr could be one,
since it would take phenomenal self-control to hide such a
thing and the so-called Iron Matriarch didn't seem very controlled at all, at least around Jame.

"Nonetheless," she said, thinking out loud, "I hurt her. That
requires an apology, even if she bashes me over the head halfway through it."

"That isn't very good sense," said the captain, "but it is good manners and good will. I'll stand by to see fair play. This way, lady."

Brenwyr had been allotted quarters on the third floor down, against the southern wall. As the captain and Jame approached, they found the escort, a cadet ten-command late of the Gothregor guard, gathered out in the hall. They were speaking together in low, worried voices. Jame recognized one of them as the cadet who had failed to stop her escape with Jorin from the Brandan compound...could it only be six days ago?

"She's in a queer mood," the ten-commander reported. "Still of a stew to be on her way. When I told her that the weirding had closed in, she made a strange sound, like choking, and ordered us all out."

"She was too on edge to stay at Gothregor either," mused the captain. "A strong-willed lady, that. When her sight returns, as the Ardeth Matriarch assures me it soon should, she's apt to bolt, mist or no, unless we look sharp. Lady?"

Jame closed her mouth with a snap. What had she said when the Iron Matriarch had cursed her? The same to you, Brandan; and now Brenwyr was also too restless to stay under a Kencyr roof? Sweet Trinity.

"I'd still like to see her, captain." Now, more than ever.

"All right, lady. On your head be it."

She knocked. There was no answer, but they could hear footsteps inside, pacing back and forth, back and forth. Jame pushed open the door.

The large room beyond was a study, full of worktables and scroll shelves. Arched windows lined the far wall, the Director's stair spidering past it outside against the growing light of day. Brenwyr's dark form stalked past it, up the room and down, up and down. Her boots intermittently rang against the oak floor and thudded as dust swirled up around the hem of her divided skirt. Her grim, blind way led through mounds of crumbling furniture, as if she had cleared a path for herself by cursing anything that got in her way.

Jame cleared her throat. "Matriarch?" Crack, crack, thud went the boots without pause. "Lady?" Thud, thud, crack. "Brenwyr?"

The Highborn stopped short, not turning. "Aerulan?" she whispered.

"No, lady," said Jame, taken aback. "It's only me."

"You." The tone was almost a curse in itself. "The Knorth mountebank."

"Careful," said the randon softly, to either or both of them.

Whatever clever questions Jame had planned to ask went straight out of her head. "I-I came to apologize," she stammered.

"What good is that?" said the other harshly. "It won't bring her back."

"W-who? Aerulan? B-but Matriarch, she's dead."

Brenwyr took a fierce stride toward her and fetched up hard against a worktable. Jame found that, without thinking, she had backed into the randon. Behind them, Jorin was digging frantically at the door. The matriarch leaned over the table, fighting to control herself, red sparking in her blind, bloodshot eyes. A choked sound came out of her throat through bared teeth, curses half-swallowed.

"Dead," she repeated thickly, and gave a terrible laugh that was half sob. "Don't you think I know that? Get out, Knorth. Now. Before I hurt you." Her fist crashed down on the table. "Rot you!" she cried at it, with all her thwarted grief and rage.

The table sagged. Dry rot dust rattled down from it as its legs started to crumble.

Jame heard the door open behind her and Jorin scramble out. The next moment she was through it herself, shoved so hard by the randon that she bounced off the corridor's far wall. The captain shut the study door behind them. Her short, sandy hair was bristling, like Jorin's tail. They heard a curiously soft, slithering, rotten sound inside as the table collapsed.

That could have been me, Jame thought.

The cadets were staring at them. They had probably never seen a Kendar manhandle a lady before.

"Stay out of there," the captain told them. "If she calls, I'll go in, but no one else. Understand?"

When she turned, Jame saw worry and more than a touch of fear in her blue eyes. She hadn't known what her matriarch was. She still wasn't sure. A maledight with berserker tendencies, so high in the power of her house. The suspicion alone was the stuff of nightmares.

"She did stop with the table," said Jame.

"Next time, she probably won't. You'd better leave, lady. Now."

There was no answer to that but to sketch a salute and go, so Jame did, wondering.

Was she to blame for Brenwyr's state? It was hard to see how, considering that Aerulan had been dead nearly twice as long as Jame had been alive. She felt as if she had wandered into an old song of passion and loss, but one as yet without an ending. It was that which might yet drive Brenwyr mad. If it did, she could do hideous damage, and stopping her could be just as costly. But that really wasn't Jame's business, was it? Anyway, how could one destructive Shanir help another? Being so ignorant made her feel stupid and weak. Worst thought of all, was she fated to end like Brenwyr, a curse to everyone she loved? Tori thought so already.

"A mistake, too dangerous to live."

Eh, enough of that. Since she had made such a mess of apologizing for something that wasn't her fault, she should find Brier Iron-thorn and try again for something that was.

Only then did she realize that Jorin was gone. Lady Brenwyr, it seemed, had been one too many for him. His disappearance didn't worry Jame too much, though: blind as he was, the ounce could usually find his way in any area which he had previously seen through her eyes. She would look for him as she did for Brier.

The morning passed, however, with no sign of either. Noon came and went.

Mount Alban's upper keep floated on over a weirding sea as its inmates set to their experiments, trying to direct their wandering home in one direction or another. As usual, the singers and scrollsmen competed. The former stationed themselves along the western edge of the observation deck and in unison chanted any song they could think of that referred to the Western Sea. (A fine thing, thought Jame, if Mount Alban should land in the middle of it.) Below, the latter engaged in more individual efforts, aiming for landfalls as diverse as Kothifir and the Isles of the Dead, using methods which ranged from solemn appeals to the masonry to one ancient scholar playing hopscotch in a corner.

Jame fell in with Index as the old man bustled about the upper keep and what remained of the lower, dispensing information and counting up his barter-profits with a miser's glee. Sometime, though, he faltered. A doggerel couplet would start him off again, if he could remember it or if Jame could supply it from those she had over-heard in the herb shed. Index apparently used the wall of herb jars as a mnemonic device, with nonsense verse as its key, a clever solution for an old man with a failing memory and no trust in the written word—except that he had begun to forget the key. Jame remembered it for him when she could, and kept her own barter score for later use.

While she saved her questions with Index, however, she asked them whenever she ran into one of the Knorth cadets. Considerably junior to the Brandan honor guard, they had been scattered throughout the keep, told to make themselves useful or at least to keep out from under foot. None of them had seen Brier in hours, and all found excuses not to talk about her.

"Vant's orders," said Rue, glowering. "We're in trouble enough as it is, he says."

"What trouble?" Jame demanded.

Rue fidgeted with the sack of chicken feathers which she was carrying in aid, ancestors only knew, of what arcane experiment. As much as she disliked him, Vant was Five, with an authority over her more immediate than that of her lord's runagate sister. Suddenly she stiffened, listening.

"Did someone say, 'Land ho'?"

"Don't change the topic," said Jame, exasperated, then broke off as the cry came again. "Not 'Land ho.' 'Sand ho.'"

Rue dropped her sack and sprinted for the nearest stairs leading upward, hard on Jame's heels.

Hot, crimson light flooded down to meet them. Up on the observation deck, figures lined the western rail, black against the glare, singers and scrollsmen both. Beyond them, a setting sun hung low and swollen in the sky. Jame looked sideways down the line of scholars, blinking away black after-images from sun-shocked eyes. Not far away stood Brier Iron-thorn, red hair sullenly ablaze. As usual, her dark face revealed nothing, but the tense lines of her body suggested someone leaning hard against a short leash. Jame looked west again, following the Kendar's stare. A vast plain stretched out before them, seemingly endless, so absolutely flat as to look unreal. A hot breath of wind blew in her face. With it came a distant, empty keening and the dry incense of desert places.

"All right," said someone, breaking the awed silence. "What clown aimed for the Southern Wastes?"

VI

"This," said the Director, "is serious."

A subdued knot of scholars had gathered around him, away from those who still lined the rail chattering like excited children. Kirien and Ashe had joined the circle, the latter hooded, an iron-shod staff in her hand. Listening from the rail, hoping to escape notice, Jame flinched as the Director turned his scarred face toward her; however, when he stared over her head, unblinking, full into the sun, she suddenly realized that he was blind.

"Ashe tells me that we're in the middle of the Dry Salt Sea," he said. "Urakarn is west of us, below the horizon but still dangerously close. I needn't remind you what happened the last time Kencyr fell into Karnid hands."

The group stirred uneasily, remembering. It had only been some dozen years ago, after all, during the long confusion after Ganth's fall. Without a Knorth Heir to lead the Southern Host, Caineron had secured the post for his favorite son, Genjar, who in turn had tried to further his own political ambitions by attacking the Karnid stronghold.

"'Black rock on the dry sea's edge,'" Ashe suddenly chanted, her harsh voice like stones grating together;

"'How many your dungeons swallowed. How few came out again.'"

Tori went in, Jame thought, and came out, with the marks of Karnid torture on his hands and soul. He must have been about her age then, if not younger. Strange. She remembered so clearly the child he had been and had met him again now as a man; but what had that boy been like, who had faced the horrors of Urakarn and barely survived them?

Ashe's song had stilled the chatter by the rail. What if the weirding stranded them here? They could see it stretching away to the east and north, a great cloud plain rosy with sunset light. Clearly, it had reached its farthest mark and now must either dissipate or withdraw. Which, and how soon? No one knew.

Jame slipped down the southeast corner stair, hopefully on Brier's heels. At least, when she had turned again to look, the Kendar had disappeared, and there weren't all that many ways for her to go.

High time that she also found Jorin. It occurred to her now that she hadn't looked for the ounce in the most obvious place. Sure enough, there in the infirmary he was, curled up asleep on Aerulan's tapestry lap. There too was Graykin, fretfully awake.

"Yellow isn't exactly your color," she said, regarding the half-healed bruises on his face, "but it's better than black and blue. Kindrie tells me that you may even have enough Kencyr blood to grow some new teeth."

"Fine," muttered the Southron, without looking at her.

Behind the mask, Jame's eyebrows rose. "If you're having second thoughts about serving me..."

"It isn't that! You gave me a job to do, something to guard, and I failed."

"Oh." She sat down on the foot of his pallet. "Listen, Gray: it isn't important. I don't want that damned book anyway. If it wants me, it will find some way to come crawling back. I never meant to saddle you with it all winter, in any event."

He was glaring at her now. "Oh, so it's not important, is it? How nice to know that I starved, froze, and got beaten up by Caineron's thugs for no good reason. But that doesn't matter. What does is that you gave me an assignment, however stupid, and I failed."

"I see. What we're really talking about here is your pride."

"My pride?" He drew himself up, indignant, clutching the blanket to his bony chest. "How about yours? You're a great lady, aren't you? The Highlord's own sister! You shouldn't run around dressed like a…a Tastigon flash-blade. You've got me now…"

"…to keep my hands clean," Jame finished. "You've said that before. Let's get something clear, here and now: if you do serve me, my hands are only as clean as yours. I'm serious, Gray. Too many of my house have tried to hide behind Honor's Paradox, from Master Gerridon on down. But you should be serious too. Look: I'm in no position to offer you security, protection, or even a crust of bread every other week. The way things are going, I probably never will be."

But Graykin was shaking his head. "You'll have power," he said stubbornly. "You must. Nothing stops you."

There was a scratch on the door and Rue entered, scowling. "You were asking about Ten," she said in her abrupt way. "Well, it's not right. Someone's got to be told, orders or no."

Jame stood up, a ripple of apprehension down her spine. "You said before that there was trouble. What?"

"Nothing, at first. The captain thought we'd been caught out in the weirding and carried along with it, the same as she was. Then someone says something to her Ten, I think it was Vant, and the next thing we know our Ten is on the mat."

"Wait a minute. This would be Captain Hawthorn, correct? Who is she, anyway?"

"You know," said Rue, impatiently. "You were talking to her outside the library."

"I was?" Light dawned. "She's the Brandan captain, with her cadet ten-command, escorting Lady Brenwyr. All right, Rue. I just didn't know her name before now. So, Brier is on the mat."

"And the captain asks her, flat out, if she ignored standing orders to take us back to Tentir when it started to weird up. 'Yes, Ran,' says Ten, wooden-like. You know her way. Did she in fact take us south, away from safety? 'Yes, Ran.' Why? 'No excuse, Ran.'"

"She didn't say anything about me or Restormir?"

"Not a word. Maybe we cadets should have, but like Vant says, we're already midden-deep in trouble, and how will it help Ten anyway? So Hawthorn says, 'You've endangered your squad, apparently without reason. You're relieved of command.' Ten's an outsider, like me. This will ruin her, and it's not fair!"

"It damn well isn't," said Jame. "Hawthorn is a reasonable woman, though. She'll understand if I explain, if she isn't still too mad at me to listen."

"She may understand," said Rue, sounding doubtful, "but it may not help. You didn't see, did you? When Ten left the deck, she went down the outer stair to the desert. I don't think she means to come back."

After that Rue left, relieved at having vented her feelings to someone, although plainly not expecting Jame to do anything but listen.

"Thought a lot of herself, that Iron-thorn did," said Graykin, with ill-concealed satisfaction. "And she was a Caineron born and bred, whatever oaths she's sworn since. You don't need the likes of her, lady."

"Jealous, Gray?" Jame asked absent-mindedly, not noticing him flinch.

She was wondering if she should leave her heavy d'hen behind. No. Without its protection, she felt naked; and besides, the sun was setting. Water? A good drink should suffice. The Southron watched with growing alarm as she drained a flask left for his use.

"What are you doing?" he demanded. "You don't...you can't intend to go after her!"

"Don't I?" said Jame. "Can't I?"

She regarded Jorin and Aerulan. Blind ounce and dead girl seemed to look back at her hopefully.

"I think not. Still. Down, kitten."

Shooed off the banner, Jorin stood by making sounds of protest as she rolled it up and slung it across her back.

"You can't!" said Graykin again, more shrilly. "Any minute now, this floating mad-house is going to snap back toward the

Riverland. I over heard people up on the deck say so! I-I won't let you go. I'll call Captain Hawthorn."

The next moment he had curled back like a frightened spider, all knees and elbows, as the other bent over him. The back of one black-sheathed finger lightly traced the line of his jaw and hooked under his chin, jarring it back with sudden pain. Silver eyes locked with his own.

"Oh no, little man, oh no. Never come between me and my honor. Never. Understand?"

"Y-yes."

The gloved hand patted his bruised cheek lightly, a panther's tap. "Good boy. Now sleep for awhile."

The door opened, closed. Graykin drew a deep, shuddering breath in the humming silence. "Be damned if I will," he muttered, shaken but defiant, trying to rally. "Be damned…"

…and toppled over sideways, asleep before he hit the floor.

VII

Jame closed the door behind her quickly, before Jorin could dash through it. Power still sang in her blood, another berserker flare successfully controlled. This could get to be a habit.

Yes: a dangerous one. If each use of her claws brought her closer to the Third Face of God, wouldn't this too? On the other hand, what she had just done to Graykin also savored of the use to which such talents were put under shadow's eaves. It was damnable, to be caught balancing between her Shanir blood and the darkling training to which the Master had subjected it, and perhaps double damned in that she understood what had been done to her.

You may still be innocent, the Arrin-ken Immalai had said, *but not ignorant. If you do eventually fall, it will be as the Master fell, knowing the evil you do, welcoming it. The abuse of power will push you in that direction. On the other hand, its mere use may drive you the other way, toward our god. That is what it means to be a Shanir, to walk the knife's edge.*

"But I don't want to fall either way!" she had cried, and that rich, ironic voice had answered her, chuckling deep in her mind:

Which one of us does? For us, alas, good is no less terrible than evil.

No less terrible. What a choice.

And how seductive power was. It was her birthright, no less than Ganth's tangled legacy and no easier to deny. But how long could she master it before, like wine, it mastered her? Now, there would be a terrible intoxication indeed. It had already made her hasty and cruel. What choice, though, had Graykin given her?

Trust honor, Immalai had said.

Yes. For her, balanced on the knife's edge, honor was more than life, its loss infinitely worse than death. And part of honor was taking responsibility for one's actions and choices, over and over, as long as one acted or chose. If she had to accept Gray as her servant, he must learn to understand that.

Huh. Knorth or Caineron, honor should be the same: Kencyr. But that didn't suit Caldane's ambition. Honor restricted his power. He would reshape it, if he could, to mean unquestioning obedience from his servants, while he used their services to keep his own hands clean. Honor's Paradox suggested that, ultimately, no one was responsible for anything. It was the knife's edge which Caldane would make all his people walk, if he could, hoping that when they fell (as they must, if only he pushed hard enough) this uncomfortable world would be remade in his image.

Come to think of it, that was exactly what Gerridon had done.

And there were other Kencyr, today, who winced at the choices which honor demanded, who would abjure all responsibility if they could.

"A lady's honor is obedience," the sewing instructress had so vehemently claimed. Don't ask questions. Don't even speak. Just obey.

Of course, that young teacher was very low in the Women's World, down where secrecy starved the mind as a seeker's mask did the senses. How clever of the Matriarchs to realize that the most may be written on the blankest slate. To what degree, though, did they carry obedience to their lords?

Jame shivered, the elation of the flare draining away. The Three-Faced God had apparently abandoned his people. The great mission which he had given them seemed more impossible year by year. The Arrin-ken had left. The women and Shanir were powerless, the priests treacherous, the lords merciless, and her brother was taking advice from a dead madman. What was left except honor, and how many secret fingers there were, picking at that last knot which held the Kencyrath together.

She had been going down the corridor glancing into each
southward-facing room as she passed. Outside a window, finally, was the silhouette of the Director's stair.

For the first time, Jame saw how jury-rigged it was. The
steps descended in a tight spiral of narrow treads and uneven
risers, precariously braced against the outer wall, held together
by a pine trunk newel. Branch stumps were their main supports. Whose work was this, anyway—that gabble of ancient
scholars? If Brier had come this way, though, it ought at least
to support Jame. She stepped out onto it, and clutched the
rough-barked newel as a tread tilted under her weight.

Gingerly, she descended several feet, then bent to peer
into the room below. Sunset lay in fading rose rhomboids on
the floor by the windows, roughed by mounds of dust. Farther in, light edged the broken lines of furniture. All the
tables but one had collapsed. The floor was rotting too.
Jame's foot sank into it, unnervingly, as she stepped down
from the window ledge. Dust billowed up. One loud noise,
she thought, choking back a sneeze, and she would find herself suddenly one story down. One soft curse might get her
there even faster.

She had started quietly across the floor, watching for soft
spots, unslinging the banner as she went, when she realized
that she wasn't alone.

A dark shape sat on the far side of the table, slumped
forward over it.

Brenwyr.

When Jame had decided to leave Aerulan in safe hands,
the Iron Matriarch had come immediately to mind. This room,
patently, was far from safe, Brenwyr even less so. Still, Jame
trusted her impulse. She hung the banner on the wall behind
the Brandan's chair and retreated on noiseless feet.

The windowsill crumbled under her weight.

"Aerulan!" exclaimed Brenwyr's voice behind her.

The Matriarch had started upright at the crash, staring
blindly before her. Behind, in the shadows, stood Aerulan.

It's only the banner, Jame told herself; but then she saw Aerulan's hand resting on Brenwyr's shoulder and met the dead girl's smiling, silver eyes.

Out the window, down the stair, run away, run—

—until a step turned underfoot, and Jame found herself again clutching the shaggy newel, all nails out, staring at a drop below her of several hundred feet.

A trick of the light, she told herself, thinking of the room above. Then, *Sweet Trinity, what have I done now?*

Whatever it had been, though, for good or ill, Aerulan was no longer her responsibility.

But Brier Iron-thorn still was.

The plain spread out below her, utterly flat to the southern horizon. Across the western prospect, half-obscured by Mount Alban's bulk, stretched a range of purple clouds like distant mountains, veined with fire as the sun sank behind it. Red sand muted to rose and coral. Dusk flooded the desert land, beautiful, unearthly—lifeless? Had Rue been mistaken, or perhaps had Brier changed her mind? Somehow, Jame didn't think so.

The climb down seemed endless, one newel-trunk succeeding another, a denuded forest laid end to end. At first, the stair descended past the wooden walls of the upper keep. Below that, as Kirien had guessed, was weirding mist where the cliff-face should have been, yet the cliff hardly seemed absent, so exactly had the weirding taken its form. Sculpted cloud gave the illusion of rock grain and feathery fern. Windows opened into vanished rooms, furnished with fog, waiting for ghosts, all aglow with pale weirding light.

The stair ended in a rope ladder dangling some nine feet short of the ground. Jame hesitated, then dropped. She would have trouble getting back without help, but then she didn't intend to return alone. Her own falling weight barely disturbed the sand crust. Beside her feet, though, were the prints of someone much larger and heavier, tiger tread to her hunting ounce. Ah.

Down the mist flank of a Mount Alban that wasn't there, out, free of its phantom western side.

Voices?

Jame paused, listening. The cadence of human speech, at least, if not words, threading in and out of the desert silence. The weirding-storm stretched obliquely back from Mount Alban's northwest corner, a billowing tidal wave held restlessly in check. The cliff's ghost shape strained forward out of it like a figurehead—anchored? Were there ruins here that could snag them as the wolvers' keep had in the Grimly Holt? She had heard of the deserted cities of the Wastes, constantly appearing and disappearing at the whim of wind and sand. If so, it must be back under the weirding mass. Was Index's herb shed still there too, trolling on its long line, catching what, or whom?

A hum rose again as if of voices, faded, was gone.

It was no business of hers, Jame thought, turning away. She couldn't do anything about it anyway, while the shed remained weird-bound and unreachable.

Brier's tracks led due west, when Jame could find them. At first there were none except where the Kendar had walked across one of the glittering mineral deposits that laced the plain, leaving a trail of powdered crystal. She couldn't be far ahead, walking, with not that much of a head start, but Jame couldn't see her.

Sink-sand? Surely no Southron would accidentally blunder into that, not that Jame herself knew what it looked like on the surface, much less what other traps the Wastes might set.

Underfoot now, the sand crust had developed corrugations like frozen ripples. It was softer too, Brier's footprints showing clearly. The ridges got bigger, their purple shadows striping the plain. Soon she could feel the pull in her muscles as she climbed them. Dunes? How could she have missed seeing these from the ladder, when everything below had looked so flat?

Then, over the crest of one, suddenly, she found Brier Iron-thorn.

The Kendar knelt, sunset light threading her dark auburn hair with fire. White grains shifted through the fingers of her raised, clenched fist, spilling back into the desert.

"Sand," she said. "Nothing but sand."

Jame stopped on the crest, feeling awkward. "Did you expect something else?" she asked, diffident.

"Expect? No. Hope? For what? This isn't even the right place."

"What place?"

"Maybe the sink-trap, where she died; maybe at the stone boat, where she returned."

"Who?"

For a long moment, Brier was silent, staring blindly at the far horizon. The purple clouds were closer, larger. The sun, shifting down behind them, traced their edges with gold, while inside tarnished silver lights flickered and distant thunder rumbled. A breath of wind rustled the raw silk of the Kendar's hair. Then, in a low voice, as if talking to herself, she said:

"They had escaped from the dungeons of Urakarn and were fleeing across the Dry Salt Sea. Rose stumbled into sink-sand. He tried to hold onto her, but Karnid torture had half-crippled his hands. All that long, terrible day, staggering northward, afraid to stop for fear of pursuit, he kept thinking that she was somehow still alive down there, under the sand. At dusk, they found the petrified remains of a boat and collapsed into it. In the night, feverish, he thought he saw the water return, all that flat sand plain changing back to the sea it had been, and the stone boat afloat on it. Under the surface, he saw Rose and reached down to her. She took his hand, pulled it down into the stinging salt water, pulled the whole boat across the sea, in a dream, he thought, born of fever; but in the morning there they were safe on the northern shore, with nothing behind them but sand.

"Sand," she repeated, again regarding the grains which trickled through her fingers.

"Torisen told you that story, didn't he?" When? Jame wanted to ask. Why? Instead, she heard herself say, "How did he look?"

"Dazed. Sick. The Karnids and infection had almost cost him his hands; but he said he couldn't sleep until he had told me how my mother died."

For her mother's sake, Tori had said, accepting Brier's bond.

Jame had wondered what her brother had been like at her age. Now she had a sudden, vivid image of him, young and haggard, wondering if Rose Iron-thorn's impassive, red-haired child understood the news he had brought, not guessing that she would never forget a word of it.

"I suppose he thought you had a right to know."

"That's what he said."

Brier let the remaining sand fall and stood up. The quickening wind lifted her hair at the temples in glowing, short-pinioned wings. Thunder growled closer.

"Storm's coming, lady," she said. "Time to be getting back."

The Kendar had always meant to return, Jame thought, humbled, as she turned to follow. Not for Rose Iron-thorn's daughter, the self-destructive, almost petulant gesture which Jame herself had made all too often. Brier was tougher than that, too professional simply to give up. Likewise, apologies meant nothing to her. If Jame's presence here didn't convey her regret, words wouldn't help. Whether the gesture itself had, she couldn't tell.

Strange. Instead of diminishing, the dunes were growing bigger and softer the farther east they went. All Jame could see now from their troughs was the darkening sky above. On the crests, a rising wind had begun to whip sand from rise to rise. It stung her face as she glanced back. The storm-rack rolled close on their heels, black against the sky's deepening blue, blotting out the stars. Bolts of searing white leaped between it and the ground. Ahead, the faint glow of the weirding cliff seemed farther away than ever.

At the foot of a slope Jame tripped over a stone—no, over the top of a shattered wall, scoured clean by the swooping wind. All around, masonry fragments jutted out of the sand like so many decayed teeth. If these were the ruins on which Mount Alban had snagged, the on-coming storm must have dislodged it. If so, not only did it seem farther away, it was.

"Run," said Brier.

Jame tried. The dunes were mountainous now, though, and her feet sank into them to the ankles. For all her weight, Brier was well ahead of her, traveling fast.

Be damned if I'll call for help, Jame thought, struggling to catch up. *Be damned.*

Salt stung her eyes like sea spray. Across her shoulders, her jacket felt heavy and damp with sweat. She floundered up the highest range of drifts yet and saw the weirding beyond like a glowing cliff against which the dune was poised to break. High above glowed the lights of the scrollsmen's keep. Below, the rope ladder swung wildly in the wind. Brier had almost reached it.

"Don't stop!" she called back sharply.

But Jame already had, panting. The slanted edge of the storm had overtaken her to the north. As it closed with the weirding, lightning leaped between them, flash on booming flash. The shock rolled southward toward the keep. In the flickering glare, the far end of the ridge on which she stood seemed to be cresting like a wave and crashing down in salt white.

"Move!" shouted Brier.

Jame took an almost involuntary step forward, and sank up to her knees. She could feel sand melting away under her. Up to her thighs, her waist.

"Brier." she heard herself cry, in a voice so thin with fear that she scarcely recognized it. Up to her chest.

And down, mouth and eyes closed barely in time, sand pressing in on them, stopping ears suddenly against the thunder's boom. Her up-thrown hands writhed free for a moment...*Here I am, here.* Then the earth gripped them. Squeezed, the breath trapped burning in her lungs as she was in this sandy grave, buried alive. How deep did Rose sink? How long did she live?

Got you now, thief, Ragga's voice seemed to grate in her mind.

But the sand was changing. Her frantic hands moved again, as if through mud, then water. Eyes opened, shut again hastily against the saline sting. Then suddenly she was tumbling forward in darkness, over and over, hammered by a muted roar. No air. Which way was up? Drowning.

Cold hands seized her, shoved her downward, she thought, and struggled feebly. Cold words bubbled in her ear: "Don't, you fool. For your brother's sake."

The roar burst full-throated around her. Air, thick with salt spray; waves, throwing her up against the glowing cliff. Underwater again, then shoved back to the surface where a strong hand grabbed her by the collar and jerked her upward. Her fingers closed on shaggy wood. She clung, gasping, still in Brier's powerful grasp. On the Director's fragile stair, in the tumultuous darkness, they listened to the boom and crash below them of the returning salt sea.

Interim V
The Grimly Holt: 60th of Spring

The forest keep lay drowned in mist as though at the bottom of a luminous sea. Difficult to say in that glowing twilight when dawn came, or noon, or setting sun.

The shadow of that other, darker keep had long since faded like a bad dream, taking with it the stench of sickness and burning. The wolvers had not discussed it, afraid that words would bring it back. There were some things about human-kind, after all, which few of them wished to know. Besides, there was so much else about which to sing.

Abandoning the outer walls of the keep to the weirding's care, the wolvers happily speculated about its interior. How thick had been the walls, how patterned the roof beams and floor, and where (whined hungry cubs) had food been stored? As debate rose and fell, weirding trickled in the long-gone windows to take the hazy shape of each detail, building its reality, a fragile shell crafted of song, cupped in a hollow of mist.

By the hearth, Torisen stirred in his sleep and mumbled incoherent words of distress. Not long ago, his breathing had changed from the deep, slow rhythm of dwar. Now he was beginning to surface, through the level of dreams. His hands twitched, as if clutching at something or trying to pull away.

"Hurting me," he muttered. "Let go, let...ah!"

His eyes flickered open. He blinked, confused, then fo-cused on the worried face bending over him.

"Oh. Hello, Grimly." His right hand hurt. He frowned at swollen, splinted fingers. Kin-Slayer lay across the nearby hearth, sullenly reflecting the pale flames which danced in the grate. "W-Where am I? What happened?"

"How much do you remember?"

The Wolver's careful tone chilled him. The last thing which he recalled clearly was trying to last out the night awake in his Kothifir quarters. Obviously, he hadn't succeeded. After that? Snatches of memory, as broken as the dreams which they might in fact be. His breath caught.

"Grimly, did I kill Burr?"

"No, no. You haven't killed anyone this time, not even a horse."

Torisen looked at Kin-Slayer, confused. "But I was supposed to. Father said."

But then Jame had shot the bolt. He could still feel Ganth's madness pressing hard against that locked door in his soul, but as long as the bolt held...

He shook himself. Just another stupid dream. Absurd, to think that it had anything to do with this blessed return to sanity—assuming he was sane.

He looked at the surrounding walls of glowing mist, at the semblance of smoking torches and the phantom flames on the hearth. It might have been a hall hollowed out of living cloud. More mist drifted over the ground, or was it a floor? He lay on something ill-defined and yielding, yet substantial enough to support his weight. A muffled chuckling came from underneath. His fingers, gingerly probing downward, touched water so cold that it seemed to burn. It was a, a brook, swift with melted snow, running down the length of a ruined hall. This was the wolvers' keep, where he had often been a guest before, and there at its far end were his hosts: dark, lupine shapes with glowing eyes regarding him shyly askance. Their song rose and fell. The misty floor seemed to harden. He jerked up his hand before it could become trapped, then lay it wonderingly down again on a surface textured like that of worn stone paving, almost gritty to the touch.

"I was northward bound on the River Road," he said slowly, remembering. "Just short of the holt, you and a weirdingstrom overtook me. And then..."

"We took refuge here," said Grimly, still with great care. "You looked at the sword in your hand and said, 'There's more than one way to break a grip.' Remember? Then you pried loose your fingers one by one. Three broke. Then, finally, you slept."

"How long?"

Grimly glanced up at the nebulous beams supporting the roof of mist. "Hard to say. Fourteen hours, at least."

Torisen nodded. Even that much dwar sleep would hardly set all to right, but he knew by the deep itch in flesh and bone that healing had begun. He wouldn't lose his right hand this time, as he so nearly had at Urakarn.

"What is it?" the Wolver asked sharply.

The old terror of mutilation had leaped on Torisen suddenly, and with it the memory of that last true dream before his present waking.

"I-I was in the Southern Wastes, trying to pull Rose Iron-thorn out of sinksand."

But then it hadn't been Rose at all but his sister Jame, sinking, pulling him down with her. "You can't bear to look at my face, can you?' she had jeered up at him. "It's the price I've already paid for your cowardice."

She wouldn't let go. Her nails were tearing the flesh off his hands.

"Let go, let go," he gasped, and found himself struggling against Grimly's restraining grip. "Let go, dammit! I've got to leave for Gothregor. Now."

"You can't," said Grimly, holding him down. "Not in this weather. Be sensible, Tori! The Riverland is over four hundred miles away."

"Then I'll weird-walk. It's been done before."

"D'you want to arrive piece-meal over the next ten years? That's been known to happen too!"

By now, they were nearly shouting. Furry ears flicked in their direction. The wolvers had chosen the wrong moment, though, to let their attention wander. The weirding outside

the keep had been stationary for some time. Now it stirred
with a sigh and began to flow northward, as if at the turning
of a tide. The song-crafted inner shell shifted with it, away
from the shadow of the brook under the floor, away from the
old ruins, taking its crafters with it.

"Now what?" Torisen asked.

Grimly had leaped to his feet, all four of them. His hack-
les had risen.

"Damned if I know. We're adrift, in a cockleshell of song.
This has never happened before—but then, you've never been
our guest during a weirdingstrom before, either, have you?"
He showed sharp teeth in a nervous grin. "I've noticed, Torisen
Black Lord, that what you want, you usually get. Maybe we're
bound for Gothregor after all."

Part VI

UPPER KEEP

HERB SHED

RUINS

UPPER KEEP

THIRD FLOOR: OBSERVATION DECK

SECOND FLOOR: INFIRMARY (WEST SIDE)
LIBRARY (SOUTH SIDE)

FIRST FLOOR: BRENWYR'S QUARTERS
(SOUTH SIDE)

Mount Alban: 60th of Spring
I

The conference was held in the library. Outside its southward facing windows, lightning intermittently lit the storm-maddened Salt Sea, patently no longer dry. In the claps of darkness between, waves crested and crashed against Mount Alban's phantom foundation. Each time, the ironwood walls of the keep shivered and lamps swayed.

Singers, scrollsmen and randon cadets crowded into the room, listening as Brier Iron-thorn made her report to the Director and Captain Hawthorn. Scholarly heads nodded. They had all heard rumors of this rare Southron phenomenon, the alluvial transformation, now demonstrated to be scrollsman's fact rather than singer's fancy. What an opportunity to investigate, even for those Kendar prone to seasickness.

Kirien stood near the edge of the crowd, taking notes in her spiky script, which Aunt Trishien's hand would also be recording in far off Gothregor. Singer Ashe, hooded and dark, stood behind her like a shadow. Both looked up sharply when Brier described in her flat voice how the Knorth had been swallowed up by the sand and spat out by the sea. Everyone turned to regard the wet, bedraggled figure in the corner, but it kept its silence. No matter. They would barter for details later.

Jame was grateful not to be questioned, especially by Brier. The sea had returned. Brier must wonder if her mother had too. Jame hadn't told her about those cold hands, that salt-chilled voice. *For your brother's sake.* Perhaps she had imagined it, and that other voice as well, the Earth Wife's gloat. Probably. But still she couldn't stop shivering.

"So it comes to this," said the Director, when Brier had finished. "If the storm flays away enough of our weirding support before we regain the rest of Mount Alban, this college will fall. Literally. The question is, can we do anything to prevent it?"

"It depends on will-power," said Index. "Either ours, or someone else's. Nothing happens by chance on this world."

That raised a fury of protest. Was he suggesting some sort of divine interference? From their god?

"Isn't that what we've been waiting for all these millennia?" snapped the old man. "But why only look within the Kencyrath? We're newcomers on an ancient world."

"'Step-children,'" said the Knorth suddenly.

Index glared at her. "Whatever. The point is, there are forces on Rathillien about which we know virtually nothing. Now, among the Merikit…"

Groans drown him out, the loudest from those the most in his debt. "Old facts, cold facts!" "Stick to remembering ours while you still can!" "How long, Index, since you last discovered something for yourself?"

"Order," said the Director, cutting them short. "If willing ourselves not to fall can help, do it. In the meantime, bail out the lower rooms."

As the library cleared, Jame stopped Hawthorn. "About Cadet Brier. Rue tells me that you relieved her of command for endangering her squad. Well, she came south to help me, and then…"

The captain raised a hand in warning. "This sounds like house business. Tell your lord brother, not me. So, you were acting as your lady's escort?" she asked, stopping Brier at the door.

The Kendar gave Jame a brief, unreadable look. "I suppose so, ran."

"Why didn't you say so before? That puts your actions on equal footing with mine, escorting the Brandan Matriarch, for which ancestors have mercy on us both. Take back your command."

That's one thing set right, at least, Jame thought as Brier acknowledged, expressionless, while Rue grinned at Vant's sour face.

As for telling Torisen, though...First, let him damn well ask.

II

It was a long night.

Hour after hour, the sea broke against Mount Alban, each blow making the wooden walls shudder while moisture ran down them like cold sweat. Everything got wet except the precious scrolls, hastily wrapped in oiled silk. Soon the highest waves threatened the keep's lowest rooms—because of a rising sea or a sinking fortress, no one could say. Scholars scrambled to save their possessions, until a wave surging into one room nearly swept a clutch of singers out with it. Upstairs, Kindrie and the infirmarian already had their hands full with a host of minor injuries. Finally, Hawthorn ordered the academic community out from under foot, and the randon settled down to cope.

Jame stayed out of their way. She knew she should use this opportunity to rest, if not sleep, but she was far too unsettled. Index's words haunted her: "there are forces on Rathillien about which we know virtually nothing." Sweet Trinity, yes. The terror of those moments under the sand caught her again by the throat, stopping her breath.

Got you now, thief.

Despite everything, she had only taken Mother Ragga half in earnest. Now how could she set foot on the earth again, anywhere, when at any moment it might open and swallow her? Had she forfeited her right not only to be among her own people, but on this world altogether?

A mistake, too dangerous to live, cursed be and cast out.

So she wandered on about the lower rooms, aimlessly, a wet, unhappy ounce creeping on her heels and standing disconsolately on her toes whenever she stopped. If the sheer will not to drown could help, Jorin was doing his part. Then his ears flicked: they were being followed. Jame turned a corner, reversed sharply, and found herself holding an indignant Graykin at knifepoint.

The Southron still looked shaky, she thought, but much improved. Perhaps when she had ordered him to sleep, she had accidentally plunged him into his first experience with dwar. At any rate, the infirmarian had judged him fit enough to make room for more recent casualties.

"I'm your sneak," he said when she demanded to know why he was following her. "Just tell me who else I should sneak after and I'll get on with it. You know," he added impatiently, as if to someone slow-witted. "Who's your worst enemy here? The Director? That Brandan captain?"

"Hawthorn? Sweet Trinity, why?"

He shot her a sly, sidelong look. "They're in command, aren't they? But you should be. The Highlord's closest blood-kin, aren't you?"

"Yes, but…"

Jame stopped, perplexed. If only custom, not law, had kept her subservient in the Women's Hall, she had no idea what her true status was. Graykin might even conceivably be right.

"Be that as it may, I can't do a better job just now than they can, so the question is moot. This is survival, Gray, not politics."

"Politics are survival," the Southron muttered, but she had already turned away.

At last the wind dropped, and then the waves. As quiet returned to the shaken keep, a stealthy rattling could be heard as all the salt water, soaking walls, furnishings, and clothes, changed back to glistening salt sand. Jame shook about a pound of it out of her boots, then went up to the observation deck with ounce and spy trailing after her.

The old scrollsman Index acknowledged her with a grunt as she joined him at the rail. They looked out over a featureless expanse of weirding mist level with the lowest rooms, faintly luminous under a predawn sky.

"Where do you suppose we are?" Jame asked.

"How should I know?" the old man snapped. "This whole junket wasn't my idea."

"But you think it was someone's?"

"Or something's. There are reasons for everything. Most people are just too lazy or stupid to figure them out. Which are you?"

"Uh, ignorant, I hope, rather than stupid. Afraid rather than lazy. About what you said in the library, what forces?"

"Among the Merikit? The Burnt Man, for one. Ha! Heard of him, have you?"

Jame had shivered, remembering nightmares of pursuit, a charred hand thrust up through campfire debris, a charcoal-smeared man laying fires in the wilderness. Out of her pocket she drew the cinder shaped like a phalange. Index snatched it.

"A Burnt Man's bone," he said gleefully, turning it over in his own bony fingers. "Bonfire, bone-fire. Tell you about that, shall I?"

"Please."

"On Midwinter's Day the Merikit burn the biggest log they can find, then bury whatever remains of it along with everyone's hearth ashes. 'Burying winter,' they call it, or 'burning the Burnt Man.' It's meant to hurry on spring, you see. Then these cinders start to turn up in their fireplaces. Not just finger bones; all different sorts. They collect 'em until they have about two hundred, a complete skeleton. Just before Summer Eve, fires are laid along the borders of the land which the Merikit claim, each with a 'bone' in it. During the festival, the chief strips naked and smears himself with charcoal to personify the Burnt Man. When he jumps over the first fire, the 'bone' in it bursts into flame. All the 'bones' in all the fires ignite at the same time. The shaman-elders claim that he passes over the whole lot simultaneously."

"This would be to draw death out of the ground, I suppose, in preparation for summer."

The old man made a face, not pleased to be anticipated. "For that, and something else besides."

"What?"

"Ha! Used up all your credit and then some, haven't you?" He pocketed the bone, looking smug. "Always keep count, my girl, and a question in reserve."

Damn. Index was a bastard and a crank, Jame decided, but not as much of the latter as his colleagues supposed. His nothing-by-chance theory paralleled her own determination to learn the rules of any game which she found herself playing. Like Index, she wanted facts, so as to understand cause and thus (hopefully) avoid being whacked on the head by effect. She had thought, after a year's research in Tai-tastigon, that she could safely dismiss all native godlings as mere byblows of her own god. That still was true of the so-called New Pantheon. Clearly, though, Index was right that there were other powers on Rathillien. Of such the Kencyrath chose to remain ignorant. Tai-tastigon's Old Pantheon, now, had it evolved from something more native to this world and not limited to the Eastern Lands, something more—elemental?

The Burnt Man and the Earth Wife, fire and earth. The Tishooo and the River Snake, air and water.

Seek the Four, the God-voice had said.

No. It couldn't be that simple—and yet not really simple at all. If the Snake was a leftover bit of Perimal Darkling, as Cattila claimed, it wasn't really part of this world either. That catfish, though, what had spoken to her through it? And how was it that, according to Kindrie, the Arrin-ken had sought the Four presumably without success for centuries, while she seemed to attract them like flies to honey? It was one thing to imagine oneself the center of the world, another to find that it might be true.

Rathillien is watching me, she thought, with a shiver. Why?

"As it happens," said Index, regarding her askance, "tonight is Summer Eve. Odd things always happen in the Riverland then, and nothing by chance, there or here. Keep track of where we stop on the way home. There'll be a pattern, you wait and see."

"Fine," said Jame wryly, looking down at the anonymous cloud-plain below them. "Just tell me where to look."

"There," said Graykin, pointing southward.

Emerging from the mist was a scrap of red cloth tied to a stick. At first Jame thought that someone was thrusting up this jaunty, improvised banner, but then she realized that rather than it rising, the mist around it was slowly sinking. An upright board appeared, to which the stick was fixed, then several bits of lumber haphazardly nailed together, and so on down, a rickety tower of debris.

"That," said Graykin proudly, "is the tallest structure in Hurlen. The tower waifs erected it last winter so that for once they could look down on everyone else. I, er, suggested it."

Jame grinned. How like Graykin, incurably ambitious.

"Hurlen?" Index demanded. "It can't be. We only snag on ruins."

So he had thought of that too.

"It's no ruin," Jame agreed, "but its island foundations are very, very old. Maybe that's the attraction."

Or maybe it was something else, not in the city but close by, one of the last places on Rathillien she had ever wanted to revisit, now shoved practically under her nose. Nothing happens by chance.

"I left some things in Hurlen when M'lord's thugs snatched me," said Graykin. "Maybe the waifs still have them." Before anyone could stop him, he had turned and darted down the southwest corner stair.

Jame started after him.

Index grabbed her arm. "Where d'you think you're going, missy?"

"Sorry, no credit," she said, wriggled free, and ran.

III

As the weirding sank, it left behind the upper portions of the cliff upon which the scrollsmen's keep normally sat. Jame ran down the main stair with Jorin on her heels, through the restored levels of the wooden maze. She could hear Graykin's feet on the treads below, but he didn't answer her call. How stupid to risk the weirding for odd bits of gear. Bad enough that she was launched on what was probably a fool's errand. Bad enough, indeed.

Below, gray mist drifted across the stair, obscuring it. Jame descended with caution, blindly, through a clammy brume more like fog than weirding, on slippery steps. Through Jorin's senses, she smelled damp earth, wet wool, and fresh dung. A muffled bleating rose to meet them. Then they were under the cloud ceiling, looking down into the soil-filled hollow of Grand Hurlen, normally a park, now packed wall-to-wall with unhappy sheep. So it had been last winter too, when the city islands had braced for a possible siege by the Waster Horde. This time, the flock must have been brought in to shelter from the storm.

Looking up, she could see nothing of the scholars' college. Presumably it was still there; but when the morning sun burned off this fog, instinct told her that it would be gone. Once again she would have to scramble not to be left behind, with much farther to go than Graykin had.

Hurlen consisted of some thirty islands at the confluence of the Silver and the Tardy, not far upstream from the Cataracts. Each isle, from Grand Hurlen down to a rock barely ten feet across, had been hollowed out millennia ago and built up ever since, into a community of towers linked by catwalks over swift water. Normally, the town would be astir by now, from the elegant confectioners on the main island down to the rowdy barges on the wharfs at Tardy-mouth. This morning, however, the citizenry was still behind closed doors, waiting for the last storm trace to blow over. Jame and Jorin thus had the passages and catwalks to themselves, likewise the bridge over the smoking Silver to its west bank.

Jame hesitated at the bridge's end. The Upper Meadow stretched out before her to the trees at the foot of the bluff on its far side. Wisps of river fog drifted across it wraith-like under a low, gray sky. The luminescence filtering through from above was still weirding-glow, but soon it would be morning light.

Get on with it, Jame told herself, dry-mouthed, and stepped to the ground.

It didn't open under her feet. So far, so good.

She and Jorin went down the sloping field, over the stone steps called the Lower Hurdles and into the Middle Meadow. No bird sang or hare grazed. How many animals the weirdingstrom must have swept away, who would never see home again. Patches of weirding glided past, northward bound. Perhaps, though, some wildlife would be able to weird-walk back, as so few men had been known to do.

Her foot slipped on the wet grass and her heart lurched, but it was only dew. The last time she had been here, the whole dark meadow had been greased and stinking with blood, like the floor of a slaughterhouse. Hard, now, to believe that so many had died on this gentle slope, where the Kencyr Host and the army of Karkinaroth had met the vanguard of the Waster Horde; and terrible to think that, in a way, all that carnage had been incidental. Few realized that the decisive battle had taken place elsewhere, on a far more intimate scale.

They turned right into the trees. It had been almost this dark and silent that night, despite the battle raging so close by, as she had run through this forest with Kin-Slayer in one hand and the imu medallion in the other, pulling her on, toward the sound of someone calling her brother's name and then the crash of single combat.

Here was the foot of the bluff, as before, and here the remembered host tree. Pale green leaves flexed on its boughs, filling their veins with golden sap in preparation for the spring migration to their northern host. A dead branch cracked under Jame's foot. The leaves sprang into the air, blades flashing, and disappeared into the low clouds. Beyond the now bare tree, the cliff face curved inward to enclose the Heart of the Woods.

Jame paused on the hollow's threshold. It was larger than she remembered, an oval perhaps a hundred feet wide and somewhat longer. Waist-high ferns carpeted its floor. Spring runoff had transformed the encircling cliffs into a hanging garden of columbine and lace frond, gilt-edged pink and trembling green. Through the vines which obscured the heights came the soft glow of diamantine. Blocks of that precious, crystalline stone crowned the bluff, each weathered into a crude, gap-mouthed imu face. Ancient power slept here, none too deeply.

Jame left Jorin crouching under the host tree, blind eyes wide with worry. That cat had good instincts. Someday she would learn to follow them.

Entering the Heart was like walking into a green sea. Dense, dripping ferns swallowed her to the waist as she waded through them, trying not to trip over their tough stems. Last winter she had entered crawling under these fronds toward the sound of her brother and Ardeth's rogue son Pereden locked in battle. Then through clearing mist she had seen the eight darkling changers who ringed the combatants. Pereden had only been the bait. They were the jaws of the trap which had been set for the Highlord from the very beginning.

The rustle of her passage was echoed by the resonant imus above.

Shhh, they hissed through their vines, as if in warning. *Ssshhhh.*

Pereden had been no match for her brother, nor he for the changers, even with a sword reforged in Perimal Darkling, proof against the corrosive blood of its servants. Disarmed, he had been seized in a changer's crushing embrace. Jame remembered her scream, which the imus had caught and echoed from wall to wall, shattering Mother Ragga's clay medallion in her hand, striking down all who heard it.

Here was the center of the Heart and, to her surprise, a raw, burned patch. The charred fragments of a platform suggested a pyre. Among the debris were blackened bones, not the Burnt Man's this time, but spongy, like misshapen fungi feeding off the hollow's floor. Only the remains of a changer or a haunt could be so obscenely tenacious of life. Jame did a quick count in her mind: Five of the eight changers and the severed head of a sixth had been removed by Ardeth's people, but they had not immediately found the other three bodies. Of these, one had been truly dead, slain by the Ivory Knife. The second, driven mad by the imus' scream, must perforce have been consigned alive to this pyre, to leave behind these hungry bones. The third, decapitated by Kin-Slayer, had crawled away.

He might still be here.

Jame tried not to think about that. She had come to retrieve the imu medallion, or rather its clay shards, hoping to make peace with the Earth Wife. And there wasn't much time.

Now, where had she stood when it shattered? In the area since burned, she thought, or close to it. There wouldn't be much to find after two wet seasons, except for one possibility: back in Peshtar, the imu had acquired a mask of living skin by ripping it off of a changer's face. If the pieces were still so encased, they would at least be together. She ducked under the fronds to search, in dim light, beneath a second, lower level of plants. Her gloved hands, questing, found only root-laced soil. Dammit, this was impossible.

Shhhh, shhhh.

She reared up through the leafy ceiling, heart pounding. The rustling hiss went on and on, from all sides. It was nothing, she told herself; the upper imus were simply echoing her.

No need to conjure that image of a second searcher, drawn by vibrations in the earth, headless, mindless, crawling toward her under the ferns.

sssshhhHHH.

A breeze had entered the Heart. It circled the hollow, ruffling ferns, swaying vines across the imu mouths. Now everything was in motion, rustling, echoing. Was it all the wind, or were any of those cat's-paws across this leafy sea the wake of a hidden stalker? Beneath the undulating leaves, something fumbled at Jame's ankle. She sprang backward with a cry, tripped, fell, was up again in a moment and plunging out of the Heart. The green sea tossed behind her.

SSSHhhhhhh breathed the imus.

Then, with the dying of the wind, they were still.

Jame stood panting on the threshold. "All right, all right," she said to Jorin as he crept to her feet. "You warned me. It was a stupid idea anyway."

The light in the woods seemed stronger. Out in the meadow, it lit the fog from above, beginning to burn it off. Patches of mist rose up from the wet grass like the ghosts of the slain and drifted northward. Out of one, suddenly, trotted a weary, blackened, naked figure. In a moment, it had plunged into the next patch of weirding and disappeared.

Jame remembered to breathe. It was the man whom she had seen laying fires in the Riverland, Index's Merikit chief, carried south with the storm and now doggedly making his way home. So should she, with little time to waste.

But as she neared the bridge back to Hurlen, she found herself slowing.

Wherever else Mount Alban might stop, it was on its way back to the Riverland. Was there anything there for her but trouble? So much unresolved business, so little she seemed able to do about any of it. Why go back at all?

Roofless and rootless.

Tori clearly didn't want her. Besides, she was dangerous to him, if there was any truth in what Kindrie had said at the wolvers' keep. Perhaps she should simply drop out of his life again.

Blood and bone.

To be free again, ah—but to go where, to do what? All roads from this place would be long and lonely, to uncertain ends.

Cursed be and cast out.

But Brier Iron-thorn hadn't run away or given up.

Jame shook herself. Brenwyr's damned curse had crept up on her again, trying to drag her down with its sink-sand grip. Interesting, that the thought of Brier seemed a talisman against it, as that of Marc had against despair in the past. The Kendar might save her from herself yet, if not perhaps from whatever waited in the Riverland.

IV

Morning light spilled obliquely into the library, spreading like a cloth of beaten gold across the table. Rending it in two, however, was a shadow. The haunt singer Ashe sat with her back to the windows, a lump of obdurate darkness defying day.

"We need..." she said in her hoarse, halting voice, "to make...some decisions."

Seated at the table's end, Kirien recorded the statement on her tablet, then added under it something in a rounded script not her own. "Aunt Trishien agrees," she said, reading the note, then looking up. "Myself, I don't entirely understand."

"Neither do I," snapped the Brandan Matriarch, glowering across the table at Ashe.

Brenwyr's sight had at last returned, although the bright light made her squint behind her mask. She kept her hand on a rolled tapestry which lay across the chair to her right, her fingers moving constantly against its nap with subtle changes of pressure.

"Jameth must go back to the Women's Halls to continue her training," she said impatiently. "No other course is open to a Highborn."

Kirien smiled. "No?"

"What a Jaran does concerns only the Jaran. This is a Knorth."

"Ah, but the Knorth aren't quite like any other house either, are they? Torisen certainly isn't much like any other lord."

"Thank...the Kendar for that."

"That's right," said Kirien thoughtfully. "He's served with randon all his life, many of them women like his steward Rowan or you, Ashe, before you took the singer's robe. More of his senior officers are female than in any other house. I wonder.

Do you suppose that's why he didn't foam at the mouth when the Jaran proposed me as Lordan?"

Brenwyr made an impatient noise. "The other houses will never agree, once they realize that you are a woman. God's claws, to have kept it secret this long!"

"No secret," said Kirien lightly, but with a slight hardening of her fine eyes. "Are we to blame that the lords can't see beyond their own misconceptions? Anyway, their agreement doesn't matter, as long as we have the Highlord's consent."

"Do you suppose that he'll give it now, with his sister to dispose of? If he empowers you, think of the precedent."

Kirien looked startled, then respectful. "You do have a brain, matriarch, don't you?"

Ashe made the rasping noise which for her was a chuckle. "Manners, child, manners."

The rasp became a deep, barking cough. One livid hand reached up, removed a tooth that had been jarred loose, and put it in a pocket.

"However," she continued, more seriously, "Torisen loathes...the Shanir."

Kirien frowned. "Who's Shanir? His sister? How do you know that?"

"The haunt that savaged her...she ripped off its face...with claws."

"Ancestors preserve us. Those gloves."

"And that sampler," added Brenwyr grimly. Adiraina had told her about the sewing teacher's slashed cloth, back in those dark, silent days at Gothregor when her only contact with the world had been the old woman's touch. "The Knorth is also a true berserker."

"And she carries...the Ivory Knife."

Brenwyr stared. "There really is such a thing? I thought it was only a Lawful Lie—no offense, singer."

"None taken. But much...thought to be myth...may come true...in the latter days, including Nemesis...That-Which-Destroys...the Third Face of God."

"The Tyr-ridan? After so long, to come in our lifetime. And you think that this girl…No. It can't be. Where are the other two, then? Answer me that!"

"Not yet matured," Kirien suggested. "Oh, perhaps come of age in the normal way, but unaware of what they are, much less ready to accept it. Nemesis would come first, in any event. Perimal Darkling has to be defeated before anything else can happen."

Her hand changed script. "Aunt Trishien says, 'Remember, the whole purpose of the Kencyrath may be to produce the Tyr-ridan and then not destroy them before they apotheosize. If so, everything else is incidental.'"

"Everything?" The Brandan Matriarch rose and began to pace. "All our long history, our trials and disasters, to no other end but that?"

"No one ever said…our god…was fair."

"I still don't understand," said Kirien. "Even granted that it's true (and it does have that horrible ring, doesn't it?), what do the four of us have to decide?"

"There have been…false nemeses…before."

Brenwyr stopped short, staring. "What?"

"It's a theory, anyway," said Kirien, now watching the haunt singer, suddenly wary. "Especially destructive Shanir have turned up before: spontaneous binders, soul-reapers, maledights—and some of them have done great harm, perhaps because no equally potent creative or curative Shanir were on hand to counter-balance them. I think that either Jamethiel Dream-Weaver or Gerridon was a nemesis, or maybe both. The latter's obsession with immortality, that is, with preservation, certainly suggests a personal imbalance. Incidentally, he also seems to have been unable to sire children, perhaps even impotent. Some historians argue that if his people had realized what he was and had dealt with him accordingly, the Fall never would have occurred."

Without thinking, Brenwyr had picked up the tapestry and was now cradling it in her arms. "Do you mean that false nemeses should be killed? If they mature before their curative and creative counterparts, though, how can you tell false from true?"

"A good question," said Kirien, still watching Ashe. "Perhaps our ordeal has gone on so long because we keep destroying the true as well as the false, assuming that there's been more than one potential Nemesis in our long history. Even if the Knorth is the one and only, though, she can only be a nemesis until the other two appear and so, by definition, out of balance. Like Gerridon, she may also try to balance herself with acts of preservation or creation, although I would be wary of the results. What exactly are you suggesting, Ashe?"

Again, the singer's answer was indirect. "According to legend…the true Nemesis can only be killed…by another Kencyr. Most dangerous of all…to him or her…are the other two potential Tyr-ridan. Other tests…may exist as well. I propose…to apply them."

"And if the Knorth proves false?" Brenwyr demanded.

Ashe didn't answer.

"Ancestors preserve us," said Kirien. "Why us? Why now?"

Her hand gave a jerk and wrote. "'Because when Mount Alban returns home, the matter will be out of women's hands,'" she read. "'Because men can't be trusted to make this decision.'"

Ashe nodded. "The Kendar would say…it was none of their business."

"And the Highborn would answer as you did earlier, matriarch. If the Knorth is Nemesis, she's the arch-iconoclast. The lords will try to destroy her out of sheer self-defense. By God, 'Some things need to be broken' in the Kencyrath all right, with a vengeance; but can't we at least trust Torisen?"

"No," wrote her hand.

Kirien frowned at its sudden vehemence, waiting for an explanation. Instead, after a long pause, she got a sort of doodle, made by someone with her attention elsewhere. Two words followed, immediately scratched out. Then came an emphatic command: "Stay out of his/her/their way," and the curt symbol that signals a message's end.

"Well!" said Kirien, letting the pen drop. "What was all that about?"

"Whatever, we appear…to be…on our own."

The haunt singer sounded almost pleased, Kirien thought. "Hmmm. With decisions to make, you say. I suspect, though, that you arrived at yours long ago. You mean to test the Knorth, don't you, and you don't expect her to pass. Why?"

Ashe hesitated. "That one…was bred to walk…in shadows," she said at last, in a low voice. "She has…the darkling glamour."

Brenwyr snorted. "Coming from you, haunt."

Ashe pushed back her hood. Snatches of yellowed hair went with it, still attached to bits of dried scalp. Sunlight, which threw her face into shadow, shone off patches of naked skull.

"Yes. Coming from me. Who…would know better?"

The matriarch turned sharply away, clutching the rolled tapestry as if to protect it. "Abomination!" she said thickly, and stalked out of the room.

Ashe resumed her hood.

"She will still make her own decision about the Knorth," remarked Kirien. "You can't shock her out of that, or me either."

"Do you decide…against me?"

Again, Kirien felt the pressure of darkness. Her childhood had ended when she had realized that such evil could befall such a person as her old friend. She didn't like to think about the shadows that would eventually, inevitably consume Ashe. Only remarkable strength physical, mental, and moral had kept so much of the singer intact this long. Kirien refused to believe that integrity had yet been compromised.

"Not against," she said slowly. "Test her, if you must. For my part, I'd rather deal with facts than theory. She's Shanir, you say. All right: I accept that. The rest is conjecture. Even

for a Shanir Knorth, though, there must be other options than
the matriarchs' hencoop. My decision is to research possibilities. Whatever Aunt Trishien says, surely Torisen won't object to a reasonable alternative."

But as she rose, her mind already on who owed her what in
barter, her gaze fell uneasily on the tablet and on those two
now obliterated words which the Jaran Matriarch must never
have intended to write:

"Kin-Slayer unsheathed."

V

Brenwyr stalked through the halls of Mount Alban with Aerulan in her arms. She was very upset, which upset her even more.

Since childhood she had known that she was a berserker and maledight, and had prided herself on having learned to control those traits. Only that cold pride, duty to her house, and Aerulan had allowed her to live with who she was and what as a child she had done. After Aerulan's death, her life had been achingly bleak but (thanks to Adiraina's training and her brother's compliance) still largely under her control.

Then the Knorth had reappeared.

And now this.

Brenwyr believed in the god of her people—how could she not—but not as an active force in her world, much less in herself. Like many Kencyr, lacking proof to the contrary, she had almost convinced herself that the old prophecies were mere singers' tales, and been glad to think them so. In that case, to be a Shanir was like having a tendency to drop plates or walk off high buildings, awkward and potentially dangerous, but manageable. But "nemesis" implied the divine, working through her, using her…as perhaps it had always tried to do? Was that upstart Jaran right? Had she been straining all her life to control a force which, ultimately, would control her?

Moreover, if Kirien was right, it was also at work in the Knorth Jameth.

Brenwyr's grip on Aerulan tightened. She didn't want to share anything with that wretched girl. Damn her anyway, when the very thought of her existence made Brenwyr's temper threaten to flare. Why, why, why should any Knorth be alive when Aerulan was dead?

"Steady, steady," she could almost hear Adiraina say, as in lessons oft repeated long ago. "Remember that the loss of control is death."

Yes. Remember. Hadn't she killed two of the only four people she had ever loved? Rather than curse Adiraina or her brother that way, she would use the white-hilted suicide knife which she had carried in her boot since Aerulan's murder. Perhaps all nemeses should be killed, false and true. If only she'd had a knife that night, she might at least have used it on that yellow-eyed assassin, the custom be damned that Highborn women shouldn't fight. It could hardly have been less effective than the curse which she had spat at him, her only malediction ever apparently to fail.

She had cursed the Knorth Jameth too.

As if thinking of the girl conjured her up, Brenwyr heard her voice, enough like Aerulan's to make her heart jump. She was approaching the half-open door of the infirmary. Inside, the Knorth was saying:

"...sorry not to appear more grateful. You see, I'd hoped that the filthy thing was out of my life for good. You were right, though, to fetch it from Hurlen: it's far too dangerous to be left to its own devices."

"I'm so glad you approve," answered a sharp voice, almost snarling. "Next time, think twice what job you give me."

"Maybe you should think again, too, about serving me at all."

"What else can I do, go back to Karkinaroth?"

"Even to Restormir, for all I care."

Brenwyr stood outside the door, transfixed by the tone of deep resentments seething up unexpectedly, perhaps disastrously. Then a moment's taut silence within was broken by an exclamation that made her jump:

"Spy on us, will you?"

No. He didn't mean her. Hasty footsteps had crossed the floor, away from the door.

"Who sent you? Tell me, you damned spook!"

"Graykin, stop shaking him. Damn. I should have warned the infirmarian not to let him over-tire himself. He's gone blank again, just as he must have done at the Cataracts."

Brenwyr suddenly realized whom they meant. She threw open the door. In one far corner, an ounce leaped off a cot and scuttled under it. In the other sat a white-haired Shanir, staring vacantly past the dark figure who bent over him.

"Bastard," she heard herself say harshly, feeling the power in her voice surge almost into a curse. "Go back where you belong."

The Shanir rose. Like a sleepwalker, pale eyes open but unfocused, he stumbled past her out of the room.

The room's third occupant had also shambled forward a step as if to follow; but his companion in black stopped him, saying softly in the Knorth's voice:

"She doesn't mean you, Graykin. Perhaps you should keep an eye on Kindrie, though."

Go, said her warning tone, anger forgotten. *Now. This is dangerous.*

Brenwyr snorted. She felt dangerous. She felt deadly.

The one called Graykin had started at the Knorth's touch, for a moment looking frightened and confused. Now he gave her a sharp glance, a half-nod, and slipped sideways out of the infirmary, watching Brenwyr askance as he passed like a cur expecting a kick.

The Knorth remained, standing her ground. Only by her voice did Brenwyr recognize her, having still been blind the last time they had met. Black jacket with one tight sleeve and one full, slim waist tightly belted, black pants tucked into black boots, black gloves and mask. Highborn girls sometimes had an unnatural craving to dress as boys, but they grew out of it just as they did out of mock berserker tendencies, at about the same time.

This girl has refused to grow up, thought Brenwyr with scorn, her own traveling gear not for a moment crossing her mind. *She's still a child, willful, spoiled, perverse.*

"Matriarch," said the child, saluting her, polite but wary. "Aerulan."

Brenwyr's grip on the banner tightened. Waking in the room below, for one aching moment she had felt Aerulan behind her, almost the touch of her hand. When she had turned, the first thing she had seen after a week of darkness had been Aerulan's face woven of the clothes in which she had died. Dead, dead—but for the Knorth, somehow, still a living presence in this room.

"She's been with you, hasn't she?" Brenwyr heard herself demand hoarsely. "All this time, she's been with you."

"Er, yes. We kept each other company on the road."

She might as well have said "on the moon," for all the sense it made to Brenwyr for a moment. Highborn girls rarely traveled, except under heavy guard. Aerulan had never before left Gothregor. It simply hadn't occurred to the Council of Matriarchs that Jameth wasn't still hiding in the deserted halls, sulking over her scratched face.

Until this moment, Brenwyr had forgotten that the Knorth had been hurt, much less how or by whom. Adiraina had spoken slightingly of the "accident," not realizing that Brenwyr had seen the blow struck or that Hawthorn had told her of the slashed sampler which the Ardeth matriarch had ordered to be dipped in the Knorth's blood on the council chamber floor.

"Your face," she said involuntarily.

The Knorth stiffened. "Yes, matriarch?" she said with chilling courtesy, as if in rebuke to an equal.

"Don't you dare take that tone with me, girl!"

The other's mouth twitched, almost into Aerulan's smile. "I apologize again. Truly, I don't mean to keep offending you. It just seems to be a talent. About Aerulan, though, I don't quite understand. I know that Lord Brandan pledged a huge sum for her contract in perpetuity, that Ganth was about to give up all rights to her forever. Your brother must have loved her very much."

"It had nothing to do with him!" Brenwyr burst out, then swore at herself and began incontinently to pace.

Her agitated path obliged the Knorth to dodge aside, swooping to snatch an old knapsack containing something pale out from under her very feet. One part of Brenwyr's mind told her that the Knorth was using wind-blowing kantirs to keep out of her way; another rejected the idea: Highborn girls were not taught the Senethar.

"Matriarch." said the Knorth, slipping aside yet again, "sometimes I'm very stupid. This concerns sister-kinship, doesn't it?"

Brenwyr spun around, almost pinning the girl between two cots, but she rolled over one and out of the way in an instinctive, flowing evasion as if from a physical attack. That must be the Senethar, Brenwyr thought, or its dance form, the Senetha. More forbidden knowledge.

"What do you know about the sisterhood?" she demanded.

"Precious little. Only that there's much more to life in the Women's World than any man realizes."

"Be quiet! You have no right to speak of such things!"

"You did ask. All right, all right." The moving pattern of her black-gloved hands seemed to deflect Brenwyr's anger. "I've offended you again. Again, I apologize. Are you going to curse me?"

"No! I can control...dammit, I could control myself before you...before you."

She stumbled to a halt, watching those hands weave before her, unable to look away. The quality of light in the room changed, thickening like honey. Lithe, black hands swam through its amber glow, deft fingers easing the knots of her rage and restraint, try as she would to keep them tight. As if in a dream, she heard herself speak:

"I've learned to control when I curse, but not what I say when I do. Then the words just come, and sometimes kill."

"You cursed me once. Will I die?"

"I don't know. I don't think so." Sinuous hands, charming her. "Perhaps we're too much alike. Snakes with similar venom. Nemeses."

"Can you lift the curse you put on me?"

"No." Seducing.

"Have you ever tried to raise a curse?"

No, no, no.

"Yes. Once. When I was six."

The knots had given way. "Forget what you can't help," Adiraina had told her over and over, but now she remembered, oh, God, she remembered.

"I borrowed my brother's clothes and dressed up in them. Mother caught me. She was furious, called me perverted, tore them off. I-I was so angry. 'I hope you break your neck.' I said that. And she did, going down the stairs with her arms full of shirts, and pants, and boots. Oh, Mother, don't! I take it back, I take it back."

She was kneeling on the floor, looking into her mother's terrified eyes, hearing the breath escape her paralyzed lungs and not return.

"I take it back."

Aerulan held her. "You were only a child. You didn't mean it. You weren't responsible!"

Aerulan, who also had died in her arms, gasping, with a severed throat.

The white-hilted knife was in her hand. What right had she to live, whose curse had slain both blood- and sister-kin?

Someone was wrestling with her, saying breathlessly, "Oh, don't, don't, don't."

Then black gloves caught her wrist and twisted. Her fingers sprang open. The blade dropped with a deadly thunk, to quiver upright in the floor which began to rot at its cold touch. It wasn't her knife at all, although for a moment she thought that her own face stared back at her, naked and hag-like, from the carved ivory pommel.

"Can't I leave you alone for a minute?" demanded Graykin from the doorway.

"Apparently not." The Knorth's voice shook. So did her hand as she reclaimed and resheathed the Ivory Knife. "Matriarch?"

"Leave me alone," said Brenwyr thickly. She dragged herself to her feet and stumbled over to lean on the windowsill. What had she been saying? What in ancestors' names had she been about to do?

"Forget what you can't help." *Forget, forget.*

But the light was still strange. It had been bright morning when Brenwyr had entered the infirmary and must be morning still, but the air had taken a jaundiced tinge with an undertaint of sulfur. She looked down on the backs of slowly swirling clouds, bounded by mountain slopes, roofed by more clouds of a darker, more sullen hue. Clearly, Mount Alban had stopped again, but where? She felt she ought to know. If only this room faced east instead of west what would she see? A side-valley of the Silver in the Riverland, the main fortress hidden by clouds but rising over them at the upper end of the gorge, the Witch's tower. The keep below: Wilden. This filthy light: Rawneth, conjuring.

Dammit. She had told that wretched Shanir to go back where he belonged, and he had taken Mount Alban with him.

But it wouldn't last. The college was only some fifty miles south of home now. The pull of its anchoring hill-fort foundation would lift it off this reef with the next weirding touch. The important thing now was that no one else disembark, least of all the Knorth.

"I did keep an eye on him, just as you told me," Graykin was protesting, full of self-righteousness but with a wary edge. "Didn't I see him walk down straight into the priests' arms? Taken him back where he belongs, haven't they? Best to let him go. You can't tangle with them."

"Oh, can't I? Watch."

Brenwyr was across the floor, between the Knorth and the door, faster than she would have believed possible. "You aren't to leave this room," she said sharply. "I forbid it."

"Matriarch, you don't understand. I dragged Kindrie into this. He's my responsibility."

"A bastard has no claims on anyone, least of all on you. I-it's indecent that you even met."

"Lady, I've led a less sheltered life than you can probably imagine. I don't shock easily. Why poor Kindrie 'least of all'? Who is he, anyway?"

"The shame of your house. Tieri's bastard, born in the moon garden at Gothregor where his mother's death banner still hangs in disgrace. There. Now are you satisfied?"

Jame stared. "He said his grandmother was named Telarien."

"Bastards don't have grandmothers. Telarien was Tieri's mother and Kinzi's daughter."

"If I had some chalk, I'd work this out on a wall, if I had a wall. Kinzi, the last Knorth Matriarch, was the mother of Telarien, who was the mother of Tieri, who was the mother of Kindrie. Tieri was my father's full sister. That makes Kinzi my great-grandmother, Telarien my grandmother, Tieri my aunt, and Kindrie my first cousin. Correct?"

"Yes. I mean, no! Bastards don't have cousins!"

"Be damned to that," Jame muttered.

She should have worked all of this out long ago. She would have, if the thought of priestling blood-kin hadn't so thoroughly appalled her. But Kindrie wasn't a priest, despite having been thrown repeatedly into their arms. There he would wake again, probably not even knowing how he had gotten there. Back in hell.

"Matriarch, I've got to go after him. Think! This is Tieri's son, the child of the girl whom Aerulan died to save."

Brenwyr hadn't moved. "You can't go down to Wilden. There are...other reasons as well. Kinzi and the Randir Matriarch Rawneth, they quarreled."

"So?" Then behind the mask, gray eyes widened. "Are you saying that I've inherited a blood feud, and no one saw fit to tell me?"

"There was no need. Anyway, it never came to blows."

"Let me guess. Before anything so unladylike could

happen, the Shadow Assassins slaughtered every Knorth woman at Gothregor except Tieri, and no one ever knew why."

This time, Brenwyr's jaw fell. "You don't mean, you can't think…"

"Don't I? Can't you? God's teeth and toenails, if it was even a possibility, why wasn't Ganth told? But that might have led to civil war, the Knorth and their allies against the Randir and theirs. Better to keep it a secret of the Women's World. Better to see my house destroyed than all the Kencyrath, except that the White Hills nearly did that anyway."

Brenwyr was backing away, hands over her ears. "I won't listen to this. I won't think about it. You're mad, Jameth. All the Knorth are. Everyone knows that."

"My name is not Jameth. It's Jamethiel."

Brenwyr made an incoherent sound and bolted out of the room, slamming and locking the door behind her. They could hear her in the hall, piling furniture against it.

"I think you rattled her," said Graykin.

"By God, she's floored me. Secrets! How many will it take to get us all killed?"

Secrets.

She hadn't meant to pry any out of the matriarch with her hand-dance, much less something so raw. That poor woman. The soul-reaping Senetha she had learned in Perimal Darkling and practiced in Tai-tastigon to control rowdy taverners should never have been put to such a use except that Brenwyr's combination of maledight and berserker tendencies terrified her.

Secrets.

Could what she had suggested to the matriarch possibly be true? All that death and destruction, to have grown out of some squabble in the cloistered halls of the Women's World? Surely not. And yet, who had told the assassins where to look for her five days ago? Who had stood by in the shadows of the Randir compound, watching while the killers nearly fulfilled their contract in the Forecourt? Whose soul had Rawneth used

to make the demon which she had sent after Jame and Kindrie?
Who wanted the last Knorth lady dead?

"I think I recognized that last crash," said Graykin. "If
your matriarch has tipped over the wardrobe beside the door,
we're trapped here until someone rescues us. Too bad about
the healer."

He sounded pleased. So much for one more rival.

Jame put an arm around his thin shoulders. "Dear Graykin.
For your future reference, a few points. First: to be served by
you is an honor, but not my only obligation. Second: as you
keep saying, very little stops me, common sense least of all.
Third: as for being trapped anywhere…"

She jerked a thumb over her shoulder. Graykin, following
the gesture, blanched.

"Oh, no."

"Oh, but yes. Where there's a window, there's always a
way."

Interim VI
Gothregor: 60th of Spring

By the dawn of Summer Eve, the worst of the storm had passed. Lances of brilliant sunlight pierced the overcast, impaling wet leaves, sparkling on the Silver, warming the shattered stones of Chantrie and melting the shadowy image that had hung above them as if of the fortress's ancient walls restored.

But the danger had not entirely passed. A river of clouds still flowed northward up the valley, trailing veils of weirding mist. Steward Rowan watched them from the ramparts of Gothregor. Out of one flew a phalanx of swans, ghosting toward the high lakes that were their summer homes. Migratory birds loved weirding weather. Much of the Riverland's wildlife had also been swept southward with the storm, but would soon begin to weird-walk back, something apparently safer for beasts than humans.

Ancestors be praised that this happened in spring, thought Rowan. In midwinter, no one would have returned. As it was, she hoped for some exotic additions to the larder when it was safe to hunt again.

And perhaps a problem. At first light, she had glimpsed something in the woods that might have been a young rathorn, except that it was pure white. There had been none of those beasts of madness in the Riverland since Ganth's disastrous hunt thirty-four years ago. Rowan turned and limped down the stair, shaking her head. An ill omen even to think that she had seen one now, given rumors of the Highlord's growing instability.

Down in the inner ward, the small Knorth garrison was combing through the grass in front of the old keep for shards of stained glass. In days of greater affluence, it had been

imported in panes from the Eastern Lands, to be worked by
Kendar artisans into those glorious third story windows, now
shattered. More precious than gold, their fragments would
be sorted and stored until the Knorth treasury could afford
an eastern glass-master to recast them—unless some clever
Kendar discovered the trick first. Rowan shook her head
again, looking up at the devastation. Blackie would not be
pleased.

"'Ware weirding!" someone called sharply.

A mist veil trailed over the south wall, then dropped like a
vaporous curtain to obscure part of it. Some twenty feet wide,
it drifted across the inner ward with deceptive speed as fast,
perhaps, as a trotting horse. Kendar moved hastily out of its
way.

It left behind a man, hairy, dirty, naked, staring about him
in dismay. The weirding had almost reached the north wall.
Meanwhile, a second, smaller veil had followed it over the
south. Given a choice, the man bolted toward the latter, braids
flying. Bemused Kendar let him pass. He stepped on broken
glass, hopped howling on one foot, and pitched headfirst into
the oncoming mist. It swallowed both him and his clamor like
the shutting of a velvet door.

"Obviously," said a familiar voice behind Rowan, "I've
been away far too long."

Ever since Urakarn, when the name rune of the Karnid
god had been burned into her forehead, Rowan had learned to
equate facial expression with pain. Therefore, although her
heart had jumped like a startled frog, her face showed no surprise as she turned.

"Welcome home, my lord."

He looked haggard, she thought: travel-stained clothes,
unkempt black hair with more white in it than she remembered, and several days' growth of beard; but large as those
silver-gray eyes were in that thin face, they looked blessedly
clear and, at the moment, clearly amused.

"Who was that naked man, anyway?"

Rowan shrugged. "A Merikit chief, by the braids, with many kills and many children. Beyond that…"

Torisen had stepped forward and caught sight of the damaged keep. "What in Perimal's name?"

"We had a visit from Old Man Tishooo. That was before the earthquake, which was before the weirding-storm, all of which was after, well, never mind for the moment. About all we haven't had is an infestation of foot-eating trogs. But come inside. Rest. Eat."

"I'm not alone, Rowan."

Rowan looked into the darkness of the gatehouse arch. Some twenty or thirty pairs of eyes glowed back at her, some man-height, others only a foot or two above the ground. Grimly trotted out of the shadows, grinning.

"That's right, steward. You're stuck with the whole pack."

"In that case," said Rowan, "we'll cope. Be pleased to enter, Lord Wolver."

Soon afterward, everyone had adjourned to the garrison's main hall, hard by the southern gate. The wolver pack came shyly, unused to so much company. The adults had taken on their most human (if hairy) aspect as a mark of respect, while the adolescents padded in awkwardly with mixed attributes and pups gamboled about underfoot. If any of the Kendar remembered that some Kencyr hunted both wolver and Merikit for sport, they didn't mention it.

"That reminds me," said Torisen. "Your people aren't to start for home until I have an armed escort to send with them. D'you hear me, Grimly?"

"I hear you, Tori."

Rowan, serving her lord wine, noticed that he took it left-handed. Torisen was as nearly ambidextrous as long practice could make him; however, unlike most Kencyr, he favored his right. Seeing the question in his steward's eyes, he defiantly held up his right hand. She stared at the splints and swollen fingers.

"Don't ask, Rowan, and don't fuss. They're mending."

She accepted that with a curt nod. In her mind's eye, though, she saw a boy fresh from the tortures of Urakarn, saying over and over, "I'm all right, I'm all right," while his burned hands festered and his mind slid toward fever-fed madness.

Torisen put down his cup with a sigh. "No use putting it off any longer. Where's my sister, Rowan?"

"I don't know, lord."

He frowned. "She did arrive safely. You sent a dispatch saying so."

"Yes, lord. I also told you that the Matriarchs had taken charge of her."

For a moment, Torisen looked confused, trying to remember. That dispatch had arrived after the lords had been at him all day to decide his sister's fate. Exhausted, he had read the first line of Rowan's message and put it aside, never to be picked up again.

"Send word to the Women's Halls, then."

"They may refuse to let you see her, lord. They did me. Odd things have been happening here. The night of the Tishooo, someone in the Halls sounded the alarm. We don't know why. We weren't allowed in. But the next day pyre smoke rose from an inner garden. Do you think?"

Torisen shook his head. "Wherever she is, she's alive, but where in Perimal's name is that?" He rose. "Time to find out."

Rowan had also risen. "You're going to ask the Matriarchs? Blackie, they won't let you in!"

He grinned at her use of his old nickname, looking suddenly as wolfish as any wolver. "Let them try to stop me."

At the gate, they tried. The guards called their captain, and she called her eight peers, while the Highlord stood outside, polite but implacable. While they were still telling him that he couldn't enter, he put his left hand on the door which everyone had thought safely locked and pushed it open. Rowan went in with him and so did Grimly in his complete furs, determined to miss none of the fun. Inside, ladies stared aghast before bolting out of sight. In a room above the Forecourt, a whole class of little girls ran from window to window crying "Oh look, oh look!" while their distraught teacher chased them.

"Where are we going?" Torisen asked Rowan out of the corner of his mouth.

"The Ardeth compound. If anyone governs the Council, it's Adiraina."

The Matriarchs were waiting for them in Adiraina's room. The blind Ardeth sat very straight in her chair, in her hands a piece of needlework oddly torn and partly eaten away by rust-colored stains. The others ranged behind her, except for the Jaran Matriarch who, as usual, kept to her writing desk, a tablet full of notes in diverse hands open before her. She was adding a new notation as Torisen walked in.

"My lord," said Adiraina stiffly, in High Kens. "This invasion is inexcusable. Withdraw at once."

"Point of law," Trishien said, looking up. "Torisen Black Lord is master of this place, and our host. He can go anywhere he pleases."

The others clearly felt this contribution to be unhelpful.

Torisen gave them a half-bow. "My lady matriarchs, I have come to visit my sister, for whom, I understand, you have made yourselves responsible."

"Jameth's training can not be interrupted," said Adiraina, in a tone fit to freeze ice. "Incredibly ignorant as she came to us, she has far too much to learn."

"I bet she's taught you a few things too," muttered Grimly, subsiding with a yelp as Torisen stepped on his paw.

"Nonetheless."

The Ardeth Matriarch twitched, as if something had given her attention an unexpected tug. Her hands closed on the stained sampler. "It's taken you long enough to show an interest," she said, answering, it seemed, almost at random. The Danior Dianthe put a hand on her shoulder. "No Knorth guard or quarters prepared, not even suitable clothes."

"I—see. And no word from you, either, that such things were required. So, if I failed to provide an adequate establishment, into whose was she placed?"

"Why, into the Caineron, of course," said the Coman Karidia, glowering. "Who had a better claim than darling Kallystine, your consort?"

Torisen blinked. In point of law, Karidia was right, but oh, lord!

"That contract," he said, without emphasis, "has nearly expired. Be that as it may, I still want to see my sister."

"Well, you can't!" snapped Karidia, discretion (as usual) failing her. "The silly twit is hiding."

"Is she indeed. Why?"

"A-a stupid spat," said Karidia, against the combined wills of all her peers except the one who could have stopped her. But Adiraina still seemed distracted, as if working out some puzzle of her own. "Dear Kallystine was obliged to slap her."

"Oh, was she. And did you sound the alarm six nights ago because of this—er—spat?"

"That concerns only the Women's World," snapped Dianthe, trying to regain control, her fingers pressing urgently on Adiraina's shoulder.

"I think not. It happened in my house."

Power stirred. They had forgotten, as so many did, that this quiet man came of a bloodline stretching back to the creation of the Kencyrath. They had not seen him below, pushing open a door which for anyone else would have been locked. But now they felt the lordship in his voice, to loose or bind at will within his own domain.

"The next day," he was saying, very quietly, "you gave someone to the pyre. Who?"

Adiraina answered, as if the words had been jerked out of her: "Eleven shadow assassins."

"What was their commission here?"

"We think—to kill Jameth. Instead, somehow, they were killed."

"And then Jame disappeared, presumably with two shadows out of a casting of thirteen still at large. Correct, matriarch?"

"C-correct, Highlord."

"You don't understand!" cried Dianthe. "It wasn't like that!"

"Like what, lady?" The deadly courtesy in his voice made her shrink back, clinging to the Ardeth's shoulder as to a rock. "That you didn't officiously remove my sister from my steward's care? That while in your charge she wasn't mistreated and then wantonly endangered? That my hospitality hasn't therefore been egregiously abused? I think, lady, that I understand very well indeed, all but what matters most: where is my sister now?"

The question hummed in the air, demanding reply, receiving none. Its weight pressed Grimly flat to the floor. In the preternatural silence, he heard a faint sound beside him, as if of a raindrop's fall, but the splash by his paw was red. Torisen's white-knuckled grip on Kin-Slayer's hilt had opened the cut on his left palm.

Trishien had been sitting with pen frozen in mid-air. Now she gave herself a shake and said, unsteadily, "Highlord, you have a right to know: your sister is at Mount Alban. Only you might not find it where it ought to be."

His eyebrows rose, but he acknowledged with a bow. "My thanks, Jaran. For this kindness, however cryptic, perhaps I won't evict the lot of you after all."

Trishien inclined her head. As her gaze dropped, she gave a half-stifled exclamation.

She's seen the blood, thought Grimly, then started, realizing what he himself had just seen: the sword's blade hanging free through its supporting belt loop, behind the scabbard. Kin-Slayer wasn't sheathed. It never had been.

Torisen had widened his salute, now half-ironic, to include the rest of the Council. Then he turned to leave, with Rowan and Grimly hard on his heels. They had almost reached the door when Adiraina suddenly shook off her friend and fell to

her knees. She still clutched the stained sampler in one hand.
The other swooped unerringly to the red drops on the floor.

"Twins!" she exclaimed, astonished and triumphant, her
puzzle at last solved with the touch of brother's and sister's
blood on either hand. "You are twins after all!"

Torisen stared at her. "Mad!" he said, and hastily left.

Trotting to keep up as they turned onto the arcade fronting
the Forecourt, Grimly said, "That was quite a trick with the
questions. I thought only Shanir had that sort of power."

"What sort? I asked, they answered. That's all."

"Oh, but surely…"

"I said, that's all!"

He had turned sharply on the Wolver, who instinctively
crouched.

"Grimly, don't do that," said Torisen, exasperated. "I am
not your pack leader."

Rowan touched his shoulder in warning, then stepped
quickly aside as a shimmering vision glided down the arcade
toward them. Full skirt iridescent with lizard scales; low cut
bodice insecurely laced with gold; the white swell of breasts;
ivory throat, fluttering mask of gold tissue, perhaps a shade
more opaque than usual; they had hardly had time to take in
her full glory before M'lady Kallystine had flung herself into
Torisen's arms, jarring his splinted fingers.

"Oh, my dear lord, you've come home at last!"

Because he had involuntarily recoiled with pain at the impact, the little puff of powder from between her breasts missed
Torisen's face. Nonetheless, he staggered, eyes momentarily
blank. Tactfully looking out into the Forecourt, Rowan didn't
notice. Still crouched on the floor, Grimly did. He growled as
Caineron's daughter raised a hand as if to stroke the Highlord's
face. Torisen caught her wrist.

"You slapped my sister," he said, as if just remembering.
"Why?"

Kallystine drew back with a hiss, hatred stronger than
policy. "Jameth, always Jameth."

He shook his head as if to clear it and put her aside. "Excuse me, lady."

She stared after him, incredulous, as he walked away, unsteady at first, then with growing assurance and speed.

A half-stifled cough made her look up. On the spiral stair to the upper classrooms crouched a little girl, the same Ardeth chit who had seen Jameth's hands bare. The child bolted back up the steps. The sorcery which Kallystine had just tried on Torisen had been expressly forbidden by the matriarchs. If that wretched brat told Adiraina what she had seen this time…

Worse, if Caldane should learn that she had failed…

"Get me a fast horse," Torisen was saying to Rowan as they turned into the Forecourt toward the gate.

"I'll saddle every brute in the stable. You aren't leaving us behind this time, Blackie."

"Or me, or me!" the Wolver cried, capering upright with excitement and trying to clap his paws.

"Or me," said M'lady Kallystine through her pretty, white teeth, watching them go. She hadn't lost. Not yet.

Part VII

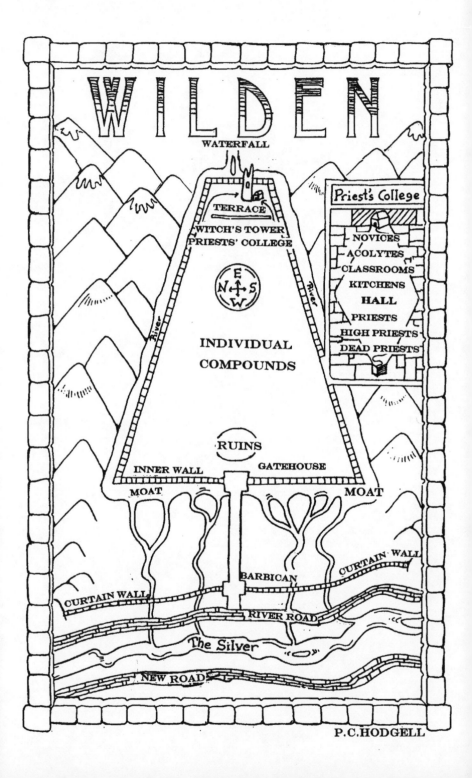

Wilden: 60th of Spring
I

The platform descended, creaking, through the scholars' warren inside Mount Alban's cliff. Jame rode it alone. Climbing out the infirmary window and swinging in the one below had been easy for her, but impossible for blind Jorin. Graykin, sulking, had refused even to try.

Creak, creak, groan.

By accident, she had discovered how the scrollsmen got their ancient bones up and down the vertical college in relative comfort. Having set this wretched machine in motion, though, she wondered if she would be able to make it stop. Ropes snaked past, tied at intervals with esoteric knots. Kendar craftsmen were certainly clever. The older scholars must find such a convenience invaluable, but Jame was beginning to wish that she had walked. This ponderous descent was giving her far too much time to think.

Of all the stupid things she had ever done, this was perhaps the stupidest, far worse than raiding Restormir. There, at least, she'd had help and an enemy prone to tripping over his own fat feet. Here at Wilden she faced a very different foe in Ishtier, and perhaps in the Randir Matriarch as well.

Clearly, a feud could run three generations or more, since Rawneth had told Kindrie that her revenge ran through him, whom she must have believed to be the last of Kinzi's blood.

Revenge for what?

As for Ishtier, what support did he have here? What had he told the other priests about her? She had called the Priests' College a cesspool of divinity, but, after all, it didn't contain an active temple. Maybe there was nothing to worry about.

Maybe.

Still, the nervous tightening of her stomach said, "Dumb, *dumb*, DUMB."

The platform sank into a layer of mist and seemed to melt. Jame tumbled down worn stone steps, for the first time missing her voluminous overskirt, to fetch up breathless and bruised at their foot in deep grass.

"Watch out for the last step," Graykin had said. Huh.

Mount Alban loomed over her, covering the sky, yet as insubstantial as the moon at mid-day. The surrounding walls of Wilden looked just as ghostly, wooded slopes showing through them as if through a misty haze. Diffuse light bathed the grassy hillock on which she stood and warmed its crown of tumbled stones, relics of the ancient hill fort around which Wilden had been built. Gap-mouthed *imus* were carved on the fallen blocks. She traced one with a fingertip. At her feet, tiny star-shaped flowers sprang open in the deep grass.

This is the morn of Summer Eve, Jame thought. *Who knows what else may wake here before nightfall?*

As she walked down the hillock, Wilden redefined itself around her. The green knoll was girt with flagstones and granite walls pierced to east and west with arches. Above and beyond, where she had seen the wooded slopes of older days, were the valley's sheer, quarried sides, cut short by an overcast sky. Mount Alban all but disappeared as she stepped off the grass at the hillock's foot. A sulfurous light smoldered down through the steel gray clouds. Was the Wilden Witch conjuring again? What this time?

Faint cloud-shadows moved over the flags between her and the eastern arch. One of them, man-shaped, seemed to pause.

Jame felt her heart lurch. Sweet Trinity. How could she have forgotten? It was near Wilden that the master assassin had attacked her and been overwhelmed in turn by Bane. Was that *mere*-tattooed killer still Bane's prisoner and mount? Had they ridden out the weirdingstrom here, perhaps in the very ruins which she had just left?

The shadow melted back into the flow.

Jame let out her breath in a sigh. *Nerves*, she told herself—or, if not, one more element in a game already hopelessly beyond her control. She had no plan except to find Kindrie and, somehow, get him out. As for the rest—well, dammit, she couldn't worry about everything at once.

The road angled upward between tall, narrow buildings. Unlike Restormir with its cantons, here each house stood by itself, gates locked, windows barred, so many fortified camps. Jame saw no one, either of the garrison or of the college. The only sound was that of falling water, which grew louder the higher she climbed. Had Lord Randir taken all his people south with him to the Cataracts? He might have, to forestall trouble at home. Randir politics were said to rival those in the so-called poison courts of the Central Lands, tangled webs of intrigue, feud, and assassination—not that anyone outside Wilden ever learned the half of it. Above all else, the Randir was a house of secrets.

One secret, though, had slipped out. The wrong lord ruled here, women at Gothregor whispered (for one did whisper about the Randir, even in their absence). The old lord's choice had been one of those Shanir who, born apparently normal, change as they mature. By the time he had earned his randon's scarf at Tentir, the Randir Heir had changed too much. Rawneth had her own grandson Keran declared lord. The whispers said that she had tried to kill the deposed Lordan and, failing that, had set assassins on his trail—much luck they'd had against a randon-trained weapons-master. The contract was still said to be open, more than three decades later.

One more link between Wilden and the Bashtiri Shadow Guild, thought Jame, resisting the temptation to look behind her.

The road ended in a high terrace almost in the clouds, its flagstones wet with spray from the cataract which plunged down beyond the fortress's back wall to form the arms of its river moat. Earth and air shook with the continual roar. Puddles quivered. Black against this sheet of white water

rose the Witch's tower. Glimmers above in the clouds suggested lit windows. Was Rawneth indeed at home, thinking
what thoughts after her demon's failure to retrieve Kindrie?
That pervading sulfurous light owed little to the rising sun,
although it did throw the tower's shadow westward, almost to
Jame's feet.

Huddled against the tower's southwest side was a plain,
stone building, about the size of a modest stable: the Priests'
College, Jame's sixth sense told her. Clever. Most people would
walk straight past, while those who did know would find nothing threatening in so humble a structure. Away from their
temple strongholds, in a society which tolerated them only as
necessary evils, the priests were wise to take such precautions.

Why, then, had they left their door wide open?

With Ishtier involved and Kindrie in his hands to use as
bait, it was very likely a trap. What choice did she have, though,
except to bite?

Still, she hesitated.

Ishtier was only one member of this community, and a
rogue at that. Jame didn't like the Three-Faced-God (what
Kencyr did?), but he (or she, or it) *had* created the Kencyrath,
and this was where Shanir trained to serve him. Likewise, she
had always felt obscurely superior to his priests (what Kencyr
didn't?); but what had her own half-remembered training in
Perimal Darkling been but a perversion of the Great Dance
which they did by right and necessity? Who was she to look
down on them? Look what harm she had already done to
Kindrie through sheer prejudice? Had she been as irrational
as...as Tori in his blind hatred of the Shanir?

No, she thought, not very clearly. *I'm better than that. I've
got to be.*

Still, it was hard to cross that terrace under Rawneth's hidden eyes to that open door.

As her eyes adjusted to the darkness within, she saw a
plainly appointed room, taking up apparently the whole interior. So, this wasn't one of those structures larger inside than

out. Presumably a minor priest should be on duty to receive
visitors and guard the inner door. However, neither priest nor
door was in sight. Nor was anyone behind her, when she steeled
herself to look—no footprints across the terrace but her own,
no empty man-shape by the balustrade defined by beads of
mist, no glint of eyes, Bane's mocking silver or the assassin's
cruel, bloodshot gold.

Jame stepped over the threshold and walked around the
edge of the room, running her fingertips along the wall. At
the back, her hand went through what had looked at a distance like rough stone. Instead, the bare warp threads of a
tapestry hung there like a dense curtain. Anyone, slipping
through it in the dim light, would seem to have walked through
a solid wall. Clever, clever, clever.

She parted the threads, stepped inside and, for the second
time that morning, fell down a flight of stairs.

Too damn much practice at Gothregor, she thought sourly, picking herself up at the bottom.

A corridor stretched away in front of her, curving downward into the earth, lit sporadically by guttering torches. Jame
descended warily. As the curve widened into a spiral, doors
began to open off its outer wall into what appeared to be novice dormitories, dark and dank, not much better than dungeon
cells. Farther down, straw mattresses and dirt walls gave way
to the cots and stone of the acolytes. Many of these culti-
vated mushrooms in far corners and multicolored molds on
the walls, the latter forming intricate murals of unpleasant
design. By their sickly glow alone, these chambers were lit.
Doors began to open off the spiral's inner curve into claustro-
phobic classrooms. Below that was a dismal kitchen, moldy
bread in discolored mounds on its tables. Under cauldrons of
pale soup, its fires were all burnt out.

Dank, sour, mean. How could anything good come out of
such a place?

But Kindrie had. True, he had made some spectacular
mistakes since, and she had often wanted to kick him out of

his sudden trances. Still, from hints that he had dropped, she gathered that he had as incomplete a memory of his childhood here as she did of hers in the Master's house. She should have remembered how many false steps one could make, stumbling out of such darkness, what courage it took even to try.

I am *as bad as Tori,* she thought bitterly. *No, worse, because I knew better.*

Where *was* Kindrie, though, not to mention everyone else? The College had an air of arrested life, almost of sudden disaster. It wasn't just the empty rooms and cold soup, either. On the hall floor was a mosaic of colored tiles, designed to help the downward spiral of power, with tessellated eddies like catch-pools in each room. She hadn't expected the savage current of a temple—as Kindrie had said, constant exposure to that would erode any half-trained mind. Even two days ago, though, standing on the far side of the Silver, she had sensed more activity than this. Had something happened to the distant temples, sources of their god's power on Rathillien, or was the problem here in the Riverland, perhaps in the College itself?

Still, there was something. As she had followed the trickle of power through Wilden to find this place, so now she felt drawn downward with it. The hall's spiral widened. From below came a rhythmic shuffling sound, massive, as if in its deep den some huge beast were dancing. Before she was aware of it, her feet had caught the pattern: step, turn, glide down and down to where the others wove the Great Dance, round and round on the tessellated floor, straining to draw in power, passing it down and down...

Jame stopped short with a gasp. She stood on the threshold of the College's main hall, and she had found its community.

Innermost stood a high priest, still eye of the storm, yet its master. Around him like black clouds circled lesser priests, feet barely touching the floor, robes a stream in wind-blowing Senetha. Water-flowing acolytes girt them with gray, and brown-clad novices with the *kantirs* of earth-moving. The whole wove a pattern of great power, each dancer caught in it, oblivious to all else.

His back to her, a young, white-clad scullion shuffled in step. His movements puzzled her until she recognized them as fire-leaping, consumed, as it were, to cinders by his exhaustion. How long had they all been at this, anyway?

The dance jerked the boy around. His eyelids drooped over burnt-out sockets. His gaping mouth was full of dried blood. He had been dead for days.

This isn't my business, Jame thought, sickened, backing away. *I can't let it be.*

But what about Kindrie? She could still feel the mindless pull of the dance which had sucked her down to fill the gap where that corpse jerked and twitched. Had the healer been snared before her? No. Of all the white-haired Shanir here, he was not one.

The stair led on, downward.

Below was the priests' domain. The lesser orders lived simply, if in cleaner, drier cells than the acolytes above. They also had better light, from diamantine panels glowing on the walls. In the high priests' quarters farther down, more diamantine filled all but the farthest corner with soft, stolen sunshine. It was as if the world had been turned upside down, the sun below and dank earth above. Jame passed austere but well-appointed rooms, many with scrolls piled high on tables. They reminded her of Ishtier's obsession with a certain pale book currently in her knapsack in the Mount Alban infirmary. These shelves weren't apt to contain anything half as priceless, but what she glimpsed looked valuable enough. She had never considered how the priesthood supported itself. An allowance from the Randir, perhaps. But that would hardly extend to this fortune in diamantine and arcane literature, or to the book chests faced with rathorn ivory which she noted in many rooms. Clearly, the high priests had access to great wealth. Where did it come from, and on what else did they spend it?

Ever since the main hall, the corridor's spiral had been contracting. No more doors opened off of it, but still it continued to descend into dimmer light, past empty niches. A curious, musty smell rose from the depths, vaguely and disagreeably sweet.

Then came a niche which was not empty. Jame thought at first that a statue stood in it, clothed in crumpling finery, wearing a mask of beaten gold. Then she saw the white of bone under the cracked maroon flesh of long-dead fingers. On the lintel was carved an unfamiliar name, a date long past, and a rank: high priest. Each niche from then on had a similar inscription, and a similar inmate.

Jame had seen something like this, descending to the secret library under Gorgo's temple in Tai-tastigon. That had been distasteful. This was obscene. Kencyr dead were given to the pyre. While one bone remained intact, the soul was believed to be trapped in it, naked before the three faces of God. To escape that hated divinity and the contract which it imposed was a Kencyr's last act of defiance, as honor was his first in life. The priests, it seemed, felt differently. Jame did note, however, as she gingerly descended between the grim ranks, that no one new had joined them in the past thirty or forty years.

The odor was getting stronger but, somehow, less disagreeable. That wasn't necessarily good. After sharing Jorin's senses intermittently for the past two years, Jame had begun to find the smell of some fairly nasty things quite appetizing. This was more of a green scent, though, as if of growing things. So far underground? Had the priests turned their world that much on its head?

Then she heard a slow, thumping sound and a voice, thick with exhaustion and hopelessness.

"Let me in," it was mumbling over and over. "Let me in."

A narrow hall curved left at the stair's foot. Around it shone a light. Jame advanced warily, then stopped, staring. At the hall's end, Kindrie huddled against a door, weakly beating against it with bloody knuckles. Above him hung a tapestry, aglow with flowers as white as the Shanir's hair. The light shone from it—no, *through* it. It wasn't fabric at all, Jame saw, but a window set in the door. On the other side, in full spring glory, was the secret moon garden at Gothregor.

Impossible, unless, unless...

Tieri had died in that garden, where her tattered death banner still hung, and there the Knorth Bastard had been born. Kindrie had been locked out of his soul-image by Ishtier, hence his inability to heal those bleeding hands. Jame wasn't trained to enter others' soul-scapes, but she apparently had walked into her brother's at the wolvers' keep, perhaps because they were twins. Kindrie must also be very close to her in blood, as she had guessed, since here she was, uninvited, on the threshold of his soul.

"Please..." the Shanir moaned, striking feebly at the closed door. Blood tricked down his thin wrist. "Oh, please..."

Jame stepped forward, then froze as cracks radiated out from under her foot. They weren't real, she told herself, any more than that lightning flash had been in Caineron's tower which had first shown her a glimpse of Kindrie's soul-garden and almost knocked the healer off the balcony.

Remember that, she warned herself, looking down at the broken floor.

Everything that happened on this level had repercussions in the physical world, hence a healer's power. But this was almost the opposite: some dangerous antipathy seemed to exist between her soul and Kindrie's, however good her intentions. She didn't dare go a step closer.

"If you want to reclaim that garden," she told him, "you've got to help yourself. Come on. Get up."

"Please, oh, please..." he moaned again.

She could have shaken him. Always whining or retreating into trances...hadn't the idiot any pride at all? But the only thing which he thought he had to be proud of was his "trace" of Knorth blood. All right.

"Kindrie, tell me again the name of your grandmother."

His bloody hand wavered in mid-air. "T-telarien, her n-
name was Telarien..."

"Good. Now, who was her daughter? Go on. Ask me."

He frowned, muzzy, as if her voice had begun to drag him
out of deep sleep. The light dimmed, no longer shining through
the door but only from the tapestry which hung against it.

Damn, thought Jame.

As he roused, he was drawing them both from the meta-
physical level back toward the real. Maybe this entrance to
his soul would disappear altogether if he woke fully. Obviously, dream- and soul-scapes were closely related.

"Ask me!" she said again, with more urgency.

"W-who?"

"Tieri, your mother, who was also my aunt. And what
does that make us?"

"F-first cousins," he stammered, sitting up, blinking at her.
"Blood-kin. A-and the Highlord?"

"Him too."

And what would Tori think of that, or of her having told
Kindrie? His skin was going to crawl off his bones. But that
didn't change facts.

"You may be a bastard," she said, "and as wet as a fresh-
dropped calf, but you're Knorth, all right, if ever there was
one. So stop shaming our ancestors. Get up and open that
damn door!"

He was looking full at her now, pale eyes at last focused
behind white lashes. "Yes," he said, climbing stiffly to his
feet. "Yes."

A tremor made Jame almost fall. She saw that the cracks
underfoot now lay between mosaic tiles which shifted like the
sullen mull of dammed waters, serpentine and lapis-lazuli, green
and blue, fretted with foam-lines of ivory. Of course, the
power gathered above must go somewhere. She had descended
into a pool of it, channeled down to press impatiently against
the sluice-gate toward which Kindrie was now reaching.

Couldn't he see that the only light now came from the molds which mottled its surface? Their spores burst, sickly luminous, under his hand. He was lifting the latch.

"No!" she cried, stumbling forward.

Too late.

II

The dark pressed in on all sides, loosening, tightening, like the guts of some great snake that feels the swallowed prey stir. Eaten alive...

But I can still breathe, thought Jame. That terrified panting almost in her ear was her own. She fought to control it. *I can still move...*

Just not very well. By the pain in her bruised knees, she located the floor. So that way was down. Her hands could feel it too, after a fashion. Now, get up. Slowly, slowly...

The floor seemed to tilt. She hit it, sprawling, before her senses warned her that she had lost her balance. *Like being drunk,* she thought, remembering the last and only time.

What had happened? Kindrie had opened the door and then...and then...

The force dammed outside had rushed in, taking them with it. Where? Clearly, not into the Shanir's moon garden. That had slipped back out of his reach, into some sealed-off corner of his soul. In the priests' inverted world, this room was the deepest, the most secret and important, the very bowels of power. And it had swallowed her with one gulp.

Nearby, someone laughed softly.

"Who's there?" she demanded, trying again to rise, again falling. Her voice sounded flat and muffled. "Kindrie?"

"You suit me better," said a dry, thin voice, "on your knees. Greetings, thief."

"Ishtier." She must not show fear. She must not. "You suit *me* better trying to gnaw off your own hand. I hear, though, that you stopped short with a finger—ah!"

The darkness around her had seemed to constrict. For a moment, she couldn't breathe. No doubt about it: her old enemy had power in this place—not the mindless maelstrom of a temple but something more considered, perhaps more dangerous, with intelligence behind it. The other seven high priests must be close by, listening.

"Renegade," she said, raising her voice. "Have you told the College how you abandoned Ganth, your lord, in the Haunted Lands to die?"

"Priests have no lords, thief. Our houses abandon *us*, when they send us here. We owe them nothing."

The rancor in his voice scraped as though against raw flesh. Such bitterness, after so many years… It must be true.

"B-but then why did you go with Ganth into exile?"

"Now, why would I tell you a thing like that? You used to be sharper-witted, thief."

He was taunting her, but he was also right. Her mind seemed full of slow moving eels, brain-suckers, eating their way out…

No, dammit. All these images of *eat-and-be-eaten*…the priest was using the Great Dance to play games with her, as she had earlier with Brenwyr. Knowing helped, some.

Don't be distracted. Attack.

"You betrayed Bane, when you used his soul to create the Lower Town Monster."

"Experimentation. You indulged in it too, theocide."

"Yes, I accidentally killed Gorgo, but I also helped his priest Loogan resurrect him afterward. That wasn't to disprove our own god's monotheism, though, as you tried to do with the Monster; and I never gave my allegiance to Perimal Darkling, as you did."

Darkness hummed. "That I deny."

"You boasted that you would bring down the Barriers and restore the Kencyrath to Gerridon, whom you called its rightful lord, under shadow's eaves."

"That I didn't."

"Liar."

The insult hung in the dark, throbbing air like a curse. Somewhere nearby, someone (probably Kindrie) gave a half-swallowed sob of fear. Jame held her breath. Despite all she knew about Ishtier, it unnerved her that he would lie so easily. In the back of her mind, though, something whispered:

Idiot. He forced that charge out of you before you were ready. Now all your arrows are shot.

Darkness chuckled again, as dry and rustling as claws at work inside a shroud, as obscenely triumphant.

"Always nosing after the truth, aren't you, little thief? Like a bitch in heat. Shall we show everyone the truth about you? Yes, oh yessss..."

Jame lurched to her feet. "Oh, no, oh, God!"

Intolerable dizziness had seized her. *He's turning me inside-out,* she thought wildly, then stumbled and fell again, retching, to the floor.

She could see it now, though the thin vomit of an empty stomach: dark stone, veined with green. Her hands shone white against it, fingers sheathed in articulated plates of ivory. Weight bowed her head, ivory helm and mask. So it had been when contact with the injured Graykin had jolted her into, into...

"No," she said again, half moaning, as the memory surfaced. "Oh, no..."

"Yessss..."

The hiss brought her head up. Around her opened out Gerridon's monstrous hall, in his house in Perimal Darkling; her soul-image. Threadbare eyes watched her from the death banners of fallen Knorth; singed sockets from the pelts of Arrin-ken piled high on the hearth. The cold air stank. Always nosing after the truth...This was what she had tried to forget, to deny, but could never escape: the abscess at her soul's core that made cruel mock of hope and honor. Bred to darkling service...She wanted to curl into an ivory ball, to hide from herself forever and ever.

"So this is where you come from," breathed Ishtier. "So this is what you are."

His white face hovered over her, more skull-like than she remembered after his winter of illness, eyes alive with scorn in a death's-mask. "Listen to me, you abomination. You have something of mine. I sent the assassins to fetch it, but they failed. I sent that whey-faced healer, but he ran away. Nonetheless, I *will* have it. Where is my book, thief? My Book Bound in Pale Leather. Tell me, or as surely as I locked that cringing bastard out of his soul-image, I will lock you *into* yours. Think about it: your mind trapped here forever; your body mine, to do with what I will…"

"No!"

She drew the Ivory Knife with clumsy, ivory-gloved fingers. He slapped it out of her hand. It clattered on stone into shadows by the door.

"Call *me* renegade, will you? Did you really think you could defy our master in his own hall? Swear allegiance where you please, Priest's-Bane, but this is where your soul lies and rots. Fool, to think that arms or armor can save you here!"

His second blow caught her on the side of the head, making her ears ring.

…the white rathorn colt, felled by her kick just where she herself had now been struck. Too immature, both of them, too unprepared…

Blood splashed on the floor between her hands, Kallystine's cut reopened beneath the ivory mask. At its touch, the green marble veins began to pulse, cracks of verdigris light spreading out around her to the hearth's edge. The flayed paws of Arrin-ken flexed stiffly.

Scree went their claws on the hearthstone. *Screeeee…*

Jame clapped hands over her ears. Inside her skull, panic babbled:

He'll let you out if you give him the Book. You never wanted to be the filthy thing's guardian, anyway. And this time, surely, it will kill him. Give him the Book.

Yes.

A ripple ran through the hall, like wind over water. Arrin-ken claws and rathorn ivory melted. Grimacing, the banners

unraveled. Walls redefined themselves around her, closer than
the hall's had been, under a low roof supported by massive,
squat columns. Mosaic covered every surface, lapis lazuli and
ivory. Green serpentine throbbed like the veins of some great
heart. No. That was up in the hall, pounding itself to death
with the exhaustion of its dancers. Here that gathered power
was stored, in the bowels of the earth, the foul cloaca of divinity...

A dark bundle with Kindrie's pale face stared at her across
the tessellated floor. "What did you *do*?" he whispered, aghast.
What, indeed?

But the black clot of priests huddled by the far wall were
staring over both the healer's head and her own. So was Ishtier.
She hadn't admitted her defeat out-loud, Jame realized. Neither the priests nor her soul-image was responding to it. Someone had opened the door.

An indistinct figure stood on the threshold. Mold-glow
glimmered on the gold mask which it held before its face.
Rotting finery crumbled away from it. The unburnt dead always return...But behind the mask as it fell, nothing—or was
there? In the shadow of the hood, someone smiled at Jame,
planes of darkness shifting around the eerie flash of stained
teeth. Yellow eyes or silver, assassin's or Bane's? Whichever,
they lifted, and the smile in them died.

"No..." croaked Ishtier, recoiling. "You're dead on the
Mercy Seat, flayed alive and crawling with flies... No!"

His maimed hand rose. Fingernails scraped the low ceiling, raking together lines of power, jerking them down. A
massive weight settled on the room. Walls groaned. Columns
crumbled at the top. With a report like the earth's back breaking, the lintel cracked. The figure standing under it disintegrated in a puff of acrid dust.

"You'll bring the roof down on us all!" someone wailed.
Good idea, thought Jame.

After all, was anyone here worth saving? These fool priests,
who had put such power in a madman's hands? The demon in

the doorway, or his half-sister, who had dreamed of walking in the light? Kindrie, who had deserved protection from so many and received it from no one?

Well, yes. Dammit.

She struggled to her feet, feeling as if the whole college rested on her shoulders. Once before, she had dealt with m'lord Ishtier, in his own temple, with an act of appalling recklessness. No helping that. Her black gloved hands were already rising, clenched in challenge not of the priest but of the god whom he feigned to serve.

"Lord," she cried, "a judgment!"

Ishtier's wild stare snapped to her face. Tendons stood out under the loose skin of his throat as he strained to keep his mouth shut. It opened anyway, muscles creaking. The God-voice boomed out through the nine spider-thin fingers which he clamped to his face, biting into them with each word:

"TRUST NOT IN PRIESTS..."

What in Perimal's name?

"...NOR YET IN ORACLES."

That *was* the Voice which she had evoked from Ishtier before, and yet not quite, as if some undernote in it now dominated. She hadn't thought before of her god's voice as a chorus, like, like...

She seized the priest by the shoulders. He felt bird-fragile in her grasp. Sinking to his knees, he drew her down with him.

"Who's in there?" she demanded of his blank eyes, of pupils so huge with shock that they looked like holes burned in parchment. "Dammit, what game are you playing?"

...not eyes at all but scorched sockets fringed with burnt fur, opening into greater darkness...

For a moment, Jame thought that she was back in her soul-image, that her spilt blood had animated an Arrin-ken pelt from the hearth to hood this wretched man, as Bane had the master assassin. Then a second possibility struck her: twice now, she had demanded a judgment and received it, perhaps not from her god at all, but from his appointed judges, the

Arrin-ken, whose plaited voices in the Ebonbane had also
forced her to judge herself. There, Immalai's mercy had prevailed; but the Riverland was the blind cat's territory.

Ishtier grinned at her around his bleeding fingers. *"In the
Ebonbane, by the chasm, you escaped my judgment,"* he said in a
voice like a winter's pyre, frost and bitter ash, *"but* these *mountains are mine. Child of darkness, do you want my judgment now?"*

She recoiled. "No!"

A rush of priests thrust her aside to get at Ishtier. The
oldest, smallest of them grabbed Jame by the arm.

"Do that again!" he cried, trying to shake her, only shaking
himself. "Evoke the Voice!"

"N-not damned likely," said Jame, attempting to free herself. The little priest barely came to her shoulder and looked
frailer than some of his late colleagues out in the hall, but he
had a terrier's grip. "You want it, you talk to it."

"God's teeth and toenails. Don't you think we've tried?
All winter, ever since we learned that the Voice had spoken
again after all these years…Oh, if only we weren't so starved
of power, now, when we need it most!"

"Why? What's happened?"

"Too few of us here, too few Kencyr in the Riverland over-
all, who knows, except that we're being cut off from the
temples. The closer to Summer Eve, the worse it gets. Not
even the Great Dance is pulling in enough power to keep the
valley ours."

"The Dance. You're killing your own people, priest."

"So? There are always more unwanted Shanir."

A harsh sound came from Ishtier.

The little man let go of Jame and darted over to join his
peers, all shouting questions at the Voice, which had just
deigned for the third time to speak through the Tastigon priest.
In their midst, Ishtier hunched jealously over his hands, tearing strips of flesh off them with his teeth and growling.

Jame pulled Kindrie to his feet. The healer's nose was
bleeding freely, as surely it would not have if he had regained

control of his soul-image. A fine pair of Knorth they were, or perhaps a trio. Discarded grave clothes lay strewn on the threshold, blind flies seething out of the eyes and mouth of the golden death mask. The pavement beneath had been smashed to powder. The assassin must have blinked in time for the shock to pass harmlessly through him. Was he still Bane's prisoner? Where in Perimal's name had they gone, anyway?

At least, there was no sign of them on the way up.

Kindrie faltered at the door of the main hall, staring at the carnage inside wrought by Ishtier's last, ruthless pulling down of power. Jame tugged him away.

"Think about it later," she said, herself white-faced beneath mask and drying blood. The Priests' College would need many new Shanir.

At the doorway of the little stone house, they paused to look warily out at the terrace. Judging from the growth of the puddles, it had rained. Now, however, the lower cloud level was beginning to dissipate.

Jame swore softly. "When this weirding haze lifts entirely, Mount Alban will be gone, if it isn't already. No time to lose."

But Kindrie caught her arm. "Wait."

The shadow of Rawneth's tower had moved since Jame had entered the College. Now it slanted southwestward, entirely across their way, where no northern sun would have thrown it.

"Don't tell me," said Jame. "The Wilden Witch can shadow-cast."

By the balustrade, a shaded puddle quivered. Out of it came groping something dark to fumble at the pool's rim and grip a flagstone's edge. A lumpish figure surfaced, out of water at most an inch deep. Gold embroidery glimmered on the muddy shoulders of dress grays. The lower half of its ruined face split into a white-toothed grin, framed by chipped, bleeding incisors.

Kindrie swayed.

"Don't faint!" Jame said sharply. "So the Witch's pet demon wasn't destroyed after all. So it still wants you. Things could be worse."

"H-how?"

"Bane could be behind us." She glanced over her shoulder. "Damn."

She had hoped that he had stayed below to deal with his betrayer—not that much more could be done to Ishtier, short of killing him. For that final mercy he could hardly depend on Bane, who in his darker days had flayed children alive for sport. Now his shadowy figure stood just behind the tapestry at the back of the room, watching her through its hanging warp threads.

Better the demon you know?

Kindrie gasped.

Still grinning, Rawneth's creature had heaved itself out of the puddle and was crawling toward them. Oily, black water streamed off its clothes, off the trailing, limp cuffs of its pants. It had no feet. The tower's shadow crept forward to give it cover, swinging in on the doorway where they stood like the closing of a massive gate.

"Quick," said Jame. "Its soul belongs to a Randir captain, late of Tentir, more recently assigned to Gothregor. What's her name? You used to live here. Tell me!"

"I-I don't know."

Jame swallowed her exasperation. After all, she had spent the entire winter in the same halls with the wretched woman without learning what she was called. Now she had made Kindrie feel as stupid and helpless as she did. Nonetheless, they must not be caught between two demons. As the shadow closed on them, she took a deep breath and shoved Kindrie out into it.

It was very cold under Rawneth's tower. They could see the white plumes of their breaths, the Shanir's so rapid that he was almost panting, her own hardly less so. Eerie twilight surrounded them like that of a solar eclipse. The splash of their feet, even the cataract's roar, sounded curiously muffled and far away. Jame wished that she were. The creeping figure had turned to follow them, sodden dress tunic bulging, pants legs now drained and flat. It left a foul, black trail behind it and sent a hideous stench on before. At least it would never overtake them before they reached the shadow's far side.

In the demon's path lay another puddle, beginning to mantle with frost. It pulled itself over the edge and sank, gurgling, through shattered panes of ice. Dark water closed over it.

Jame and Kindrie stopped, staring. Bubbles, then nothing.

"It's under the pavement," she said suddenly. "Run!"

Kindrie shot her a terrified look, then bolted. She floundered after him through such water as lay in her path, too much in haste to detour. The Shanir's bare feet scarcely cracked the growing sheet ice, but her boots crashed through it, sinking with each step from ankle to shin to knee.

Fifteen feet to the light, ten, five...

Kindrie burst out into it.

Jame lunged to catch up and fell heavily, half on mist-chilled pavement, half up to the waist in freezing water. Something had grabbed her foot. Now it pulled. Her nails rasped on icy stone, clawing for a grip. Kindrie clutched her wrists. Behind her, something surfaced, stinking like a week-old corpse, chuckling thickly.

"C-cum an' play, liddle girl..."

Kindrie nearly let go. He was staring up at something, aghast. The grip on Jame's foot broke. She shot forward into the Shanir's arms, both of them going down in a heap.

Bane stood on the other side of the puddle into which she had nearly sunk. Out of it he had fished the demon, which he now held one-handed by the scruff of its dress-gray neck, fastidiously, at arm's length, as it squirmed and mewled and stank. In his other hand was the Ivory Knife. With great care, he began to slit the uniform's seams. As each gave way, black liquid filth poured down. Those grinning teeth fell last, bloody at the roots as if just pulled. For a moment they floated white in the befouled pool, then sank. Bane held out the coat like a trophy skin and dropped it at Jame's feet.

She had risen and was standing just barely within the light, close enough to touch him or to be touched.

Not since that last night in Tai-tastigon had she seen him so clearly. Never before had she realized how much like Torisen he looked, especially in the elegant lines of his face and hands. But although his eyes mirrored the true Knorth silver, almost luminous in this half-light, they hadn't the depth either of Tori's self-doubt or of his intrinsic strength. Bane had always believed that in the end he could defeat his own damnation, that an honorable death would wipe away stains even as black as his. How often she had seen the arrogance of that faith in his lazy, mocking smile.

He wasn't smiling now.

In his hand he held the Ivory Knife, gripped perilously by the flat between thumb and forefinger, its point resting lightly on his palm. He was offering it to her, hilt first.

Could the dead die? *Was* Bane dead? Perhaps he himself didn't know. A scratch from the Knife would make certain. It might even be the honorable death which he had sought, if given by her hand—or then again, it might not.

His voice didn't carry beyond the shadow's pall, but she saw his lips move: *"...your choice, sister..."*

Choice. She had been so proud of her ability to choose and to live with the consequences. That had been her honor, or rather her arrogance, more than a match for any of Bane's. But what did any choice matter when under it lay that cold, dark hall, that predestined damnation?

"Who am I," she said bitterly, "to judge you?"—and, with great care, she took the Knife from his hand. "Follow, if you choose."

Behind her, Kindrie caught his breath. He was staring up at the Witch's tower, at a low balcony just now cleared by the wispy, thinning clouds. Yellow light streamed from the interior, silhouetting the tall, slim figure motionless by the rail.

Come out to see the fun, had she? Let her fish for her servant's teeth, then, in foul puddles and the rain which had again begun to fall. Jame sketched the proper salute—more insulting under the circumstances than a rude gesture—and turned her back on the Witch of Wilden.

"Time to go," she said.

They did.

III

The platform ascended, creaking.

Kindrie sat cross-legged on it, shoulders drooping with fatigue, a shock of white hair hanging down over his face. Jame wondered how much more of this he could take. True, the Knorth were tougher than they looked, but most of them hadn't depended all their lives on a healer's talents.

For that matter, how long had it been since she herself had last slept or eaten? About forty-eight hours in both cases—not that she hadn't often gone longer than that without sleep. As for food, sore as her face had been and now was again, thanks to Ishtier, the prospect didn't much appeal. Anyway, she wasn't tired or hungry, just numb.

Empty.

She seemed to remember, a lifetime ago, when her mind had teemed with plans. The narrow halls of Gothregor had taught her to think more...modestly, the Women's World would say. Since then, the world had seemed to close in on her, prospects slamming like doors along a dark corridor down which she had run, increasingly alone with that which followed. One could never outrun one's past. Now she couldn't seem to plan ahead at all. Tomorrow didn't exist; this afternoon, just barely. She supposed, making an effort, that they should sneak back into the infirmary before their absence caused a stir.

One thing at a time.

The platform stopped with a jolt in Mount Alban's upper reaches. Jame pulled Kindrie to his feet, then threw an arm around him as he staggered. She could count his ribs by touch.

Not until they had turned into the corridor did she remember that Brenwyr had toppled a wardrobe across the infirmary door. However, it had been removed. From within came voices, one patient, the other sharp with frustration. Both ten-commands had crowded inside to listen while Captain Hawthorn tried tactfully to learn from her matriarch why they should risk war by raiding Wilden.

Graykin stood by the door, biting his nails. He nearly bit off a finger when Jame spoke softly in his ear:

"What did you do, shout for help through the keyhole?"

"Someone had to be told," he muttered, regarding her askance.

"Huh," said Jame.

"Someone," apparently, had been Brenwyr, who must have summoned the guard posthaste but now couldn't bring herself to explain why the Knorth had gone down to Wilden, much less what specific danger she was in.

Women's secrets had some use after all.

Glancing back over the heads of her restive squad, Brier Iron-thorn met Jame's eyes. The Kendar's expression didn't change, but the sharpening of her attention made others turn as well, including the Brandan captain and her matriarch.

"Er..." said Jame, trying surreptitiously to shift Kindrie into Graykin's reluctant arms. "Is anything the matter?"

"Suppose, lady," said Hawthorn, sandy brows rising, "that you tell us."

Jame's mind went blank. Earlier, she had broken one of her own cardinal rules by making herself forget an unwelcome fact. Now her brain seemed to have closed shop altogether, lights out and nobody home. The truth wouldn't do, nor would a lie, leaving...what? Twenty-four pairs of expectant eyes and the hiss of rain falling past the windows—except that part of that sound came from Jorin, followed by his low, throbbing growl.

The cadets had cleared a path between her and the two principal Brandan. In the shadows behind Brenwyr, Aerulan's banner lay unrolled across the seat and back of a chair. On her tapestry lap crouched the ounce, ears flat, fangs bared, moon opal eyes aglow, but what was he seeing, and through whose eyes? In the room's gray, rain-washed light, Aerulan's white hands glimmered, one clutching the cat's ruff, the other pressed against the crimson line across her throat. She was staring, transfixed, at something behind Jame.

Jame felt the hair on the back of her neck rise. Someone stood behind her in the open doorway, so close that she smelled its rotten breath, but the cadets' fascinated gaze hadn't shifted from her face. Whoever—*what*ever—it was, only the dead girl and the blind cat could see it.

A hoarse, mocking whisper breathed in her ear: *"...my choice, sister."*

The master assassin's voice, Bane's words. "Follow, if you choose," she had said, and they had. Oh, lord. Now what?

First, clear the room.

"This is house business," she said to the infirmary at large. "Everyone, please leave."

Hawthorn's brows rose even farther, but she acknowledged with a wry salute and hustled her cadets out of the room. The Knorth cadets hesitated, hopeful, but Jame waved them out too, including Brier. The latter paused on the threshold.

"Lady, are you all right?"

Jame sighed. "Have I ever been?"

Only after the Kendar had gone did Jame realize what an insult she had just dealt her, now a Knorth herself, as good as told publicly that she wasn't trusted with family business.

Ishtier was right, thought Jame. *Where are my wits? Be damned if you must, but don't be stupid.*

However, this really didn't concern the ten-commander. Nor did it Graykin, who had slunk out with the greatest reluctance and would probably listen at the keyhole, if he could. Kindrie had tumbled over asleep on a pallet. What good that would do him without access to his soul-image, Jame didn't know, but still she hadn't the heart to wake him up.

"That was good thinking," said Brenwyr gruffly. "They won't challenge a house secret."

"Wait," said Jame as the matriarch started to pass her. She shut the door in Graykin's avid face. "I might as well have called this sister-kin business. About Aerulan…"

Brenwyr stiffened, still facing the door. "She's yours again. What more do you want?"

Jame frowned. The matriarch *had* been about to leave without the banner, er, Aerulan, whom Jame could still plainly see, one hand on her throat, the other raised as if in supplication.

"But I gave her to you," she protested.

The Iron Matriarch turned on her. "One does *not* demean a lady by giving her away! Have you and your brother no decency at all?"

Her throttled rage drove Jame back a step. Then she thought, perhaps, she understood.

"Lord Brandan asked for Aerulan's banner," she said slowly, sorting it out, "and Torisen simply told him to take it."

Of course. Any other lord would have insisted on the fabulous price which Ganth had demanded for Aerulan's contract in perpetuity, paid in full. The Knorth were poor. Torisen could certainly use the money. But he had refused to profit from old grief and his father's rapacious bargain. Neither he nor, perhaps, Lord Brandan had realized what an insult this charity had dealt to the Women's World, where a lady's price confirmed her rank. Aerulan wouldn't have minded. Brenwyr did, terribly, for her sake.

A berserker and a maledight. Of all people to have enraged.

"We meant well," Jame said awkwardly, wanting very much to be believed. "We just didn't understand. I think, now, that I do. I'll explain it to my brother. There must be some way to send Aerulan home with honor, to you."

The older woman had turned away again, as if better to keep her precarious self-control. Without thinking, Jame put a hand on her arm. It felt as hard under her fingertips as the Iron Matriarch's nickname. A tremor passed through it.

"Adiraina said that you would instruct him."

For the first time, Brenwyr turned to look at the banner on its chair, and gave a sharp exclamation. A hasty stride took her out of Jame's reach, but then she stopped short, hands curling into fists at her side.

"Knorth, are you trying to drive me mad?"

Jame stared. "What?"

"Taunting me with glimpses of her, then snatching her away... Traveling with her, sleeping with her, do you think I don't recognize seduction when I see it?"

God's teeth and toenails. She was *jealous*.

"Lady, I swear..."

"Liar!"

Jame felt her hands go cold. A terrible clarity filled her mind—what she would do to this...this hag, with her disheveled hair and red eyes, who had dared to impugn the only thing of worth which she had left: her honor. She wanted the release of a flare, to feel its power burn away doubt and self-disgust. She craved its intoxication. Her claws were out through her glove tips, ready.

No.

This was the onset of a berserk seizure, against a woman striking out in pain, against another berserker. She must not, *not*, NOT.

Brenwyr was shouting unforgivable things in her face.

"Self-restraint, endurance, obedience-be-damned!" she shouted back as she retreated, to drown words which she must not hear. "Self-restraint-endurance-obedience-be-*damned!*"

Brenwyr grabbed her arm just as, groping behind her, she touched the death banner. The matriarch's other hand was poised to strike. Jame knew, with detached certainty, that if Brenwyr slapped her, Jame would kill her.

But another hand closed on the matriarch's raised fist. Joined by touch, the three of them stood frozen—two alive, panting, and one dead.

"Aerulan..." said Brenwyr hoarsely. "Knorth, do you see her too?"

"Yes. I have off and on for days, but never so clearly as now. And no, you aren't going mad, unless I am too."

Thunder rolled, retreating. Gray rain fell, gray light in a gray room—but there the dead stood, smiling, in her rust-red gown.

"She was given to the pyre thirty-four years ago. How is this possible?"

"I'm not sure," said Jame.

Her left arm was going numb from the older woman's iron grip. Her right hand felt the rough tapestry nap, and beneath it a shoulder which flame had reduced to ash long before she herself had been born. *Had* they both gone mad?

Aerulan smiled past her, at Brenwyr.

"Perhaps," said Jame slowly, "the dead are more persistent than our priests have led us to believe." *The ranks of hieratic dead beneath the Wilden college.* "Perhaps the rules have changed here on Rathillien." *Bane, at her back, with his enigmatic smile. Where was his body?* "Or perhaps…" *Aerulan's dress, woven of threads taken from the gown in which she had bled to death.* "Can blood trap the soul as well as flesh and bone?"

"If you say so," said Brenwyr, doubtfully.

Jame felt her scalp prickle. The matriarch had not been speaking to her.

Brenwyr stiffened. "He's *here?*" She spun about, her fierce gaze sweeping the room.

In the farthest corner, a flaw moved in the shadows, dropping the *mere*-tattooed hand with which it had hidden its eyes. The yellow irises were as blood-shot as fertilized egg yolks from being kept open so long and the spirit in them raged with impotent fury. Bane's features overlay the whole like a shadow-spun cowl, smiling.

Brenwyr rounded on Jame. "*You* brought him here!"

Jame recoiled, hands clenched behind her not this time to forestall a berserker response but to keep from dancing down the matriarch's rage. Ancestors only knew what she might unleash, trying *that* trick again.

"It's all right," she said hastily. "Aerulan's killer *is* in this room and I *did* more or less invite him here, but he's under control."

"Control? Yours? By God, Knorth, if you've sold yourself to the Bashtiri Shadow Guild…"

"Oh, don't be silly."

Brenwyr boggled, suddenly deflated. "That's what Aerulan said."

"You can actually hear her? I can't, but then I don't know what her voice sounded like."

"That's something." The matriarch glanced back at the banner, mere tapestry again without Jame's touch to bridge the gap. "Then too, at last her blood-price will be paid."

"That isn't enough. I want to know who took out a contract on my whole family."

Brenwyr blinked. She had forgotten the larger massacre whose aftermath had almost destroyed the entire Kencyrath. Kinzi, Telarien, all those Knorth women dead and unavenged… But what if the old quarrel between Kinzi and Rawneth *was* to blame? Could the Kencyrath survive such a terrible discovery?

"It was all so long ago," she said, hearing the echo of Adiraina's warning in her voice. "After all these years, is it wise to ask?"

"Vengeance aside, it isn't just ancient history. Everyone keeps telling me that the Shadow Guild never gives up. So why did the assassins let Tieri live, and will they keep coming after me?"

Brenwyr rubbed her temples, which had begun to throb. "Tieri lived because everyone except Adiraina thought she was dead."

"But this man knew better: he's the one from whom Aerulan hid Tieri. Why didn't he enlist the rest of the casting to help find her, instead of leaving his precious contract unfulfilled? What happened? Bane, make him talk!"

Out of shadows, he looked at her unsmiling, as he had under the Witch's tower with what passed for his life balanced on the edge of the Ivory Knife. *Choices…*

"Yes," said Jame unsteadily, meeting the yellow glare of the captive, set unnervingly in his captor's face. "I choose this. It's necessary."

Bane nodded.

He seemed about to speak, but instead his mouth opened wide, wider, stained teeth and coated tongue shaping a mute shriek. The corner seemed full of writhing shadows, indistinctly at war like snakes in a bag. Then staring eyes and bared teeth lunged out into the room. The distortion of a *mere*-tattooed body showed against the windows, naked shoulders beaded with sweat and rain. Its faint shadow danced with it on the floor, all but consumed by the darker shape which clung to its back.

"Watch out!" Jame said sharply. "If he closes his eyes…"

The yellow glint vanished. Raindrops spattered on the floor. Away from them streaked the guild master's living shadow, flat to the ground, free. If the Bashtiri had made straight for the closed door, blind, he would have slipped out under it. But at the last moment his nerve failed. He looked—and bounced off the panels with an oath, back into his pursuer's grip.

The sound of struggle thrashed across the floor. Brenwyr snatched Aerulan's banner off the chair and Jorin scuttled out from under it a moment before the chair was smashed to pieces. The assassin's cursing changed to a cry of pain. One of his eyes filled with blood, then the other. Red brimmed over bony sockets and down hollow cheeks, defining their invisible planes with bloody tears.

"What's happening?" demanded Brenwyr.

"Bane has torn off his eyelids."

"Who in Perimal's name is Bane?"

The uproar abruptly stopped. Harsh panting came from amid the chair's wreckage, then a sharp gasp. A crimson line appeared beneath the grimacing face, following the winged arch of the collarbone. Blood trickled down the incline, down the sternum. Another cut traced the major pectoral of the right breast, then the left.

Brenwyr's fingers dug into Jame's shoulder. "What...?"

"He's got the assassin's *mere*-knife and control of his hand. The pattern of cuts is called *kuth*. It's used in the public execution of child-killers." It might, Jame thought, have been the last thing which Bane himself had felt on the Tastigon Mercy Seat under the flayer's knife, unjustly accused of Dally's murder. "In the Eastern Lands, it would be considered just punishment for the assassination of Aerulan, her...blood-price."

With a deft flick, Bane cut off the assassin's right nipple. The bastard was enjoying himself. He would stop, though, if she asked.

The assassin spat out teeth, with fragments of gum attached. Demon-ridden for two days, he was doomed, whatever she did. The left nipple...

"This will only get worse," she said, hearing the truth in her voice, knowing how it was meant to mislead. "Talk, while you still can."

Yellow teeth bared in a ragged snarl. Parallel cuts marked prominent ribs as Bane continued to sketch in details of surface anatomy as if with a brush dripping red. A sinewy torso was taking shape in mid-air, slick with blood.

"Cut lower," said Brenwyr.

The assassin burst out cursing. The cut down his side skidded awry, into the fold of the groin.

"Bitch! Red-eyed, sodding whore... D'you want to hear how I cut that one's white throat?"

"Yes," said Jame, reaching behind her to restrain Brenwyr. Her hand closed on Aerulan's cold fingers.

"Gaaah... She came in with the little bint behind her, just when we'd finally pulled down the matriarch. 'Aerulan, Tieri, run!' she says—the old witch, brains half out on the floor and still squawking. They ran. I followed. Lost 'em both in that damned maze, then caught up with one again in the arcade. 'Brenwyr!' she was calling. 'Brenwyr!' You, huh, red-eyes? Came too late, though, didn't you...but still too soon for me, before I could make her tell me where she'd hidden t'other one. It should've been a double kill..."

"What happened?" Jame demanded.

The bloody mask of a face worked. Bane never paused. Left ribs, external oblique...

"Told the others both bints were dead, didn't I? The contract had been honored, I said. Get the hell out, get out, get out..."

Abruptly, his voice sounded younger, the terror in it stark. Was Bane at work in his mind, slitting open the seams of memory as he did those of flesh?

"'*Shadow, by a shadow be exposed.*' I *felt* that curse strike, sink in. Had to get away, contract be damned. Thirty-four years I waited for it to catch up with me, dreaming of red eyes, rising in the Guild. More rank, more tattoos, nothing is going to expose *me*. Then that dog-shit Ishtier sends word: the little bitch lived in hiding for years after our raid. *Years!* Says he'll tell the Grand Master that I lied, have me stripped of rank and tattoos, exposed, unless I do what he wants: steal a book (me, a *thief!*) and kill a sodding girl."

"So I didn't come under the terms of the original contract?"

The question jerked him back to the present. "Stupid cow. Had it down in blood how many to kill, didn't we? But I told the Grand Master that I wanted to go back anyway, to make a clean sweep. My turn to lead a blooding. My choice of target. Let the brats steal the book, kill the girl and all the red-eyed women they can find. No need to meet that cursing whore again, no need..."

"But you have," said Brenwyr. "You son of a yellow bitch, who paid you to kill Aerulan?"

He knew where he was again, and who faced him. Bane brought him up short as he lunged forward. Jame slipped in front of the matriarch, drawing the Ivory Knife. The assassin strained inches from its point like a dog against its leash, attention fixed on Brenwyr.

"Curse *me*, will you?" he spat at her, spraying Jame with bloody froth. "Thirty-four years, snapping at my heels, ruining everything, *me*, the next grand master! Soil my hands with your sow's blood, should I? You should have been the brats' meat, but they failed. I won't!"

He strained forward, twisting to be free. The cuts opened red lips. Beneath, from collarbone to groin, muscles rotted by the Bane's touch tore like wet butcher's paper. Black intestines spilled out. His feet tangled in their coils, bursting them with a fecal stench. On his knees now, incredulous, he clutched at his abdomen as if somehow to cram back in its contents, but everything inside was tearing loose, falling. Then the aorta and femoral arteries ruptured. He collapsed, a look on his face of outraged disbelief. The red tide on the floor swelled twice with the failing heartbeat, then slowed to a spreading creep.

Out of the reeking cavity that had been his abdomen rose a miasma, a shadow. It stood over him, a mere thickening of the air against the windows' gray light. Then Bane raised his eyes. In their silver depths Jame saw mirrored her own pale face, her complicity. She looked away, back at the red ruin which lay at her feet.

"*Shadow, by a shadow be exposed,*" she quoted in an unsteady voice. "That's exposed, all right."

Brenwyr made a choking sound. The next moment, she had thrust Jame aside and thrown open the door. Hawthorn and Brier Iron-thorn made way as she plunged blindly past them out into the hall, Aerulan's banner clutched to her breast.

Of course, the two Kendar would have waited beyond normal ear-shot to ensure family privacy, but not so far as to have missed the latter uproar. They entered in haste, probably expecting to find Jame reduced to chitterlings on the floor. Instead, there lay a complete stranger, completely disemboweled.

Hawthorn's sandy brows rose. "Lady?"

"Argh!" said Jame, snatched up her knapsack, and bolted out the door after Brenwyr, Jorin scrambling on her heels.

IV

The rain declined into a gray drizzle as fine as the heart of a
cloud. Impossible to see from one side of the observation
deck to the other, much less down to the ground. Mount Alban
might be anywhere. Jame thought, though, that it had probably returned home at last—everything back where it belonged
except her. Appropriate, that she couldn't even see her feet as
she sat on the deck's waist-high wall, legs dangling in space.
What use were feet, anyway, with no place left to run?

Huh. There are always *options,* she told herself. *There have
to be.*

From behind the wall came a low, reproachful cry. Jorin
was not happy.

Still, thought Jame, she must be at least as wet as he, and
as cold. At least her hands didn't feel the chill: the Ivory Knife
had numbed them as she idly turned it over and over. Soon it
would start to rot her already tattered gloves.

Someone stood behind her.

Bane, she thought, and said, without turning:

"So. Just what did we gain by that little exercise below?
You, of course, enjoyed yourself. As for me, well, I already
knew that Ishtier was behind this last raid on Gothregor. He
bragged about it to me at Wilden. Presumably, he learned
about Tieri from the Randir Matriarch when they traded information. A nice lever to use on an ambitious guild master,
caught in a lie."

At a guess, she thought, *Rawneth didn't know that Tieri had
survived until Adiraina was obliged to tell all the matriarchs after
the poor girl's death. Some council meeting* that *must have been.*

"As for the original massacre, would we have found out
who contracted for it even if Brenwyr hadn't precipitated
matters? Now, I'm not so sure. That wretched man would

only have been an apprentice then. He probably wasn't told. Perhaps he learned later, as he rose in the Guild—but 'perhaps' is a thin excuse for a death like that, Aerulan's blood-price notwithstanding."

A death you *chose for him,* she almost said. *Was I to blame for that?*

But she hadn't stopped him, and now she couldn't hide behind his actions. Honor's Paradox was a pretty thing in theory; in practice, it bit. Nor did recent revelations free her from it. Damned or not, she couldn't turn her world upside down the way the priests had their college. Honor was still honor.

"Wait a minute," she said. "Honor and obedience…"

She had fled from Bane all winter, but what had he done except answer her summons? Now, down in the infirmary, he had obeyed her again, if in the most gruesome manner he could contrive. That was his style, after all—but since when had obedience been?

"Perhaps…" said Ashe behind her, "since you blood-bound him."

Jame's start almost dislodged her from her perch. Unconsciously, she had depended on Jorin's senses for warning. What a time for the bond to fail. But Ashe was Torisen's friend, she told herself—and her enemy, instinct told her. In Kindrie's case, though, "instinct" had turned out to be another word for "prejudice." Maybe so again.

"Do you read minds, singer, and what in Perimal's name d'you mean, I bound him? I'm no blood-binder!"

Even as she spoke, though, she remembered Bane's mocking whisper: *"Blood binds,"* and felt her heart sink.

Could one be a binder and not know it? Her brother Torisen was, and didn't. The trait was said to run in particularly potent Shanir families. Like the Knorth. In the old days, before the Fall, it had allowed them to bind more Kendar more tightly than the mere mental discipline commonly practiced today. It had been the ruthless parallel to their God's binding of the Three People as a whole to his service, the antithesis of honor because it was said to abolish choice.

"I don't think," she said mildly, "that I can stand much more of this. When did I blood-bind Bane? How?"

"To answer…first questions first…I don't read minds. But some thoughts…are louder than others. Then too, haunt-sickness nearly killed you once. That forms…a bond. So did Bane's farewell kiss…in Tai-tastigon. Your blood in his mouth…his in yours. He was trying…to blood-bind *you.*"

It was said to run in families. Of the three of them, only Bane had played with blood and knives enough to make such a discovery on his own.

Then the implication struck her.

"Why, you bastard!" she said, twisting about to search for his amused eyes in the shadows. "You wanted me any way you could get me, to the very last!"

The ghost of a chuckle answered her, from the opposite direction in which she had looked:…*worth a try…*

"So the hunter got caught, uh? Like Tirandys with Torisen."

"Not quite," said Ashe. "Not between…two binders."

"Snakes with similar venom," Brenwyr had called destructive Shanir, with limited or at least unpredictable responses to each other. Perhaps that was why she hadn't seen any sign of binding in Bane at the Sirdan's Palace. Even now, how affected was he, really?

"Wait a minute," she said again. "How do you know these things, Ashe? 'Haunts know what concerns haunts,' you said once. *Is* Bane dead?"

"His state…peculiar. Did you know…that the Brandan Matriarch thinks he is…a projection of the nemesis in you?"

"Brenwyr. How is she?"

"Better. She is a strong woman…for all that you've seen her…only at her worst. She should be stronger still…if Aerulan stays with her."

"We'll work something out," said Jame, absently.

Stronger? Maybe. But Ashe didn't know that Brenwyr thought she had killed her own mother. The Brandan had learned to live with that, apparently, but if Jame were to dredge up her guilt again...

A shiver ran up Jame's spine. For the first time, she knew exactly what spot to touch, to destroy someone.

"You *are* a nemesis, aren't you?" said Ashe softly. "But are you...the definite article?"

"*The* Nemesis, Regonereth, That-Which-Destroys?" Jame held up the Ivory Knife, the Maiden's cold, white face on the pommel so like her own under the mask, before Kallystine's handiwork. "You tell me."

"I can't. Not...without tests."

The shiver nestled between Jame's shoulder blades, light as the touch of a phantom hand.

"You're thinking about pushing me off this wall, aren't you, haunt? Why?"

"Because...I mistrust your blood. Because...you have the darkling glamour."

Bred to darkling service...

Could that have been in Gerridon's mind when he sent the Dream-weaver across the Barrier to Ganth—to breed a nemesis, perhaps *the* Nemesis, bound to serve him? The abyss within her plunged down and down, to the cold hall, to the banners of the dishonored dead...

Ashe caught her by the collar. "Not...yet."

Jame found herself leaning forward against the other's grip, staring down into milky nothingness. Almost over the edge...

She reared back, appalled (how far to fall? a hundred feet? a thousand?), swung her legs inward over the wall, and stepped on her knapsack. The Book within shifted under her weight. She staggered, an inadvertent lunge with the Ivory Knife that sent Ashe hastily backward. The singer's iron-tipped staff swung up on guard. Bane rose behind her, a thing of clotted mist and cold eyes, reaching.

"No!" said Jame.

Haunt and demon stood still, the former almost enfolded in the latter's arms. Ashe could have been said to hold her breath, if she'd had any.

Let him take her, Jame thought. A crumbling dead thing, half-sunk in shadows already, how could a haunt be anything but her mortal foe? Then she remembered the dead in the Haunted Lands keep, rustling. Which one of her childhood friends had attacked her outside the keep's broken walls, its mind decayed to gray scum, its rotting teeth buried in her arm?

"Haunt-sickness nearly killed you once," Ashe had said.

...the darkness of infection under her skin, in her blood, festering, undeserved...

Who was she to judge Ashe, anymore than Bane?

"Let her go," she said. "D'you hear me? Now."

If Bane didn't agree, at least he obeyed, melting back into the mist with the ghost of a whisper:...*'s your pyre, lady*...

Ashe leaned on her staff, the hood overshadowing her haggard face. In a mortal woman, the slump of her shoulders would have looked much like vast weariness.

"Whatever he could have done to me...perhaps would have been only a mercy. That too."

Jame realized that she was still clutching the Ivory Knife, that she had almost used it on Ashe—inadvertently? The damn thing had killed as if by accident before. It always had been and would be avid for death.

"Dammit," she burst out, "how can I survive Honor's Paradox saddled with things I can't control?"

Ashe straightened slowly. "What...things?"

"This." Jame held up the Knife. "And this."

A kick slid the knapsack within the singer's reach. Ashe flipped back its cover with her staff and stared at the contents.

"Ancestors preserve us. Carried around like a...change of underwear." She looked up sharply. Light caught her sunken, death-clouded eyes. "And the third object of power...the Serpent-skin Cloak?"

"Last seen slithering back into the Master's house. It didn't seen to fancy my company."

"No," said Ashe, as if to herself. "It wouldn't. Argentiel never favors Regonereth...preserver...against destroyer. See here. This is dangerous. Without the Cloak, the other two are seriously out of balance. The Knife...is bad enough, but the Book...! You don't know how to read it, of course...but if it should fall into the wrong hands..."

Jame turned away. The wretched creature was calling her ignorant and irresponsible—with reason. The Book *had* gone astray three times since she had become its guardian. Ishtier, the Sirdan Theocandi, and Graykin had all possessed it briefly, the first two with the knowledge to make fearful use of it. And she had almost given it back to Ishtier, to save herself. As for her own misuse of its master runes, the less said, the better. If the Book and the Knife *were* intended for her, patently she didn't yet have the wisdom or strength to wield them responsibly.

Jame sighed. "If I could safely put them aside, I would."

"I think..." said the haunt singer, "that I know...a way."

V

Ashe's way led down into the wooden labyrinth, almost to the lower hall.

At no level did Jame see any sign of weirding. Mount Alban must indeed have regained its foundation and encasing cliff-face. So, at least, Index clearly believed, pattering past without seeing them, so eager to reclaim his beloved herb shed that he again scorned the slow-moving platform. Otherwise, the college rested except for the groan of settling timber. Most of its elderly inmates had at last put aside their experiments. Their voices murmured down the stairwell, then faded as they retired to their diverse lodgings in the upper levels for a well-earned late afternoon nap.

Jame knew that she should also rest. Much longer without sleep would impair her judgment, if it hadn't already. Ashe's dark figure shambled ahead of her; behind crept Bane's shadow, almost but not quite treading on her own. This might have been the descent into some dark dream, except for the brush of Jorin's whiskers against her hand as the ounce trotted close at her side.

They came to an ironbound door, set in the college's eastern wall, hard against the mountain face. The cool, dank breath of stone met them when Ashe unlocked it, and darkness waited beyond. The haunt took a torch from a bracket and lit it, revealing a rough-hewn passage. Jame and Jorin followed the singer down it for some twenty feet before it ended at the edge of an abyss. Torchlight could reach neither the bottom, nor the top, nor even the far side of that great emptiness. The drip of water in its depths echoed upward, distorted.

"Is this what you brought me to see?" Jame asked.

No answer. No Ashe. Only her torch moving to the left, apparently along the sheer wall of the chasm. Then Jame saw a walkway carved out of the cavern's side and hurried to catch up with the light.

Sometimes the walk crept under low ceilings jagged with stalactites; sometimes it careened with a perilous slant along the chasm's sheer drop. Parts of it had been damaged by the recent tremors; parts, by quakes long past. A wonder, thought Jame, that the whole honeycombed mountain hadn't collapsed in on itself ages ago. Possibly Mount Alban's ironwood skeleton had forestalled that. The tips of her gloves began to soak through as she ran them along the wall to steady herself. The stones wept continuously, tears turning to drops of fire as they caught the torch light, tumbling past the black, crumpled forms of sleeping bats clustered in fissures. Blind, white crickets the size of her fist scuttled away from the brand's heat. What if there were trogs?

The light vanished.

Jame pressed back against the stone wall, blind in the sudden dark. The emptiness of the abyss seemed to tug at her. She remembered the chasm in the Ebonbane snow-field, the terror of falling, the Arrin-Kens' suspended death sentence.

Dammit, no one is going to push me, if I don't want to jump...

A few feet to the left, light glimmered. Jame edged toward it, and discovered a side-cave. Down three stone steps, there was a low-ceilinged antechamber cut from living rock and at its back, an iron door scabrous with rust. Ashe had laid down the torch and was struggling with a key. It turned, groaning, in the lock. She dragged opened the door.

Jame stopped at the foot of the steps. She didn't need Jorin's senses to hear the mad scurry within, as if of countless multi-segmented bodies seething away from the light. Through the crack, she saw a bare stretch of rough stone floor, the ruins of an iron chair, and a small iron table still half obscured. All the shadows' edges blurred with the torch's flare and furtive movement.

Ashe stepped aside. "Enter," she said.

For a moment, as clearly as she had felt the haunt's impulse to shove her off the wall, Jame saw the door slam shut—behind her. Her eyes filled with darkness; her ears, with the obscene in-rush of swarming life.

"Haunt," she said thickly, "you're joking."

"Afraid of shadows, darkling? I remember…what shadow stands guard, behind me. Put the Book and the Knife…on the table."

She could refuse. Leave. Back to the stalemate that had trapped her before? No. Wherever her way led now, it didn't retreat.

She ducked into the room. Good as her night vision was, she couldn't see its walls, nor did she wish to: that stealthy rustling surrounded her, all too close. It was a very small room, she sensed, and was glad for the cap that protected her hair. A tall man couldn't have stood upright, even if he had wished to. She put the Book Bound in Pale Leather on the lit side of the table. The darker half seemed surreptitiously to boil. When she placed the Ivory Knife next to the Book, however, the tabletop emptied with an unseen, verminous cascade off its far side.

"All right, haunt. Now what?"

"Now…leave."

"Just like that?" Jame turned to glare at her, surprised at how cheated she felt. This was no solution after all. "Even locked, that door isn't going to keep out anyone determined. Believe me. I know."

"I didn't say…that there would be…no guard. Tell your pet demon…to stay."

A moment ago, disappointment had made Jame feel almost sick, but this was worse. "Ashe, no. I wouldn't confine my worst enemy here—well, maybe Ishtier, or Caineron, or Kallystine. Dammit, why does Mount Alban have a pest-hole like this, anyway?"

"Kendar builders discovered it. A secret Hathiri prison…perhaps for a secret prisoner. Who…we don't know."

"Well, I'm not going to order Bane to fill his place."

"Perhaps…you don't have to. Look."

He sat at ease in the rust-eaten chair, long, elegant legs stretched out before him. His black scale armor rustled with the overlapping wings of a million death's-head beetles. The spiders that had woven his fine gray boots hung inside them like ornaments. Silver wireworms ringed his long, white fingers. All the finery of the tomb…

But his smile jolted her back in memory to the night she had returned to find the Res aB'tyrr held hostage by his thugs and Bane himself waiting, just so, to welcome her home. Then as now, she had come from causing a man to be flayed alive— a hanger-on of Bane's, a miserable sneak-thief who had ambushed and nearly killed her friend Marc. Her revenge, like the smell of blood, had brought the thief's master down on her; not to claim vengeance in his turn, but kinship.

They had talked of honor.

It wasn't his fault, he had said, that Marc had been hurt. Nothing was his fault. Forced into the Thieves' Guild, hadn't he tried to protect his soul by entrusting it to Ishtier? Wouldn't he redeem it and honor both in the end by an honorable death? Until then:

"Better to fall. Life loses all boundaries. No one can tell you where to stop. Freedom…"

Jame shook herself back to the present. Here was the dead, consumed with hunger for the living; the seducer, seduced by his own argument; the man, whose soul she had once offered to carry, and would again, if he asked.

"Is that what you want me to do?" she demanded, suddenly very angry. "To make myself answerable for your soul? To tell you where to stop? To *order* you, by the blood-bond which you contrived between us? Dammit, Bane, you always try to put responsibility off onto someone else! On Ishtier. On me. Without choice, there is no honor, and I will *not* choose for you! If you want to sit in this hell-hole, in the dark, ancestors only know for how long, it has to be your decision. Well? D'you hear me?"

Only his smile answered her, enigmatic, infuriatingly intimate.

"Fine. Stay, then, and be damned to you!"

She stalked out. The door shut behind her, with a screech of rusty hinges cut short by a dead thud. She pivoted, full of sudden misgivings, as Ashe with difficulty turned the key in the lock. In her mind was an image which she had been too late to see: Bane's sleeve trailing across the Book Bound in Pale Leather, his fine-boned hand at rest on the Ivory Knife. Shut away in the seething dark...

"This isn't going to work," she said, dry-mouthed. "Dead or not, he has to eat. We can't just let him starve."

"He won't." Ashe turned to face her, key in hand. "The door will keep out...only the idly curious. Keep it quiet as we may....word will spread of the treasure inside. From time to time...he will feed very well indeed."

Jame stared at her. "My God, you're cold-blooded."

"Of course. I'm dead."

She slipped the key through a slash in her robe, into the corresponding sword-cut underneath, as if into an inner pocket. The lips of the wound were shriveled and bloodless, the rib glimpsed through them, discolored white. The key's outline showed clearly through the skin, against the bone.

"Why don't you just swallow the damn thing?" Jame demanded.

"Because...it might fall through."

Jame sat down abruptly on the stone step. No sleep, no food, and now this.

"All right, kitten, all right," she said to Jorin, whose forepaws were on her knee, his nose anxiously touching her own. But inside she was raging at herself.

How easily she had let Ashe and Bane manage her. Should she have given up the Book and Knife, when they had chosen her as their guardian over and over? Should she have agreed to Bane's living burial, assuming he was still alive? Only now did she realize how desperately she had wanted to be rid of

both them and him—enough to have let herself be tricked
into consent?

"That knife may have been given to me to use," she said.
"What if I need it someday?"

"Then call. I think...he will bring it to you...with help."

Jame shuddered. Into her mind had come the image of that
"help": a trail of disintegrating victims, chosen at random, ridden and discarded as Bane ate the soul out of each in turn.

"More guts on the floor," she said, shaken. "Perhaps across
the breadth of Rathillien and beyond. Sweet Trinity. Whose
responsibility will *that* be?"

"His...who feeds," said Ashe, clouded eyes merciless with
the logic of honor. "And hers...who calls."

A rumbling tremor passed through the stones surrounding
them, followed by a series of loud cracks and crashes outside.

"Bloody hell," said Jame. She found herself on her feet, without remembering having risen. With one hand she was steadying
herself against the wall; with the other, clutching Jorin's bristling
ruff as he stood on her toes. "Haven't we had enough of this?"

But she spoke to herself, in abrupt darkness. Ashe had
snatched up the torch and darted out of the antechamber.
Swearing, Jame scooped up Jorin and followed.

The brand already bobbed far ahead, throwing contorted,
confusing shadows behind. Jame called on her trained memory
to show her the way, but memory didn't encompass the changes
wrought in the past few minutes. Echoes crashed farther and
farther away, as if a dozen unseen cave-mouths had caught
the sound and were gnashing it to pieces. Sections of the
ledge had fallen. Others shifted, grating, under her feet as
Jorin wriggled with fright in her arms. More light would have
been welcome. Ashe might hesitate to push her, Jame thought
grimly, but clearly wasn't above letting her fall.

The earth growled again deep in its throat, as though trying to clear it. Bats exploded from a crevice almost in her
face, a black cataract ascending. Ten feet, five, and here, ancestors be praised, was the lip of the tunnel.

"Earth Wife, Earth Wife," she cried, turning, shouting into the abyss. "Leave us a*lone!*"

"That," said Ashe, behind her, "was not helpful."

Darkness swallowed the haunt's hoarse voice, but Jame's still echoed from wall to wall, down to the depths, up to the heights. From far, far above came an answer—a crack like the splitting of worlds and then a massive downward rush. The wind of it threw Jame back into Ashe and sent the latter's torch flying, a moment before something smashed off the tunnel's shallow lip. Jame had the dazed impression of a giant's jaw full of ragged teeth, savagely biting down. No. A plummeting section of cave roof, studded with stalactites. The echo of its fall crashed off into the distance, starting more rock-falls farther and farther away. From above, light filtered down, full of dust and broken bat wings.

Jame disentangled herself from the haunt faster than was strictly polite.

"The tremor must have breached the cliff-top," she said, leaning perilously out to peer upward. "But why is it getting brighter?"

The answer came billowing down the opened shaft.

They bolted down the tunnel with weirding on their heels and tumbled into the college. Too late to shut the door. Mist rolled in after them, over them, a soft, sighing avalanche. Jame clung to the floor, all her nails out, Jorin pinned squawking under her. She could see and hear nothing else, except the pounding of her own heart.

Then the mist began to subside. It drained between floorboards into the supports beneath; it twined up load-bearing piers and across ceiling beams like tendrils of dry rot. Whatever ironwood it touched, it sank into and replaced. The bones of Mount Alban were becoming ghosts of their former selves which still, hesitantly, upheld the college's weight. The floor boards beneath Jame shifted uneasily, like a raft launched on a troubled sea.

"Adrift...again," said Ashe.

She sounded pleased.

VI

It's all coming loose, Jame thought as she followed Ashe through the maze toward the presumed safety of the main stair.

Underfoot, floorboards bobbed. Overhead, the ceiling rippled. Weirding glowed and smoked through every crack like cool fire smoldering inside the walls. Nothing was settled, after all, nothing finished. Was she disappointed, or relieved?

At least, Bane had definitely been left behind. And the Book. And the Knife. She had done without all three often enough before. Why did their absence now make her feel so vulnerable?

Having to trust a haunt didn't help, even in so small a matter as finding a flight of stairs. Moreover, it seemed to her that Ashe was deliberately going as slowly as she could.

Some thoughts are louder than others...

Over her shoulder, the singer gave her a rictus grin. "D'you want...something to fall off me?"

The deceased she could deal with, thought Jame, or even the demented, but the decayed? Fragments of Ashe's thoughts crawled through her mind like maggots. The haunt was glad not to see Mount Alban's journeys end with unfinished business, not when she still had the right test to find.

The right test for what?

More glowing beams, studs, and stanchions, their reality elsewhere, their boards left resting uneasily on weirding support. Before, the college's main framework had resisted much longer, the softer woods melting away first. If this replacement held true throughout, Mount Alban had been boned like a fish.

The rooms of the lower maze were mere attics for the Bashtiri halls below, or cellars for the keep far above. At least, they seemed never to have been used for anything but storage.

Strange shapes loomed out of corners. Rotting crates spilled their contents across the floor, centuries' worth of scholastic pack-rattery hidden under a gray pelt of dust.

But here was a room where the muddled stacks had been pulled apart—recently, judging by the torn webs still fluttering about them. Something in their disarray suggested curiosity rather than a deliberate search, and a certain amount of disinterested vandalism.

The dust on the floor was roiled with foot prints. Jame bent over them. In the soft light streaming through the door from the landing beyond, she saw that the feet that had made them were naked, one set huge, the other no bigger than a child's.

"Ashe," she called. No reply. "Ashe!"

The haunt singer stood looking up at the main stair. It glowed, treads, risers, supports, all sculpted in the finest detail in weirding mist. The spine of the college, gone too.

"We...are not alone," said Ashe.

The ghost of a snicker seemed to answer her.

Crooked halls opened off the landing in all directions. A murmur of approaching voices came from one, but which?

Kirien and Kindrie emerged from a doorway behind them.

"Ashe," said the former. "Ancestors be praised. Have you any idea where we are?"

"Dislodged from the Alban cliff. Upstream...given the weirding's northward flow. Probably caught...on the ruins opposite Restormir...or at Tagmeth beyond that. And the upper keep?"

"Left behind. We were on the stair coming down when the weirding surge rolled over the cliff top. The curtains weren't up to keep it out. It came down the stairs, sinking in and changing them. Brier Iron-thorn was right behind us, but before she could jump clear it lapped over her feet. Odd, but I could have sworn that I heard someone below call her name. Anyway, she set that ironwood jaw of hers and just kept walking down into it."

"L-like a ghost," said Kindrie, obviously still shaken. "More of her insubstantial with each step. T-then she just vanished. Ancestors only know where she is now."

"With the stair, presumably," said Jame, "wherever *that* is."

She spoke lightly, but her stomach had tensed. They had been incredibly lucky to weird-walk in one piece all the way north from Wilden to Restormir. Their sheer number—ten cadets, two Highborn, and a cat—might have helped. Now Brier was on her own in the mist, perhaps several places simultaneously if the stair had displaced in steps.

"What about you?" she demanded of the Shanir healer, dropping her voice. "You should still be safe in the infirmary, asleep."

"I woke up." Kindrie shot her a pale-eyed look, frightened but defiant. "Captain Hawthorn was trying to decide what to do with that, that mess you left behind. Brier said she had better go after you. I-I followed, and met the Lordan Kirien looking for Index. I thought..." He swallowed and tried again. "I thought you might need me."

Jame bit back a sharp reply. In the past few hours, she'd had to acknowledge bonds with both a demon and a haunt. Now here was another connection, just as strong, twice as natural. All winter, searching for her dead family, and she couldn't stomach a live first cousin simply because he had fallen into the hands of priests?

"I did need you," she said, rubbing her tired face with a gloved hand, feeling the scar ridge like a knotted cord under the mask. "I still do. But I don't trust myself or my reflexes. I'll hurt you, Kindrie Soul-Walker. I can't help it. Stay away from me."

"This little side-trip may not amount to anything," Kirien was saying to Ashe. "My guess is that we well and truly hooked onto the Mount Alban fort ruins, before the tremor and this last surge of weirding swept the college core temporarily northward. We're like a...a plucked bow string, vibrating, the middle out of line with both top and bottom—or the upper keep and the lower halls, in our case. Everything should snap back together again soon."

"Not soon enough to prevent visitors," said Jame.

She told them about the disarranged storage and the naked foot prints in the dust. For a moment, they looked at each other in dismay, then up, as someone above suddenly bellowed, in a voice trained to carry:

"If you lot of egg-heads can't sleep, we singers can. Shut *up!*"

For the first time in Mount Alban's travels, the academic community wasn't in the upper keep, prepared, safe—nor, apparently, did it realize that the college was on the move again.

"Where are the two randon ten-commands?" Jame asked.

"All in the upper keep, except Brier Iron-thorn," said Kirien, still looking upward, a frown drawing together her fine, dark brows. Her house was the protector of Mount Alban; its safety, her personal responsibility as the Jaran Heir.

"In that case..." said Ashe, watching her, "we had better find out...where we are."

The main stair being unavailable, they used another, older one nearby, which corkscrewed drunkenly down a narrow shaft into what should have been a minor Bashtiri hall. Wooden treads gave way to fire-blackened stone. The well opened out. They were now descending a mural stair, circling a stone walled chamber some forty feet across past the charred stumps of floors. Mount Alban roofed them, its under-structure a seeming chaos of wooden planks and phantom, weirding beams.

More wood filled the bottom of this stone structure—logs, branches, brush, piled promiscuously together, red-tinged by the light falling from narrow apertures above. Jame paused to look out one. The cloud ceiling had lowered again, almost to within reach of this third-story window. A setting sun had kindled the weirding inside it, brightest above the hidden mountains to the west but already deepening to blood ruby with the fall of night. Crusts of snow sheltered under boughs on the opposite bank of the Silver. How far north had the weirding taken them? There was no sign on that dark slope of Restormir or the ruins opposite Tagmeth.

"This," said Ashe, looking over Jame's shoulder, "does not ...bode well."

"What?" Kirien demanded, instinctively keeping her voice low. "You think you know where we are, don't you...What's that?"

Ching! went a jangling bell-tone. *Ching, ching,* approaching from the left, passing by out of sight beneath the window. *Ching, ching, ching,* on to the right, northward and then east, circling the outer wall.

They followed its progress clockwise down to the tower's second story front door, which stood open. At the foot of a flight of stairs lay a flagstoned courtyard, an open well shaft gaping at its center. Most of the surrounding buildings, like the tower keep, had been touched by fire, rain, and long neglect. The barracks to the left in particular had been gutted, its roof collapsed, trees growing up through the ruins. Wild grape vines sighed against the wall behind it. Faint lines showed on the weathered stone, nearly washed away—a series of circles, each with three smaller circles inside, like so many round eyes and mouths gaping.

"Kithorn," said Ashe.

Then Jame recognized it too, not because she had ever seen this sad place before, but because her Kendar friend Marc had described it to her so clearly—his childhood home, until Merikit had slaughtered everyone in it almost eighty years ago. That, and Marc's revenge, had closed these hills to the Kencyrath ever since, except for boys slipping up to these ruins on a dare to search for relics of its garrison. Last winter, her brother had come here on a similar mission and accidentally left the old tower in flames behind him.

A shiver ran down Jame's spine. From these walls, Tori had seen the Burnt Man face-to-face.

She ducked back. Seven figures had trotted into the courtyard through its eastern gate, one after another. Four of them were not the Burning Ones, as she had for a moment feared, but half-naked Merikit elders, smeared white with ash, each carrying a sack. Breasts made of goat udders swayed under gray hair loose to the waist.

Ching went the bells strapped to their ankles. *Ching, ching!*

Between them came three figures if possible even stranger: an over-padded parody of a woman with a hard, male face framed by a wig of straw; a dripping wet youth festooned with bladder weeds; an incredibly hairy man, aflutter with black feathers knotted to every elflock.

The whole procession jogged solemnly sunwise around the courtyard, *ching, ching, ching.*

"First close the outer circle," said Ashe softly, "then circle the inner square, to create sacred space. The summer rites begin."

"And we," said Kirien, "are inside the circle."

The first shaman-elder and the "woman" stopped at the eastern corner of the square which their perambulation had defined. The second elder halted with the feathered man to the south; the third with the wet boy, to the west; the fourth by himself to the north. While the three squatted patiently in their corners to wait, the four ash-smeared elders emptied their sacks respectively of clay, wicker, bucket, and kindling. Along with this last came tumbling out what appeared to be a crude, black skull. The solitary elder began to arrange the kindling around it, crooning softly in an age-cracked voice.

Jame recognized that chant. Four days ago, north of Falkirr, she had heard the charcoal-blackened Merikit sing it as he laid a Summer Eve bonfire. The Burnt Man's bone which she had taken from that site was no longer in her pocket. Now where...Ah. She had forgotten to reclaim it from Index.

Index, who had come down here before them. Sweet Trinity, where was *he?*

Other Merikit emerged from the surrounding ruins—a good dozen of them, half-naked like their elders and intricately tattooed. A nervous young man in green homespun appeared last, with obvious reluctance, gingerly holding an ivy crown.

Kindrie made a stifled sound. A huge, young Merikit stood close beside them, wearing scarlet drawers and nothing else. His long, fox-red hair was all combed to the left into a dozen or more braids. His heavy arms and chest were black with tattoos. He must have come down from Mount Alban, for surely those big, bare feet matched one set of the prints which Jame had seen above. Green, slightly crossed eyes widened in wonder as he touched the Shanir's white hair. He gave it a tug. Kindrie gasped, almost falling. The big man grinned and took a firmer grip.

"No," said Jame, as if to a large, chancy dog, and put her hand on the Merikit's elbow.

Her nails found the nerve. He let go of Kindrie with an exclamation, eyes bulging at first with astonishment, then with outrage. He was, thought Jame, looking up, very, very big.

Something crashed down the Mount Alban stairs: a storage crate, disintegrating as it fell. Butterflies caught perhaps a hundred summers ago shimmered azure and amethyst, gold-veined and bronze, their wings turning to dust with the first frantic beat. The crimson moss that had preserved them rained down like a shower of sparks. From above, quite clearly, came a snickering laugh.

The big Merikit laughed too, but the grin which he turned down on Jame was bright with malice. He juggled one of the moss clumps from hand to hand, as if it were as fiery as its color, then tossed it onto the jumble of dry branches below.

"Oh my God," breathed Kirien, staring down at the wood pile, then up at Mount Alban's vulnerable underpinnings.

More bonfires than one had been laid for Summer Eve.

Interim VII
Mount Alban: 60th of Spring
I

"So this," said Torisen, "is what the Jaran Matriarch meant about Mount Alban not being where it ought."

He was standing in the college's vaulted lower hall, which looked perfectly normal, with one exception. So had the entire establishment as they had approached it, apparently untouched by the surge of weirding which had just rolled past at cliff-top level and the tremor which had run before it. He should have guessed, though, that the ghostly light spreading inside the cliff-face from window to window had had nothing to do with welcome. Now here was this ghostly stair molded in weirding mist and all the internal structure above too, as far as he could see, except for the shadowy lines of its ironwood skeleton.

"Hello?" he shouted up the glowing well. "Is anyone there?"

"They'll never hear you above," said Grimly.

The Wolver sat down on his haunches and began to lick a raw foot-pad. They had come over thirty leagues since sunrise, exhausting several changes of mount, but he had insisted on running most of that distance. Better sore paws than more saddle sores. Now, however, he wasn't so sure.

Torisen had turned away, swearing under his breath. To have come so far, only to be thwarted again... After a winter of hiding at Kothifir, this rush to reunion had caught him up like a spring thaw. He didn't know to what end he was hurtling, what would happen when, at last, he and his sister met—but meet they must. Soon.

Frustration sharpened by urgency turned him back to the stair's foot, set loose the innate power of a Highborn in his voice: "Dammit, COME DOWN!"

Grimly goggled, the fur slowly roaching up along his spine. Something *was* coming down the stair. At first, it seemed no more than wisps of smoke rising off each step in turn, then indistinct feet, legs, body, head—a complete ghost silently, steadily descending.

Torisen went back a step, almost tripping over the Wolver, who had scuttled around behind him. His throat felt scraped raw by those ill-chosen words of command. What in Perimal's name had he summoned? Something in the set of those broad ghostly shoulders, that deliberate, grim tread…

"Iron-thorn?" he breathed. "Brier? Dammit, Rowan, shut that door!"

Too late. A gust of wind swept into the hall around the steward's stocky form, rattling last autumn's leaves under her feet. The ghost on the stair faltered, then unraveled. Gone.

Rowan hadn't seen it. Expressionless as her scarred face always was, her tense carriage as she hurried down the hall betrayed a problem of her own.

"Don't tell me Kallystine has caught up with us!" Torisen exclaimed involuntarily.

Rowan almost smiled. "Not that. My lord, Blackie, we've found something you should see."

II

South of Mount Alban, the damned horse slowed again, stumbling, ropes of bloody lather hanging from its lowered muzzle. Kallystine kicked at it savagely.

"Lady, ease up," warned the captain of her guard. "It's nearly spent."

M'lady cursed behind her mask. Damn Torisen anyway, for grabbing all the remounts between Gothregor and the scrollsmen's college, as if *that* would stop her. One by one as their horses failed, she had lost all her escort except its captain. She wouldn't catch the Highlord with a force behind her, but by God she *would* catch him, if she had to kill every horse in the valley.

A breath of wind teased her heavy travel mask awry. She jerked it back into place. Not since the assault by that Knorth bitch had she dared to look in a mirror, not that she had one left intact, but the potion's effect was only temporary. It *must* be.

...don't think about the maid's withered hand, clawing at the braid twisted around her neck, don't think...

What did she have but her lovely, lovely face? What else was she? A glittering gown, a hollow mask...

No. She was and always would be beautiful, *beautiful*— which was more than could be said, now or ever again, for the Knorth Jameth.

Remembering that, Kallystine smiled.

"Weirding coming up fast behind, lady," said the captain, looking back. "Another bank that should pass well overhead and a smaller patch at river level."

"Shut up. How far to Mount Alban now?"

"After the weirdingstrom, lady, that's hard to say. I haven't recognized half the land we've traveled through today."

"Damn you, how *far?*"

The randon sighed. "With luck, around the next bend."

Kallystine set her eyes on it and her heels to her horse.

Soon, she thought, with a hidden smile less pleasant even than the first. *Very, very soon.*

III

The gorge north of Mount Alban echoed with the muted roar of the Silver. Overhanging trees dripped with spray and the stones of the River Road shone darkly. Bats flitted through shadows that had grown deep and cool with the sun's setting. Then larger shapes were among them, clowning in the spray, snapping bats out of mid-air and letting them drop; foxkin at play.

Their appearance preceded the clop of hooves, the jingle and groan of harnesses. Down the River Road came riders grimly upright in the saddle with the blood-shot eyes and strained faces of the hideously hung-over. One of them carried, drooping, a standard with the device of a serpent devouring its young, gold on black. A curtained horse litter followed. Beside it plodded an enormous draft-horse on whose back, hunched like a golden toad, rode Caldane, Lord Caineron.

His daughter Lyra followed him. Claiming that litter-travel made her sick (which it did, if she stuck a finger down her throat), she had been allowed to ride her little hill-pony. Consequently, at the end of this second day's travel, she was not only cold, tired, and hungry (as when was she not?) but also very saddle-sore. Nonetheless, how wonderful finally to be off on an adventure! She even took pleasure in feeling so much better, saddle-sores notwithstanding, than most of the Caineron Kendar. Once in Karkinaroth she had tried to pass on a stomach ache from too many sweets to her servant Gricki, without success. Father must know a very special trick to have so thoroughly inflicted the aftermath of his five-day binge on his Kendar.

She bet that he wished he knew a trick as good, to get out of escorting Gran on this visit to the Women's Halls at Gothregor. He had better, Gran had said ominously, after incapacitating all her servants—except, of course, the Ear, whom nothing ever seemed to upset.

This would be their second night on the road, and they had come scarcely twenty-five miles south of Restormir. Gran complained of being jostled if they went faster. Besides, groggy Kendar kept falling out of the saddle, which Lyra had found hilarious, the first dozen or so times. By now, however, two-thirds of their company had been left behind and they had picked up a bare score of those Kendar who had been caught out on patrol when the weirdingstrom had swept down on them. The rest, it was hoped, would make their way home eventually. How long it would take some of those still at Restormir to recover from that terrible night's madness, no one could say. Lyra missed a dozen familiar faces in her father's retinue, without thinking much about it. She didn't know that they had quietly been slipped the white knife—and assisted in its use, if necessary.

Meanwhile, Gran had been hectoring Father for two days about the over-indulgence which had left them so short-handed, and about any other of his faults which she could bring to mind. Now, with sunset, she turned to his lack of foresight. If they had followed the New Road on the west bank, they would have been at the Jaran's Valantir by now, snug for the night. Did he *want* her to catch her death of cold out in this wilderness? Well? *Did* he?

Father hunched ever lower in the saddle, muttering.

Lyra nudged her pony closer, trying to eavesdrop, and ducked as Gran's foxkin Precious swooped close overhead, big ears cocked.

"*What* did you say, young man?" demanded Gran, peering at him through the leaf-patterned curtains of the litter. From behind her came the Ear's earthy chuckle. How *could* the two of them fit in so small a space? "You'd like to do *what?*"

Father started to answer, but a hiccup stopped him. He clutched wildly at his horse's mane, as if to anchor himself. Lyra wondered if that was also why he had put on every scrap of heavy gold he could wear. She knew for a fact, having seen it, that last night his servants had staked him down like a tent. His mount, the largest in the farm stable, laid back its ears, set its prognathous jaw, and plodded stolidly on.

They rounded a bend. The river divided around a wooded island, plunging down on either side in rapids and falls. Father straightened, staring from his superior height at something below still hidden from his daughter.

"My barge," he said thickly. "My beautiful barge," and spurred his mount into a heavy trot toward Mount Alban.

IV

Rowan led Torisen out the smallest of the hall's three inset doors and through the old fort ruins beyond. Stones still rattled down from the cliff after the most recent tremor. Such aftershocks might be expected for days, Torisen had been told, assuming (dire thought) that they weren't instead a prelude to worse. No one knew yet what permanent changes so severe a weirdingstrom might have wrought down the entire length of the Silver. He noted, however, that not one leaning stone of the ancient fort had toppled. In their midst, ready for Summer Eve, someone had laid a small bonfire.

On the shoulder of the foothill where the fort stood, Torisen paused to look down the valley. The sun had just set over its western rim and purple shadows were lengthening down its slopes. The river threaded through them, alight in the afterglow of sunset with that argent gleam which had given it its name. No sign yet of Kallystine. Good.

It was strange that he had ever felt attracted to that gilded lady or, for that matter, that he thought of her with such aversion now. Both emotions seemed unreasonably strong, especially in that he preferred not to feel strongly about anyone: it was too much like being in their power. He had long suspected Kallystine of trying to manipulate him through unnatural means. Soon their contract would expire, ancestors be praised—but Caineron had made it clear that he would consider failure to reinstate as a mortal insult. Oh, for an unequivocal excuse to break clean away.

Patches of weirding drifted by down by the Silver, tinged red by the setting sun. Their silent passage reminded him of Brier Iron-Thorn's ghost-like descent and disappearance...where? Northward, presumably, with the weirding-flow. That was probably where Mount Alban's innards had gone as well—taking Jame with them? Oh, to slip away like that, out of everyone's reach, as he used to do into the Southern Wastes...

"This way, my lord," said Rowan impatiently. "Around on the south side."

The "something" which she wished to show him hung tangled in cloud-of-thorn bushes at the cliff's foot. It was a canvas sack, as long and thin as a rolled carpet, but disturbingly articulated. It must have fallen or been thrown from high above, to have smashed its way so far in among the tough branches before stopping, impaled. Blood ran down the long thorns from the punctured bag. The sodden ground beneath shimmered with the azure wings of feasting jewel-jaws.

Torisen realized why Rowan was watching him so anxiously.

"No doubt," he said, "someone will eventually stuff my sister in a sack and throw her off the highest cliff available, but not this time."

How he knew, as at Gothregor, that Jame still lived, he couldn't (wouldn't?) say, even to himself. Once again, Torisen was uneasily aware of questions unasked, of unwanted answers.

"Highlord!" said a voice overhead.

A randon officer dropped down beside them, seemingly out of the sky.

"Captain Hawthorn, isn't it?" Torisen looked up. Those naked trunks which he had taken for dead trees growing out of the cliff-face..."Is that thing some sort of a ladder?"

"Yes, lord. 'Some sort' is about right, but it's come in handy despite itself. Not very good for carrying bodies down, though."

"So I noticed. Would it be tactless to inquire...?"

"Who? Highlord, perhaps you can tell me."

Gingerly, the Brandan officer reached into the cloud-of-thorn and loosened the mouth of the sack. Out of it lolled a head. The Wolver growled. Those dead eyes seemed to stare at him, yellow irises and whites so suffused with blood as to be almost indistinguishable. The rest of the face, too, was blood-smeared—over skin that didn't seem to be there at all.

"*Mere*-tattooing?" he demanded.

Torisen nodded curtly. "A Bashtiri Shadow Master, unmasked."

The assassin's jaw fell open, as if about to answer, and then fell off. It rattled down through the branches to the ground, scattering the jewel-jaws, but only for a moment. The Brandan captain flipped the canvas back over that terrible face. As she withdrew her hand, a thorn laid open the back of it.

"Damn," she said mildly, brushing away eager azure wings.

"That's the last Kencyr blood he will ever cause to be spilled," said Torisen, hard-voiced. He had always known what misery the Shadow Guild had caused his house, but never before had it seemed…personal. So this was the creature who had come to kill Jame. "Shove kindling under these bushes. Burn the carrion where it hangs. Now, captain, will you please tell me where my sister is?"

Somehow, it didn't surprise him that the randon didn't know.

"She ought to be back soon, though," Hawthorn said, as if Jame had merely stepped out on an errand.

Both glanced up as two Brandan cadets dropped down from the hanging stair, followed by a scruffy young man. The latter slunk off to one side, trying not to catch anyone's eye.

Hawthorn shrugged, dismissing him. "At least," she said, "with the whole college as chaperon, the young lady can't get into too much trouble."

"Huh!" said Grimly.

Torisen had turned to look down the valley, which dusk was beginning to obscure. The Silver, tarnished, had lost its gleam except to the south, where it disappeared around a bend. There, the light on it grew, and on the cliffs facing it. A cloud billowed silently around the turn, its heart coolly on fire as if with continual heat lightning. It filled the valley from side to side, its raised skirts trailing over the top of the foothills, its crown just below the cliff summits.

It wasn't the approaching cloud, however, at which Torisen stared with such dismay. Under it came two riders on limping, lathered mounts—a randon officer incongruous in dress grays, and a heavily masked lady. The randon's horse fell. Its rider jumped clear and reached for the lady's stirrup, either to stop her or to run along at her side. The slash of her riding crop made the randon spring back. Then the lady caught sight of the watchers on Mount Alban's hill. Her whip fell again, this time on her mount's bloody flanks. The beast tottered into a trot. Those above could hear the tortured wheeze of lungs long past healing.

"On to Tagmeth?" suggested Grimly.

"Good idea."

They started down the hill toward their own tethered horses, Hawthorn accompanying them to get safely below the oncoming mist; but here came one of the Knorth Kendar, anxious with news.

"Highlord, our scout to the north reports a company approaching on the River Road. She thinks Lord Caineron is leading it."

Damn. "How many troop?"

"Two one-hundred commands. My lord, we're outnumbered ten to one."

"I *can* still do simple arithmetic," said Torisen dryly, but his heart had sunk. The last time Caldane had caught him at such a disadvantage, the previous winter at Tentir, he had almost ended up permanently confined as a dangerous lunatic. This time, the High Council wouldn't be so hard to convince.

"You still have nine cadets above, lord," said Hawthorn, "and I have eight more. Shall I call them all down?"

"Five to one, counting you. No, captain, I won't involve the Brandan."

Rowan appeared at his elbow, her expression as shocked as it ever got. "Blackie, in the herb-shed, you won't believe who we found…"

"I don't care," said Torisen, "if it's the High Council, three ducks, and a goat." He was staring northward, at the huge horse which had just lumbered into sight on the River Road. "Sweet Trinity. Where d'you suppose it left its plow?"

"You could climb up to the cliff keep," suggested Grimly.

"Like a treed cat? Too late, anyway."

The leading edge of the mist passed overhead, obscuring the hilltop and ruins. Its glow caught the silver in Torisen's black hair, the fine bones in his face as he looked up at it speculatively.

"Oh no," said the Wolver, seeing him suddenly smile. "Oh, Tori, no."

V

Lyra's pony scampered on Caldane's hairy heels. The litter swayed wildly behind her, its position urged on by Gran's excited, bird-like cries from within. Foxkin dived around it. The Kendar vanguard kept pace, but didn't look as if they were much enjoying themselves.

They could all see Mount Alban now, over the broken wall that ran beside the road. Figures moved on the college's hill, under a passing mist bank. That slim one in black might be Jame, Lyra thought. Oh, splendid! Father seemed to think so too. He gave a hoarse shout and flailed his mount into an earth-shaking canter. Here was the front gate...

...and suddenly from around the wall's southern curve came a masked lady on a blood-lathered horse. It skidded into Caldane's massive steed, staggered back, and stopped splay-legged, trembling.

Lyra almost didn't recognize her half-sister. She had always admired Kallystine's beauty and cool poise, both noticeably lacking in this disheveled creature shrilly demanding that Father avenge slights which she had suffered at the Highlord's hands. There Torisen was now, going up the hill. Hadn't she followed him here all the way from Gothregor, he running before her like the yellow cur he was? Was she to be thwarted of her revenge at last by Caineron cowardice? No, dammit, that was *not* Jameth!

Father insisted that it was, so that he might finally have the pleasure of tearing the wretched brat limb from limb.

He and Kallystine were shouting at each other now. The raw, undisciplined power in their voices shoved the Kendar back as if from the heat of a pyre. The little position fell off his horse and lay motionless at its feet. Lyra retreated, frightened.

She glanced up the hill. The dark figure, whoever it had been, had disappeared into the glowing mist, followed by what looked like a huge dog. Other people were gathering around a man incongruously clad in desert gear who had just emerged from a wooden shed on the hill's north side. Why, that looked just like old Lord Ardeth. How very peculiar.

A stifled exclamation made Lyra look down. Out of the bushes growing by the front gate, a thin, familiar face stared up at her in horrified surprise.

"Why, Gricki!" she exclaimed, but softly: even as she had recognized her former servant, she had remembered what sport Father had made of him in the tower at Restormir—because he couldn't lay hands on Gricki's new mistress? Now Jame had escaped again. Father would want to make someone suffer for that, horribly, but what could she do?

"Psst!" hissed Gran through her leaf-patterned curtains. "Psst, boy! I *never* forget a voice. Get in."

Gricki shot her a doubtful look.

"Go *on!*" whispered Lyra, almost faint with this, the first time she had even obliquely defied her father. Nonetheless, it must be done. She might have treated Caldane's Southron bastard like the excrement after which she had named him, but he belonged to Jame now; and Jame, not Kallystine, was the sister of her choice. What had she renamed the wretched fellow? "Graykin, *go!*"

He looked up at her, astonished, then suddenly grinned. Her dancing pony gave him cover as he darted across to the litter and dived into it, head first. Lyra expected him to shoot straight through it, out the other side, but he didn't. He, Gran, and the Ear must be sitting on top of each other.

Kallystine gave a startled cry, abruptly cut off. Lyra looked up too late to see her vanish, but there went Father, swallowed whole by a rolling patch of mist. It billowed up over her like a cresting wave. As she stared, too frightened to move, the Ear's strong, grimy hands plucked her out of the saddle and pulled her into the litter.

She expected to fall on top of someone, but instead found herself sprawling on a cool, yielding surface, with loam under her hands. Weirding threw into relief the foliate pattern woven into the curtains. Foxkin dove in through the leaves. In the dim light, she saw them hanging upside down from the litter's framework...or were those branches? Graykin crouched near her, staring open-mouthed about him. Gran sat on a puff of pillow moss, grinning toothlessly at their amazement. The other end of the litter was occupied by the Ear, on a throne of roots, canopied by leaves. She loomed as big as a bear, indistinct except for the gleam of her eyes. Weirding sighed around them. The foxkin rustled furry wings and then were still.

"All gathered up?" asked Gran.

"All," said the Ear's deep, gruff voice, a sound licked together out of darkness. "Now, let's go to a fire."

Part VIII

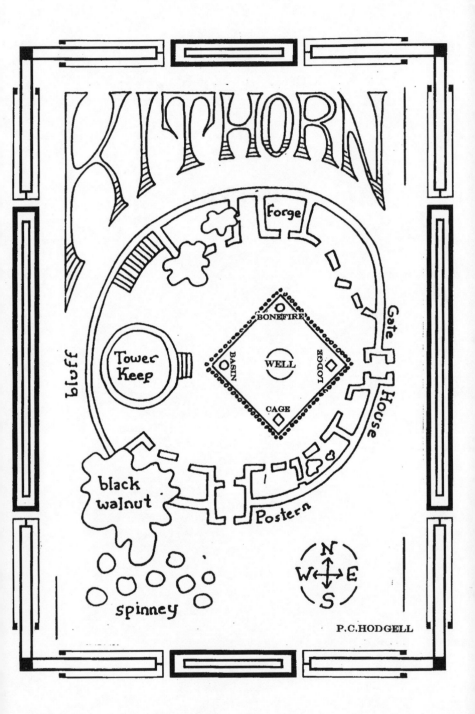

KITHORN

Forge

Gate House

bluff

Tower Keep

BONEFIRE

BASIN   WELL   LODGE

CAGE

Postern

black walnut

spinney

N
W E
S

P.C.HODGELL

Kithorn: 60th of Spring
I

The sun had set, but the lowered clouds still glowed with the sullen rubescence of banked coals. The air had grown very still. Its unseasonal warmth pressed down on the Merikit as they swept Kithorn's courtyard, renewed the imus drawn on its crumbling walls, and placed long-shafted torches in sockets around its inner square. These last hadn't yet been ignited. The shaman-elders continued their preparations under that flaming sky, watched by the three fantastically dressed Merikit squatting behind them and, less stoically, by Jame, through the smithy's barred window. She supposed that the intricate patterns which they had drawn on the four quarters of the square were the sigils of their gods. She also recognized the bone-fire being laid just outside at the square's northern corner. What was the purpose, though, of the box constructed of clay slabs to the east, or the wicker cage to the south, or the basin to the west?

This last had been revealed by the tipping back of a flagstone and appeared to be of great antiquity. Like the hill fort ruins to the south, Kithorn's court must be much older than the surrounding keep. Just look at that well at its center. Who in recent times would have dug so wide a shaft in such a remote place or rimmed it with what looked like serpentine marble? Damage to the stonework suggested that the Kencyr garrison had covered it with a more conventional hood and winch. The elder now straining to draw up a bucket of water must wish that the gear had been left in place. Feet braced, muscles quivering under age-loosened skin, he might be trying to reel in the River Snake itself.

Huh. That monster. Hadn't the cadet Rue said that its head lay under this very well and Cattila, that the Merikit would

send down a hero to master it? Maybe they had already done
so to stop the weirdingstrom—except that under this angry
sky it hardly seemed over. Anyway, did she actually believe in
the Snake, much less in the great Chaos Serpent that was said
to have spawned it? More likely, such stories were only the
Merikit version of a Lawful Lie. Rathillien couldn't be that
much stranger than the Kencyrath thought—could it?

The shaman's bucket finally rose, full of shimmering silver. Over one side hung a great tail; over the other, a gap-
mouthed head abristle with whiskers. The catfish flopped out
onto the marble rim. For a moment, the elder goggled at it.
Then he grabbed. Its barbed dorsal slashed his hand. He hastily bound up the cut with a switch of gray hair, but not before
a drop of blood had fallen into the well.

From deep underground came a low rumble. The ground
shuddered and flagstones ground together like teeth. Jame
clutched the bars, feeling once again the terror of the living
earth. How did one distinguish between fore- and after-shocks?
What if all that had come so far had only been a prelude?

The tremor subsided. A vast sigh breathed up the well
shaft, echoed by the catfish, which had crawled on its stubby
pectoral fins over to the basin and gratefully plopped into it.
The youth cast his mantle of weeds over the fish and hastily
backed out of the square.

"Bloop," said the fish, spitting out a frond.

Jame remembered the catfish that had leaped out of the
Silver during the last big quake and especially the one in the
barge which had prevented her from drowning. This fellow
looked not unlike the latter. Odd, how her encounters with
the river seemed by turns primordial and personal.

Well, she wasn't on the Silver now and no fish was going
to save her from her current predicament. Kirien had insisted
that they not fight for fear of calling attention to Ashe, the
Merikit having no tolerance at all for haunts. As a result, they
had let themselves be made prisoners in this smithy, one of
Kithorn's few intact buildings. Kirien, pacing back and forth

behind her, clearly chafed at their helplessness even more than
Jame did. Kindrie had retreated to a back corner with Jorin to
keep out of her way. In the far shadows, Ashe and Index had
resumed the discussion of Merikit fertility rites which the
tremor had interrupted. The singer had pulled her hood well
forward to hide her livid face. Perhaps Kencyr should learn
from the Merikit, Jame thought, glowering at her. Why had
she been so eager to put both the Book and Knife out of Jame's
reach, just before they would have been really useful? Whose
idea had it been, anyway, to trust a haunt?

Perhaps, at least, Mount Alban was safely away. But no.
Moving to a chink in the western wall, Jame saw the panels
which lined its inner wall still hovering ghost-like above the
ruined tower, its upper reaches swallowed by low clouds red-
lit as though already sullenly smoldering. Perhaps the weirding
had already done its strange work there above. Perhaps the
most valuable scholars in the college now slept in rooms detached from the firetrap below. Perhaps. If not, they must be
roused and brought down to safety.

Abruptly, her peephole was obscured. She jerked back as
a stick was thrust through it. From outside came a hoot of
laughter. That damned boy again. Tired of throwing boxes
down Mount Alban's stair, he had descended to cause what
trouble he could in the courtyard.

So had the large, young man in red, who was now swag-
gering around the square, trying to browbeat one elder after
another, being waved away by each in turn. He looked like
someone accustomed to getting his own way, unwilling to believe that this time he might not. The boy followed just out of
reach, jeering. The big man stopped at the north corner and
tried again.

Jame found Index at her elbow, listening avidly.

"Sonny-boy wants to play the Burnt Man," the old
scrollsman said. "That's his father's role, Daddy being
Chingetai, the tribal chief, but he's also not back yet from laying bone-fires around the Merikit borders for Summer Eve."

"I take it that there's to be a mummery," said Jame, who had seen such seasonal playlets often in the Old Pantheon section of Tai-tastigon's Temple District. New Pantheon priests sneered at their crudity, but they sometimes had surprising results, such as the year when all within earshot, including the men, had suddenly found themselves pregnant.

She understood now why the elders were so strangely attired. By the four-fold contradiction of male and female, human and animal, age and youth with unbound hair, life and ash-smeared death, they were trying to render themselves invisible to their gods. As important as they might be in the up-coming ceremony, they wished like puppet-masters to draw attention only to their puppets. But one of these, patently, was misbehaving.

"Hasn't, er, 'Sonny' already got a role? With those red pants, he's certainly dressed up for something."

"I told you she had a brain," said Kirien, coming up behind them.

Index sniffed. "Huh. But no more credit."

Kirien took a deep breath. "Index, I swear, if you withhold information now, with the entire college at hazard, I'll never barter with you again."

"Or I," said Jame. "Of course, if you don't want to be reminded how that precious herb shed of yours is arranged, or why…"

Index glowered at her. "All right! Yes, Sonny has a role. Since last midsummer, he's been the Earth Wife's Favorite, the darling of the hills, although obviously not a very successful one."

"How can you tell?"

Index looked embarrassed. "For one thing, all his braids are on the left."

To signify the men Sonny had killed, Jame remembered. The absent right-hand plaits would have been for children sired.

"Disappointing," she agreed solemnly.

"Er, yes. Also, it's dangerous. The Favorite's failure weakens the Earth, which consequently is less able to keep quiet the Chaos Serpent and its brood, including the River Snake. Hence this season of tremors. Therefore, the elders aren't waiting for Midsummer's Day, when the Favorite traditionally fights to retain his position. See that nervous fellow in green? That's the Challenger, already in possession of the ivy crown. The elders have told Sonny to lose."

"I can't see him liking that. If he obeys, though, what will happen to him?"

"In a quiet year, not much. To propitiate the River Snake, a goat would be thrown down the well in his place. This year, though, the Merikit believe that a hero has to be reborn in the Snake's belly so as to master it."

"An honor," said Ashe dryly, "that most people...would rather decline."

"Including Sonny," said Jame, working it out. "Anyway, he'd prefer to play the Burnt Man—who, I gather, is always the chief. Would substituting for his father now give him a claim on the chiefdom afterward?"

"Yes. Which is something else the elders want to avoid. They'll keep the midsummer part of these rites as intact as they can, to please the Earth Wife, to quiet the Snake, and to provide the Burnt Man (that is, the chief) with this year's best choice of an heir."

"One out of three for Sonny," said Jame. "I wouldn't care to be snake-bait, either. Just the same, if we're dealing with real powers here, not just local politics, this is filthy dangerous. Not," she added, with a passing thought to Graykin, "that politics aren't. But with Earth and Fire involved, who knows what a mess Sonny may make of things? The elders must be worried sick."

"Index," said Kirien, looking out the front window, "when you studied the Merikit some eighty years ago, didn't you have a special crony among them? He was a shaman's son, I think."

"All right!" said Index again. "Yes, yes, yes! Tungit. That's the silly bugger out there now, singing to a pile of wood."

"Well, then, talk to him! He's been a guest at Mount Alban, He can't mean to incinerate all his former hosts."

But the old scrollsman was shaking his head. "We went through all that before you arrived. Tungit doesn't want to hurt anyone, but there's a Burnt Man's bone buried under the college as well as one out here. Both will kindle spontaneously if the rite succeeds. I'm telling you, a crisis like this supersedes the rules of hospitality, now, as it did eighty years ago. Bad enough that Sonny is playing the fool and we've stumbled in. Tungit won't even let the rest of the college come down for fear of upsetting things more."

"Wait a minute," said Jame. "Go back a bit. Are you saying that the Kithorn massacre was caused by a situation like this?"

"Very like." Index turned to her, eager to escape Kirien's insistence. "This courtyard has been a ceremonial site since time out of mind. The old lord who held this keep didn't mind. He even got his people out of the way so as to give the Merikit a free hand, so he didn't know about all the goats that'd been pitched down his well over the quiet years. The River Snake got 'em all, you see, so the water never suffered. But then there was a season of bad quakes and the Merikit planned to send down a hero. The lord got wind of it, though, and refused to have a corpse thrown down his only well. The Merikit were desperate. They thought, if they didn't do something, the Snake would destroy the entire Riverland. So they planned to seize Kithorn on Autumn's Eve and hold its garrison captive until their work was done. No one was supposed to be hurt."

"But the Merikit hall-guest who opened the gate cut the throat of the Kendar guarding it," Jame protested, remembering the story as Marc had told it to her.

Index nodded. "So he did. They knew that there would be a blood-price to pay for that, and they panicked. The barracks was sealed and set ablaze; the tower, stormed; the people—men, women, and children, Highborn and Kendar—

slaughtered. Tungit wept when he told me, the last time we met before the hills were closed. And then, despite it all, the price fell due, because they'd missed someone."

"Marc."

"That's right." He gave Jame a sharp, surprised look. "A nice boy, that, despite everything. Big for his age."

"He still is."

"That's all ancient history," said Kirien impatiently. "Index, for the last time, will you ask your friend to stop this?"

"No! Dammit, I've done all I can!"

Jame wondered at his tone, at once exasperated and obscurely excited.

Even more, though, she wondered about the Merikits' purpose. There was something more to it than Sonny and the Snake, something that she should be able to guess, based on what she had seen and heard over the past few days. The Merikit were trying to combine two ceremonies this time, the first to quiet the Snake, the second...the second...

She groped after the thought though a sudden haze of fatigue. The others' voices grew dim. *Too damned long with-out sleep...* But then she was struggling back to the surface, away with a shudder from Ashe's cold, supporting hand.

"Trouble," said the haunt singer.

"You want this ceremony to continue, don't you?" Kirien was saying to Index, almost gently, but with a stir of power that made Jame's scalp crawl and Jorin growl in the corner where Kindrie held him. "You claim to be an authority on the Merikit, but the truth is that you have never before been permitted to witness a major seasonal mystery."

Index sputtered. "One needn't...Grindark rituals ...Nekrien mythology...if one draws intelligent comparisons..."

"But that isn't first hand experience, is it? For eighty years, since Kithorn fell and the hills were closed, you've been denied primary research, reduced to cataloging the details of others' work. Now comes this opportunity."

"Nothing happens by accident!" the old man cried. Before, he had sounded as defiant as a child trying to snatch a forbidden treat. Now he was backing away, as if from an assault for which his defenses were proving unequal. "A chance like this…"

"'Chance' implies 'accident.'"

"Knowledge is everything!"

"Certainly, scrollsmen have died for it before, and killed."

So might this inexorable inquisition, slicing away the self-deceptions necessary to the old man's self-respect. At last Jame understood Ashe's concern: anxiety had pushed the young scrollswoman into the academic equivalent of a berserker flare—a ruthless drive to lay bare the truth, regardless of the cost.

"Kiri…" she said, awkwardly, out of her depth, "this isn't helping."

Cool, unblinking eyes turned on her. Their attention, focusing, drove her back a step. Too late, she realized that here lay the Shanir power not only to demand the truth, but to compel it.

"Helping what? Do you contend that self-knowledge is not of itself a worthy end?"

Jame winced, remembering the awful revelation of her own soul-image. "Perhaps," she said, "we can't endure to know ourselves too well. Perhaps, the truth can sometimes destroy."

"That which can be destroyed by the truth should be," said that implacable voice. Could any Arrin-ken have spoken with more authority? "Of what would you choose to remain in ignorance?"

Involuntarily, Jame started to answer, but then she stopped herself, swallowing hard. She felt a horrible sinking inside, as though fatigue had eaten out her heart and all was crumbling in toward darkness. Dammit, she would not be forced back into her own shadows. In a curiously detached way, she felt her anger try to spark an answering berserker flare, but exhaustion had dampened the tinder. She didn't even have the energy to argue, leaving…what?

"If I had a choice," she said, reaching up, "I would ignore this."

The mask came away in her gloved hands.

Kirien blinked. "Oh," she said, in a small voice.

"Effective," Ashe remarked. "As a point of debate, though…"

"Agreed." Jame resumed the mask with fingers grown suddenly clumsy with fatigue. "It lacks subtlety. But then so did M'lady Kallystine."

Kirien had turned on Kindrie. "Healer, why haven't you done something about this?"

"Because I wouldn't let him," said Jame. "I may be a nemesis, Kiri, but I won't be his. Oh, hell…"

She put a hand on the anvil to steady herself. Her reserves had been almost exhausted before. Resisting the Jaran had nearly finished her. Still, in justice to her cousin she must explain and did so, haltingly.

"When did you last rest?" Kirien demanded. "An injury like that requires dwar sleep. Lots of it."

"Not dwar. It'll set the scar."

"Oh, I suppose you'd rather just drop dead. Fools who won't sleep sometimes do. Listen. Nothing will happen here for…how long, Index?"

"An hour," said the old scrollsman sulkily. "Maybe two. If you'll accept a mere, informed guess."

"Very well. Until then, lady, you'll sleep, if I have to hit you over the head with a brick."

Jame laughed. "I have already been hit quite often enough, thank you," she said with careful enunciation. "Wake me when the fun starts."

She lowered herself stiffly to the floor by the west wall, finishing with a thump as her legs gave out. "Oh, my," she said, gathered Jorin in her arms, and tumbled over, fast asleep. The ounce licked her chin, then stretched out beside her with a deep sigh.

Ashe stood over them. "'Nemesis,'" she repeated softly.

Kirien regarded her with alarm. "We still don't know that for certain, nor yet what kind, if it's true. For pity's sake, Ashe, if you still have tests in mind, postpone them. Haven't we enough trouble as it is?"

The haunt singer didn't reply.

"Ancestors know," said Kirien, after a pause, "she's got trouble enough. That face…! Well, healer, what are you going to do about it?"

Kindrie's white head jerked up. "L-lordan, she told you…"

"And I believe her. She was right to point out the risk. Now it's your decision whether to take it."

If Kindrie could have shrunk farther back into his corner, he would have, loathing himself all the more. After all, the young scrollswoman was only asking what he had already tacitly volunteered to do by coming down after the Knorth. Even then, though, he had doubted his ability to succeed, and been relieved to escape the test. Now it seemed that he hadn't. Dammit, what had happened to his nerves? Maybe he wasn't a hero like his two purebred cousins, but neither last winter had he been so very craven. No, just foolish, plunging into one misadventure after another through sheer ignorance, protected by the ability to heal himself of virtually anything. Now he knew where the risks lay, and, thanks to Ishtier, what their true costs were. Without the priest to unlock the way, perhaps he would never know the healing peace of his soul-image again.

If not, then what? Hide in dark corners the rest of your life?

No. Whatever he had lost, he had gained two things which he had never thought to have: a house and a name. He must try never again to be unworthy of either.

Get up, then, Kindrie Soul-Walker, and walk.

As he rose, his joints cracked like an old man's, full of shooting pains. This, too, was the mortality which Ishtier had made him taste. The others made way as he circled the anvil and crouched stiff-kneed by the Knorth. His hand, reaching out, shook. From her slow breath, she was already deep in dwar sleep. All barriers would be down. This was like standing on the edge of a precipice, all darkness below but in it lurking that monstrous house, that cold, blighted hall.

Take the plunge, Knorth. Go.

He touched her face.

II

The red clouds began sluggishly to stir over the square, crimson patches silently appearing and disappearing, streaks of blood and fire swirling at the touch of no breeze felt below. The elders crouching, each in his corner, might have been so many fantastic statues, the "woman" and the feathered man hardly less so. Outside the square, the on-lookers also stood motionless. All the workers had gathered at the southern corner, the challenger as if by chance keeping out of sight behind them. At the northern corner, in solitary splendor, even the big Merikit had lapsed into an expectant if morose silence.

Kirien wondered what they were waiting for. How much did any Kencyr, even Index, know about these wild hill-folk who had occupied the Riverland before the Kencyrath, before the old empires? If knowledge was power, surely this was its opposite. Therefore, she must also wait—for the Merikit to start, for Mount Alban (please, God) to escape, for the healing to finish.

"Why is it taking so long?" she burst out, speaking despite her anxiety barely above a whisper. "Obviously, no major muscles or arteries were cut. Early attention would have healed it without a trace. Even now…! How long does deep healing usually take?"

"How long…is a dream?"

"Ashe, please: no riddles."

"Rather, a metaphor, as are all dreams and soul-images. To a healer at work, time is subjective."

"Not entirely," said Index, screwing up his clever, monkey's face. "How long can a dream seem to last—a minute, a day, a lifetime? Sometimes, a healer ages accordingly. Why, I know one young chap who gained a century overnight."

As he spoke, he shot Kirien a malicious, sidelong look—his revenge, she thought, for having scared him so badly before. Not that she blamed him. What had possessed her, to have been so tactless? Oh, it had been exhilarating at the time, as debate so often was, but afterward…!

Still, the old bastard would raise a subject about which she had been trying very hard not to think.

Facts before theories, practical needs before speculation. She had said as much before to Ashe in conference, and had acted on it in pressing Kindrie to deal with Jame's injury. Still, a healer and a nemesis…

Should she have forced two such people together, against the wills of both? What if they could only be mutually destructive? She wished she could see Kindrie's face, but his hair hung down over it, stained by the sullen light to a bloody fringe. His thin, sensitive fingers rested on the other's masked face with a moth's trembling touch. That fragile contact reminded her how precarious the balance between them must be. She flinched as Jorin whimpered and twitched, as if he were straining to plunge as deeply into sleep as his mistress. This time, however, she and the healer had gone where he could not follow.

"Listen," said Ashe softly.

Outside, at a distance, someone was shouting. That voice, although faint, carried as across a battlefield, an insistent rally-cry: "K-north! K-north!"

Back in the shadows, the breathing changed.

III

A thick, black thread stitched together a fold across the cheek of a death banner. Eyelid dragged down, mouth twisted up, that handsome, arrogant face seemed to sneer at its own deformity.

Look at us, your precious ancestors. Are these honest faces? Are these kind?"

"Shut up," muttered Kindrie. "I'm not listening."

He shouldn't be talking, either. All that protected him was that his patient slept more deeply than he, although their dwar breathing matched. He must finish and extricate himself before she woke. He concentrated on ripping out that clumsy seam, one stitch at a time. How cruelly tight it was sewn. He worked a finger under the black thread and pulled. His nail split to the quick.

What is there here worth saving? We are a fallen house, a people utterly corrupt. Your house, your people…

His torn nail caught on the tapestry's warp. The moldering strings broke and bled, like ruptured vessels, as he fumbled to retie them.

And what are you, who need us to prove your own worth?

…shut up, shut up…

There. The warp stings were knotted back together and that damned black thread was free. It twisted like a whip-worm in his blood-slick hands, out of his grasp, up his sleeve. He felt it wriggle down to join the seething mass of scars already inside his jacket, inside the naked cage of his ribs. Fifty banners repaired. How many more to go? Row after row of disfigured faces lined the Master's cold hall, watching him askance, their rustle in the dwar wind snide with laughter.

You fatherless fool, you motherless bastard.

Kindrie slumped against the wall. He would never be able to mend them all, thereby restoring this soul-image to health. It had been mortally diseased to begin with. *(A fallen house, a corrupt people*—I will not listen!")* Perhaps a lifetime spent laboring here, but only a healer with access to his own soul would have the strength to attempt so epic a cure, though it might age and kill him in a night. Kindrie couldn't even control his own physical aspect on this level. That obscene roil eating out his guts—the symbolic equivalent of jewel-jaws in the stomach or of worms, feasting in the grave?

There it was again, that devouring fear of death which had made such a coward of him before. To enter this soul-scape, he'd had to match dwar-breathing with his cousin. It still whistled in and out of him, his jacket acting as bellows to his fleshless ribs. He couldn't stop it. He couldn't wake. Without his soul's reserve, his real body would die of exhaustion in its sleep. At least it would go to a proper pyre. What if no such cleansing flames could reach here? Kindrie hugged himself, feeling the voracious churn within. His mind would be devoured inch by inch by his own fears, as real to him here as maggots in the flesh.

...crawling up his throat, about to spew out his mouth...

"Stop it," he whispered behind clenched teeth. "Stop it, STOP IT!"

What allowed him to swallow that surge of panic, more than anything else, was a nagging doubt. He might not always like Jame, nor did he yet know quite what to make of her, but he no longer believed that she was the monster which Ishtier had claimed. If she really had come from such a vile place as this, it seemed to him that she had long since left it behind. How, then, could it still be the model of her soul? True, the death banners of these fallen Knorth accurately mirrored her injury. Any healer would look first for such a correspondence, and usually be right. They might represent her darkling fear of dishonor, but still...

Had he been tricked into looking at the wrong thing? As his own soul-image consisted of an outer blind and an inner reality—the garden hidden within the priests' college—perhaps hers also was unexpectedly complex.

Think. Remember: that flash of white just before he had first been knocked out of this soul-scape and across a forest clearing—had it only been four days ago? What had struck him? What in this dark, accursed place was white?

One thing only, which he had deliberately avoided: an indistinct glimmer on the cold hearth at the far end of the hall. Graykin, he had thought, thankful that his fumblings hadn't brought that bitterly jealous spirit down on him. It occurred to him now, though, that four days ago Jame hadn't yet given Graykin's soul her grudging permission to occupy this place. What a maggot-seethe of fears that distant fireplace stirred between his ribs, the worse because he didn't know why.

Then find out, his training prompted him. An unnamed fear is an unconquerable one.

Disfigured faces grimaced at him through warp and woof as he passed. Whispers followed him down the hall:…but what about me, and me, and me…? Healer, kinsman, come back…!

The walk seemed to take hours. Under his bare feet, the green-shot floor was numbing cold, but the wind that blew over it was the sirocco of human breath. Kindrie inhaled as it pushed at him, exhaled as it pulled, deep and slow. In his terror, he ached to breathe faster, but couldn't. The sense of suffocation fed his fears and had to be fought down, as did the gorge continually rising in his throat.

Three steps led up to the hearth. Over the top one hung the flayed paws and snarling masks of Arrin-ken pelts, some a ghostly silver gray, others iridescent as pearl.

That was what I saw, thought Kindrie. *I can turn back now.*

But he kept walking.

The black vault of the fireplace was full of charred, twisted limbs, fantastic in their deformity. The eye kept trying to make sense of them. They seemed to organized themselves around a pale block of ash and an ashy stick, lying flat as though on a table. A distorted figure as if of a man sat beside them, there one blink, gone the next as Kindrie drew closer and his perspective changed. He remembered that Ishtier had wanted him to learn from Jame's soul-image where she had hidden the Book Bound in Pale Leather. Perhaps the strange, shifting image in the fireplace could have told him, except that, ironically, he had no idea what it meant.

If he found out and dealt with it as the priest had demanded, maybe he could still regain his own soul.

...do it, do it! the banners whispered.

Kindrie started to mount the steps.

A pale shape rose from among the furs and lunged at him. He was knocked back to sprawl in the floor, cringing as the other ravened over him on the end of its chain. It was naked except for a ridge of dark hair which ran from the head, down the curved spine, along the tail curled up between its legs as if for modesty. Its rear legs bent backward. Its dangling hands were half-paws. The muzzle and bared teeth were also canine, but in those baleful eyes Kindrie recognized Jame's stray dog of a servant, chained to the hearth and starved by her reluctant acceptance, but grimly on guard as she had bidden him. The man-dog fell back into a crouch on the second step, slackening the chain, panting. Famine-gaunt, his bones seemed about to burst through the taut skin which covered them.

"Liddle man, liddle bassstard!" A thick growl, barely articulate, as few people are on the soul's level. "Go 'way! My hearth. My lady!"

"B-but Graykin, she needs me..."

"No!" Snaggle-teeth bared. "Needs me. No one else. No one needs you, no one wants you, 'cept fed-chi priests. Go back where you b'long, priestling!"

The Knorth had called him that at first, with no less scorn. Kindrie hunched over, gut-sick with the remembered sense of his own worthlessness, frantic to escape from it into the garden of his soul. How could he ever have hoped to out-grow Wilden? The priests had had him too long, made him too much their own—he, who had been nothing to begin with.

"Bassstard," the man-dog was crooning, eyes bright with hungry malice. "Worthless Shanir bassstard..."

All this stress on bastardy, by someone more unfortunately bred even than himself... Kindrie's training pricked him again into observation. The creature was actually salivating. A self-professed sneak and mongrel, Graykin fed on other's weaknesses to...to hide from his own devouring sense of worthlessness.

Understanding slowed Kindrie's panic. With a jolt, he realized that Lady Rawneth had played on him much the same way all his childhood, telling him over and over what trash he was, rubbing his nose in his misbirth until he could smell nothing else, except in his garden where he had run to hide. From what weakness had she been trying to hide by demeaning him? What a fool he had been, to have let her do it for so long!

Indignant, Kindrie found himself on his feet without remembering having risen. He saw now what the man-dog had been trying both to guard and to hide: A second pale figure laying asleep in a nest of Arrin-ken furs, partly clad in rathorn armor. No, not armor exactly. Mask, gorget, breastplate, gauntlet and greaves all grew out of that slim white body in bands of ivory, as they would have on a young rathorn—and as on so immature a beast, not all the plates properly overlapped. Out of a gap over one cheekbone, thick blood welled. The ivory band across the small breasts rose and fell with the slow rhythm of dwar.

A-ha, thought Kindrie.

Through the halls came echoing a sound from beyond its walls, drawn out, distorted by echoes: "K...k...k..."

The sleeper's breathing changed. She had heard; she was beginning to wake.

The man-dog grinned wolfishly. " 's torn it. Get out while you can, white-hair!"

Louder, closer: "...norrrRRR..."

The quickening breath of wind pushed Kindrie back a step, then dragged him forward almost into Graykin's jaws. Behind him, banners clutched at the wall with threadbare hands.

Rrrrun! their voices cried, with the sound of ripping cloth.

"Yesss," Kindrie breathed, pushed back again, perforce exhaling. What chance had he, half-trained, against a soul-scape so complex, so malignant?

But if he ran now, he would be running the rest of his life. Where was there a corner so dark that he could hide from himself? He had no garden to escape to now. Ishtier had cut off that retreat. Run, or advance. To do the latter, though, he must master his fears, or lose them.

Bastard, worthless...

No. Look at Graykin, a mongrel in his soul because he accepted that judgment in life. And he, Kindrie? A cringing coward with a belly full of death, disgracing his house, disgracing himself. The thought set his guts roiling, but this time he didn't swallow it back. He retched again and again. No more cosseting of weakness, no more excuses. Purge them all.

With a whine, the man-dog flung himself down the steps in a hunger-frenzy to snap at the seething mess. Kindrie edged past on unsteady legs.

"...THHHHHH..."

Sleeper's breath and the exhalation of sound matched in the wind hissing in his face, tearing at his hair. Arrin-ken fur rippled. Banners flailed. He touched the cool ivory of the cracked mask.

Nothing.

"...HHHhhh..." The sound died with a sigh. Then, somewhere in the distance, it gathered itself again, faster this time, like a wave rushing for the shore: "...k...k...knorrRR..."

Why hadn't his healing power engaged? What was he still doing wrong? Torn banners snickered against the wall: failure, stupid failure…

Why should they be glad?

Then he thought he understood. Tricked again.

"Listen!" he cried, raising his voice against the approaching roar. "These banners aren't part of your soul-scape! Perhaps, perhaps none of this hall is. It's a trap, to make you think that the shadows still own you, but here you are, in armor against them. Fight, d'you hear me? Fight!"

He had to shout, but he must have been heard. Under his hands the ivory was growing together again. Behind him, banners unraveled in the wind, swirling nets swept away even as they cast themselves to ensnare him. Green light laced the dark floor. Just another moment…

"…THHHHH!"

The eyes behind the mask snapped open: mindless silver, the soul's pure reflection. A flash of white. Oh, no. Not again…

CRACK!

Pain. Confusion. The blow of that ivory fist, lashing out by reflex, sent him flying sideways through a forest of charred limbs. No, into the fireplace. No, into a black room where a man with silver eyes looked up, smiling, from a pale book ('welcome to the family, little cousin'). Crashing into the iron fireback. No, through a hidden door into…into…

Green, and white self-heal. Wild heartsease drooping against the night, white herbs abloom, white moths dancing in the moon-garden of his soul…

Home. Safe. Sleep now. Sleep.

IV

Jame fought her way out of sleep, crying, "Who calls the Knorth? Who? Brier?"

Cold hands held her down. Over her bent a livid face, leprous with death.

For a moment, she was back before the broken walls of her old home keep, under the dead weight of the haunt about to sink its rotting teeth into her arm.

"Don't," said Ashe.

Against every instinct, Jame sheathed her claws. But she had attacked someone, she thought, still half-dazed with sleep. Who?

Jorin stretched out limp beside her.

Oh, God, surely not.

The ounce twitched and began to snore. She remembered now, how he had tried to follow her into the depths of dwar and been left, crying, in its upper reaches. Obviously, he was still there.

A confusion of legs and hands moved toward the front of the smithy, taking with it a limp form.

She had struck...Someone had staggered backward...

Over the haunt's shoulder, Jame saw the anvil squat on its ironwood stump. One of the horns glistened darkly.

"Oh hell," she muttered, shaking off Ashe and rising unsteadily.

In the stripped light that fell through the barred window, Kirien bent over Kindrie. "I should never have forced this!" she was saying. "A healer and a nemesis...don't!"

Jame's hand stopped in mid-air.

Index shoved her aside and pressed a clot of cobwebs to the back of the Shanir's skull to staunch the blood.

Kiri was right, Jame thought, sitting back. It would be dangerous for her to touch the Shanir when he was so vulnerable. Damn her poisonous soul-image, anyway!

But someone (Kindrie?) had said something about it being a trap. What had he meant? She groped after the memory as if after a rapidly fading dream. The details were already gone, but the suggestion lingered. It implied a deception on the most intimate level, a deceiver closer to her than her own skin. Just the same, if she could disown any part of that ghastly hall...!

Steady, she warned herself. Whatever the truth is, it won't be simple or perhaps so easily discovered.

But still...!

Ashe stood behind her, a hooded death mask hovering in the shadows. "Why...did you attack him?"

"I couldn't help it. He was too close."

"Huh," said Kirien. "Remind me to keep my distance. That's dwar breathing, at least."

So it was, deep and slow. Trinity. She had warned Kindrie that the next time she might knock him through a wall, and she had—back into the healing embrace of his soul-image.

Then she remembered: "Did someone call the Knorth?"

As if in answer, they became aware of an approaching disturbance outside. Struggling forms passed the window. The door was flung open and a large, gagged figure was thrown in, almost on top of them. It was Brier Iron-thorn.

"Ancestors be praised," said Jame.

The Kendar lurched to her feet and stood for a moment swaying. Muffled noises came from behind the gag, which she made no effort to remove despite her free hands. Breath smoked from her nostrils in faintly glowing plumes. Her eyes were screwed tightly shut. Oblivious to their questions, she set off across the room with a determined if unsteady stride and bounced off the far wall. Slipping up behind her, Ashe whipped off the gag.

"...north!" the cadet was crying. "K-north!" Over and over.

Her voice seemed to come from a considerable distance. Its tone, however, was no less compelling than when it had reached Jame in the depths of dwar sleep. It conveyed no fear, only a grim determination to evoke an answer.

The old shaman called urgently from his corner of the square.

"If she won't shut up," Index translated, "they'll kill her."

Jame grabbed Brier's hand as it groped past her. "Cadet, stop it. I'm Knorth!"

Brier paused, head cocked to listen. "Lady?" she said in her far-away voice. Her glowing breath made Jame's face tingle. "Where are you?"

"At Kithorn. So are you. For pity's sake, look at me!"

The Kendar's eyes opened warily. Luminous mist filled the sockets, throwing into relief her high, strong cheekbones. "All I see is weirding," she said in a tight, slightly louder voice. "The Highlord called me down into it and now I'm lost. So is he."

Jame gave a stifled exclamation, involuntarily tightening her grip.

Brier's hand closed on hers. "I feel...something."

She was half-crushing Jame's fingers. Her voice seemed perhaps two rooms away now instead of half a field.

"Keep calling!" Kirien said.

"I, no. If my brother is lost in the weirding too, he needs help. A guide. Brier Iron-thorn, do you remember how your mother came back under the sand to bring Tori safely across the Dry Salt Sea?"

The Kendar's dark face hardened. "That story. A fever dream. A sop for an orphan."

"Maybe, maybe not. When the salt sea returned yesterday and I nearly drowned in it, I-I think Rose saved me too. It was wrong of me not to have told you before, but I was unsure, and scared."

Brier's face would never be good at showing emotion, whatever she felt. "What do you want me to do?" she asked at last, gruffly, almost in her normal tone.

"Will you go back into the weirding to find Tori? No, don't move." She pushed the Kendar down to sit against the west wall, next to Kindrie and the still sleeping Jorin, and knelt before her. "Just think about doing it. The Senetha can be done purely in the mind, perhaps this too. Will you try?"

Brier had squeezed her eyes shut again, like a child afraid to see. She was afraid. Jame could feel it through her grip. Never before had she been asked to do something so much on faith, for a girl whom she must think half-mad and a house which she had only begun to trust. Then she gave a curt nod and began again to call: "K-north, K-north"—each cry more faint than the last, as though she were resolutely walking back into the mist which enveloped her mind.

Kirien shivered. "I wouldn't care to do that, even with an anchor. For God's sake, don't let go!"

She had been stealing sidelong looks at Jame. Now, abruptly, she said, "Forgive the rudeness, but I have to know: would you please take off that mask?"

But Kiri had just seen her face, when she had used it to cut short the scrollswoman's berserker flare. It couldn't be such a treat as all that...

Then Jame remembered. Kindrie had been in her soul-scape.

Not daring to think, much less to hope, she fumbled at the mask with her free hand. It came loose. She took a deep breath and turned to look at Kirien.

The Jaran regarded her critically. "A few minutes more would have been better. Still, not bad. Not bad at all."

Jame touched her cheek. Apprenticeship to the best thief in Tai-tastigon had trained her fingertips to abnormal sensitivity, even when gloved. As Kirien had said, a few moments more had been needed, and lost, thanks to Brier's call. There was still a scar. It was so faint, though, that she could hardly feel it. Kindrie had done his work well enough: she was no longer disfigured.

Outside, someone cried in alarm, echoed by Index. Kirien hastily joined him by the front window, Ashe only a step behind her. Red light flared across their startled faces.

"Oh!" said Kirien, staring.

Jame tried to rise, but couldn't break Brier's grip. "What?" she demanded.

"The weeds in the courtyard's cracks, they're bursting into flames from the inner square out. Watch it!" She jerked Index back as lines of fire laced the windowsill, following the mossy cracks. In a moment, they had burned out, without spreading to the interior.

Outside, Sonny's voice rose again.

"Huh," said Index. "The fool acts as if he's never seen a purification before. He claims that the fires show the Burnt Man's disapproval. The chief isn't coming, he says, but someone's got to represent the Burnt Man here tonight, or the entire Riverland may be torn apart. Guess who volunteers."

"He may have a point," said Kirien. "Whatever they're up to, annoying the powers that be can't help. I wonder where that precious chief of theirs is, anyway."

"Four days ago," Jame said slowly, "he was near Falkirr, laying a bone-fire. Then he went on southward."

"Don't be a fool," snapped Index. "I told you: the silly bugger is off defining the Merikit borders for Summer Eve…"

"Right down the Silver," Jame finished, as her wits finally woke. "He's preparing to reclaim the entire Riverland."

Index and Kirien stared at her. "Impossible!" they burst out. "The lords…the priests…! They'd never permit…"

"The lords have been gone all winter," said Jame. "So has most of the Kencyrath. You don't realize how empty and strange the valley has become. And the priests have been…preoccupied. Now they can barely draw in the power they need to maintain contact with their temples. The Merikits' plan only takes things one step farther. They probably haven't had so good an opportunity since they closed these northern hills to us eighty years ago. How did they do that, Index?"

"My God." The old man stared at her. "With bone-fires."

It could have been more thoroughly done, Jame thought. After all, here she and others were. In her travels through

Rathillien she had encountered areas such as the Anarchies so strong with native power that they could literally eat an unwary Kencyr alive. These hills were hardly as voracious, but she doubted that her people would ever live here again. And now that might become true for the rest of the Riverland as well? How ironic if the entire Kencyrath was about to become as roofless and rootless as she herself had been made to feel.

She remembered the dinner party at the Cataracts, those self-satisfied lords so sure that they had every right to dispose of her as they wished. The Kencyrath was theirs, wasn't it? Of course, they could do with it whatever they wanted. But what did they know about the blood feud between the Knorth and the Randir, still festering like an abscess after all these years, or the priesthood malignant in its foul hole, or the secret life of their own women? Nothing was as sure as they blandly assumed, not even their suzerainty over this northern land, perhaps about to be snatched away from them forever.

And these were the people who had told her that she could only belong to the Kencyrath if she played the role which they decreed, living in public and private behind the mask of their conventions.

And she had accepted that, even when she had fled Gothregor, just as she had been prepared to live with Kallystine's handiwork as the mark of her failure.

Jame looked at the mask still in her hand. Seeker, seeker...the children's taunt. That damned game of confusion and lost identity.

But the game's object wasn't to find out who you were. Rather, you escaped the eyeless mask by catching someone else and taking her name, which the next seeker might in turn take from you. Well, in trying to play by their rules she had damn near lost herself altogether.

No more of that, Jame thought, letting the mask drop. Thanks to Kindrie, she had her own face back again, and by God she was going to wear it.

"It could really happen," Index was saying. "We could really lose the Riverland. Sweet Trinity, what a catastrophe!"

"Why?" Jame asked.

They all turned to stare at her.

"I mean," she said slowly, thinking it out, "we've tried to make it home by ignoring its true nature, by...masking it, as it were. But it's always been a sort of trap, hasn't it? We can't support ourselves here, so we have to hire out our people as mercenaries—prostitute them, almost. Then too, it keeps the nine major houses preoccupied with the High Council's idiotic political games, while isolated minor families near the Barrier guard against Perimal Darkling alone. If you look at it that way, life in the Riverland is perverting everything that makes us what we are, or should be."

Index snorted. "You sound like crazy old Cattila, always harping on how we're failing our trust, as if that damned god of ours hadn't failed us first."

"Does that change our responsibility? Why is it that no one can keep in mind what we Kencyr are supposed to be doing?"

"Perhaps," said Ashe, "because none of us, are as close to it, as you are, nemesis."

"You might also consider this," said Kirien tartly: "To lose the Riverland now would tear the Kencyrath apart. I admire your brother. He's a far better man than we deserve, and the only one who could have held us together so far. But not in the face of this. Besides, remember that success for the Merikit tonight means the immolation of Mount Alban. Are you now in favor of that?"

Jame stared back at their suddenly hostile faces, dismayed. They were seeing her unmasked, the outsider, the potential destroyer. And so, perhaps, she might be. All the weaknesses which she kept uncovering among her people, all the secrets— for a moment, the whole Kencyrath seemed to lie in her gloved grasp, flawed and fragile.

Some things need to be broken...

But it was Brier Iron-thorn's hand which she actually gripped, or rather which gripped her with a mute desperation that threatened to break her bones. She owed it to Brier, and Marc, and yes, even Tori, not to do anything stupid.

I will think first, and take responsibility afterward, she told herself, trying to ease her fingers in Brier's grip. *I will, I will, I will.*

Outside, there was a muffled whoof and a flare of blue light, then another and another. The moment's startled silence after the first broke with a babble of urgent voices, Sonny's rising above the others.

"What is it?" Jame demanded, then, getting no answer, "Scrollswoman, describe!"

"Spontaneous, sequential ignition of torches," Kirien reported, obedient to her training. "Cyanic flames and smoke, indicative of unknown properties. Conclusion... Damn. Ready or not, here we go."

Index crowed with excitement. Whatever the outcome, he would have his treat after all. "The elders are ordering Sonny and the Challenger to get into the square before it closes. Green-britches looks ready to shit in 'em. Sonny is arguing. He's stripping naked. He's picked up a lump of charcoal, no, he's dropped it. Got his fingers singed, the idiot. Talk about the Burnt Man's disapproval! Tungit is pointing..."

The three scholars watched with deep interest.

"What? What?"

Index cleared his throat. "It, er, has to do with those missing right-hand braids."

The old fool. Whose innocence did he think he was protecting, anyway?

"D'you mean," said Jame, "that he's more impressive with his pants on?"

A shriek of laughter answered her. The ragged boy leaped up from beneath the window where he had lain eavesdropping and shouted to the big Merikit.

"Damn," said Kirien again. "D'you suppose that brat knows Kens?"

In answer, the smithy door crashed open. Sonny stood on the threshold, a naked, black hulk against the courtyard's glare. His head turned rapidly, searching. Before, a masked female had dared first to hurt him—him, the Earth Wife's Favorite—and now this...!

Only one mask was in sight. He lunged at Kirien.

Ashe stepped in front of the young scrollswoman. The Merikit elders had taken the singer's iron-shod staff, so she met the big man's charge with a water-flowing move that sent him careening into a dark back corner. From the complicated crash which followed, he had blundered into the smithy's scrap heap. Yells of rage mingled with the clatter of rusty iron and the rip of rotten bellows. Any moment, though, he would extricate himself.

"You're the nemesis," Index shouted at Jame from across the room. "Do something!"

Jame growled. She would at least have liked the freedom to maneuver, but Brier still clung to her hand, so far into the weirding that only wisps of luminous mist came from her moving lips. How could Jame betray the Kendar's trust or, for that matter, break her grip?

Sonny emerged from the shadows and stumbled toward the front corner where Ashe stood guard before Kirien. The singer spoke a word in Merikit and pointed at Jame.

Damn all haunts anyway, teeth and toenails.

Jame pinched the nerve in Brier's elbow. The Kendar's grasp involuntarily loosened as her fingers went numb. Her unheard voice faltered. Jame pulled free and scooped up Kindrie's limp hand. Brier's grip clamped like a vice on the Shanir's thin wrist, with an audible crunch of bones. She began again soundlessly to call "K-north, K-north," but now sweat shone on her dark brow and weirding poured from her lips with each strong exhalation.

Sweet Trinity, thought Jame, recoiling. *What have I done now?*

No time, though, for second thoughts: Here came Sonny with a roar. He hadn't learned from Ashe's water-flowing move; possibly, he hadn't seen what had sent him flying into a far corner and now into a wall. Jame was out the door before the crash.

A row of torches burned blue down the northeast side of the square. Their pale, glowing smoke, drifting inward, filled the enclosed space like a box, from the bottom up. Blossoms of flame seen through the haze marked the progression of fire from torch to torch down the southeast side. Inside this closing perimeter stood the elders' indistinct figures. Their anxious voices sounded as thin and distant as Brier's in the weirding.

Hurry, they must be calling. *Hurry, hurry!*

Jame had paused for a moment to stare. Behind her, she heard big, bare feet slap on stone. The Merikit's arms swept over her head, snagging off her cap, as she ducked and kicked backward, as it were, at the bone of contention, connecting. Free, she bolted toward the court's eastern gate. If she left Kithorn, the outer circle would at least be broken. If Sonny followed, the rites might fail without him and Mount Alban be saved by default.

The ruddy light from above mixed with the blue glower of the torches to cast violet highlights on Kithorn's shattered timbers, shading to deep purple—a glowing world except in the velvet shadows under the gatehouse where indistinct shapes waited. Some rose at her approach to stand hunch-shouldered in the gloom. Others only gained knees and elbows, their feet and hands having long since fallen off. Blackened skin cracked with their movement. Red fissures opened in seams of blood and fire. From their huddled mass came a long, questioning sigh:

"Whaaaaa...?"

Jame stopped. A breeze under the gatehouse brought to her the stench of burnt flesh and its taste on her lips in charred flecks.

"Thaaaaa..." breathed the Burning Ones, disappointed, settling back down outside the circle, like hounds at bay, to await their master.

A shuffling sound behind her and a furious curse. Here came Sonny, hopping on one foot as he pulled his red britches back on. Made him feel vulnerable, had she? Good. Oh, but what a fool, to be playing such games before such an audience...if he was aware of it. Ancestors knew, he was close enough now for the black specks of that terrible conflagration to freckle his fair-skinned face.

A thought struck her: Maybe he was one of those people who simply couldn't see certain things. She had met a few in Tai-tastigon, oblivious to its teeming supernatural community and contemptuous of their neighbors' belief in "such nonsense." If so, he literally couldn't see the reality behind the ceremony he was being compelled to perform.

Still, he wasn't the real problem. The ways north and east blocked, Jame veered southward along the square's southeast side, to gain time, to think.

The breeze followed her. Overhead, glowing clouds began slowly to wheel as though around the axis of the now invisible well. Blue smoke swelled up within the enclosure to met them, undisturbed by the wind except at the edges, where a few wisps were teased loose. One of these blew in Jame's face, and her senses lurched.

She was following the path which the elders had taken earlier, circling sunwise to close the square. Her feet fell with the remembered beat of theirs, the memory of their bells ringching-chinging in her mind—no, millennia of feet, and bells, and power called up from the earth, down from the sky. The Merikit, clustered at the south corner, stared but let her pass: they would as soon have stopped their own elders, treading the sun's path. It seemed to Jame that she was pursuing suns, one after another of them born in bursts of blue flame, one for each day of the summer to come.

Then she had out-paced them and was slowing, shaking her head to clear it. The wind seemed to keen in one ear and out the other. No. That whistling came from her right, inside the square, and the wind swerved inward at the west corner to answer it. What had she been doing, and where bound? In a damned circle, back to where she had started with nothing gained, nothing changed...

But it had.

Ahead lay the smithy, with light streaming out of it. Index burst out the door, pulling Kirien with him. Jorin wobbled on their heels. A shape of darkness followed—Ashe, backing out. After her, billowing out the door, came weirding.

Jame stopped short. "My God," she said to the Challenger, who had just come up beside her. "Now what?"

In answer, the Merikit clapped the ivy crown on her head and shoved her between the torches, into the blue smoke of the square.

V

At first, Jame thought that she would die. Acrid smoke burned in her eyes, throat, and lungs, inhaled all the more deeply with each racking attempt to cough it out. Kencyr might not poison easily, but they could certainly choke.

Bit by bit, however, breathing became easier. At last she was able to wipe her streaming eyes on a sleeve and look up.

Kithorn was gone.

Sacred space stretched out before her to horizons lost in a hazy distance, pale blue below, shading upward through lavender to mauve. Above, angry red clouds wheeled in a slow vortex, centered over the well. The latter's rim of dull green serpentine loomed in the middle of that interminable plain like a volcano's mouth, half-obscured by drifting smoke. A low, continual rumble came out of it, felt more than heard. The mottled veins of the marble rim extended into cracks and some of these into quake fissures. So far, however, the latter appeared to have been stopped by a network of dark lines lying across the granite-white plain. Ah. Those must the god-sigils which she had watched the shaman-elders draw in the square, the power of the Four still containing that of the River Snake's mouth.

While the sigil lines near the well looked spidery with distance, those close at hand lay in bold strokes across the plain. Jame had nearly fallen on top of one a good twelve feet wide...or would she have fallen into it? It was so impossibly black. When she tried to touch it, her hand disappeared as though into sunless water, feeling nothing.

A harsh sound came from the left. At a distance, beyond two more inky bands, the Favorite doubled over, as racked with coughing as she had been a moment ago. He must have plunged into the square just before it closed, driven by his blind rage exactly where he had no wish to go. Jame reached up to remove the ivy crown. Whatever Sonny's role, she needn't play the one which the Challenger had thrust onto her...

"BLOOP," said something behind her.

The basin, like the square, had grown. So had its inmate. A flat, fishy eye the size of a buckler gazed down at her dubiously. The huge head in which it was set seemed otherwise to be mostly mouth and whiskers. Four of the latter rasped on the basin's edge as the creature chinned itself there. Two more extended from its upper lip like downed spars, one passing almost over her head. The thick, wide lips parted. Out of them came a small, dreamy voice.

"There was a maid," it said. "Oh, so beautiful, so proud."

Jame stared. She almost thought that she knew that voice, sleepily gloating over its new secret.

"No chief's son would do for her, oh no. When the earth shook, what must she needs try but to seduce the River Snake itself."

The monster's maw gaped wider and wider. Deep inside that pink-ribbed gullet nestled something that glimmered like a viscid pearl. Jame had heard that some catfish carried fertilized eggs in their mouths to hatch them, but this "egg" had shadowy markings under its mucous sheath—no, features, as if under a caul: a face, which Jame knew only too well, despite never having seen it before without at least a tracery mask.

"M'lady? Kallystine?"

This was moderately strange, Jame thought, but perhaps no more so than Loogan stuck in Gorgo's craw. Did aquatic relationships always end in eat-or-be-eaten? So she asked again, only half in jest, "Did this fish swallow you, or are you wearing it?"

"Poor maid," said the voice, suddenly dolorous. "Poor, pretty maid. The Snake ate her all-l-l-l up."

The Caineron device was a serpent devouring its young, but that couldn't be what Kallystine was talking about, could it? Despite the similarities (pride, ambition—downfall?), this was someone else's story.

"Who are you?" Jame demanded, leaning into the creature's mouth, hands between teeth which, on a fish of normal size, would have been small. "What are you?"

A smile made the face under the membrane shift and flow, like a changeling fetus in its embryonic sack.

"The Eaten One," it said, in a different voice, in Merikit.

"I understood that!"—but then, why shouldn't she? In this space sacred to gods not her own, ancestors only knew what might happen. Keep to essentials. "Why are you here?"

"To find a hero to feed the Snake to save the world."

"Oh, that's helpful. 'To feed' in what sense?"

"Pretty maid, guess."

That did it. What was this but another game of seeker's mask, one victim substituted for another? But when she tried to tear off the ivy crown, its leaves were so entangled in her hair that it might have sunk rootlets into her skull. Perhaps it had. No wonder the Challenger had been loath to put on the damn thing. Now, short of scalping herself, she was stuck with it—and with the victory which it implied?

Not if Sonny could help it. He had recovered from his coughing fit and was groping toward her, drawn by the sound of her voice. Whatever blindness had prevented him from seeing the Burning Ones now kept the blue smoke in his eyes. He came to a sigil stroke and stepped into it—except that for him it was still only a charcoal line drawn on the flagstones. On he came, stumbling across the abyss.

"...such very, very good friends..." murmured Kallystine's silken voice.

Huge pectoral fins surged out of the water, hooked on the basin's rim, and pulled. The leviathan rose over Jame like a ship's prow about to dash itself on rocks, then crashed down. She found herself flat on her back, her head over the sigil's void, surprised not to be smashed flat. The darkened sky was vaulted with ribs, from which hung an improbable moon with Kallystine's distorted face.

"...eat you all-l-l-l up," it crooned.

A rumble swallowed her voice. It came from behind, approaching fast, accompanied by a rending crack. Jame clutched the monster's chin whiskers for support as the stones beneath her back split and fell away. Looking down over her shoulder, she saw a seam of glowing red open deep in the darkness below. Then a rising wave of heat took away her breath.

"Let, me, up!" she gasped. "Dammit, it's...not...your turn!"

The moon-face shifted, pouting, and the great fish surged backward into the basin, hauling Jame with it and displacing a wave which almost swept her away. The vast mouth snapped shut: WHOMP. Steaming water seethed around it, red-lit from beneath. Looking behind her, Jame saw that a quake fissure had breached the sigil, running from the distant well mouth almost up to the basin. The ground shook again.

"How do we stop this?" she demanded.

A sulky, Merikit voice answered from within. "I told you: feed the Snake."

"Ugh," said Jame. "There's got to be another way. Where can I find the Earth Wife?"

"In her lodge. Where else?"

"In Peshtar?"

"Dumb, dumb, dumb."

"Listen, chowder-head: you're the one in boiling water."

Or perhaps they both were. Here came Sonny, groping toward them through the steam. Damnation. Could he walk straight over fissures too?

The thick catfish lips parted slightly, the voice inside grumbling: "Someone has to feed that damn Snake. Here, boy, here, here!"

"Oh, go stew," said Jame, disgusted, then turned and fled.

On reflection, she thought she knew where to go, if not exactly how to get there.

The enormous sigils sprawling across this plain and complicating her route were made up of many lines, some connected, others not. Whatever their other properties, they clearly served as a series of entrenchments. The quake fissures must thus break through each in turn in order to breach the square, as one had already so nearly done in the western corner by the basin. Others had broken lines closer to the plain's well-mouth center and spewed into them the Serpent's hot blood. Rising heat met the cool breath of the sigils in smoke and stream, turning the expanse into the semblance of a burning battlefield—which, in fact, it was. The prospects south and west appeared only intermittently through a drifting haze. North and east had disappeared altogether.

Of course, it was some consolation that Sonny couldn't see anything at all; but then neither was he hindered by the sigil lines nor, much, by the fissures, which must be no more than cracks in the real courtyard. He was also stumbling around in an area only some fifty feet square, while the plain which Jame had seen before this last tremor had looked as if it would take days to cross, or months, or a life-time.

However, she'd had some experience in Tai-tastigon and the Anarchies with the quirks of distorted space, including their deceptive distances.

What she wanted lay to the east. She set off as nearly as she could in that direction, guided by her memory of the sigils' shapes and by the vortex flow of the clouds above, hoping for the best.

It was hard, hot going. A dozen fissures now laced the plain, reaching ahead through the branches of the sigil strokes which they had overwhelmed. Veils of smoke and wavering heat rose from the red fires in their depths. If they did indeed break open the square, would sacred space itself be breached? A cataclysmic thing, certainly. Perhaps this plain was Rathillien's soul-scape. In that case, events here might reverberate across an entire world.

She skirted yet another sigil line, trying to remember if one side or the other led to a dead-end. Another damn maze. Sometimes, her whole life seemed like one huge labyrinth whose key kept changing.

It was getting very warm. Oh, for a breath of wind.

One came, as if in answer to her wish, fretted with black feathers. Hundreds of these, the spoils of entire flocks, had been tied to the hairy Merikit. More fluttered past, many of them broken. She turned her face into the fitful breeze and followed it.

Ahead loomed a skeletal structure: the wicker cage, like the basin, grown huge. Loose feathers swirled inside it, vast, disorganized wings flailing at the bars. In their midst, an indistinct shape plummeted toward the earth…

No. Jame's heart had leaped, anticipating the smash of flesh to bloody ruin on stone. Her nerves still flinched at the expected impact, but the figure seemed to fall on and on, as though through infinite space, without ever reaching the ground.

"Who are you?" she demanded.

A voice answered inside the cage, speaking a singsong language which she had never heard before and yet, somehow, understood. "There was an old man," it said, "oh, so clever, so ambitious that he claimed to be a god. To prove it, his followers threw him from a high tower. Now he falls, forever and ever. He helped you at Gothregor, little girl. Help him now!"

Jame stared, remembering that storm of black wings above the old keep's broken roof at Gothregor. "Tishooo? Old Man, you nearly got me killed! What do you want?"

"Out, out, OUT!" Frenzied feathers beat against the bars, broke, and hurled their fragments forward again. "Oh, those foolish priests, to have whistled the wind into this cage when only he can blow away the Serpent's Breath! Oh, let him out of…HIC!"

The half-obscured figure began to rise, frantic, hiccupping. Hands thrust through the feathers to clutch at the bars, golden rings half-embedded in rolls of fat.

"No, no, NO!" babbled a different voice, in Kens. "Who-ever you are—HIC!—out there, open that door and I'll have the living hide off of you!"

What door?

Going back a step, Jame saw a hinged panel on top of the cage, secured by a latch. From the latter, a string hung down outside the cage, swaying in an errant breeze. She caught it.

The plump hands tried to shake the bars, ineffectually since by now the other's heels had risen well above his head. "An-swer me! Damn—HIC!—you, don't you know who I am?"

"Yes," said Jame, and pulled the string.

The trap door fell open. A riot of wind-borne feathers streamed joyously out of the cage, in its midst a pudgy figure tumbling up into the sky. The angry red clouds swallowed them all. Caldane's wail, trailing after, faded into the distance.

"Damn," said Jame.

The overcast showed no sign of dispersing. So much for the Old Man's boast to blow away the Serpent's weirding breath and so, incidentally, to send Mount Alban home.

Time to move on, quickly, before M'lord's clamor brought Sonny down on her again.

More weaving through the maze, more fissures like ruin-ous, blind fingers groping outward. Finally, here was what she sought: the house of clay slabs.

At first, it seemed as small as when the shaman-elder had built it in the square's eastern corner, no more than a model. As Jame approached, however, it grew. The walls which had appeared so low were half-sunken into the ground and lined by imu faces whose mouths gaped wide enough to swallow her whole. Serpentine forms rioted over the lintel and down the posts. For days, traveling northward up the Riverland, she had caught glimpses of that door standing farther and farther ajar. Now it loomed over her as though over the smallest of children, gaping wide open into darkness.

"E-earth Wife?" she called, flinching at the loudness of her own voice.

An earthy, musky smell flowed out into her face, as if of some animal's lair but massively, indefinably, female. If only Marc were here, as he had been at the lodge in Peshtar. Him, at least, the Earth Wife had liked.

"Mother Ragga?"

A faint voice answered, sounding incredulous: "L-lady?"

Jame frowned. Graykin? What in Perimal's name was he doing here? Eh, no helping it now. She entered.

VI

It took Jame's eyes a moment to adjust to the gloom.

Opposite the door, a fireplace smoked and flared, throwing a fan of uncertain light on the low beams and the sunken floor. Spread out on the latter was the earth map of Rathillien, composed of materials taken from the corresponding parts of that world—hills of rock, fertile plains of black soil, sandy wastes, river and sea beds of stone and coral. With her ear pressed to any of these features, the Earth Wife could hear what was happening far away, as she had the previous winter when Marc had consulted her about events in the Riverland.

The map looked much larger to Jame than it had that day in Peshtar, almost as though she might walk into it here at Kithorn and emerge wherever else on Rathillien she chose. Well, stranger things had happened. But it also looked less stable than it had then, with sections rawly altered—the weirdingstrom's work, perhaps, or the tremors' that had accompanied it.

"Lady!" said Graykin's voice again, almost whining.

A misshapen figure crouched to one side of the hearth, out of the fire's light.

Jame stepped down to the dirt floor and almost lost her balance. At the eastern edge of the map, sink-sand was pouring down as though through a hole in the floor. A nice pitfall for the unwary, she thought. Sidestepping it, she began to circle a room which seemed to have no walls at all, only space opening out to the rim of night, crowded with motionless, watching shapes black against a scattering of stars.

Don't look at them, don't look...

Two pairs of eyes, not one, waited for her by the hearth; not a single shape but two, clinging to each other. She indeed knew that thin, sharp face, although she had never seen it before with so long a nose.

"Why, Graykin," she said, staring. "Where did you get that muzzle, or that tail?"

The Southron showed sharp, white teeth in a snarl. "Don't ask!"

The thin girl with her arms around his neck hugged him tightly, as one would a trusted hound. Her eyes gleamed with a more feral light than his did, but she wasn't the Earth Wife's imp, who had given Jame the imu medallion in Peshtar. Jame snapped her fingers in the girl's face.

"Lyra, do you hear me?"

Caldane's daughter blinked, and smiled. "Oh, here you are! Will things start happening now?"

"Very likely," rumbled a voice on the other side of the hearth.

Someone very large sat there in the shadows. Firelight caught the twisted lines of a chair like a tangle of oak roots. Bone-white splinters flashed and clicked in hands scarcely less gnarled than the chair, or less strong. Jame couldn't yet see what was being knit, except that it appeared to be alive.

"Earth Wife," she said, rising and giving the seated figure her most formal if shaky salute. "Honor be to you and to your halls."

The Earth Wife grunted. "Very pretty. Think you can honey-talk your way out of anything, do you? Not yet caused enough trouble, hey? The map, girl. Look at it."

Jame looked, as another tremor rippled through the fabric of the lodge. On the floor, lengths of the Silver as far away as the Cataracts twitched and shifted. All across the map, seams of unrest stirred, and sink-sand poured down into hungry maws as the Serpent's Brood awoke.

"This is trouble, all right," said Jame, "but I don't understand: are you saying that it's somehow my fault?"

"Had to look you over, didn't we?" the shadowy figure muttered. Her voice was a toothless mumble, but in it lay the strength to gum mountains to dust. "All four of us, here in the north, treading on the River Snake's back…woke him up, didn't we? He thought he'd blown you out of our reach with his weirding breath, down to the Wastes to feed his brothers under the sand, but back you came, and your people with you, just in time to muck up our ceremonies. Now his hunger rouses all the Brood, who may wake the Chaos Serpent itself and so end all. Of course it's your fault."

Jame shook her head to clear it. Index had said that there were reasons for everything, including Mount Alban's journeys. The weirdingstrom—all to flush her out of the Riverland? And the sand which had swallowed her in the Wastes—pouring down some vast, subterranean gullet?

"No. It's too much. How can so many things hinge on me? Why should they?"

"As we are," that great voice grumbled, "so you may become. But there are three of you to our four, and different, so different! If I kill, I also give life, and I abide. That's balance. But you, what are you becoming? Pure destruction, Nemesis! Whose, girl?"

"If the Serpent and its brood belong to Perimal Darkling, perhaps we have the same foe. Is destruction always evil? Earth Wife, I know we haven't behaved well on this world. Our lords can be so arrogant and stupid…! Trinity knows, I seldom act wisely myself. But if your enemy is ours as well, can't we also call Rathillien our home and you our mother?"

Stony silence, on which no seed grows.

"Why are you begging?" Graykin demanded in a low growl. "We're Kencyr, the Chosen!"

"Not this time," said Jame, chagrined. She felt like a whining child who had been pushed contemptuously away. This was so important, and she was handling it so badly.

"All right," she said, collecting herself. "You say this crisis is my fault. Help me to understand it. How can the River Snake be subdued?"

"Feed it."

Damn. "Is the hero at least reborn in its belly?"

"So the Eaten One says, but she seldom gives the same answer twice."

"And the Burnt Man—must he set all the bone-fires ablaze, including the one under Mount Alban?"

"Who knows what charred thoughts flake off that cinder of a brain, or what rules keep its fire banked?"

The Four didn't seem to know much about each other, Jame thought. What an odd way to run a world—if, indeed, that was what they did. Such almost human ignorance. Hmmmm. A maid eaten by the River Snake, an old man falling from a tower...

"Earth Wife, tell us a story. 'There was an old woman...'"

"...who dug her son's grave. And when it was done, he buried her in it. Tcha, men!"

"But she didn't die. Neither did the Eaten One or the Tishooo or—ancestors preserve him—the Burnt Man, by water or wind or fire. Nor you, it seems, by earth. As I may become, so you were: a mortal, transformed. But when, and why? Did it have something to do with our temples suddenly appearing on this world? I know they raised hell with the Tastigon godlings. The New Pantheon arose, feeding off our temples' power, while the Old Pantheon of native forces declined. Was that when Rathillien's essential divinity was precipitated out into the four of you?"

Impatient huffs of wind had been coming down the chimney.

"Hooom!" it now said, as though the flue were clearing its throat, and exhaled a billow of smoke and ash into the room.

Jame slapped at a swarm of sparks determined to nest in her hair. The singed smell triggered a pang, almost, of guilt before the fact: sometime recently, she had overlooked something obvious, perhaps deadly, for someone—but who, and what?

"Huh!" said the wind in the chimney, a short, self-conscious cough that swept smoke from the hearth and made the flames there leap.

The Earth Wife's skirts rustled, or rather the ferns did, that cascaded over the cliff of her knees down to the floor. Between the fronds, as out of hidden caves, bright eyes caught the firelight. Far above, dimly lit, was a face like a granite out-cropping with cavernous eyes and a bird's nest crown of twig-tangled braids.

"Ask a lot of questions, don't you, girl?"

"Uh," said Jame. Her mind had gone blank. Who was she, anyway, to demand answers of this hanging garden that was Rathillien?

The tree-root hands turned their black knitting inside out, around the delicate bones that had served as needles.

"Quip?" said the knit-work, tentatively flexing dark, furry wings. "Quip!"—and scuttled down the Earth Wife's skirt to disappear within its leafy folds. A chorus of welcoming cries greeted it.

"Was that the foxkin that Cattila lost, investigating the weirdingstrom?" Jame asked. "She'll be glad to get it back."

"She is."

Jame shot Lyra a questioning look.

"Yes," whispered the girl. "That's Gran, or was before we got here. Isn't it exciting?"

Another substitution, the Caineron Matriarch for the Merikit "woman" who was to have played the Earth Wife, and now Ragga herself for Cattila. Puzzling was more the word, though, for the relationship between the matriarch and her sometime Ear.

"Does, er, Gran know with whom she's been dealing?"

"Yes," said Cattila, from the other side of the fire.

A log had burst into brief glory. In its glare, the Matriarch perched on the oak-root throne, blinking like a toad, tiny, ar-thritic feet dangling well above the ground.

"Well enough, anyway," she amended, gumming at the ad-mission as though at something not quite palatable. "Ragga hears the most amazing things through earth and stone. Oh, what gossips we two old women have had! That fool Rawneth,

trying to compel and control with her hedge sorcerers and rogue
shamans, when all that's needed is a love of talk—oh, and a
gift or two."

"What gift?" Jame asked, with deep misgivings.

Cattila glowered. "Think I'd do anything to harm our
people, missy? The reverse, if anything. Ragga can only enter
a Kencyr keep by invitation and me, I don't get around as
much as I used to. So I made her my Ear, for both our sakes.
That's all."

"All? To make an outsider privy to the Matriarchs' Council? You didn't even warn them, did you?"

The old woman squirmed. "As if they have much by way
of secrets these days! Anyway, once she's inside, no tricks by
earth or stone work, do they? Ragga has to use her own ears,
like any silly maid, and maybe risk her own silly neck too.
Hasn't figured a way around that one yet, has she? Well, for
once she gets to listen through me."

"As the Eaten One does through Kallystine, the Falling
Man through Caldane, and maybe the Earth Wife's imp through
Lyra. Quite a family affair. I understand your involvement
now, matriarch—more or less—but theirs?"

"Huh. Another damn trick of the weirding, to have put
them in the right place at the wrong time. The Snake's meddling, I'd almost think, if it had the brains. How're Wind and
Water supposed to think straight now?"

"They aren't," said Jame, remembering how both kept losing control of persona and power. "Your kin—our Kencyr
people—have meddled with this world's balance and now we're
confusing its soul. We don't belong on Rathillien, much less
in its sacred space. Only you were invited, matriarch. Only
you know how to play seeker's mask with a god. What are we
going to do?"

The Earth Wife's rumble answered her like distant thunder: "What do you mean, girl, 'we'?"

The fire had sunk. Cattila had melted back into a shadow
which had again become the substance, like a cliff up reared

against the night. No. They were circled by cliffs with a glimmer at their heights, under a roof of southern stars. Ferns sighed. Jame, Lyra and Graykin stood on the pyre's blackened ground, beside a false-fire that was the efflorescence of spores on the bones of a darkling changer.

"Where are we?" demanded Lyra.

Her sharp voice echoed from cliff to cliff, a volley of blows rebounding from rock to flesh to bone.

Jame grabbed both girl and man-dog, a hand clamped over each mouth. "This is the Heart of the Woods at Hurlen," she breathed in their ears. "This is killing ground. For pity's sake, shut up."

As debris rattled down from above, pale imu faces weathered out of diamantine emerged all around the summit, half obscured by vines as though by hanging hair. The Earth Wife's indignant voice muttered down from all their gaping mouths.

"Look at the mess you've made in my heart—just look! Fire and fungus, death and decay… Give me one reason, Nemesis, why I should let you leave this place alive."

"Well, there is this," said Jame, almost apologetically. "If you shout me to death, Lyra will die too, for which her Gran will hardly thank you."

"Ohhh!" Lyra said, not listening. She had picked something up from the ashes.

"Nice of you to remember me as well," Graykin snarled. "A fine lot you've involved me with!"

"And you such an innocent. I did warn you, Gray."

A tremor made them all stagger. If Ragga's heart lay here at the Cataracts, so did the River Snake's, in strong contention. The shaking had set loose spores like a cloud of sparks from the changer's bones, diminishing the false-fire glow. When it died, they might well find themselves stranded.

(But oh, what was it about bones and fire that she couldn't quite remember?)

"Look," she said, scrambling after her wits. "Here and now, I am not the problem."

"THIEF."

"Present," said the Earth Wife's imp, out of Lyra's mouth. Grinning, she thrust the ash-covered imu medallion into Jame's hand.

Jame stared at it. Her first thought when she had searched the Heart earlier had been right: the imu had fallen near the center of the hollow; but she hadn't considered that its sheath of changer's skin might resist the pyre's flames, much less that it would restore clay as it would have flesh. For whatever reason, the imu was whole again.

Lyra blinked, the feral light fading from her eyes.

"And that," said Jame, gesturing at her, "is exactly how I acquired the damned thing in the first place: as a gift from your imp. Here."

"You make me a present of my own property?" Despite everything, greed crept into that gravel voice, Ragga's master passion beneath the Earth Wife's stone. She leaned forward out of her root-chair, drawing them back to lodge and hearthside by her covetousness. "If I give you Mother Ragga's favor, girl, what will you give me? Eh?"

"I-I don't know," said Jame. The Earth Wife might be offering her exactly what she had begged for before in vain, or "favor" might mean the medallion itself. Either way, she understood from Cattila the importance of exchanged gifts. "What do you want?"

"Mmmm. You left behind more than one mess, girl."

Ragga nodded toward the hearth, where a moment ago the darkling false-fire had danced at the Heart's core. They might almost still have been there: on the iron fire-back in high relief was wrought a pattern of fern fronds that seemed to wave in the flickering light. Among them, motionless, crouched a grotesque figure, without a head—the changer whom Kin-Slayer had decapitated.

"It's been long ages since I last had a pet. On the whole, though, I'd prefer one able to hear—say, a dog. Give me yours."

Graykin cringed.

Jame gulped. To lose the Earth Wife's favor in any sense of that word could be disastrous, for the entire Kencyrath. If Rathillien became actively hostile, they had no place to go except back into Perimal Darkling. And if they did finally defeat the shadows that lurked there, what was the point without a home to return to—for, as with the hills above Kithorn, she doubted that her people would ever live on the fallen worlds again. Compared to all that, what was the life of one scruffy half-breed?

Then she meet Graykin's scared eyes, and sighed.

"The only ears I have to offer," she said, turning to Ragga, "are my own. For whatever good that is to you."

But there was that nagging fear again: if she made a present of herself to the Earth Wife, she would be letting someone down (who?) by not warning him (of what?) Fire, bones... Sweet Trinity, Index! The old fool still had a Burnt Man's bone in his pocket.

"I'll be right back," she said, and ran for the door.

"The map!" cried Ragga behind her.

But Jame had already stepped on the nearest rocky ridge. A blast of cold air hit her in the face. Through watering eyes, she saw white peaks spread out before her under the sliver of a moon and under her leading foot, a sheer drop. Over and down, falling, stepping on a rocky slope among bitter scented flowers, floundering in a morass among flies, stumbling up a hill...

"...sorry, sorry, sorry..."

The Earth Wife's voice roared after her like an avalanche: "GirrRRLL...!"

...treading on the River Snake's back...

Icy water up to the knee. The Silver's bed twisted under foot, throwing her sky high in a moon-spangled spray. Beneath, she saw another mountain chain, then plains, then the Eastern Sea, leaping up at her. At the water's edge, swallowing it, was the vast maelstrom known as the Maw, a hundred miles across—the mouth of the Chaos Serpent itself? For a moment, she thought that she would fall into it, but it was dirt onto which she crashed: the lodge floor beyond the eastern edge of the map, where sink-sand poured down as if into a hole. Still, the ground rippled under her like water, while the beams overhead groaned and the nearby steps cracked. Another tremor.

"Woke the River Snake, didn't we?"

If the Four hadn't, she now surely had.

"Nemesis," muttered Ragga, holding down her skirt as its hem seethed with the black wings of terrified foxkin.

"Sorry," said Jame again, staring at the five indentations her feet had left across west and central Rathillien, trying to remember if any cities had lain in her path.

She stumbled up the cracked steps and grabbed the door's edge for support as the lodge shook again. Chittering foxkin streamed into the square over her head. She leaned out after them.

"Index! Take the bone out of your poc...uh!"

A yelp of warning from Graykin, too late: a big hand closed on her collar.

VII

Far away, someone was shouting her name.

Jame tried to follow the voice out of the maze of pain throbbing inside her skull. She must have hit her head. No. Someone had struck it against...against a doorpost. Yes. Jerking her out of the Earth Wife's lodge. Now she was being dragged, her knees banging on uneven pavement. When she opened her eyes, though, the bruising abruptly stopped. Beneath her lay utter darkness. Had she been stricken not only numb but blind? No. Beneath her lay the abyss of a breached sigil, through whose depths even now a ribbon of fire was unrolling.

The moment she had seen it clearly, she was falling—only to be brought up short, half-choked, by the grip on her collar. Her captor jerked her impatiently out of the void and stalked on across pavement marked by charcoal lines which his bare feet scuffed and broke in passing.

"Lady!" Graykin howled somewhere off to the right. "Where are you?"

Obviously, in the square, being hauled by Sonny to the well to serve as snake-bait. Damn.

Jame twisted out of the Merikit's grip and rolled to her feet.

"Can't we discuss this?"

In answer, he lunged at the sound of her voice. She tripped him and ran.

By now, most of the sigils were breached and reeking, the angry pulse in their depths reflecting on the bellies of the low, sullen clouds, red on red. To keep track of where she was had taken a constant, conscious effort. Jame supposed that she must now be somewhere west of the well mouth, unless Sonny had gotten lost. North was to the right, then. Best to get out of the square as quickly as possible, hoping that that, in itself, didn't rupture sacred space. Ancestors knew, she had done sufficient harm already.

Huh. Yes. Bad enough that she'd let herself get stuck in this mess as the most inadequate of Challengers, like a player in the seeker's mask when everyone else had run away. Since then, not only had she failed to win over any of the Four but she had wreaked havoc on the Earth Wife's map and, inadvertently, run off again with her precious medallion. Ragga probably even blamed her for the Caineron involvement, since neither Caldane nor his daughters would have been in the weirding's way if not for her. What rotten luck to have such a trio mixed up in this...

But had it been pure chance? Cattila claimed that the Chaos Serpent and its brood were a primordial part of Perimal Darkling, which had also long sought to make that fallen highlord Gerridon its Voice. If he had become a part of it, perhaps it had gained not only his scheming mind but also his perverse desire to implicate his people in the fall of this world, as he had in that of the previous one. What a tool stupid, ambitious Caldane would be in such a plan—and what a mess they all were in, Kencyr and Rathillien alike, if there truly was a link between Gerridon and the Chaos Serpent.

Ahead, beyond one of the last sigil lines, veils of smoke shifted around upthrust, blackened timbers that loomed like a pair of gigantic, knobby knees. Beneath them, the cinder skull of Tungit's bone-fire rested like a scorched boulder on a pelvic cradle of half-burnt beams.

A current of fresh, cool air stung Jame's eyes, just as the smoke had at first. Inhaling, she saw the quake-ravaged square, its pattern of charcoal lines nearly obliterated by cracks and Sonny's careless stumbling, Kithorn's broken tower still crowned with Mount Alban, and Tungit's small fire a bare twenty feet away. The old shaman himself crouched by his handiwork, a gray, shaggy gnome with anxious eyes. She had forgotten that he and his three colleagues were also in the square, as invisible to her as presumably to their gods.

More fresh air. Through shifting mist, she saw that the torches in the northern corner had been knocked over by the tremors and blue smoke was bleeding out through the gap. There stood the smithy, weirding boiling out of it like smoke from a house on fire. Kirien, Ashe, and Index watched with helpless fascination while a bundle of silver-gilt fur snored at their feet. Index held something black gingerly between forefinger and thumb—the Burnt Man's bone, Jame saw with relief. So, whether he had heard her or not, he'd had the sense to remove that potential inferno from his pocket, if not to let go of it altogether. The old miser.

But if scrollsmen weren't so tenacious, their knowledge would long since have turned to dusty rumor. Instead, Index clung to his morsel of primary research at the risk of his fingers, as single-mindedly as Kirien pursued truth or Ashe defended her humanity with songs full of terrible wisdom. Jame felt sudden gratitude to all three of them, for their basic worth. Perhaps there was a reason to go home after all, not to a place but to a people.

Or perhaps not.

Out of the mist rolling from the smithy's door walked Brier Iron-thorn, grim-faced, carrying Kindrie's limp form. In her dire need she'd had the support of a Knorth, but not the one in whom she had put her trust.

I didn't keep faith, Jame thought. *Neither of us will ever forget that.*

At the Kendar's heels slunk a shaggy form: the Wolver Grimly, terrified, in his complete furs. After him came Torisen Black Lord.

Jame hadn't seen her brother's face at the wolvers' keep. How haggard he looked, shadows under his silver-gray eyes, black stubble blurring the sharp line of his jaw, white fretting his disordered hair. There was white, too, on his right hand. Bandages. Splints. But in his left hand shone bright, naked steel, stained with red light as though already dipped in blood: Kin-Slayer unsheathed.

Oh shit, thought Jame, stopping short.

The earth growled. Flagstones shifted uneasily in their beds, edges grinding together like teeth, pebbles spitting up from the cracks to dance around Jame's feet. The tremors were getting worse. Kithorn wavered in and out of sight as other torches fell to the east, confusing the currents within the square.

Then from the direction of the well came a disgusting noise, half scaly rasp, half wet slobber. Over her shoulder, Jame saw the well's lip rise. Under the green mottling of the serpentine rim was a band as pallid as an earthworm's belly. Then the well mouth jammed back down again, hard.

The concussion sent an earth wave rolling outward. Flagstones tipped and shattered over it like thick ice, throwing Jame from her feet. On the shock surged, rapidly diminishing but still frightful, to scatter the bone-fire and crack the smithy wide open. Torisen tried to catch the doorjamb with his injured hand to steady himself, missed, and fell heavily. Jarred from his grasp, Kin-Slayer skidded into the square. His eyes, following it, met his sister's.

The currents shifted again. Back in sacred space, she saw Tungit's bone-fire overthrown, like the remains of some primordial giant strewn across the earth. Their fall had almost but not quite broken the last sigil, lying black between sacred space and ruin, between her and safety. Kin-Slayer flamed on the other side, out of both her reach and Tori's.

Jame lurched to her feet and turned to circle the obstacle— but here came Sonny stumbling toward her, huge and glowering. Reeking fissures cut her off to right and left. No breath of outside air disturbed the trap in which he had caught her.

Was it one, though? Before, she had only started to fall when she had clearly seen the abyss beneath her.

The Merikit advanced. Jame stepped backward without thinking. Her heel came down on empty space. She fell, mouth open in a yell of terror, eyes screwed shut. The yell became a startled grunt as the up-thrust edges of ancient paving knocked the breath out of her. She was back in real space.

No, don't look… Run.

Impossible, over that shattered terrain. Jame dropped to all fours and scuttled, barking knuckles, banging knees, eyes screwed shut against the shock of each blow, against the urge to check her course. It was less than thirty feet to the north corner of the square. How far wrong could she go?

Far enough.

As she shifted her weight forward, her hand came down on air and she fell. Something stopped her with a blow to the stomach, jarring open her eyes. She was half over the edge of a broad pit. The ridge jammed into her middle was its rim, no longer smooth serpentine but green-mottled and leathery. Just below her hand was a ring of yellowed spikes; below that, red, padded walls studded with down-turned, horny projections. Out of the depths came a rumble and then a hoarse sigh—haaaah—laced with wisps of weirding and an unholy stench.

Jame found herself on her feet, backing away from those scaly lips which had been the well's mouth. The River Snake's empty belly growled again, and the ground shivered.

Behind her, Sonny stumbled out of the smoke. His bare shins, seen through tattered red cloth, were bruised and bloody, likewise his feet. He kept tripping…on the patch of smooth plain between fissures which she saw? No. For him, as for her moments ago, scrambling blind, this was Kithorn's quake-stricken courtyard. He was lurching across broken pavement which she now neither saw nor which would hinder her in a fight. For the first time, the advantage was hers.

But still something made her hesitate. She was remembering all the times in the past when she had been mistaken for easy prey. "A baited trap," her friend Darinby had once called her, too slight for some men to take seriously or to forgive when they found they were wrong. Unlike those bullies, though, Sonny was an overgrown, not very bright child. The scowl distorting his face squeezed all his features toward the center, like those of a small boy in a tantrum. He must have always gotten what he wanted through sheer size and strength. He was trying to bull his way through now, in near panic, against odds he couldn't begin to understand.

Just then, with a startled grunt, the big Merikit toppled forward.

A shift in the air revealed Tungit standing over him, the Burnt Man's cinder skull raised to strike again, if necessary. The other three shaman-elders flickered in and out of sight as they trotted up, goat-udder breasts swaying under gray hair. Jame heard their words in snatches.

"...too ambitious, too dangerous," Tungit was arguing. "...can't even walk the Way of the Four...for the best."

"...you mad?...will make the Challenger the new Favorite, and he isn't Merikit."

"...not even a 'he.'"

"Quiet!...in trouble enough already? Only men...allowed here, so he's a man."

"You are mad! What will Chingetai say? What about next year?"

Graykin would love this, Jame thought. Local politics at their most ruthless: the choosing of a scapegoat. Should she be glad that Tungit preferred to sacrifice Sonny? And what about next year?

Another hungry growl came from the River Snake's belly. The elders looked at each other. Then, with one accord, they grabbed the young man and dragged him, stumbling, dazed, toward the well. Jame found herself in their way.

"No," she said.

They had stopped, staring at her, when, far off to the south, the bone-fires began to ignite.

At first, Jame thought that they were only sparks. Everything was red—the clouds ribbed with flame, the conflagration in the ground, the tongues of lightning flickering between earth and sky—but those distant points of fire multiplied like glowing rubies added to a string, one after another, faster and faster, flashing up the Silver's curve.

The elders had dropped Sonny and were groping frantically for the bells which they had stowed in their goat-udder
breasts. Out came the leather anklets, to be strapped in haste
to skinny legs.

Ching! went the bells as the old men stomped, already far
behind in the count, dancing like maniacs to catch up. *Ching,
ching!* How many bones in all? One hundred? Two? All the
Burnt Man's disjointed body, rising out of the earth in living
flame, out of winter and night...*Ching, ching, ching!*

Jame glanced up at Mount Alban, still hovering ghost-like
above Kithorn's ruined tower, which the quakes had not yet
overthrown. All the old scholars sleeping above, the irreplace-
able knowledge locked in their memories as in the most fragile
of scrolls; and below, waiting for the first spark, the inferno...

The bells jangled to an uncertain halt. The progress of the
fires had stopped.

Why? thought Jame, peering southward. *Where?*

Somewhere between Falkirr and Wilden. Sweet Trinity.
That was where she had removed the Burnt Man's bone from
the Merikit's bonfire.

She found herself counting, as though between lightning
and thunder, to gauge the distance. One, two, three...No more
sparks appeared, but something still might be coming up the
valley in a dark, vengeful rush. Seven, eight, nine...

With a hollow boom, fragments of kindling blew out the
doors and windows of Kithorn's tower to rain down on the
square. Billowing smoke followed. Tungit yelped and kicked
the cinder skull away, its eyes and mouth trailing fire. A faint
cry from Index outside the square echoed him as the old
scrollsman at last perforce gave up his prize.

Jame began to laugh. All that worry about Mount Alban
and she had caused this debacle days ago, without even realizing it. How typical.

Then laughter died.

Black smoke had been pouring from the Burnt Man's skull.
Now it stooped over them under the low, red sky. A sooty

shape half-emerged, as confused as Tungit's scattered fire—
the jut of a knee, a leg bone becoming the knotted ridge of a
spine, smoke streaming down into ribs, gathering in a domed
darkness which rose slowly on a disjointed neck, hollow sockets searching the ground beneath...

From a world away, under the gatehouse, came the welcoming cry of the Burning Ones: "Tha! Tha! Tha!"

Tungit crouched, cowering. The other elders seemed to
have melted into the ground. Jame wished she could.

"What next?" she hissed at the shaman, wondering if he
could understand her as she had him. "It's all gone wrong, but
there's got to be something we can do. Tungit?"

With the return of sacred space, he had disappeared.

Cattila hobbled out of the mist, supported by Lyra, surrounded by darting foxkin. When the latter saw what loomed
over them, they dived inside the old woman's loose outer vest.
She approached, seething physically and mentally.

"A fine mess! Can't anyone do anything right these days?"
The presence above had turned at the sound of her shrill voice,
still blindly seeking. A muted growl as though of distant thunder came out of it. She glared up. "You—burnt-breath!
Where's chief Chingetai?"

Lyra tugged at her sleeve. "Gran!"

"All right, all right. What's the point of a mummery, though,
if the real thing barges in? Faugh! Now the Earth Wife is supposed to present her lover, the new Favorite, to her consort, the
Burnt Man, as their son. Life out of winter and ashes, d'you see?
Spring fertility and frolics. It's called 'fooling death.' Not too
bright, our friend up there. Of course, once in a while he catches
on and the Favorite spontaneously combusts. Charming, eh?"

"Very," said Jame, with another futile tug at the ivy crown.

"Oh!" said Lyra, staring upward.

Above them, the nebulous, smoky skull seemed to be emp-
tying itself out through mouth, eyes, and nostrils. Fat, smudgy
fingers drifted down. A wave of heat preceded them, fetid
with the pyre's breath.

"It wasn't supposed to be like this," Catilla was complaining, oblivious. "We should have lost the Riverland, been forced to mind our own business for a change. Stop tugging at me, girl! Nothing less will save that idiot father of yours. Going to Perimal in a pushcart, that boy, and dragging his house after him..."

The smoke fingers groped toward her rising voice. Foxkin, peeking out through the armholes of her vest, withdrew abruptly. Lyra buried her face in the old woman's gown as smoke brushed over Cattila's face, then slid past, leaving her in soot-smeared, sputtering outrage.

Sonny sprawled in the way. Smoke fumbled blindly around his fallen body, sparks scorching holes in his red pants, singeing his tattooed skin. He twitched. Loosened strands of his red hair rose in the heat's updraft, crinkled, and stank. He would burn as though on his own pyre, alive.

"Tha," breathed the murky air, a croon of hunger. "Thaa, thaaaa..."

"Matriarch," said Jame loudly. "I won the challenge. Present me as the new Favorite."

The smoke rose from Sonny's body and drifted toward her. She went back a step involuntarily but stopped, rigid, as her heel struck the well's rim.

The fingers closed loosely about her in a stifling wave of heat. She held her breath against their stench, as though pressed face to face against the dead. Through streaming eyes, she saw the sparks dance, two by two by two. Not sparks. Eyes: the Burning Ones unleashed and circling hungrily, waiting for the first flinch. She felt them brush against her. Their charred fingers rasped, crumbling, across her face.

Don't move. Don't even blink.

"Burnt Man!" she faintly heard Cattila cry. "Stop messing around! This is the Challenger, triumphant, your true child in destruction, if ever Nemesis was. Now bugger off!"

Breath scorched Jame's ear in wordless protest. A moment more, must have been that hoarse plea; just a moment more...

"Thaaa-HA!"

The command boomed like thunder too close to the lightning strike, a vast impact more felt than heard. The smoke
shredded with a cry, torn away into the distance: "KI-Ki-ki-
iiiii...

Jame gulped air a moment too soon and went off into a
coughing fit. When her eyes cleared, she found herself tottering on the edge of the well, and the Burnt Man standing not a
score of feet away with his head in his hands.

No.

That black thing was the cinder-skull, consumed to a brittle
shell, already crumbling. The charcoal-smeared man let the
pieces fall through his fingers. Through a profusion of singed
braids, he was glaring at the erstwhile Favorite as the latter sat
up with a groan.

"Somehow," Chingetai growled at his son, "this is all your
fault."

What the Merikit chief meant by "all" he immediately made
clear, from Sonny's failures as a mewling baby to his many
shortcomings as a man. It was an epic list, its details honed by
repetition. Its subject rose and listened with a sullen scowl.
The shaman-elders flickered in and out of sight beside their
naked chief, reaching up to pat him as though to calm an enraged stallion.

"Even that," he roared, pointing at Jame, "would make me
a better son!" Then he looked again. "By the Four, who is
that?"

Tungit stood on tiptoe to whisper in his ear.

"My new what? The Burnt Man approved?" He made a
half-choked protest as though at a world gone mad and tore at
his hair. A scrawny right-hand braid, burned through near the
root, came away in his grasp.

Out of the well rose a low, impatient growl, and the ground
shivered. One rite might have failed, thought Jame, stepping
hastily back from the quaking edge, but not the more important one. Not yet. The River Snake still hungered.

"You see?" Chingetai thundered at his son, brandishing the plait. "This was yours, started with four hairs on the day of your birth." He threw it into the shaft. The earth swallowed it, muttering, unappeased. "You're dead, boy, discarded by the Burnt Man and by me. Now do what you were born for: Jump down that damn well!"

In the midst of this denunciation, Graykin appeared breathless beside Lyra and Cattila, clutching Kin-Slayer. Jame was staring at him when Sonny grabbed her by the arms and swung her out over the well mouth.

"No!" she and the Southron cried simultaneously, he at Sonny, she at him as he stumbled forward, swinging up the sword.

Too late. With a butcher's dull thunk, the war-blade sank into the Merikit's side. Sonny staggered, and dropped Jame.

She fell a dozen feet down the well's throat before her nails caught on its red wall. The surface shuddered and bled as she hung from it. Her boots skidded on its slime. From below came a swift up-rush of foul air—haaaAAA...—and a sense of something vast, rising fast.

Her foot gained purchase on a down-turned projection, then another. She clawed her way between the stained spikes, feeling the wall begin to bulge as its sheath of muscles contracted. Here at last was the lip...

And there stood Sonny, swaying, arms wrapped around himself to stop a tide of blood. Graykin had somehow disengaged Kin-Slayer and fallen back, aghast. From the dumbfounded look on the Merikit's face, he couldn't believe that such a thing had happened—to him, of all people. In shock, he hadn't yet felt the bite of his own death.

"HaaAAAAA...!" said the River Snake rising, ravenous, to the smell of blood.

The rim surged upward. Jame launched herself off of it, over Sonny's head, into Graykin's arms, nearly onto the sword. As they rolled, a terrible impact bounced them off the ground and down again, hard, in a cloud of dust. Into the ringing

Seeker's Mask

silence which followed came a shrill but oddly muffled sound: a scream that seemed to go on and on, until a rasping slurp cut it short.

All too close, something massive scraped over stones...questing? No. Receding, gone with a viscous gulp as the earth swallowed it back.

"Another fine lot...you've involved me with..." Graykin gasped, choking on the dust-thick air.

"So quit! Or at least...get off of me. Matriarch? Lyra?"

Coughs answered her, then Lyra's voice, shaking and piteous: "Here, both of us. Will things please stop happening now?"

Perhaps they would. The last upheaval had overthrown all the remaining torches and the blue smoke had dispersed. The square was left quake-wracked, still partly obscured with dust, under red clouds beginning to unravel with dawn. Had everyone really come through this alive? No. Beside the well was a circular indentation as wide as the well mouth and two spans deep. The pavement inside had been crushed almost to powder. At its center, however, in solitary splendor, were a pair of large, hairy feet, sheared raggedly off at the ankles.

A rumble not unlike a belch came from the depths. A hero had fed the Snake to save the world.

"I hope he gives you gas," said Jame.

VIII

"Friend or foe?"

Jame's heart jumped at the sound of her brother's voice behind her. For a moment, she thought he meant her, but then she turned and saw that he was looking down at the orphaned feet.

"Neither, really. Just someone in the wrong place at the right time."

"Somehow, I'm not surprised." He surveyed the surrounding ruins. "Your friend Marc warned me that I would probably find the Riverland reduced to rubble and you in the midst of it, looking apologetic."

"Er, sorry."

A winter of things waiting to be said, and that was all she could manage before this cool, strangely elegant man who was her brother. She could feel him withdrawing into the mantle of the Highlord's power, out of reach. Even now, he wouldn't deal with her twin to twin if he could help it.

Then he saw her face, and the mask of his expression slipped.

"Oh." Despite himself, he raised a splinted finger as if to touch her scarred cheek. "I dreamt…"

A noise made him turn sharply, his uninjured hand leaping to the empty sheath at his side.

Graykin stumbled out of the dust. Narrow face set and ashen, he looked more like Genjar's death banner than ever—a bastard Caineron, clutching Kin-Slayer in his dirty hands.

Torisen went white under his dirt and stubble. "Treason!" he said, in a deep, hoarse voice. Terrified, the Southron fell back before him, unsteadily raising the sword's blood-stained point.

Jame slipped between them. "Tori, no!" She seized her brother's arms, feeling a strength in them far beyond her own. "The bolt is shot!"

He blinked at her, confused and suddenly—frighteningly— vulnerable. "What bolt?"

Impossible to explain, then or perhaps ever, that she had barred a door in his soul-image against their father's madness. Enough that he had asked in his own voice, not in Ganth's.

Graykin had knelt, face averted but with a wary look askance, to offer Kin-Slayer hilt first—a dedicated sneak, embarrassed to find himself in so prominent a position.

"Company," said Jame softly.

On the far side of the indentation stood Chingetai. His shaman-elders huddled about him, their helpers, including the erstwhile Challenger, close behind them in a gray, wary clot. The chief was staring at Kin-Slayer. The Knorth war-blade had come into these hills before, in different hands, to leave stories repeated for generations. Neither he nor his followers were armed at all except for Ashe's confiscated staff.

Still, they outnumbered the Kencyr more than two to one.

Torisen accepted Kin-Slayer and turned to face the Merikit, casually grounding the sword's point. Sonny's blood ran down its blade to form a small puddle at his feet. Jame had fallen back a step to his side. The brush of a furry shoulder against her leg heralded the arrival of the Wolver. The shift upward of the Merikits' eyes told her where Brier Iron-thorn had come to stand behind Torisen, and an unbreathing coldness at her back announced Ashe. Graykin scuttled to the rear, where Index and Kirien could be heard greeting him with surprise.

The two front lines regarded each other warily.

"All right," said Torisen quietly. "I'm open to suggestions."

"Can you use that thing one-handed?" Grimly muttered up at him out of the corner of his mouth.

"You've got Father's ring on your sword-hand," Jame said, "and Kin-Slayer has just tasted life's-blood. I'd be careful, if I were you, what you swing at."

He shot her an impatient look. "You can't mean that it's all a trick, as simple-minded as that. Anyway, how in Perimal's name would you know?"

Jame grimaced. "The same way as usual: trial and error."

Chingetai suddenly launched into a speech. At first, his attention still fixed on the sword, he inclined to preoccupation. Soon, however, he hit his normal, loud stride, with a piping echo from the back row where Index translated in paraphrase.

The Kithorn massacre of eighty years ago was mentioned, with the implication that it had been the fault of its misguided victims. Marc's collection of the resulting blood-price nearly sidetracked the Merikit, but after a brief boggle he plowed on, gaining vehemence.

"What is all this in aid of?" Torisen asked over his shoulder.

"Hush! He's finished with ancient history."

Chingetai jumped into the depression.

"It's all his fault!" he roared in Merikit, scooping up and brandishing his son's truncated remains.

What followed, up to a point, was the same denunciation as before, not at all hindered by Sonny's inability to hear it. Although sacred space had departed, Jame found that she didn't need Index's gleeful translation to understand; therefore, she knew what Chingetai was saying even when the old scrollsman broke off and began apparently to choke.

"No!" she cried, chagrined to discover that her new knowledge of Merikit didn't extend to speaking it. "Index, tell him that that's impossible!"

His indictment of Sonny's feet concluded, Chingetai seemed momentarily at a loss what to do with them. Then, with a shrug, he tossed them into the well and clambered out of the indentation. Jame fell back a step as he limped toward her, all fear of Kin-Slayer forgotten, a broad grin splitting his blackened face. She had barely time to note that under the charcoal much of his skin was tattooed when she found herself swept up in a bear hug that made her ribs creak.

"No, no, no!" Index was gabbling as he clung onto Tori's sword-arm.

Hearing Brier's quick footstep behind her and a growl from the Wolver, Jame made a flailing gesture for them to hold back. "It isn't—umph!—what you think!"

The next moment she had been dropped to regain her breath as best she could while the Merikit swept out of the courtyard after their chief. On the way, they nearly ran into Cattila and Lyra but skirted them, glaring. Jame remembered the Merikit trophy skins in Caldane's apartment.

Meanwhile, Index had collapsed into another coughing fit, which turned out to be laughter.

"A Kencyr girl, foisted on Chingetai as the new Favorite, his heir for the year! And what does that madman do to save face and get his people safely away? Declares her his new son, to take that young idiot's name and fill his boots—for which, ancestors know, he has no further use. What do you say to that, hey?"

"Only this," said Jame, glowering: "If that man expects me to earn any right-hand braids, he's in for a long wait."

"Hoo!" The old scrollsman wiped his eyes and nose, both of which had run copiously. "There is this, though: we're still on Merikit land. Chingetai has gone to raise his village. He'll be back as soon as he can with the whole tribe to kill us all—except you, of course, favorite son. Time we are leaving."

High time, thought Jame, looking up.

Mount Alban showed through rifts, its exposed inner walls glimmering ghostly silver in the gray dawn. The red-lit clouds had begun to disperse, the fire within them dying with the onset of summer's first day. The weirdingstrom was finally breaking up. The college was about to depart.

Below, glowing wisps trickled out of the broken shell of the smithy. In the back by the forge, where the chimney still upheld the rear wall and part of the roof, weirding light shone briefly as though seen through an open door.

A dark figure moved against it, then came forward, brushing tendrils of mist from white, desert gear with a silken handkerchief.

"Well, really!" said Adric, Lord Ardeth, surveying the shattered courtyard with fastidious distaste.

IX

"My boy, are you quite sure that you're all right?"

"Yes, Adric," Torisen said patiently, for the third or fourth time in as many minutes. He wiped Kin-Slayer on Ardeth's proffered handkerchief and sheathed it, to everyone's ill-concealed relief. "You seem almost disappointed."

Shamelessly eavesdropping with Lyra at her elbow, Cattila chortled at Ardeth's protest. Even from the far side of the well, Jame had heard the wistful note in the old man's voice. A mad Highlord would have been easier to manage than her unpredictable brother, given his family penchant for absurd situations.

This time, though, it seemed to her that the Ardeth had rivaled the Knorth. Adric had been explaining, with a shade less than his usual aplomb, how he had been overtaken in the Southern Wastes by the weirdingstrom. Why he had been there in the first place, he hadn't cared to make quite clear, except that he had apparently expected to find Torisen there before him. Finding Index's herb shed instead had inclined him to question his own sanity, nor was he particularly grateful for the timely shelter which it had provided.

"I don't know how long we were storm-bound in that wretched little shack," he was saying peevishly, while Index sputtered with indignation in the background. "Two days, at least. As well to have been lost at sea in a closed dinghy, all groaning timbers and swaying herbs and seams leaking mist. My Kendar servants were hideously sick. Then we fetched up where Mount Alban should have been and I, at last, emerged, only to be swept up again by more weirding. Someone in it was calling your name, my boy. Such a forceful voice! I simply followed it here."

That would be Brier Iron-thorn, thought Jame, now with the Wolver on Kithorn's crumbling battlements, keeping watch northward for the Merikits' imminent return.

She wondered if she would ever win back the cadet's trust. After this, Brier would return to Tentir to resume her ten-command and training, no doubt glad to put this whole insane adventure behind her. Perhaps she would eventually become one of the great randon, whose memories live in song for generations. She had the potential. But she was also as much a prisoner of her past as Jame had been of hers—no, more, since Brier only knew how to fight what the Caineron had done to her with their own weapons of cold distrust.

What things we could teach each other, thought Jame.

Then with a jolt she remembered that Bane had once said something similar to her. What wisdom had she to impart less dark than his? The best thing she could do for Brier Iron-thorn, probably, was to leave the Kendar alone.

As for herself, though, what now?

Kirien and Ashe had withdrawn to the edge of the courtyard where Kindrie lay in dwar sleep with Jorin curled snoring in his arms. The scholars' low voices had half-woken the ounce, through whom Jame had overheard a conversation never meant for her.

"So you didn't try a test after all," the Jaran Lordan had said to the haunt singer. When the latter hadn't replied, Kirien had stared hard at her for a moment and then sworn under her breath. "So that was it. According to the old songs, only a Kencyr can destroy a Tyr-ridan. When you pointed Jame out to Sonny, you thought that he would prove she was a false nemesis by killing her. Trinity, Ashe, that's cold-blooded...and lame-brained. His failure doesn't establish anything, except that she's damned lucky."

"Next time," the haunt had muttered, "I'll do better."

Even her own people wanted her dead. No wonder she felt safer with the well mouth between her and any of them.

Seeker, seeker...

She had thought that it was enough to drop the mask, to be only herself. But who was she?

Maybe she should complete her withdrawal, run away to become the "son" that the Merikit Chingetai had proclaimed her, the first Kencyr in eighty years with free license to roam these hills. Jorin would love that.

Yes, but then what would she do about Graykin, now skulking around the edges of the courtyard as if afraid either to draw more attention to himself or to be left behind?

And if she did flee up into the hills, whom might she encounter there? According to Merikit beliefs, she was now also the Burnt Man's son, or was that the Earth Wife's lover, or both? This was getting not only complicated but potentially messy.

Anyway, Mother Ragga must still think of her as a thief. That damn imu. She took the medallion out of her pocket, as always feeling its power tingle unpleasantly through both her gloves and its covering of changer's skin. But this time something had been added to it. Eyes, mouth, ears...

Ears, framing the crude imu face like bits of leathery, dried fruit.

"If I give you Mother Ragga's favor, girl, what will you give me?"

Not Graykin's ears or her own, after all, but the imu's, to be carried into Kencyr houses where the Earth Wife feared to go, to listen for her as she had for Cattila at Gothregor...

"Is that it, Ragga?" Jame whispered into one of the shriveled flaps. "Have I your favor after all?"

The imu's lips moved against her face. She jerked the medallion away, unsure if it had meant to bite or kiss.

"We'll just have to see, then, won't we?" she muttered, slipping it back into her pocket.

A descending cry and a great splash drew all eyes to the basin at the square's western corner. In it floundered a great welter of wet skirts, making angry noises. Out of this confusion emerged Kallystine. Waterweeds crowned her straggling hair and inch-long catfishlings cascaded from her clothes. She clawed a slimy caul from her face. Under it, her wet mask clung to her features with unbecoming fidelity.

Lyra, after a moment's open-mouthed gawk, burst out laughing.

By then, Kallystine had caught sight of Torisen. However, her half-sister's laughter made her pause, furious, to try ineffectually to set herself to rights.

Torisen had also recognized her, with difficulty and dismay.

His expression would have amused Ardeth, except that as the old lord's gaze had swept across the square toward the newcomer, he had for the first time noticed Jame on the other side of the well. Fifteen decades had made his far-sight unusually keen. Still, he hesitated to believe what he saw.

"My dear boy! That can't be…but the family resemblance…it is!"

"What?" said Torisen, his attention wrenched from the sight of his consort angrily shaking fish out of her bodice. "Oh. Yes, I'm afraid so."

"But, but this is appalling! A Highborn lady in this place, barefaced, in that indecent garb… See here, my boy, this must never become common knowledge! When I think how difficult it was to explain away your eccentric departure from Kothifir…"

"How did you, by the way?"

"During my years as a diplomat, I earned a singer's right to the Lawful Lie. I told the High Council that trouble in the north demanded your immediate attention, which seems, after all, to have been no more than the truth. I tell you, though, your reputation won't survive another scandal!"

"But you just said that you successfully concealed my, er, eccentricity," said Torisen, a glint coming into his eyes which his old friend would have done well to notice. "As for our reputation, everyone knows we Knorth are as mad as a gelded rathorn, to use Harn's elegant phrase."

But Ardeth wasn't listening. The Highlord's affairs had obviously gotten out of hand, as he had always predicted they

would, and must be saved by an older, wiser head. If he felt
satisfaction that events could finally be turned to his own advantage, he dismissed the thought. After all, it only made
sense that Knorth honor should be saved and his young friend's
position strengthened by an alliance between their two houses.
If his son Pereden wasn't alive to oblige, grandsons were. It
only remained to decide which.

Torisen tried to stem this tide of plans, without so much
as fully getting the old lord's attention. He himself impatiently
brushed aside Kallystine when she swept down on him, her
remaining charms in full if dank display.

"Lady, please. Not now."

Kallystine recoiled with a venomous hiss. "Jameth. Always Jameth…"

She swung back her hand to slap him. In her palm, steel
flashed.

"No!" Jame cried, starting forward, but she was much too
far away.

Lyra caught her sister's back-flung arm, pulling her off-
balance and bearing her to the ground. Kallystine's hand, striking the pavement, sprang wide open.

"Why," said Ardeth, staring, "that's a razor-ring."

"You slapped my sister," said Torisen slowly, "with that."

Lyra hastily rolled away. Kallystine was left crouching like
a toad in her sodden finery, mask askew, perfect teeth bared
behind wrinkled lips. The Highlord stood over her.

"Caineron," he said, in a voice through which the cords of
his power ran like steel. "I curse you and cast you out. Never
come near me or mine again."

His words drove her backward, yammering, on hands and
knees. Then she was on her feet and would have bolted out of
the courtyard if Cattila hadn't stood in her way. The Caineron
Matriarch opened her voluminous vest, dislodging foxkin, and
wrapped her great-great-granddaughter in it.

"There, there," she said as Kallystine buried her face against
her ancient bosom and burst into tears. "There, there." Her

rheumy eyes met Torisen's over the bowed head, power speaking to power. "A poor, disgraced thing, Highlord, but of my blood. I will care for her."

"That was well done," said Jame softly to Lyra. "You'll need a new title soon: 'Lack-wit' doesn't seem so appropriate anymore."

"Actually, it is," Lyra whispered back. "Tackling Kallystine like that, it wasn't exactly on purpose: I...sort of tripped."

"Huh. Just the same, in future I'd keep out of M'lady's way if I were you."

"Now what?" Torisen demanded.

They all heard it: another shriek that seemed to plummet out of the sky, although no one saw any falling body. It ended with a crash. At the southern corner of the square, the wicker cage which had held the Tishooo had been smashed flat. On its ruins sprawled a fat, glittering figure. Graykin ducked out of sight as Lord Caineron sat up with a groan. Ardeth went to help him rise under the weight of his golden accouterments which, nonetheless, had not prevented the Tishooo from carrying him off. He rewarded the old lord's assistance with a blurry snarl.

As the two made their way back across the broken pavement, Jame decided that, shaken and confused as Caldane undoubtedly was, he would have been much more so if he'd had a clear memory of the past few hours. For him and Kallystine both, their possession respectively by the Falling Man and the Eaten One must now seem like bad dreams, rapidly fading.

Meanwhile, Ardeth was taking this opportunity to inform Caldane about the new alliance, making "Jameth" sound at best a poor bargain. If he hoped to slip this news past the lord of Restormir when he was in no state to protest, however, he underestimated the Caineron will, if not the wits.

"Wha' do you mean, a contract with your house?" Caldane demanded, stopping short. "The young fool's already contracted to my daughter, isn't he? Can't keep his hands off her."

"Not with Torisen. With his sister. Anyway, M'lady Kallystine has, er, rather badly disgraced herself. She just tried to slash the Highlord with a razor-ring. In front of witnesses. I'm afraid," Ardeth added smoothly, with no evident sorrow, "that he had quite sufficient grounds to cast her off."

"What?" Glaring around him, Caldane caught sight of his daughter cowering in Cattila's arms and advanced on her. "Here, girl, what's all this nonsense, and what in Perimal's name has happened to your face?"

"You, boy," said the Caineron Matriarch, stopping her great-grandson in his tracks. "Leave be. This business is mine."

Caldane turned, shaking his head like a bull that had charged a sapling and hit an oak. His blood-shot eyes fell on Lyra. He grabbed her arm. "Then here's younger meat, Knorth, good enough for the likes of you. She even comes to you unbroken. You laughed at me for contracting her to that Karkinoran princeling, but I wasn't fool enough to grant him full rights."

He shoved the terrified girl into the Highlord's arms, jarring the latter's splinted fingers. Torisen swallowed a grunt of pain. Over Lyra's head, his eyes met his sister's. It had come into both their minds simultaneously that Lyra didn't know what being "broken" meant.

"Don't be afraid," he said to the girl gently and put her aside.

"Not the Highlord," Ardeth repeated patiently, "Jameth."

Caldane, following his gaze, flinched. "Oh, my God! Not her." Then, in a surprising act of self-control, he pulled himself together. "That is to say, yes, of course she must be contracted out—to a Caineron. In my house, we know how to keep women in their place…"

"Ha!" said Cattila.

"…and believe me, that one needs it."

On this, the two lords agreed. Then they fell into a wrangle over Jame's disposition which, from its abbreviated points, must have summarized all their previous arguments.

Torisen rubbed his eyes, looking suddenly exhausted.

Jame wondered why he didn't just tell them to mind their own business. Then she realized that it wasn't this squabble alone but a winter's worth of them which had worn him down and now threatened to grind out the sparks of his authority. Not knowing what to do about her, he couldn't fight them. At stake here was not only her fate but that of the Kencyrath: would its Highlord rule, or be ruled by the self-interest of such men as these?

"Listen!" came the Wolver's yelp from the battlements.

His ears, keener than theirs, had caught the sound first, but in a moment they all heard it: a distant, bone-jarring throb of drums. The Merikit were coming.

"What these people do to captives," said Index, "you really don't want to know. Believe me, we need to get out of here."

"Well, I and mine won't," snarled Caineron. "Not without a decision! Knorth, you've danced around this long enough. To whose house do you send your sister?—and if it isn't to mine, be prepared for war!"

"Oh, really," said Ardeth. "Caldane, I keep telling you: it's already decided. My grandson Dari will probably be the best choice," he added, thinking out loud. "His breath may smell like a rotten eel, but no woman ever contradicts him twice."

With that, they were off again, the chance of an imminent, messy death secondary to their winter-long obsession.

Graykin sidled up behind Jame. "Let them stay," he hissed in her ear. "We can go."

Then he ducked away again as Torisen shot him an annoyed glance.

"Who is that person anyway, and what does he mean, 'we'?"

"Gran?" said Lyra, in a small, frightened voice.

Cattila shook her head. Although she had faced Caldane down in a woman's matter, now they were bound by his word.

"We won't leave you," Torisen said, turning back to them.

Kirien cleared her throat. "Highlord, it sounds to me as if the Ardeth and the Caineron are deadlocked. May I suggest an alternative? 'Lordan' is an ancient title applied to either the male or female heir of a lord. Nothing in the law forbids the latter, as I've told you before. Since then, my research has progressed. By ancient custom, the heir always has the status of a man, and 'he' doesn't form any contracts before coming of age at twenty-seven. Why don't you take a lesson from the Merikit Chingetai? He's made your sister his son; likewise, you can declare her your lordan."

Caineron gaped, then sputtered with laughter.

Ardeth smiled. "You academicians will have your little jokes."

"The joke," Index snapped, "is that we should be debating this now."

Indeed, they were all aware of the approaching uproar. "Boom-wah! Boom-wah!" The Merikit could hardly be accused of stealth.

"There are about two hundred of them," Brier reported, coming up with the Wolver close on her heels. "They're bringing fire. Highlord, this is not a defensible position."

From far above, in Mount Alban's tower, a voice trained to carry floated down: "Will you please stop that racket? People up here are trying to sleep!"

"That does it," said Torisen. "Kiri, I accept your suggestion."

"Mad!" Caldane exclaimed, staring. "D'you hear that? Raving mad!"

"Really, my boy, this farce has gone on long enough…"

"There is this too," said Ashe. "Traditionally…the Knorth Lordan trains at Tentir to become a randon."

Was the haunt singer proposing another test? If so, the only way Jame saw to pass it was to get herself killed by some enraged randon. Or Tori might wring her neck on general principles. Instead, after a moment's blank surprise, he looked thoughtful. Sweet Trinity. Could he actually be considering

the idea? It would buy time, and give him an excuse to drop
her as his heir if she failed. It took Ardeth, however, to make
up his mind.

"My dear, dear boy," said the old lord, with an air of much
tried patience, "you simply cannot..."

"I can do anything which the law allows and custom ap-
proves. This seems to be covered by both. And I'm tired of
you or anyone else trying to run my life. Understood?"

He looked at Jame, with a sudden, wry smile. "When I
was a boy, serving the Ardeth, I would have given anything to
become a cadet at Tentir. But Adric forbade it."

"You know it was impossible!" the old lord protested.
"Why, if anyone had so much as suspected who you were before you came of age..."

"So you told me, Adric, when you dismissed my request as
if it were a child's whim. So I lost my chance. Now, it seems,
my sister is to have hers—if she wants it. Do you?"

"Yes," said Jame. "Very, very much," and burst out laughing at Brier Iron-thorn's expression.

"Right. Then I assume that we can leave. Caldane?"

Caineron glowered at him. What an ugly face that man
had when he was thwarted, Jame thought—or anytime else,
for that matter. "No doubt, as always, you think you've been
very clever. Well, Knorth, if your 'lordan' can enroll at Tentir,
so can mine, and it's my war-chief's turn to serve as the college commandant. So we'll just see, won't we?"

Torisen sighed. "I suppose we will. About all sorts of things.
In the meantime, if I've understood this correctly, our way home
lies above Kithorn's tower. My lords and ladies, will it please
you to climb? I shouldn't dawdle about it either, if I were you."

They didn't, taking Kindrie's limp form with them, Graykin
skulking behind, with an anxious glance at his mistress as he
sidled past her.

At Kithorn's front door, Jorin draped over her shoulder
and snoring in her ear, Jame had paused to look northward
over the battlements. The Merikit were flowing toward Kithorn

between dark hills, torches flaring in the gloom beneath dawn-lit clouds. Drums echoed back from the mountain slopes above:

"BOOM-Wah-wah... BOOM-Wah-wah..."

It looked more like a procession than an attacking force.

The Merikit would undoubtedly kill any trespassers whom they caught, but Jame didn't think that their chief really wanted to catch anyone. Even someone so flamboyant must feel, as Lyra did, that Summer Eve had already provided enough excitement. If Chingetai had known that the Caineron lord was here as well as his womenfolk, he might have felt differently.

And how did she feel about all the strange things which she had learned concerning the Merikit gods (if that was what one called the Four) and Rathillien itself? If even half of it was true, the Kencyrath had totally misjudged this world and their relationship to it. Two years ago, in Tai-tastigon, the mere suggestion of such a thing would have half-panicked her. Now she felt an old, familiar excitement: there was so much to learn and, thanks to Chingetai, such a wonderful opportunity to do it.

Last up the steps, Torisen stopped beside her. "You can't go back to the Riverland wearing that." He disentangled the ivy crown from her hair and threw it away. "Next Midsummer Day, the Merikit will expect you to return here. Of course, you won't."

Jame didn't answer.

She had wondered what to tell her brother, about not only the Merikit but also the strange things going on among his own people. Nothing, she decided, unless he specifically asked. The scrollsmen were right: Knowledge was power. She would need much more of both to survive, lordan or not, as long as Torisen could reduce her to nothing again with a word if it suited him.

The clouds over Kithorn still simmered red, but they were beginning to lift and disperse. Soon the Tishooo would return to blow them away and Mount Alban southward with them. To the east, over the Snowthorns, a sickle thin crescent moon rose barely before the sun.

Torisen remembered how he and his sister had watched it rise over the trees at the Cataracts, the two of them reunited after so long and such strangers to each other.

"This is going to be hard," he had said. "For both of us. But we'll find a way to make it work. We have to."

That was still true, and no easier than it had been before. He felt as if events had out-paced him, too much happening too fast and he too little in control.

"The moon is waning toward the dark," he said somberly. "I should have known about Caldane's man being in charge of Tentir now. Did you know how our father came to power? His older brother, the Knorth Lordan, was killed in training at Tentir. The college has its own rules. If you're…hurt there, I can't even demand your blood-price."

It was on the tip of his tongue to renounce his offer. What was it but madness to think that any Highborn girl could become a randon? At best, she would fail and make them both laughingstocks. At worst… But he had proposed this before his oldest friend and worst enemy. To back down would look like weakness. He couldn't afford that, and his sister knew it. He heard it in her silent refusal to protest or point out the obvious. Her strength frightened him.

Your Shanir twin, boy, your darker half, returned to destroy you…

No. He wouldn't listen. The bolt was shot.

The sun raised a blazing rim over the mountains' spine, striking him momentarily blind.

"The moon may wane," said the darkness beside him that was his sister, "but this is also sunrise on the first day of summer. Warm days and new life. You've earned that, and so have I. Let the bastards take them from us if they can."

Then she laughed and whistled, a clear, soaring note. The wind came as if in answer. Its wings brushed his face as he blinked to clear his tired eyes—or was that her fingertips in a phantom caress?

"Here's Old Man Tishooo at last. Come on, brother. Let's go home."

Author's Biography

Pat Hodgell can't remember a time when she wasn't passionately interested in science fiction and fantasy. "'David Star' Space Ranger by Paul French was the first novel with which I fell in love, so much so that I started making my own copy of the library book, long-hand in a spiral notebook, complete with a carefully drawn facsimile of the frontispiece. Long afterward, I cam across a paperback reprint and learned that my beloved 'Paul French' was none other than the ubiquitous Issac Asimov."

Over the years, as her interest grew, Pat collected piles of paperback science fiction and fantasy novels and comic books. Soon, however, reading and collecting genre fiction wasn't enough for her and, after college, she began to write it as well.

"It would be nice to say that, after the long suppression of the writing impulse, the dam burst—but it didn't. Due to lack of practice, I simply didn't know how to put a story down on paper." Pat began to learn, however, and by the next summer she had several stories finished and an invitation to the Clarion Writer's Workshop. "There, for the first time, I found a whole community of people like me—storytellers, wordsmiths, an entire family I never knew I had," Pat says of the Clarion experience. "Even more wonderful, here suddenly were professionals like Harlan Ellison and Kate Wilhelm telling me that I could indeed write. I could hardly believe my luck." She made her first professional sale two years later. Since then, she's sold stories to such anthologies as *Berkley Showcase*, *Elsewhere III*, *Imaginary Lands*, and the *Last Dangerous Visions*. Pat has also published three novels: *God Stalk*, *Dark of the Moon*, and *Seeker's Mask*, all part of an on-going fantasy saga concerned not only with high adventure, but also with questions of personal identity, religion, politics, honor, and arboreal drift.

Both of Pat's parents are professional artists. Other reputed ancestors include a decapitated French Huguenot, a sheep thief tried by Chaucer, and a "parcel of New York Millerites who in 1843 sold their possessions, put on white nightgowns, and sat on the chicken coop waiting for the world to end. When it didn't they moved to Wisconsin out of sheer embarrassment."

Pat earned her Master's in English Literature from the University of Minnesota, her doctorate at the University of Minnesota with a dissertation on sir Walter Scott's Ivanhoe, and is a graduate of both the Clarion and the Milford Writer's Workshops. In addition to her work with WDS, she is a lecturer at the University of Wisconsin-Oshkosh in modern British literature and composition, and teaches an audio-cassette-based course on science fiction and fantasy for the University of Minnesota.

Pat lives in Oshkosh, Wisconsin, in a nineteenth-century wood-framed house, which has been in her family for generations. In addition to writing and teaching, she attends science fiction conventions, collects yarn, knits, embroiders, and makes her own Christmas cards.